MY TRUTH, YOUR LIES

HEIRS AND DESCENDANTS

BOOK FOUR

DANIEL KEMP

Published 2023 by Next Chapter

Edited by Lorna Read

Cover art by Lordan June Pinote

Large Print Edition

PREVIOUS WORK BY THIS AUTHOR:

The Heirs and Descendants Series:

The Desolate Garden

Percy Crow

What Comes Before

The Lies and Consequences Series:

What Happened In Vienna, Jack?

Once I Was a Soldier

The Widow's Son

A Covenant Of Spies

Novellas:

The Story That Had No Beginning

Why? A Complicated Love

Self-Published under the Name of Danny Kemp:

A Shudder from Heaven

Falling Greenhouses and Digestive Biscuits

And for children:

Teddy and Tilly's Travel Series

CHAPTER ONE
A DESTITUTE POET
WITHOUT A POEM

I had a decent enough dinner but there was no sign of Sir Walter Scott, the famed Scottish novelist, who I'd read had dined here in bygone days. His attendance at a meal was noted by a grim-faced portrait of the great man hanging on one of the walls of this fine dining room. Instead of him for company I had the two main officers, as well as the Chief Petty Officer and, as a further break from tradition, Second Officer Lucy Walton, WRNS.

Apparently, it was not normal practice for the non-commissioned officers to have cocktails with the commissioned ones, let alone dinner, but my arrival had loosened the traditions for a while, but not the drinking of a pink gin or three!

Before I left the evening company, I asked Captain Lloyd to signal the Admiralty for an increase to the number of ratings available to use as prison guards. I did not want to draw attention to the place by asking the Home Office for private security guards. I thought having them around in garish uniform would be a backward step for local relationships, but what presently existed was lacking sufficient numbers.

The inevitable question of why the sudden need of an increase to security, came from the Lieutenant only micro-seconds before that from the Captain; however, the answer was the same no matter who had asked. "Call it my natural ministerial worry now she's temporarily in my charge. I hope she will be moved by the time I leave your warm hospitality."

That night, the naval guard was doubled, with four now on perimeter patrol, and ratings ordered to closely accompany Fields when in the garden. Using my name for the instructions, Captain Lloyd petitioned the Admiralty for additional service personnel to strengthen the contingent at Gardie.

Within an hour, his signal to Admiralty House in Whitehall was answered with a corps of naval personnel arriving by boat from a frigate, *HMS Prudent*, presently on shore patrol duties. I later learned the warship was to be posted to a British-led carrier group which was cruising near the South China Sea. Without a full complement the posting was postponed. Was it an omen or a case of an unexplained coincidence? I don't know about you, but I'm not a great lover of coincidence.

I asked about Judith, using her Home Office ascribed surname of Fields, and was told she was in the library. Over drinks, Lucy Walton, the WRNS officer, told me she spent practically every day alternating between the library and the garden, where she was detailed to work. It was too dark for the garden so she would be back in the library at this time of night. Lucy Walton was not only the officer in charge of the WRNS unit; she was the person with overall responsibility for Judith's welfare. There were seven Wrens on the island. The number was included in the overall strength of eighteen.

Privately, I could not fully understand why Meadows was still alive and being kept in reasonable comfort, having been the number two to probably the greatest Russian master spy since World War II. She had not told her original interrogators anything, but that was not known to her Russian masters, who must be worried. Or, perhaps not!

From inquiries I'd made before I left to travel here, I discovered the visitor she'd had in her first prison was not part of the solicitor's team she had engaged for her trial. The papers he'd carried had been false. It was highly irregular to get entry into the state-of-the-art prison she was held in at the time, so the lengths that person had gone to in order to see her were, to say the least, extreme. Knowing the intensity of Russian retribution, I wondered why she had been left alive.

* * *

It was a little after nine-thirty when I left the dining room fully satiated but tired and in need of a cigarette. The two naval ratings in the guard room at the end of the garishly lit, broad corridor leading to the open front door recognised me and, after I signed the duty-register, allowed me to pass.

* * *

I had the specifications of Gardie House, which had yet to have a full complement of cameras and microphones added to all the open rooms, but outside the main building it was different, with practically all areas covered by cameras. There was also a directional microphone hand-controlled from inside the camera room, behind the guard room. There was nothing in Jerry's notes to say the microphone had ever been used, nevertheless, I considered it to be a useful addition. After smoking my compliment of cigarettes during my stroll under the stars, I went to find my room.

With the weight of Gardie's information overwhelming the contemptible yet confusing memories I had of Judith, my night's sleep in the austere room I'd been allocated, was agreeable, if on the ascetic side of life. I woke in time for the uninspiring breakfast, then, with nicotine from my Dunhill cigarettes fortifying my reserve, I went for another stroll.

Fortunately, I had never discussed the feelings I've mentioned to you before I discovered her to be the murderer she was. Not only was she responsible for two murders, she had successfully shielded a traitor for years. Surely this 'love' I'd professed to myself to feel, in a palpable state of achievability, had been eclipsed by these memories of murders. Let me now be strong enough to murder the infantile longings I'd named as love.

It was still early. More importantly, it was earlier than one of the many times on the checklist Lucy read out to me when I declined the after-dinner port. The timing of her work in the garden was one of the few I consigned to my memory, so I knew there were thirty or more minutes to go before Judith's tidy-up in the garden would commence. I knew where she would be at this time of day, because I'd asked. I took myself off to the library for the start of the reversible roles played out with a murderer I'd had developed uncommon feelings for. I didn't have long to wait!

I have never before broken down moments in my life into ones referred to as life-changing, but if I had to decide when it was my life changed with the realisation I could finally handle my feelings towards Judith, it was now, as she altered her walking pace from slow to swift, leaving me feeling as though I was in a silent movie as I watched her close the gap between us. It was then, in that moment, it registered I'd been a colossal fool. I was no longer a fool. My once strong but idiotic resolve to chase love, had changed to one of the same tenacity found inside the barren heart of a poet searching for a poem where none exists.

* * *

"Oh, Harry, how I've missed you! Have you come to rescue me?" Her hands were clutching my face. I left them where they were.

"They never told me it was you who was coming. They only said someone from the Home Office was coming to see me. I got a brief glimpse of someone, who must have been you, earlier through the laundry room windows, but I couldn't make out for sure who it was. From the inside they have a coating on the glass that makes everything blurry. Are you back working at Thames House on Millbank?"

She withdrew her grip on my face and took a hasty half-step backwards away from me instead of planting her full, luscious lips on my lips. What was I thinking of? Was she the only one of us thinking straight? Maybe those two murders had once and for all made a mark on her subconscious, compelling her to face the same shame and remorse I felt. Was my remorse a sham? After all, it was true to say I felt no affection for either Edward or Elliot. Was it possible for me to feel shame? I could not find any rationality anywhere inside my head.

I had killed in the past. Two of those I'd killed were married, leaving wives after I had taken their lives. One of those men had a mother still alive to mourn his death. So why am I blaming my loss of love on the murder of two relatives for whom I had little or no feelings? No, I'm not debating this. In the business I'm in, we kill first, love last. Let's get on with it, Harry, and stop f...... about!

"I'm in a position where I can help you, but you must assist with a matter predominately concerning Russia. However, we will cover other subjects." Thankfully, I had rediscovered some of my professional side.

"Whilst we are conferring, you will refer to me as Mr Williamson. You will not call me by my real name, nor my rank. When we are discussing our business, you will refrain from being whimsical. You must listen to what I'm asking and answer what I'm asking of you. This is a new opportunity, so use it, Judith. It's in your favour to treat this examination sensibly. I will start this examination with a name."

I indicated the table she had just run from as our place of questioning. The irony of me being the one asking the questions did not escape me, nor her, as I saw a wry grin on her face as she sat. Then I thought the grin could be for a matter I had no knowledge of and my confidence started to drain away.

She closed the open book on the table, adding a gold-coloured leather bookmark with some letters embossed on it. From where I was standing I could not make it out. I wanted to ask if the lettering meant something to her, but decided against it. I wanted to keep everything as impersonal as I could.

I began in Switzerland, with Paulo Sergeyovitch Korovin and the first time she used the word 'ruffled'.

"There is a Russian who holds a very high position inside a part of the Russian security service who is an American double agent. Recently, he contacted me by using the word 'ruffled', alongside another clue leading me to you. I was told the sender of the message carefully selected the surname of his messenger he sent all the way to New York. I'm hoping you can unravel its lettering in such a way that it could be the opening to something important."

"Important in what way?" she asked.

I replied that I wished I knew, but then I was lost for words. Her large, hazelnut-shaped, green eyes still held the same fascination they had done the first time we met in daylight at King's Cross Station. As I remained in this wordless state, she offered to make a cup of tea which I declined, preferring to leave what thoughts I had undisturbed by any social nicety.

I held the thought of when she had proudly proclaimed her father's title—Lord Edwin Meadows.

How did he feel on being told of his daughter's treason? I could not guess the magnitude of his heavy-heartedness, but I do know it would have been a colossal blow to someone as wrapped in tradition as he must have been. He had then to face his employer, Her Majesty the Queen, to offer his resignation from the position as her private secretary. I wasn't ready to resign, silently I shouted at myself.

"Does the Russian surname of Oborka mean anything to you, Judith?"

She withdrew a pen from the small, brown leather, oblong bag I hadn't seen her with before, and she wrote the letters of the word OBORKA in a small, flip-top, lined notepad after asking how I spelled it. It was a different notepad from the one she used at The Hall with what was then a pen, but was now a pencil. In less than a minute she had discovered quite a few.

"It could stand for book, brook, boa, boar, rook, the vegetable okra. I think I'm stuck there."

She fell quiet for a moment, staring into my eyes. I thought she wanted to ask a question, but also appeared worried in some way. I fashioned a stifled half-smile, hoping to encourage her to ask whatever was troubling her. It worked, but I was disappointed in its subject.

"I shall not say his name, Mr Williamson, but if I was to ask if you knew what had happened to a certain nameless person who was arrested for treason at the same time as I was arrested, would you know who I mean, and would you tell me what you know?"

"Yes, I know who you mean, but I have no idea what happened to him," I lied. "I could make inquiries in the morning, if you wish. But I doubt I would turn up anything nice."

She chose a view of the table instead of my eyes. Not being wanted, I invented some plausible excuse and left to look at her collection of books on art stacked on top of one another, next to a computer screen showing the words, *Art and its Condemnation.* I wondered if I shared another of those coincidences with the word condemnation?

I left her with the word puzzle, off to seek my own answers to finding the room where I'd emptied the grey canvas bag I'd carried all the way from London, as if I was off to the northern wilds of provincial Scotland in search of a malt whisky trail, which in a way I suppose I was. Only my adventure was concerned with the hunt for the real Harry Paterson who had just poked his head above the battlements.

Thoughts of comfort insisted on the carriage of three bottles of single Jura malt, so it was with a glass of this refuelling liquid in one hand, that I used the spare one to open the bedroom door to the unexpected knock.

Knock, knock. A rehearsed knock. A practised and bold type, not a timid knock. It was not a 'can I please come in?' Oh, no, not this. This was an 'open this door at once' kind. A military knock. Yes, I was right. Petty Officer Boyce stood there. Upright, shoulders back, arms behind his back, feet apart. He was standing at ease. I was not.

'Never rush to answer a door, Harry, my boy, bad news can wait to find you. Whereas, if good news is kept waiting, it will be enjoyed the more.'

Such was an example of another pearl of wisdom my great-grandfather Maudlin and I would mull over when I was in London visiting him.

On my visits in those faraway days, I would travel to London by car, with John, the now retired chauffeur, going stoically about his business without speaking to the young me in the back of 'his' newly polished red and burgundy Rolls Royce for the journey to see The Old Man before he died.

I was with The Old Man in his office of Annie's, when there was a similar knock on his cream-painted office door, the door marked *Chief Executive,* written in black-inked calligraphy onto the middle rail separating the two translucent glass panels from the lower wooden half. I had risen quickly from the black, cushiony leather chair at the window overlooking Birdcage Walk only to be softly rebuked by him who, by a single hand motion, ushered me to sit. With his spare hand he took a slow draw on the cigar that almost filled the silver, glass-bowl ashtray and then, when satisfied, called "Enter," in a deep, self-reliant voice.

I can't recall if Maudlin had good news that day or bad, it mattered not to him; what mattered was the dignity applied to the incident. I answered my knock in the same leisurely way I had learned from him.

"Sorry to disturb you, Mr Williamson, but I have a message from the prisoner," the Petty Officer announced. I held out my hand expecting a written message. I was wrong.

"She said," he cleared his throat, "it means Lady's Fingers, and she knows the hidden meaning of that word, sir." His eyes reflected the same obedience and duty I had seen on non-commissioned officers, as well as on the faces of the rank and file soldiers of the British army, in all the places I'd served.

"Thank you, Petty Officer," I replied.

"Would you like me to take a reply to the lady, sir?"

"You could do, Petty Officer." I looked down at my hand with the glass of my favourite whisky, then looked at him.

"What would you like me to say, sir?"

"Please tell her I will see her in the morning. The journey was far too tiring, I'm afraid."

I shut the door on the appeal she once held over me, leaving it to sink into the sea that surrounded my island.

CHAPTER TWO
REPRIEVE

"Yes, I got it quite quickly. Okra is a derivative of Oborka, it's a vegetable. But the word Okra means Lady's Fingers. It leaves the letters BO, but who wants that, hmmm? And the Lady's Fingers belonged to a sculpture called *Samothrace*, or, more correctly, *The Winged Victory of Samothrace*. That's its full name. Not bad, hmm?

"In all the books I've read it's supposed to be quite nice. Mind you, statues are not my type of thing. As I say, most of my knowledge comes only from books, but it's a marble Hellenistic sculpture of Nike. It was, apparently, created in about the second century BC. No, Harry, it's not the trainers or sweat-shirts, if that's what you're thinking. This one is another Nike. In ancient Greek civilisation, Nike is the goddess of victory. I looked it up last night before going to sleep. Since 1884, the statue has been on display at the Louvre, in Paris."

It was the following morning and I was with her in the library for what felt no longer than a few minutes, but I couldn't be definite. Time seemed to have stopped for me. One moment I was at home, leading horses across the cobbled paddock yard, waiting to ride out, next I was here, either asking questions or listening to answers.

She had read all about the statue with its missing hand, an open palm and two outstretched fingers being found on the Greek island of Samothrace. It was, according to Judith, fascinating. She didn't stop for air whilst she was describing the importance of Okra's Lady's Fingers.

It was as she was speaking of Samothrace that I remembered when Gerald Neil and I were gossiping in the Bottomly library. He told me he had a yacht tied up in the harbour as well as having property on the same island. Could the torture he'd suffered be connected to this statue in some obscure way? It seemed as though it was one coincidence too many for it not to be true. I was silently thinking of that whilst facing Judith in this library, with neither of us speaking since her explanation mixed with my worry. It was a question from her that broke the silence.

"Did the question I asked yesterday, about you-know-who, upset you? Only your mood changed immediately after that and you left. Also, I hope you notice how reticent I'm being with the name of you-know-who. Walls have ears and all that! Are we still enemies, Mr Williamson?"

Did that question come from her mouth or mine? I wondered, as she stared at the walls, alternating the stare from one to another, literally driving me mad with those big eyes of hers. God should never give green eyes away to traitors, or murderers. Certainly not for free. He should have made it a prerequisite that green eyes had to be earned in a way only He would have been able to figure. I thought about her question for a short moment before quickly realising we were precisely what she asked.

"How could we not be enemies? What else did you expect, Judith?"

It was as though the Heavens were against me today, as outside it was continuous rain, keeping my frustrated body from venturing into the fresh air for any length of time. I grabbed a cigarette while walking under a garrison umbrella, but I didn't want to walk while questioning Judith in the rain. Besides, there were other matters to consider.

The previous day had indeed been tiring, not only because of the journey, at least in the open air I could relax, but I could not relax with the calls to and from Serena. She and my solicitor were the main contributions to my feelings of fatigue. I skipped both meals, breakfast and lunch, settling on a bag of peanuts eaten on the flight, by which time I had decided I could not fight my ex-wife any longer.

The second night I couldn't sleep and it was useless to try. I think it was some moral sense of right and wrong that kept my mind alive with my eyes closed. Closed as they were, sleep deserted me and there was no point in using my stock of Jura as a sleeping tonic. I had informed Judith of the plans for tomorrow, an early start after breakfast, but I hadn't told Lucy of those plans.

* * *

It was no good! I got out of the bed and walked down the stairs to the ground floor, continuing to where the guard room was. I asked the guards to unlock the front door, then, once it was opened, I went outside for a walk around the outer area of the base with a cigarette in hand and the packet in my pocket. I hoped the walk or the cigarette would make me feel sleepy, but it didn't work. I tried another cigarette and another walk. That ended with the same result. There were two naval ratings on patrol whom I passed twice, with another standing to one side of the front door. I wondered if they were all there to stop Judith escaping, or to stop someone wanting to break in. I didn't wonder long. There was no respite to find in thinking.

Inside the building, there was a small reception

desk to the left of the front door, on the opposite side of where the guard was standing. I'd had no reason to take more than a cursory look at it when first entering the house, nor a few minutes ago before setting off for my walk, but now was different. I opened the visitors' register book, purely because I was bored.

After thumbing through the first three pages my boredom was worse, nevertheless tiredness was still a long way from me. Fixed on the wall, to the left of where the register was lying, was a highly colourful wooden newspaper and brochure rack. Predominately the colour was yellow, but even so, there was room for blue, red, and orange randomly painted streaks. All in all, it made a rebellious statement against the old standard, brown-varnished wallpaper, with the even darker stained wooden panelling.

Curiosity got the better of me. I started to look through the colour-strewn racks holding the local newspapers, edging me closer to the weariness I wanted to find. There were maps of the island, alongside timetables for the ferry and train connection times from Lerwick to other parts of Shetland. There was also a directory of local arts and crafts that interested me, in particular the photographer who Jerry Furley, at Vauxhall, had mentioned to me prior to coming. There was some of her work included in the six-page local free newspaper. On the last page there was a collection of her photographs of the island.

There was one photograph that grabbed my fervent attention, so much so it caused the guard, the other side of the open door, to inquire if I was okay after his eardrums were assaulted by my scream of incredulity.

* * *

It was a little after four in the morning with three and bit hours to wait for the first ferry to leave the island. All thoughts of weariness disappeared as a more practical side of me took over. I left a message for Lieutenant Murray with the ratings in the guard room, stating I was catching the first ferry into Lerwick and would not be present at breakfast. I left another message for Second Officer Lucy Walton to the same effect but adding I would not want Fields for questioning until my return to the island. I estimated that to be around midday. Most of the remaining time I spent chatting on the phone with the duty officer at Thames House, Millbank, where I hoped the information I needed could be found.

* * *

In London, Jerry briefed me on the universal codes to be given to Home-Casuals, the name given to the volunteers like the Lerwick photographer, in order to set things in motion.

"This is Timothy, from Stepney," I said into the

telephone recorder, hoping someone would pick up, but no, nobody was there. I had asked Jerry how long this woman photographer had served as a volunteer.

"Not sure, exactly, but quite possibly a long time. I got her name from Millbank immediately after you said you were going to Shetland," was the answer I was given. I asked him how long since she was last contacted? To which I got another indefinite answer. All I could think of was now would be a bad time for her to forget her tradecraft and find Timothy from Stepney meant nothing to her other than there was an escaped mental patient who had her telephone number. If the name Timothy had meant nothing, then the rest of the message was also a waste of time.

"Please, make your call to London to verify the authenticity. I'll be at the dock at Lerwick as soon as the first ferry from Bressay docks. For the purpose of this operation I'm named Williamson from the Home Office. I'm visiting Gardie in search of a special avian species. You will easily recognise me. I'm quite scruffily dressed and I have fair, red hair."

I added a bit more about the photograph I was interested in, saying I thought I'd noticed the bird I was looking for in the corner, leaving it there. I closed my mobile phone, more in hope than belief that she would come.

:* * *

My hope paid off. It had not been a waste of time.

"Mr Williamson? I'm sorry to trouble you if you're not, but I'm Mrs Tate and I'm looking for a Mr Williamson."

"How did you guess?" I replied with a smile that, for a split second, I worried gave away volumes of uncertainty. She was also smiling as she replied.

"You looked so out of place, that's all. I can normally spot the locals. Up here, they all look so Scottish as they're normally rushing everywhere to keep warm, but I can't tell them that. I would be ostracised if I did!" She laughed, then carried on.

"It's much better in the holidays. We are all generally much busier then with tourists. It's tapering off now, as you can see. The ferry can get very busy. It's good for the local business, but you haven't come to discuss the tourist situation, now have you, Mr Williamson?" she stated, adding a charming smile to the trite conversation.

"Do you include yourself as a tourist, Mrs Tate, as you don't sound very Scottish to me?" I asked.

She was very similar to how I had pictured her. Small in height; five foot would have been a compliment. Petite in size; if my estimation about Judith Meadows being a size zero was correct, then Mrs Tate was at least a minus one, zero. She was roughly seventy years of age, but my powers of guessing people's ages are woefully poor. I think I may have said that already, but if not, it's something you should bear in mind whenever I estimate age.

She had thick grey hair tied in a bun and wore stout, brown-framed glasses that did not quite hide her aged, grey, round eyes which must be suffering from short-sightedness as the lenses she wore were thicker on the edges and thinner in the middle. I thought I knew this to be the case as a lady I know in Harrogate was, I'm sure, short-sighted, and the lenses in her spectacles were made in a likewise fashion.

Mrs Tate had a small, oval face with very few lines worth the mention, other than one narrow groove across her otherwise unsullied forehead. In my imagination, I saw her in a studio quietly sitting in front of a canvas whilst inwardly she fretted over how to paint the awkward scenes, the ones that caused the line to appear on her forehead.

I thought her too minute to bear children, but what did I know about children? Her clothes were certainly colourful and summery, perhaps somewhat bohemian, with a wide, silk, blue and pink scarf with a matching-coloured linen blouse. Open-toed, yellow slip-on canvas boating shoes, which complimented her not old-fashioned, nor outlandish outfit. Most of this was how I imagined her to be; what I hadn't expected her to be was English.

The pre-recorded message on the Tate's telephone was in a strong, male, Scottish voice, with slowly spoken directives. On the ferry crossing I had said 'good morning' to a local delivery driver, who was standing beside his bread van looking towards Shetland, probably dreaming of the coming day. I could not understand a word of his reply, because of his broad local accent. I was expecting the same from Mrs Tate.

My offer of a cup of coffee was refused, as apparently she never drank 'the stuff', as she put it, adding that she doubted anywhere would be open at that time of day, so we settled on ambling along the wooden landing platform when I broached the subject of why I had caught the first ferry to Lerwick.

"In the photograph from the newspaper I sent you, there was someone I thought I recognised. I was wondering when the photo would have been taken?"

"Well now, the paper is a weekly edition in summertime, then it goes out every two weeks in late autumn as well as in the winter. We get a fair lot of those tourists I was talking about up here for the birds in the autumn and the winter months, you see, but the weather can be very harsh for venturing too far. I spend that time consolidating my collections.

"The east coast of Bressay is famous for the birds, but across Noss Sound is where the real treasures are. The island of Noss is one of many National Nature Reserves in this part of Scotland. Boats are hired from here to take the bird fanciers around Bressay. Or, for the brave and hardy, there's an inflatable dinghy for hire, to go across to Noss Sound.

"Dunlin and Great Skua are just two of the breeds one can find on Noss. I go there, but not as often as I used to. I can see by your blank expression you're not a twitcher, Mr Williamson? Ah well, it's not for everyone. Yes, anyway, the photograph you're interested in. I'm sorry, I get carried away when speaking of the attractions of the island, don't I? You're unfortunate that I've not found anyone else out and about at this time in the morning to use up my energy of speaking." She was smiling again as she stopped for breath.

It could have been an effect of the early morning sun on my unusually uncovered head, but to my knowledgeable ear of women's voices, I thought Mrs Tate's voice carried a smile on every note wrapped inside mixed melodious tones.

"The images for the edition you're talking about would have been taken in the week they're included. It's my husband's paper, you see, and he selects the photographs from whatever's in my weekly diary. He does sometimes look further back into my portfolio, but that's unusual. Very fastidious is Mr Tate, a man of skilful habit.

"He was the compositor for one of the big London newspapers before he retired. It was his first and only job working for that newspaper. He did fifty-three years setting print on machines. He started part-time on the delivery side. I won't tell you at what age he started, but what I can tell you is he loved every second and found he couldn't give it up when he got here." The smile was still there, as though it was a joke worth sharing. I smiled in return.

"It keeps him busy and out of my hair," she added as an afterthought.

Whatever caused her amusement, was finished as she returned to the reason for our meeting.

"I brought the original photo with me. I just hope it's the one you meant. You can keep it if it is. I sometimes use photographs as a form of motivation for the canvas, but I don't usually paint people. I find them a little difficult." I thought I detected a slight frown when she confessed.

"I'm much more a landscape person, but I might try painting people again." I thought I detected a sigh, before—"I shouldn't. I should just accept the fact I find painting people too difficult. No, I should tackle it. What do you think?"

I had complimented her, but maybe I hadn't praised her enough. I tried to remedy any mistake I may have made in that department before thanking her and moving off to catch the returning boat, saying I would pass on word of her good work when I got back to London.

The photograph was the one I wanted. When I was satisfied I was far enough away, I put the photo in the envelope I'd already addressed to Jerry Furley, at his home address. I would ring him later to explain it was taken earlier this week.

CHAPTER THREE
HUMVEE

Judith was waiting for me, seated in the library with a ruled notebook on the table in front of her, her sharpened pencil lying neatly beside it. She was facing the open door.

"Harry! Out on the tiles all night, were we? I hope she can remember your name this morning. The poor girl."

I ignored her use of my first name, thinking I would be rather petty by bringing it up. I didn't need to admonish her to reinforce my dislike. The laugh was as false as the rest of her. It seemed as though she had built a wall between herself and what was real, wanting to live in the world of fantasy she had created. I tried to use that to my advantage. I introduced the name of a Russian illegal I wanted her to think about, who had worked for Microsoft in America until he was arrested by the FBI in 2010. He then skipped bail, never to be seen again.

Christopher Metsos, real name Pavel Kapustin, was a professional Russian agent who travelled from Canada into America to bankroll an operation, code-named Ghost Stories. Amongst other things, the operation concerned the transmission of misinformation communicated to local news outlets, intent on causing as much unrest as it could. The FBI believed Metsos was the Russian banker for other sleeper agents, similar to the 'illegals' London wanted information about. First, though, I needed what she knew of this statue of Samothrace.

"I have the information you want, but there's a price-tag to it. You being the person you are would expect nothing else. It could be said what I know about the island is the Russian equivalent of the British Crown Jewels. Yes, H, don't look so surprised, it really is. But, is it worth my while to tell you?"

"Before we test the ground with that, I want all the information you have on some smaller points that will show me if you're worth trusting or not. I'll put it another way, one that's easier for you to understand; if I can trust you, then I'll recommend you are reprieved to Russia. Maybe we can get you to Moscow."

"I most certainly do not want to go to Moscow. Why would I? I want to settle here in good old England. Maybe near you on that estate of yours. How about I move in as Lady Paterson? I could live on the edge of your estate in one of those houses you have there. Where on earth did you get an idea I wanted to go to Russia? I gave you credit of having one brain cell more than a unicellular organism, but after that idiotic suggestion I'm not so sure."

"If you've stopped showboating, we'll play the game of 'let's see if you're worth anything', shall we? I'll put the salient points to you and you concentrate on what I ask. Your starter for ten: have you ever met or heard the name of a Kuwaiti, named Sabah Al Salim?"

"Yes and no. I never met him but I have heard the name mentioned. I came close to him when I was attached to a Special Projects Team having direct orders coming from Vauxhall. It was a long time ago, Harry. If you're fishing for an introduction you might be out of luck. I've been out of circulation for a while."

I asked another question, about how long ago it was since she heard his name. There was a prolonged silence whilst she estimated the time since she'd heard it. The answer surprised me.

"It must have been over ten years ago. You have to remember that I was in deep-deep cover with absolutely no possibility of ever being sdiscovered, before your Russian relative started to look so very closely into what was going on inside British intelligence. I have been posted to many private military contractors, or divisions of MI6, Special Projects being just one. During the occupation of Iraq there was an operation against a Kuwaiti with the same name. I have no access to my notes of the time, so the year and other such points are guesswork. May I?" she asked, just before helping herself to a cigarette from the packet of Dunhill International that lay on the table in front of me.

I nodded my agreement and pushed my lighter towards her. We had been here before when she had no cigarettes. That was when we were at The Hall, in Yorkshire. To alleviate the same problem arising, I had brought some packets of her usual brand, but being the forgetful person I am, I'd left them in my room. I promised to send them to her later.

"When this Sabah Al Salim was on the ops table, he was financing what was then a small group of idealists before they became the Islamic State of Iraq, or ISIS. My section were instructed to work up a plan to take him out. Apparently everyone was on the same side, even my Russian handler agreed with British intelligence. They were, so I was told, an unsettling influence in an already unnerving part of the world that held one fifth of the world's oil reserve. Instructions coming from Moscow were to make myself conspicuous to those in charge of Al Salim's assassination.

"I did all I could with those orders in mind and I was selected, but not in the first assigned pairing. I was in the second. The first kill team was all American Delta. I was one of three from twenty-two SAS regiment in the second grouping. My unit, about twenty of us, was transferred to a base camp near Karbala, in central Iraq. We had two kill teams, both with a four-strong back-up.

"A drone strike was a no-go as he operated in densely packed areas of Baghdad or Karbala. He was a very cautious man, often using a public bus to travel in between the two cities. At the time, GCHQ were providing the up-to-the-minute intelligence on his entourage and his movements. I wasn't told until afterwards there was a Russian agent in his grouping. There was nothing sinister about being told afterwards. In a way that shows how good my cover was.

"Both teams were incorporated into a battle group comprising a Rangers section, a unit from the US 3rd Infantry Division, supported by the 101st Airborne Division. The idea was that we blended in with this battle group so as not to look as though we were assassination units.

"Our four vehicles separated from the main party as it passed through a place called Ar Razzazah. When Sabah Al Salim was identified by the agent inside his group as being in the supermarket on the corner of a built-up area, we moved in as planned. It was all done by the forward ranged operational control system in the vehicles of teams one and two. More importantly, we got times of convergence along with preferred escape routes forwarded on via the Global Positioning System.

"At the set time, team one, which was, as I said, an all Delta unit, rammed the grey Land Rover that should have been carrying Al Salim in the rear seat. The team were out of their transport and whilst the front crew were laying down fire on Al Salim's vehicle from one side, I saw a figure who resembled him running from the other side of the vehicle towards his second protection team who were coming fast and starting to open up with the top-mounted M2 heavy gun.

"Our Humvee and the front team started to returned fire, but there was little chance of either team hitting the target. The order came to withdraw and that's what we did. I know of three terrorists who were killed and I saw another two, on the ground, who looked cold. Sorry, service speech. I mean dead or wounded, but definitely—out of play.

"At the collective debrief, intelligence was blamed for the escape.

Evidently, the intel indicated there would be two terrorists with Al Salim on the rear seat of the Land Rover. Al Salim would be seated on the outside of the three, next to the door where the reinforced Humvee would ram. The collision would make it impossible for him to jump clear, therefore being killed where he sat. That's not how it worked out.

"It meant nothing to me. I'd fired a few rounds off

in something not a drill, making me feel good, had the old adrenaline pumping up and down, and my profile went up without me doing anything towards it. I slipped back into my personal protection role inside the intelligence service at Vauxhall with a little tick against my name, carrying on with life as it was."

I decided to let a lot of what she'd said go over my head without comment. For example, when she'd said everyone was in agreement and even her Russian handler agreed with British intelligence. The truth was she had no Russian handler. She was the handler! I changed the subject, asking a question that could cause her some embarrassment.

"Have you heard the name of Alexi Vasilyev before?"

"What's wrong with you, Harry? Have you become more stupid on purpose? Are you looking for a big payoff for being an idiot, so you can put your feet up counting the cows on your estate? I do seriously wonder about the quality of what's called counter-intelligence in Britain today. You notice I didn't say Great Britain? Well, I didn't, and it was your fault for being so imbecilic. Of course I know that name. We spoke of him when we were together in Switzerland on the night I felt sorry for you. So much for my support.

"You were grieving and I was a bitch, a hard bitch with a soft centre, though. Later on from a night in a hotel with Paulo, it was Alexi Vasilyev who gave the

Americans your Katherine. I guess he got fed up with her. I don't remember how, but we worked out he was working both sides. Oh yes, I remember now. He hadn't changed all of Katherine's names. Had he? He was showing himself to us. You surely cannot forget that? It was you who said he was with the Yanks. Big moment in both our lives was that."

"Yes, I suppose it was a big moment. Not as big as when I found out you were working for the other side though, was it?"

I left my question hanging, not needing any answer. The only question needing an answer was, why had I not remembered how we uncovered Alexi Vasilyev? Surely I wasn't old when counting the years between my birth and now, but if fifty-one was reversed, then I would be even younger. But playing around aside, my memory was not what it used to be. I didn't need the woman I'd held emotionally driven feelings for laughing at me because of a failing memory. It wasn't the first time I had forgotten a date on a calendar, or a time of year, or the number of the year, or, far more worrying, the name of a woman I shouldn't have forgotten. The specifics of that sorry episode of my life is one I will not commit to paper, nor mention in company. It was a one-off, I can assure you.

"What of Valery Agapov? Remember him, do we? Now your honesty's being tested without the use of any mechanical, or electrical machines. Is his name known to you in more ways than being mentioned in Switzerland, Judith?"

I was hoping the obscure mention of a polygraph might have regained the ground I could have lost if Judith had suspicions over any failing memory I might have. She replied she didn't know him in any other sense and I left it there for now. There were still matters Sir Leonard Miles and Charles Wallace had added to my brief that Judith may have been in a position to assist, in those enquiries.

"Take me back to Pavel Kapustin, or Christopher Metsos as you may have known him. You were saying he was in the same business as Al Salim, as a banker for terrorism or espionage. Were you ever told the two men may have met, or do you know of such a meeting?"

"Oh, Harry, I do worry about you. I have not said I know him. You may have thought you mentioned his name, but you haven't. You really must go and see a doctor, a scan on the brain-box might be favourable.

Either that or more sleep, or, come to think about it, a drastic reduction in the amount of whisky could be a good point to start with. If we want to recount on the work we've done so far, then please do, but you never asked me about Kapustin or Metsos. You have asked me about Sabah Al Salim.

Memory, Harry, memory."

She was right. I was going to ask but then got sidetracked. I asked her now and she had heard his name. Even more compelling was that she had an idea where it was he absconded to when not answering his bail. Her story started when she was being held in custody in a top-security prison in South London before being sent here to Bressay.

When in custody in HM Prison Belmarsh, she came in contact with a man who claimed to be from her court-appointed solicitors. He carried the correct credentials and his name was checked against the list held by the supervising prison office at the time. All was found to be satisfactory. But it wasn't satisfactory. The man was Valery Agapov. I asked what purpose was served by this visit, which Russia must have gauged as vital considering how much work it would have demanded.

According to Judith, Agapov came to tell her how she would be treated by the English. He suggested she would be offered resettlement with a good financial income in exchange for all she knew about Russian procedure, agents and any codes she may know. He said he was in a position to not only match whatever the British offered, but offer her far more, with her resettlement being in any English-speaking country of her preference.

This is where Metsos came into the conversation in a positive way. She asked her visitor if he knew where the favourite place was for defecting English-speaking spies. He told her a story about a man named Christopher Metsos who spoke English, with a broken Ukrainian accent. If she wanted, he said, she could move close to him, in Ottawa, Canada. He lived in a lovely area, he told her. A place called ByWard Market, spelled with a capital 'W', in a suburb called Halls Mills.

One conclusion I could draw behind Meadows giving me the whereabouts of Metsos was for her to feel more important, but was there something else? Had the Russians given Metsos to Judith as a Get Out Of Jail card, or had someone inside whichever resettlement division was responsible, simply given him up?

I made my excuses and left her in the library whilst I messaged my control at Section 9 with the information I had on Christopher Metsos. He was now known as Christopher Signalman, having a fresh Canadian food delicatessen, called The Signals, in the ByWard Market area.

It crossed my mind how his first name of Christopher had not been changed, which, as Judith and I had once remarked, would be the first rule of an identity change. To have a better chance of not being recognised by name, one must change both first name and second, not just one. Was this a signature of Alexi Vasilyev, who had left Katherine's first name unchanged when he gave her over? Perhaps, the whole structure of Russian espionage ignored any basic precautions for the safety of their operatives?

Not likely, I reflected. In that case it must be a message.

For many inexplicable reasons, I have lived a life more inclined towards spontaneous reactions than calculated ones, and that rule dictated my newly found reluctance to ask about the island of Samothrace, even the statue of the same name. It had been the first issue to discuss with her for some time, but somehow it had slipped down the list of 'things to do'.

I asked the question I knew had to be asked; even so, I can honestly say I feared the answer. I had no need. Her answer was she had never heard of a Winston Bottomly being mentioned. It was not as though it was a name you would forget. Thankfully, she never made a joke about it. While I was introducing names from my own part of the world, I touched upon the names of Sir Leonard Miles and Charles Oswald Wallace. Sir Leonard was in Government when she was arrested and as far as I was aware Wallace would have held a significant position in the Civil Service, if not the one he now held. Her reply to each name was the same—she had never heard of them.

I'd had enough negative answers to last a fair while, so, cigarettes and lighter in hand, I walked the garden alone, but not without purpose. There wasn't a lot of ground for me to cover and that should have made my search easier. I wanted to find a place where it was possible for Judith to be out of sight of the naval guards, for long enough for someone on the other side of the double perimeter wire to throw a note over.

After a short brick wall, that effectively only hid the hard-standing patio, there was no solid barrier between prison and freedom other than this double wire-link fence I'd mentioned, with double razor wire running the whole length along the top. It didn't take me long to find a place out of sight. In fact, after finding one, I found quite a few places where she could conceal herself from view of the house and take advantage of the privacy either the sizeable trunks of some trees offered, or the spread of several large shrubs.

When I finished my time spent walking, thinking and juggling clues with actuality, I sought out Captain Lloyd, suggesting he request the removal of the offending tree trunks and bushes.

Although Judith sat through many question and answer sessions inside the high security prison, my thinking when questioning her depended on the far more relaxed surroundings Gardie House presented, combining with the incentives I was authorised to offer, hoping the two would persuade her to be more cooperative. I was not conceited enough to believe my technique of interrogation was better than the military professionals; the difference I relied on was the fact that no matter how our relationship was looked at, it had been somewhat unusual.

She continued to be cooperative as I broached the subject of the French. I asked her how she thought the Russians managed to have such a sizeable presence inside strategic French establishments scattered around the world. When the French communicated with allies, the Russians were able to listen to the conversations, modifying their foreign policy in line with what they heard. When Judith was an active operative, MI6 had two Russian placements benefiting from the dexterity of their counterparts in French organisations, getting first-hand information from the top.

Page Boucher was a name she had heard mentioned quite a few times, in various conversations covering many topics and interestingly, one of them was South Africa. She had met Boucher once when he was in the company of a woman much younger than him. I asked her to describe the woman and if she'd heard a name. A name she had not heard, but I wished I had a photograph of Samantha to show her, as I thought the description she gave fitted Samantha to a tee.

How long ago was that, I asked, and it turned out it was the year before she murdered my father. She used that occasion to calculate the time from. Was it her intention to harm me by utilising the word 'murder'? Or was the word so trifling and the act so trivial to her? Her unhesitating admission stopped me from asking any further questions.

I suppose it was my acceptance of the finality of her actions that I found frightening. Of course it was personal and as such, all the more painful, but my reaction was so... what? Pragmatic, sensible, unfeeling? Hmm. I mimicked her favourite exclamation when lost for a reply to an answer of mine when we were alone in The Hall. Now, it was me alone.

I silently wondered how many lives we live in the life we have. I was sure it was not just one life we travel along in one straight line. No, I think we travel several lines of life during our allocation of time. Some are long, some are short. Some relationships, built on firm ground, can last for many years if honesty and loyalty count for anything in the morality of the characters of those involved.

Whereas, lives consisting of nothing other than the undoubted pleasures and gratification of sex survive only as long as desire is present and desire has no rigid base. Desire is a simple fancy. Judith was a fancy, I decided.

My leg folded under me as I rose from the table. I have damaged knees, not as a result from playing too many games of rugby, but playing too many games when the knees were not thoroughly mended. To make medical matters worse, I once fell heavily from a horse onto hard ground when riding in a competitive point-to-point race. The fall left me with a spinal complaint that will never improve. With all that going on, it leaves my legs liable to unexpectedly give way. This was such an occasion.

"Is it your leg or your knee, Harry?" she asked, as she bent down to help me regain, my... what again? This time, perhaps, my composure? No, how could I be composed when having to sit opposite the murderer of two members of my family?

Perhaps, some would say I needed to regain my pride. That could be an answer, except pride could demand revenge and I would have to question whether I could kill her in cold blood to bring revenge down on her head, then face the consequences. Could I sit and wonder? Could I kill her with my bare hands then leave the room aided by the stick I always used? I chose to exit without her death, reminding myself there were many things I needed cleared up before thoughts of revenge could fill my head. One of the mysteries I needed clearing away, was the mystery of Samothrace.

"I see you're still as obstinate as you ever were, but age is catching up on you, Harry. Perhaps you should look for a desk job, or take a pension and feed your chickens," was her sarcastic remark when I did regain my feet and sat opposite her.

"Don't mock it, Judith. Counting chickens could be the highlight of your future life if you're not careful. Your future lies in your past. If you want to live the remainder of your life in a positive, creative way, then find what London wants. Put this repetitive agony away for good."

I punched the top of the table with a closed fist causing everything on there to rattle. I didn't care if the whole house knew I was angry. Pride before a fall, eh?

"You've been in this business long enough to know when you're in a corner with no place to turn, and you're given a chance to get out of it—you take it, with both hands. This is your chance. Stop playing to the house, as I'm the only spectator and I'm about to leave! Take the chance I offer, or some faceless bureaucrat in London will make travel arrangements for a single ticket to the British research position deep inside the Artic Circle. Do you fancy spending the rest of your life in sub-zero temperatures? Let's see if we can complete this today, shall we?"

"Whatever you say. Just remember it was your family, specifically your great-grandfather, who started the mess that had me singled out as the bad guy. Yes, I killed two members of your family, but you didn't care much for either of them. Your great-grandfather only cared about women and his Russian bastard son." She paused, but there was no stoppage.

"You should remind yourself more often how he encouraged that son to spy on Russia and provide this country with the intelligence he had no right to have. Had that not happened, then your father and brother would probably still be here and I would not have entered your life."

I interrupted her.

"Who put the bomb in the car we were using in London? Your dog, or was it you who planted it?"

"Yes, it was me. I wanted to spend more time with you. I knew it wouldn't take you long to unearth your traitor. It then followed it wouldn't be long before you—" She didn't finish and I didn't want to finish it for her.

"Do you want me to tell you all I know of Samothrace, Harry?"

"First, I want more of Sabah Al Salim, but not in Iraq. Can you place him in Afghanistan for me? London says it's important—why, I don't know, but it is."

Why did she want to open up so readily about this Samothrace place?

Suddenly, I distrusted her memory of that island.

CHAPTER FOUR
IT'S NOT ALWAYS WHAT YOU KNOW

Sabah Al Salim was, as they say in the military, often mentioned in despatches from both Afghanistan and Iraq after a coalition invaded those countries at different times. Whereas in military terms, to be mentioned as I've described would mean distinction for some heroic act, Sabah's mentions were not for acts of heroism.

He was mentioned by those in positions to know as associating with known Daesh, ISIS members. Unfortunately, facial recognition in those days was still in its infancy, effectively not much use when applied to the satellite photographs the CIA examined at the Royal Air Force, Menwith Hill base, not far from my home at The Hall.

There were, however, some faces who could be

named from databanks. In the main, they were all of low-level interest already being serviced by Special Branch or another divisions of counter-intelligence, both here and in other NATO countries. There was one name that stood out, but first we had to sift through the rest.

From communications, I put several of those names to Judith, late afternoon on the first day of September whilst the two of us walked around the gardens of Gardie House. As we sauntered along, I continued to question her.

"During the time when Sabah Al Salim's name was being mentioned, did you hear the names of Jackson, or a woman's name of Colette? And thank you for being straightforward with Al Salim." I didn't think it any harm to compliment her.

"You're certainly the most polite interrogator I've come across, and thank you for being so polite, dear Harry. It makes a welcome break from the impolite world I've encountered so many times. Yes, I did hear the name Colette mentioned. Unfortunately, it was mentioned a few times both to me and within my hearing." She gave a detached sigh when she finished, but did not explain her hardship.

"I can't be sure if I've got it in the right chronological order, but here goes. Colette was a Russian agent, operating out of Paris, who was running a South African double agent. The asset she was working was a serving English military, as well as serving as a South African intelligence officer.

"On any of the counter-intelligence desks her name would generate great interest, but we were told it was 'Top-Floor only'. Which meant someone high up on the feeding chain had her on their list and the rest of us were to stay well clear. Obviously, she was designated as a very important figure, as was her asset, this British military guy."

"How do you know her double agent was not female?"

"Two reasons, really. The first came when some detail was introduced into the operational sphere, when the South African officer concerned was referred to as a 'he'. Even though you-know-who was on one of the lower floors back in those days, he knew of the agitation her name caused when mentioned to Control on the top floor. I don't think I was told why that was at that stage, though.

"Round about this time, one of the intelligence desks in the British military post in Bagram, Afghanistan, requested London send a female officer to work with them on something they had going with an Iranian, Shia female. It was not until I was on an RAF plane out of Brize that I was told the full version of why The Box was sending me, because it may surprise you but my uppermost qualification was not the debriefing of agents in the field.

"I was going for two reasons: one's my inherent skill at killing, that you know all about, and the other is, I speak several languages. Farsi is one and I can speak it fluently. I speak Persian and Dari as well. Farsi was the old Persian tongue so it's more of a common language of Iranians than of Afghans, although it is spoken in Afghanistan. They are all much the same, but it is in the dialect where there are differences. I can speak the various nuances.

"The Iranian woman was to be regarded as surplus at the end of my job. She would have to go when I'd finished. I'm never told why that is the policy, I'm only told to get the job done as cleanly as possible. I'm sorry if that part of my background brings bad memories to you, but it is what it is, and it's the main reason why I was sent. I'm off the subject a bit, I'll get back on track." I thought I saw her blush but that couldn't be. Could it?

"What I'm getting at is, I bumped into her. I mean this Colette woman, not the Iranian. I literately bumped into her when I was on my way to the Intel centre after passing through security. She had a press pass and certainly spoke French, another language of mine."

"What on earth made you think the woman was Colette?"

"I'm sorry. I'm misleading you. No, I didn't know at that stage, silly me."

Her statement ended in one of the characteristic

mocking laughs she would always be famous for, in my life. An indecorous, shamelessly scornful laugh I remember hearing so many times in The Hall. This time, as with many before, her taunting ended with a rhetorical question.

"Do you think I have the powers of a clairvoyant to go with the rest of my capabilities?"

There was a short pause with her characteristic grin, before she continued.

"I'm sorry. I keep forgetting the bad bits that happened between us, as well as forgetting about the bad bits of me."

A nonchalant shrug of her shoulders followed on from her all-too-real statement.

"I promise you it's not that I'm insensitive to what I did, it's just that—well, it was my job, my role. It was what I was trained to do." Another silence, then, "That doesn't help, either. Does it?"

"No, it doesn't!" I harshly replied, perhaps a little too quickly.

"What's happened has happened and nobody can change the past. I know that. But you might be able to change the future. Carry on with the story of how you knew this member of the press was the Colette you'd heard about."

* * *

Having completed the debrief in Farsi, then the assassination of the Iranian, Shia woman in Afghanistan, in which she took greater delight in her expansion of the details than I thought gracious, she was assigned to eliminate Colette. The photographs of the target she was given were of the same woman she had accidentally bumped into when in Bagram. That was the same Colette.

A résumé of the Russian Colette's work history, where it related to Great Britain, and/or her subjects, was displayed on the computer screen in the office where I had a chance of a private examination. It showed the names of three compromised individuals, beside their photographs. It also showed the faces of two British civil servants where it could not be proven beyond absolute doubt it was Colette's work; even so, the investigations alleged she killed both. The first was in 2009, the last was three months before Judith's assignment. The one thing that stood out in the details of the last two alleged murders was the position the two civil servants held inside the British Government civil-service-driven, perpetual machine.

She carried on with her story, which I was eager to hear, making allowances for her voice when it became acerbic in places, other times when honeyed with false sweet tones.

It revolved around a time when she was provided with a new passport, driving licence and credit cards and instructed to go to Paris by train, arriving in the afternoon. Once there, she was to proceed as quickly as possible to the British Embassy where she was issued with the standard British sidearm; a Glock pistol, together with a full clip. She was to sign and date the issuing papers.

Her next destination was a bookshop on Rue Saint-Eloi named after its owner, Pierre Ducard: Librairie Ducard. The apartment above the shop was where Colette lived. That night, after making sure her target was home, she entered the premises by climbing over a rear wall, then opening the door on the patio by using a miniature drill shaped like a pen, very similar to the one she was to use at Eaton Square to gain entry. At my father's London house there were cameras to avoid, at the Paris bookshop there were no cameras. She had no worries either about squeaky treads on wooden staircases, as there was a metal spiral staircase leading to the locked apartment door, which was opened in a similar manner as the front door.

It didn't take much searching to find the room where the two were. Colette was lying on her left shoulder next to her lover, who was lying on his right shoulder facing her. Using the noise suppressor for the Glock plus a cushion she had taken from a sofa in the room next to the bedroom, she fired two shells into Colette's head from close range, then two more shells into Ducard's head. First, she satisfied herself each was dead by feeling for a pulse, before she removed all four spent shell cases from the scene. And that was what made me ask why!

Why pick up shell cases from a clean gun? The embassy would always have issued a clean gun which, if I'd read all standing orders correctly, could have been left at the scene. Clean, in the sense I use it, meant every traceable number had been filed off the gun so it didn't matter if it was found. Conversely, if by chance the assassin was stopped in the street by police, then found in possession of a weapon, let alone a weapon with spent shell cases, then it's a different matter entirely. One from which the assassin would not escape the consequences, even by claiming diplomatic privilege.

I couldn't understand why she had not been assigned any back-up to the operation, which would have been normal practice in the situation. Instead of back-up, or leaving the gun, Judith was ordered to return the weapon to the embassy. The absence of any back-up was very strange.

There could never have been enough back-up to shoot her way out of France, but one other person there to take the gun would have helped. The business with the gun could have been suicidal. I couldn't detect any sense of fear in her voice, or regret, although I would have thought she must have felt some sadness at having killed a Russian operative similar in many ways to herself. Had that made any difference to the way she felt? I asked.

No, was the unequivocal answer to my question. Duty was duty and orders had to be complied with, was her cold-blooded response. I asked who had given the orders to kill Colette and return the gun to the embassy. It was who I thought it to be—the man whose name we were both avoiding. So a Russian ordered the assassination of another Russian and it was carried out by a Russian operative. Somewhat poetic, I thought.

I can't give you an answer as to why I kept away from the questions about the Greek island of Samothrace. I have none, other than I still did not completely trust her. Even my questions about South Africa were tempered by mistrust. My opening remark about the ANC was met with an empty grin, accompanied with an acrimonious verbal attack I did not expect.

However, later that night when alone with my single malt, with its desecration of added ice, I applied the reasoning of guilt having affected her reply. Judith and guilt, words that ordinarily would not be related, like single malts with ice. On this Shetland Isle irregularities were allowed to happen.

She loved, as well as hated, the man who made her murder this Russian Colette. Loved him because of the way he treated her and hated him for the same reason. She knew a secret she should not have known. She hated him more for that secret.

From the desk on the African-floor where this

man, who has no name, worked, it was relatively easy for him to shape the things to come in the African continent by directing others against the African National Congress from inside the organisation. Meanwhile, he directed more chaos from within the white supremacists of the Afrikaner Weerstandsbeweging, the AWB. Both organisations were endangered by his simple rerouting of an arsenal of weapons, which arrived in Cape Town from China, carrying documentation for the remnants of the People's Liberation Army of Namibia, the military wing of the South West Africa People's Organisation, or SWAPO for short.

The plan coming from the London desk was exactly the same plan as the AWB's—a black explosion against a black government. The only difference between the two was that this time, the People's Liberation of Angola did not only have Cuban weapons. They would be additionally armed with weapons that could be traced all the way back to the invisible stamp—*Made in China*. If the Chinese guns were found, as indeed his London desk intended them to be, it would be hugely embarrassing, perhaps bringing forward severe sanctions with increased political tensions on all concerned.

* * *

The only one who would know whether this plan had re-emerged under another English signatory, would be Winston Bottomly, and he was in South Africa. All I could say for certain was if the plan was active, then at the end of what would be a short, bloody conflict, the White AWB would say: "Only we can save your home from the yellow men with the slit eyes from the faraway East. We can prove they supplied the rebels with the guns and missiles, because they want your country for themselves by giving the ANC, the Angolans, and the Cubans, the upper-hand. It was the AWB who stopped them this time! Give us your vote and the real South Africa will rise again. We will stand shoulder to shoulder against tyranny from any race or colour."

Apartheid would return, but with a different tune this time. If the plan worked, then Blacks, approved by the AWB, would be in charge of the country. The Chinese would be left raving with incensed anger, which the rest of the world would either laugh at or, probably, ignore.

The secret about the guns from China being rerouted to the Cuban rebels, was the secret Colette knew about because Bottomly had told her and it was why, by knowing it, Judith was sent to kill her. For Judith, who held no conceptual belief of saving South Africa, for any White man, Black man, elephant, or lion, it was just another job.

She could be defined as a liberal communist

having only one idealistic belief; love could be found in the arms of a militant Marxist working at The Box, at Vauxhall. Perhaps, it was a match made more in the old KGB Lubyanka basement prison gazing out on the Urals, than in Heaven.

CHAPTER FIVE

WINGED HORSE OF PEGASUS

I was acutely aware of the timetable that was operating in Southern Africa, particularly the five men who were trekking down from Zambia heading for the meeting in Gaborone in Botswana which was, perhaps, the lynchpin to launch it all. Everything became particularly more threatening after learning of the Chinese weapons rerouted from Cape Town to the Cuban mercenaries who Alice reported as travelling from Angola to the same location, to meet there, at the same time. It would seem General Albert du Preez's supposition about it being the Cubans who would be used against the ANC's government, was correct. If that was so, then the General's AWB would be on hand to fill the gap left when the fighting stopped and the final count of the dead and wounded would have to be made. It could be a matter of, to those hiding at the back go the spoils.

As Judith elaborated on what she could remember of internal South African politics, it became clear her knowledge of the Angolan conflict came from a strictly Soviet Union perspective. She told me how that perspective intensified when the Russians learned the Americans had supplied Stinger missiles to the South African Defence Force, who in turn, had used these missiles to stop the MIG 23s the Russians had supplied the Angolans. The South Africans had recovered the crashed fuselage of one such jet airplane.

For political leaders in the West, the confirmed use of Russian-produced war planes in the Angolan conflict caused the already fraught tensions to run higher, and when the same South African Defence Force captured a highly sophisticated Russian-developed SA-8 anti-aircraft missile system, the first of its kind to be seen by western military leaders, the international peace organisations were seen to be pulling each other's hair out in a search for a solution.

Unfortunately, the SA-8 was not the last item of Russian weaponry discovered in the conflict. Large quantities of equipment were destroyed or fell into SADF hands when the Cuban mercenaries, along with the Angolan freedom fighters, broke away from the fighting, causing the Russians to withdraw their so called 'advisors'. This action left those fighting for the liberation of Angola without the leaders they so desperately needed.

This was not the only time liberation was left in search of leadership.

Various armed forces, wearing badges of liberation of one kind or another, had looked upon Russia as the one to unshackle them from their despotic regimes, but not now. Russia had lost the respect it was trying hard to grow in Africa. The Politburo did not want a commonwealth of nations, it did not want dependencies, what it did want was to be held in high esteem as well as to be respected in fear. To be looked up to whilst shaking. How was that possible when its weapons had been humiliated?

From the despondency I heard in her voice as she told me this story, I deduced it was round about this period of time that her abhorrence of all things American was born.

I asked several times why she had so much interest in South Africa, trying to establish if it was the truth she was telling, or not. Each time I asked, I heard the same answer only told a different way. It wasn't long before I came round to believing her.

As a child, she went everywhere her family went. Changing schools or changing her domestic teachers was never a problem for someone as influential and affluent as her father, who I understood had relinquished his role as an equerry to Queen Elizabeth II when his daughter was arrested for murder and treason. She did not add any comment of his, or any opinion he had of her.

Before becoming equerry, Judith's father, Sir Edwin Meadows GBE, Knight Grand Cross of the Most Excellent Order of the British Empire, was an advisor to a select group of worldwide business entrepreneurs. He could boast of having clients in every corner of the world. After becoming the Queen's equerry, a few of his more wealthy clients could boast of having prestigious titles bestowed on them by Her Majesty. Apparently, if he said something was a viable proposition, it was a viable one, so buy it and either *flip it*—a term that meant apply for and get whatever permission was needed to increase its value, then sell it on, with that underpinning profitability—or hold on to it, expanding your business as it too expanded.

His percentage for professional advice varied depending on various standards, including the individual wealth of the client. The same criterion was followed in regard to his fee for his name and status to be added to their investment prospectus, which, if he was paid, was permitted to bear the gold-leaf embossed heading of CEO Strategist, Sir Edwin Meadows GBE, Knight Grand Cross, Equerry to HM Queen Elizabeth II. An impressive inscription, until, that is, Judith dropped the ball, and his name was dropped from every boardroom where his face had been seen.

Judith displayed no appreciable sorrow for her father's demise, but for her mother it was a different matter. Here, she actually asked me if I would take a message to her. When I started to explain it was prohibited, I never had a chance to finish my explanation before she had interrupted me with her apologies for asking. However, I made a mental note to maybe drop a line to the address I had for her mother on file under next of kin. That's if I had time and I remembered, of course.

I wonder if this habit of talking to myself is a widespread illness affecting part-time spies, as it did full-time ones, or is it just me who does it? Sitting here listening to Judith's overflowing, vivid reasons for her love of South Africa was founded on it being a stop-off point for four-year-olds like her, in her early life, adored from the back of a Range Rover, enjoying the safaris when her mother and father took her.

There she was, on her chair imitating the ride of a bumpy old vehicle that sounded as if it would fall apart in the next ten-foot hole it crashed through, somehow never disturbing the basking lions. Why was it? She deliberated on this question until arriving at the answer, which involved a leaf that fell from the baobab tree just as they passed under its upside-down branches. Why? Because the lions knew where the Range Rover would break down, of course, and any minute soon they would lazily saunter to the spot with their claws sharpened and their teeth primed.

But no, they would not dare do that. The two guides were armed, as were Mummy and Daddy. And, of course, the lions, together with all the other wild animals, knew they were English. Could I ask Judith if she spoke to herself? Perhaps I shouldn't.

This time, I asked if she knew someone who was known as Liam to some, and Mike to others. But no matter what he was called, he used the same surname —Gibson. I knew something was wrong as soon as I'd asked. But not wrong with the name Liam, nor the person. No, not wrong with him, surely? I was soon asking myself how many more times am I going to be wrong on this mission?

Liam Gibson joined the communist party after learning his family had agreed to the extension of the underground arms depot built on neighbouring Bottomly land. The need was there, he learned, for when the ANC were kicked out of government and placed behind the rusty barbed wire of the apartheid camps.

He joined the Communist Party of Great Britain, a year before it was disbanded following on from when the Soviet Union was dissolved. It was easy for him to hide his membership using the family money to buy his anonymity. He loathed the fascist philosophy shared by his and Bottomly's father, but like so many of the red-sock brigade, loved their money.

Liam's father was one of Sir Edwin Meadows' clients and when Judith was born, the Gibson clan, along with other wealthy families, were entertained and cosseted at the Meadows' sprawling English home in Surrey. The two families' association continued for many years, but she was unclear as to whether or not it had withstood the scandal of her arrest. I asked her how she felt about Liam, and she said she thought Liam would be loyal to the edicts of the party.

He was around twenty or so when Judith was born. She was uncertain of his exact age as she could not recall asking him, but other things she did remember asking. Like the day when she asked Liam why he had joined the British army when his father's money would have bought him a nice job behind a desk? She repeated what he'd told her, what he had seen in South Africa, how the Whites treated the indigenous Blacks and how the only answer to fascism was to become an honest and true passionate communist learning how it's the truth to fight for your ideals. But "fight for the British?" she'd asked in a high, disbelieving voice. To which he'd offered some lame excuse about undercover work, which she had imagined meant lying in bed all day reading books on Leon Trotsky.

To her juvenile ears, he had the solutions to all the problems in the world so, when she was in university, she followed his instructions of mixing with students and earmarking those who shared the philosophy of 'from each according to his ability, to each according to his needs'. But she found her most pleasurable moments came when she identified those whose ideals opposed her own communist ones. As she added the names of her unbelieving students into the little red and black book, with an ink pen of course, the anticipated delights of turning them encompassed her whole body.

It was partly her education, plus the expected nepotism, that pushed her into the higher reaches of British security system where, through Liam Gibson, she met the man of her dreams, the man I uncovered sleeping inside the British intelligence service. The one who was exchanged for an American.

It was Liam who first taught her the skills she would need to became a lethal government assassin. When he was undergoing his SAS training courses, more so when he had finished, he would take Judith away with his wife and family, showing her what he been taught, such as breathing when silent, when the adrenaline is screaming for air and the heart wants to come through your chest. He taught her where the 'kill points' were for a bullet, knife, or hand attack. He showed her how to remain calm when killing a man with her bare hands. How to concentrate on the act itself of killing. It was designed to give her a head start in the elements she had left to learn of unarmed combat.

She said she hadn't finished being a shining light for me. Now she wanted to speak of the Pegasus Mercantile Company. Yes, that was what she wanted to talk about. She brought up the subject, not me! We went from the SAS to the bank, in one leap. The day had begun in the library, but we'd transferred to the garden where the sun was strong. Winston Bottomly and his aunt Alice were on my mind, as she began to speak.

"I learned from my father how the last White government of South Africa under F. W. de Klerk, funnelled money into somewhere called the Pegasus Mercantile Company. Apparently, it was one of the companies he recommended to his opulent clients for excess cash funds. De Klerk's cash-rich government ministers were trying to intensify public opinion on continuing the apartheid policy.

"For that controversial action to succeed, they wanted to broadcast all of what they saw as its advantages. The level of unemployment, they said, would rise sharply if apartheid was ended because business owners, along with the investors, would flee South Africa for anywhere a white-skinned man could safely open a business. That was the flag they flew; one of safety first. Upgrade what you've got without risking the safety.

"Unscrupulous unions would spring up, easily becoming corrupted by money. It would mean prospective workers having to pay for work after being compelled to join one of the unions. The 'union wage gap', often complained of, would widen as a consequence of the brutality union leaders would bring to bear on Black workers exercising their right of not wanting to join.

"The picture the government wanted to portray was that under apartheid, the workers knew exactly what they were paid and where they stood for things such as pensions, holidays and sick pay. They had certain rights that would be taken from them when apartheid was abolished. The government would increase the rights they had, where it was due. It was a joke really, but they argued that by spending astronomical amounts of money on bribery and advertising, they hoped to extend the life of the fascist oppression."

When Judith celebrated her first year's anniversary of working for the British intelligence service, the Meadows family held a dinner party for forty guests in their inner London home in Cumberland Terrace, inside Regent's Park. Here was where Edwin introduced his daughter to an American whom he said was a CIA operative working from their European desk. The man made no attempt to dispute his connection.

As with everything to do with her father, the conversation inevitably came to focus on money with the CIA agent showing no embarrassment when Edwin spoke openly about the amount of South African gold, especially the minted Krugerrands, being funnelled into the banking arm of a company named the Pegasus Mercantile Company, not on South African soil so not subject to South African ownership, or export limitations.

Another occasion Judith readily recalled, was when her floor at The Box was ordered to locate all the Weapons of Mass Destruction, WMDs, hidden in Iraq, along with the nuclear weapons the Bush administration in the White House were positive Saddam Hussein had in his armoury. There were in total one hundred and fifty-seven false alarms the teams on the counter-intelligence floor at Vauxhall identified from the accumulated intelligence their sources uncovered. Some of the intelligence came from the agent who had been carefully placed inside the centre of the group known as Daesh.

Although Daesh was multifarious in its aims, as well as in its capability, it was the group's finances that were the single topic under discussion at a high-level meeting attended by Meadows with one other from her floor. In all, it was an assembly of representatives from various intelligence bureaux along with the Deputy Governor of the Bank of England.

Nothing was particularly odd about the delegates, other than one, a young man from cyber security who looked completely out of place. Where everyone, apart from Judith with the one other woman present, wore suits, shirts with ties, the young man in question wore a pair of ripped jeans and an untidy shirt, without a tie. He was the invited technical speaker, introduced by Judith's counter-intelligence female colleague.

Her summarisation of the meeting was, I'm sure, accurate, but without any explanations of the esoteric terms, I was no wiser about cyber security than I was before I had heard of its name. I genuinely hoped the tape-recording I was making of her summary meant something to whoever had the pleasure of listening to it.

She spoke of a report from the National Intelligence Service of Iraq that revealed the combined assets of Daesh, held as traceable bank deposit assets, totalled more than seven billion dollars, plus change. They got their money in various ways, but again there was one way that caught my avid attention—kidnapping for ransom. Judith told a very tragic example.

A Swedish gas extraction engineer, working for the Iraqi Ministry of Gas and Oil, was kidnapped, not by Daesh, but by a group calling themselves The Rapid Extraction From Iraq, or REFI for short. It was treated by the Iraqi Intelligence as part of ISIS. He was taken from what was considered to be a secure site just outside the city of Basrah. I had knowledge of Basrah as it was somewhere Sabah Al Salim was known to have lived.

Nobody had heard of this group, nor was it on

any outlet that could be factored by the usual worldwide development agencies. Once again, it was a team containing Judith who were given the task of identifying who was in charge of this Rapid Extraction From Iraq.

"We found them within an hour of looking, Harry. You would have been so proud of me. After we exposed the members of the group, we located two of the founders who also belonged to the Popular Mobilisation Forces of Iraq. It didn't stop there. I bet you can't guess where the groups banked all the money they got from extortion?"

"It wasn't Annie's, was it?" I asked, unable to control my concern about there being another scandal at the once owned family bank.

"No, but you were close. I'm joking, Harry. Not close in the sense of being in a close proximity. Although there is an element of that enmeshed in it. Oh, okay. Don't look so glum. I'll give sweetie-pie a clue to stop him from crying. There are facilities in one bank in the City of London for payments deposited into the bank to be transferred into the bank I'm talking about."

"Judith, you can use virtually any high street bank to pay money into an account held in another bank."

"I know you can, but as I understand things, you can't if the bank has no British, or European branch. No matter, it's immaterial. The bank in question is your pet winged horse kind, dearest; Pegasus. We'd found another player who's paying in money, and shed-loads of it. I wonder why all this money is going into a private bank of the Central Intelligence Agency via a private investment bank in the City of London you're well aware of?"

Once again, she was looking straight at me as if probing the facts to find the lie that was my condemnation. This was not an innocent game of hiding the truth she wanted to play. This was straight from the book on Communist interrogation. She was reaching out for the mistake she was yet to find in the fiction I was giving away free.

CHAPTER SIX
BIG FEATHER

"Yes, you were right about there being a place in the fence secluded enough to throw a written message over and update me on various affairs, and yes, you were right again in believing at least one meeting took place. Do you want to go for three correct answers in a row? No coconuts to win, I'm afraid, but if we shout loud enough and long enough, we might get a cup of Rosie Lee. That's if our luck is in. What do you say, eh? Eh, sir?" She was pushing me, but it wasn't into a place I didn't want to go.

"Come on, Mr Home Office man. What does that plaque say on a wall at that iconic bastion of Englishness, Lord's Cricket Ground? P'lay up, play up, and play the game'? Eh? You know I'm right. The outcome is unimportant, it's in the game where one's virtue is decided."

I didn't ask another question at that moment; instead, I smoked a cigarette whilst trying to grasp all the conflicting information I had on this Pegasus Bank. The bank was clearly an American clearing house going back as far as when they bailed Hugh Pickering out of a hole to get an established foot in Europe. My mind was estimating the amount of money from the cleared away excess defence budget along with excesses from other government agencies, including the CIA itself. Wow, I thought. How many billions must be in there?

Going back a few years, I had discovered a similar bank in Panama that was used by elements of American intelligence agencies to fund incursions, then interference, with other governments in other countries. Back in those days, this would be disguised as government foreign policy. For example, when the American government refused to pay ransom to Hezbollah, who were holding American hostages, the money was raised from an account in the same Panama bank. If ever a journalist managed to trace it to its source, it would show up as coming from a deceased American philanthropist who, as an act of benevolence, had left sufficient funds in an account for such eventualities.

However, it didn't stop at relatively small amounts, collected as ransoms. From other accounts came monies to fund anti-communist fighters, government changers if you prefer in the case of Nicaragua leading to the Iran-Contra scandal that almost destroyed the Reagan administration. At that time, the American government had been embarrassed by implication.

Then along come the Popular Mobilisation Forces of Iraq, with strong connections to ISIS, or whatever the groups were calling themselves, banking the combined ill-gotten funds into a bank that somehow the CIA had managed in secret. How ironic was that? I asked, whilst trying not to look too disillusioned with life. Life around money was complicated, it seemed.

Whilst there was a hiatus as we slowly walked around the perimeter, I asked again about Bottomly. Did she know him? I was expecting the same denial, but, for some reason impossible to explain, there was more than just hope in the back of my mind.

"Yes, I'm sorry I lied, but I wasn't trusting you completely when you first asked. I think I have, or better still *we* have, got past that stage of mutual mistrust."

It will probably sound silly to you, especially as here it is, in print for eternity for all to see, but to me there was still an element of mysticism about this woman. How she could change from being a little girl in need of her mother's love to a sophisticated woman dealing in the secrets of life with the agony of death rolled into one, showing no distinction between the two, I did not have enough wisdom to understand. I simply listened.

"Again, I'm sorry if sometimes I sound flippant and insensitive. I'm really neither of those things. But I find it difficult to relate to the fact I murdered two members of your family, yet here we are talking, both of us being impeccably mannered. You should be wanting to rip me to pieces with your bare hands. I should be wanting to get out of here, with zero thought to giving you the whole shebang too early. If I did give you it all too soon, I couldn't trust you. That's how I felt, until now. Now I can trust you. Can you understand that, Harry?"

Yes, I could understand her and yes again, I might have withdrawn the offer of clemency to the self-confessed murderer and a traitor to the country I was meant to be protecting. I needed a break from this protocol. A break from me forbidding the use of my name.

* * *

It was a photograph I'd seen in the magazine rack at Gardie House, of the Russian, so-called, meteorologist, Valery Agapov, who was there getting off the Lerwick ferry before I visited Judith's place of incarceration, that had me wondering first, why did she have to be told of my visit, and second, why had he not killed her by throwing something sprayed with polonium over the wire? Why allow her to live?

I guessed the answer to the second part of the questions could depend on the man who Judith had fallen in love with being kept alive. Was it true, if he were to die, then her secrets had no value? Perhaps it was a plain question of as long as he lived, she lived. Yet how did she keep him alive? Just maybe, Judith had something else that did not rely on the man whose name we are not mentioning.

When I put the name of Valery Agapov to her, she agreed it was he who came to pass on the message about my probable arrival. I thought there was little point in asking if she knew it was Alexi Vasilyev who had composed the underlying meaning in the message—*emissaries having more information can be found where the pastures are closed in the north.* Nor, I thought, was there much point in telling her it was this message that had brought me to the island. I did, however, tell her the name of the man who was chosen to deliver the written message to Katherine in New York, Dimitri Georgievich Oborka. But now I decided to ask and tell her everything I knew, and I was pleased with myself that I had.

According to Judith, who I was now trusting to tell me the truth, both the hidden meaning in the cryptic messenger's surname of Oborka, and the hidden meaning in the passed-on spoken message, were typically the type of clue used by one of the departments Alexi Vasilyev might either have served in, or commanded, before the attempt on his life.

I wondered if not changing a surname when composing a legend was a clue he'd leave if it suited his plan? I did not ask. Not asking suited my plan. As I was contemplating what could it be that Vasilyev wanted from me, Judith decided to detonate the bomb that swallowed my brain into the crater it created.

"After the attempt on Alexi Vasilyev's life, by electrocuting the door handle to his apartment, his field work for any Russian intelligence branch was curtailed for quite some time. His work for the Americans was also finished. He would be too easily recognised to be put to work in any covert fashion, equally he was too valuable to allow to lose himself sailing boats on the Caspian Sea. As far as the Americans were concerned, he could be even more valuable, depending on where he could hang his hat, as it were.

"When he was, eventually, assigned to work, he was co-opted to a coded signalling traffic unit, where he applied the same amount of energy and vigour as he'd done to everything he had ever touched. Agapov told me how Vasilyev built up lines of listening and siphoning stations, zig-zagging across Russia, from Africa and the Middle East, through which all radio traffic was streamed before being deciphered.

"Very recently, one of his so-called delineation portals discovered some messages communicated between a Syrian ISIS group and a mobile communication hub using a system nobody had ever seen before. One they believed to be unbreakable. Vasilyev's immediate overseer wanted answers he was unable to supply, causing—and remember, Harry, this is coming from Valery Agapov, not me—a sense of fierce hostility between him and his commanders.

"Agapov then said to me, 'Alexi Vasilyev wants to defect.' Yes, defect! That's what he said. Then he confirmed Vasilyev was working for the Russians as well as the Americans. Can you get your head around that?

"Neither Agapov nor Alexi could contact you directly with this. It would be impossible for Alexi to leave Russia to meet you before a plan is worked out. As far as Agapov goes, he said you would not believe him if it came from him. There was also the possibility of directional microphones on him and you when he was in London talking to you, but there were none here. He'd checked! It was Alexi who thought you would believe me.

He admired how you handled Korovin's departure."

I tried to protest.

"Yes, I realise it was Korovin who made most of the arrangements, but Alexi is looking at it in a different way. He knows how Valery Agapov works. Alexi is not the type of man who trusts easily. He's bought Valery Agapov's loyalty. He doesn't have to do that with you. You, he can trust.

"If Vasilyev goes, so does everything he knows about Russian signalling traffic, interpretation capabilities, coding, everything in communications. As I understand things, the depth of Russian decrypting and encrypting is immense. Then there is the ability to penetrate cyber networks across the world. There is, of course, a caveat that I have yet to mention." I wanted to let her continue, but I couldn't. I had to ask.

"Why would you want to help a Russian such as this Vasilyev escape to the West? I can understand Agapov doing anything if he's being paid. But you? Maybe Agapov wants to defect as well, that makes sense, but why are you helping? I don't get it, but Agapov clearly does. What is it he knows that I don't, Judith? Please, enlighten me."

"You know how it was Valery Agapov who came to see me inside Belmarsh top-security prison, posing as part of my solicitor team. He's an ultra-clever being, Harry. If I were you, I would be very careful of him. I think he knows people very high up the chain."

I found that remark troubling. I had a traitor telling me to be wary of a Russian traitor. One who might want to defect and who would be a huge asset, but to be careful of him. What on earth did she think I am? I was about to ask, but thought it best to leave her to tell more of him, hoping more interesting stuff would be divulged. I was coming round quickly to the thought that she didn't know if Agapov wanted to defect. He hadn't told her.

"The reason why Valery's been in the London embassy for so long, is because so many Russians are in London, having property in the capital as well as scattered around the English countryside. He is a careful man and in the time he's been here, he's learned what he calls 'London habits', and the way things are handled in the capital. Money speaks volumes to him.

"He came here to make certain I stayed onside and on plan, as he put it. All nonsense to me, but by the time he'd finished I understood his meaning. He told me what I've told you about settling in Canada. Then he said something I found very complimentary, but also very strange. Alexi had told Valery he thought it best to have a native English-speaking negotiator presenting his petition to settle in the West. Agapov suggested me.

"If you can land Vasilyev, well, I don't know what to say, you can name your own price for the sizeable feather to add to your cap. Alexi Vasilyev needs some special care. I mean, not only because of his medical condition, but, as we now know, he's been an American asset operating in Russia. He asks for you to be his protection and his personal help to navigate around the hurdles. He wants you to organise his escape without him being... ruffled.

"Which leaves only me. What I would like I cannot have, so I'm going to make you work hard to get all I know you want out of me. I'm also going to need a good whisky, which I know you must have and another of your cigarettes, then we can make a concerted start."

I asked the nearest naval rating to organise the retrieval of the opened bottle of Jura from my room along with two glasses. Also the open packet of cigarettes that was on the table. My latest resolve to stop smoking was not holding up. I had some of her brand in the room and I promised again to bring a packet the next time we met. Reasonably, I figured an apology for forgetting was not necessary. It was then I asked her if she feared for her life, being here in an open prison.

She had noticed the increased naval presence and now she knew why. I was castigated for it, but it was done with a smile.

"Tell me something, Judith. Why would this Russian, Alexi Vasilyev, who I've only heard of, want me to help him defect when he must have better placed contacts in the CIA who would be only too pleased to help?"

"That's where you're wrong. I asked Agapov the same question, but in a different way. I asked him what the CIA would do if they knew Alexi Vasilyev wanted to defect. It didn't take much time for him to reply they would kill him and everyone else who knew. He said it really was as simple as that.

"Vasilyev has worked both sides of the fence for a long time. He's got so much information stored in his head. The things is, Harry, if you help in his defection, you run the risk of being killed by the Americans as well.

"I'm sure Mr Jeremy Isaac Furley would be only too pleased to share a cup of tea with Alexi Vasilyev, looking out at the Houses of Parliament, whilst the discussion is about the CIA. He could even provide all the relevant departments with the facial recognition of all the CIA and FBI agents ISIS have a lucrative association with. What would Mr Furley and the Foreign Secretary recommend if one of the British top operatives was about to go over to the other side? Hmm, Harry?"

I didn't answer her question. I couldn't see the point.

CHAPTER SEVEN
THE COUNT

"Earlier in the week, you asked me about a Kuwaiti named Sabah Al Salim. I gave you an answer, but I was a bit vague when I answered. I would like to enlarge on what I've told you."

It was a warm start to the day, with both of us, I thought, in good spirits. I had wondered what the day would bring forth, following on from the revelations of the day before about Vasilyev wanting to defect. That news had come with his request to have a native English speaker on his defection team. The thought of being first in line for this role had made Meadows begin the day with Sabah Al Salim, without any preamble from me.

We were outside once again, this time seated at one of the only two tables on the stone patio, in the process of taking a leisurely cup of coffee whilst smoking cigarettes. On the face of it, we were two people without a care in the world. Well, at least that's the image she wanted to portray.

Part of the reason for my good mood was because I had fulfilled my promise of making sure Judith had her own cigarettes. I had bought her brand on the mainland whilst waiting for the flight to the Shetlands, but kept forgetting to take them from my room. Despite my genial optimism, the laissez-faire attitude of mine was to change quickly after her opening submission.

"Now we're into the bargaining stage, I'll be more open with you.

Although I told you about the assassination attempt on this Al Salim, I've never given you as full an answer as I should have. I would like to put the record straight now. However, before we start, you have to understand you will not like much of what I have to say, which is not just confined to Sabah Al Salim. As unsavoury as it may be, Harry, you must listen, and listen carefully.

"Sabah Al Salim is a tremendously powerful man. He is immensely wealthy with, as I understand, most of his vast fortune coming from historic investments his family has made. In the chain of command of the Pegasus, he answers to your friend Viscount Winston Bottomly. Yes, as I've said, I know Bottomly. It's he that, first my father, then the man whose name we are both avoiding, told me was in charge of most things that happened in Southern Africa. Especially to do with the AWB. My father called him by a shorter name—he called him the Count. That was Bottomly's constantly used sobriquet.

"My father told me who the Count was when we were first invited to stay at the Bottomly home in Somerset. A place I was told you are aware of. Valery Agapov told me you know it. He also said you were involved in a cover-up of a murder. Both barrels, eh! He certainly made a mess of her.

"Before you say anything, whatever happened is not important. I heard the name Count fairly recently. It was when I was told of a shipment of weapons from China that Bottomly had interfered with. I won't go any further on who told me, but it was the title of Count that was mentioned. This Count is the man who has the last say over who gets an introduction into the Pegasus Mercantile Company and who gets an invitation to use any of the facilities of the bank.

"I've never heard the names of those at the top table of the Pegasus Bank. I know Valery Agapov knows them because he loves telling me who he knows, but I don't know. So there's no point asking me. All I can say is, what I knew about the Mercantile Company may well have changed by now. But big corporations like this AWB, an intricate organisation with a structured code of command, take years to build. It would take something crucially important to have the structure fundamentally altered."

* * *

I met with Jerry Furley the day, following the coffee in the garden when Winston was elevated to the highest chair of Pegasus by Judith Meadows. I wasn't sure yet if I could add the word 'liar' to her present titles of known traitor and murderer, but if I was asked, as I was about to be, did I believe her or not, then my answer would be—yes, I do believe her.

Jerry and I met in Aberdeen, on mainland Scotland. Whereas Shetland was relatively small, peaceful, quiet, scenic, with few people but plenty of sheep, the city of Aberdeen was full of large, grey, granite monuments of office blocks with gleaming industrial oil storage containers. It was certainly modern, without any sheep, for most of the time, but for all of the time, it was cosmopolitan.

I had retaken the taxi journey across Shetland from the ferry terminus, in the north at Lerwick, to the quaint Sumburgh airport at the southernmost tip of the island. It really was a beautifully drive, one I was thankful to have enjoyed before a bumpy flight in a twin-engined plane to Aberdeen airport and an extremely bumpy, wind-affected landing.

I blamed the landing for the urgent need to get my hands on a glass of whisky. Believe it or not, that was something I wouldn't normally do before lunch. It was just a bad day, I told myself, looking for biased reassurance. We met in an understated, friendly restaurant with a fantastic view across the sea, the port area and oil storage being in the far distance, that Jerry had found on the internet. Nobody at The Box knew where he was.

Apparently, since I had been away here in Scotland the Iranian desk at Vauxhall had been busy. They had identified the South African agent who was inside this ISIS group. Not only had they identified him, they had successfully lifted some intelligence he had on the position Sabah Al Salim held inside the Ministry of Intelligence and National Security of Iran. It made a compelling accompaniment to my whisky with a superior lunch to the one I would normally be having at Gardie House.

I raised the subject of Colette and Jackson, the two people Bottomly said he reported to in Afghanistan when posted to the communications hub. Furley had read through the accumulation of paper files, along with the computerised data on Judith Meadows's involvement in the assassination of the French national, known to us as Colette, in Paris, before setting out from London.

Like me, he was surprised there was no escort or extraction security team allocated to France, either before the operation, or on its completion. He was shocked that her orders were to return the firearm to the Embassy, which, incidentally, was over two miles from the bookshop where the two murders took place. That was not the only thing he was surprised at.

He could find no further reference to the gun once it was returned from the British embassy addressed to a little known building, under the Ministry of Defence umbrella, in Hatton Garden, the centre of jewellery shopping, in Holborn, London.

The only thing he could find was the printed name applied to the issuing document as well as its accompanying signature. It was the name of the man I'd already exposed as Judith's treasonable agent. The same one we had allowed to be exchanged for an American flier, held by the Russians. Only he, it seemed, knew of its final location.

" Why was the gun's location a secret?" Jerry asked, as I finished the first glass of whisky and had a stab at answering.

"I think it's been kept to discourage Meadows giving us intelligence which only she has on the man who was exchanged. If the French found out a British agent was authorised to assassinate a French citizen on French soil, all hell would break out on the front pages of the French newspapers.

"I think it would be safe to assume the stink would cause a massive schism on the diplomatic front, with Parisian bureaucrats baying for our blood. Your department would be hugely embarrassed. We could never give her over to the French in case she opened her mouth about the man we gave away for the Americans to facilitate an exchange. They would laugh at us. Our relationship with the French, plus the rest of Europe, is strained enough without adding two murders to it."

Having spoken of Colette, our conversation turned to Bottomly and the man known to him as simply Jackson, along with the nameless man with freckles on the backs of his hands Winston said he'd spoken to before going to Beaulieu House, via Poole in Dorset, from Iraq.

.Jerry knew nothing of this Jackson, never having come across that name being used as a pseudonym or code name from British intelligence. His lack of knowledge didn't stop there. He could not find any report where a flight by any aircraft, let alone a C-17 Globemaster III military transport aircraft, from anywhere in the Middle East to the Royal Marine Barracks at Poole, had been authorised.

After my first mention of Jackson, Jerry had turned his many and various departments upside down in attempting to discover who he could be. There were no reports in any computer folders or anywhere else from an agent named 'Jackson', when Winston was 'working' with a Russian operative called Colette, in Iraq.

What's more, despite another exhaustive search, the code name of Jackson was never allocated during the time Bottomly told of the name. The only remaining conclusion was it had been invented, but Jerry could not tell me why.

The quality of intelligence Bottomly was given to pass to Colette was always low-grade, according to the mandate Furley had received. Nothing of any consequence, he told me, promising to keep an eye out for any more developments. I was at a loss to understand why Winston would go to that much trouble if there was nothing to gain from it? Perhaps he wanted to play the game he was shown at Beaulieu without harming our intelligence service, while giving Colette to us? As I sat staring out to sea, I wondered again if I ever did know a man named Viscount Winston Bottomly.

I changed the direction of our conversation to cover the defections. It was my understanding that whoever it was inside the American CIA controlling the Pegasus Bank, dealt solely with Yuri Bogden. Valery Agapov was a shrewd Russian agent, especially when dealing with this bank. I thought I might know the reason why he used another name with the bank, but I was unable to prove my suspicions unless certain documents were opened to me.

Agapov had told me how he had used the identity of Yuri Bogden to build a series of special relationships going back many years with just one particular man inside the CIA, who had top-level access to every section of the Pegasus Mercantile Company. From that, I understood Valery kept his other dealings with the CIA entirely away from the company. So, provided what I'd been told was correct, his defection was made considerably easier.

When it came to Vasilyev, things were progressing far quicker than I'd thought possible, but as I listened, I realised they were along a different road entirely. Jerry briefed me on a Skype connection between Vasilyev and Sabah Al Salim which was successfully broken into by the dedicated cyber-intelligence unit at Menwith Hill. Vasilyev had informed his CIA control, an intriguing figure for us to identify, of the conversation which focused on the island of Cyprus, in particular the British Sovereign Base Areas of Akrotiri and Dhekelia. There had been no reference to the present arm of the British military who occupied the sites, the RAF.

Whilst they were speaking of our two RAF bases, they made no mention of a current mission operating out of Akrotiri, code name Shader, an RAF mission mounting strikes on Daesh, ISIS, in Iraq and Syria, but, as the conversation developed, reference was twice made to a figure known as the Count. Both mentions of the name were during a discussion on the evolving situation in South Africa, where it was decided to leave matters to 'the Count'.

Having heard Judith's account of Winston Bottomly, we were both aware of the Count and Bottomly being the same person. The CIA needed to be approached for an expanded explanation from Alexi Vasilyev, on the reason our signal reading posts on active RAF stations were of interest.

Of course, both of us wanted to know more of why two Russians were discussing the RAF bases, but any enlarged explanation was hampered by the delicate nature of Vasilyev's close association with the American intelligence service. We had a good enough idea about the subject, so it would be prudent to wait until after a successful defection. Unless I could persuade Valery Agapov to divulge anything about it.

Secrecy was foremost in our minds when it came to the RAF bases the Russians were speaking of, as it was the ability we had of seeing over the horizon which the Russians obviously wanted. We needed to know how they intended to go about getting it.

One thing that worried me about it all was the fact that signals from Cyprus were seen by Charles Oswald Wallace, with possibly others from the civil service, before being seen by Jerry Furley at MI6. I could do nothing about it, but Jerry was in a position where perhaps he could. He could raise his concerns about the complex radar structure having being breached directly in front of the Joint Intelligence Committee. Then, to strengthen his mythical worries, have the retrieval system for the signals overhauled directly from GCHQ, where it should have been from the beginning. This he agreed to do at the earliest opportunity.

Our main anxictics now rested on the defections themselves and the fact that Judith Meadows knew nothing concrete of Agapov's desire. As I've said, Valery Agapov would be the easier of the two, simply because he was regularly seen away from his posting at the London Russian Embassy. That ease of movement could not stop questions being asked when his absence became a lengthy period of time. One thought Jerry was toying with, was for them to defect to a country other than us. That, he argued, could help to keep their relocation sites more securely secret. Every advantage we could grab, we should. It was as I was thinking of grabbing hold of things, that a negative thought entered my mind.

I was talking in my head again and it seemed as though the seascape in front was reflecting my changing concerns. As the wind was picking up the crashing waves, so the individual worries rushed through my head, crashing into one another, until at last they merged together, pushing the strongest, most pressing worry to the front. Was Alexi Vasilyev's reason for me to help with his defection because he wanted to kill me for what Paulo Korovin did to him?

* * *

The meeting in Aberdeen lasted a little short of three hours, with fading daylight for the flight to Shetland and then more so for the country drive from the airport to Lerwick. Autumn was coming quickly in this part of the world at the top of the British Isles, where parts are nearer Norway than Scotland.

Humans can do most things nowadays, from the exploration of space to discovering different ways to cause pain to each other, but fortunately they cannot stop the contrasting red and yellow colours of the leaves in the hedgerows or on the myriad of trees we passed, when autumn approaches. There was one special request I made of Jerry with my mind on his variety of departments; where I did want to alter the stability of one particular possibility, yet to be decided upon.

I was reflecting on the simplistic arguments going on in my mind as I looked through the list of missed calls on my phone and I read the messages from Serena, as well as the one from Katherine. Serena's were the more straightforward. She wanted me to read, then sign, the divorce papers her solicitor had prepared, ready to send to Harrogate. From what I could understand, these papers referred to the properties in Portugal and Brazil, on which I was prepared to make no claim, but that decision relied on reciprocation on her part, and no claim from her on the estate at Harrogate or on the two properties in the Paterson name in London: Chester Square and the one in Eaton Square.

I had signed that house in Eaton Square over to George Northcliffe, Paulo Korovin's illegitimate son, as a wedding present, preferring not to listen to my wife's protests. It was the first time I think we had argued over money. For some reason, I had anticipated this insignificant rift becoming a cumbersome affair by the fairly easy way she announced the name of her solicitors, adding how I should be prepared to sign the legal documents, served at my London solicitors, 'as I was always somewhere unreachable'. I was right, as it was a matter of a few days after that dispute when the divorce proceedings began.

She saw the transferred deeds of a thirty-five-million-pound home in central London, her valuation, as a betrayal of trust, disloyalty to my legal wife and son, as well as being generally dishonest. I should have seen it coming, I guess, in the way she alleged I was scheming with George to keep the Eaton Square home in the Paterson name. " That way," she said, "it would be beyond Breno's reach." I alleged she was mad. On my solicitor's overpriced advice, I had withdrawn the allegation.

Katherine's message was far more pleasurable. Our son, Luca Tovanisch, had been presented with a Medal of Achievement from the Musical Academy of Vienna. It was a supreme accolade, especially for someone so young. He has a bright future which I am sure his mother and I will do our utmost to safeguard.

Katherine had changed one letter of her father's patronymic name and taken Tovanisch as her surname, passing that on to our son. She wanted the Russian connection, rather than my own English heritage. Initially, I regretted her decision, with some of that regret still remaining, but as she was bringing up our son, with my only contribution being financial, I felt as though I had no moral right to insist on any alteration.

Her father, known by his pseudonym of Paulo rather than his full, traditional Russian names, had invented all his false identity with help from his mother, Andrea, when the two had arrived in Russia as part of the Children of Russia campaign being coordinated in Spain. It was in Spain where great grandfather Maudlin and Andrea had met.

This Children of Russia movement helped almost three thousand children, with some single parents, to be evacuated by the Spanish Republican authorities to Russia. They came from communist sympathisers to the Soviet Union, to avoid the rigours of the Spanish Civil War. By the time of Andrea's death in 1955, Paulo was known as Comrade Tovarisch Sereyovitch Korovin, inside the KGB.

He served three years in the Russian KGB, after leaving Leningrad University, where he had kept himself busy writing his final thesis on international law. Luca had the Paulo bloodline running strongly through his veins.

Another strength he had inherited was his grandfather's tenacity to succeed, only it was a long way from the espionage career his grandfather followed. I was sure Paulo would have been as proud as I was. Only now I had the added stimulus of Alexi Vasilyev presented into my son's upbringing, when Katherine was made fully aware of her previous lover's impending presence.

No matter how proud I was, or how angry Serena was likely to become, I was needed in London, to leave a message in Gerald Neil's club, now being operated by Gerald's only son, Ryan Neil. On my first evening back in town, I paid him a visit at Crocketts to offer my condolences. He made me welcome, saying his father had often mentioned my name.

Whilst we chatted about the ills of the world, I happened to mention Winston's surname and the name of Upington, in the North Cape area of South Africa. Ryan knew it. He had stayed at the Bottomlys' spacious home for two weeks, when he was twelve. He was there with Gerald, his father.

We spent a good hour talking about his South African memories, which left me with no idea if his knowledge would prove useful or not. It was most certainly enlightening. As was his father's close relationship with Bottomly, which I was definitely not aware of. On the way out, I left a message with

Agapov's recommended croupier, proposing a meeting for the following lunchtime. No doubt when Ryan saw me in conversation with one of his attractive croupiers, he believed all his father's salacious stories about me. I hoped he would keep an open mind.

CHAPTER EIGHT
WOOLWORTHS

The house at Chester Square was empty. It wouldn't take much for me to move in for a few nights. I kept a wardrobe and a razor, etc. there. More importantly, the trusted forty-year-old Isle of Jura single malt was in the decanter with the ice machine in the cellar, along with more bottles of the Jura as reinforcements. No doubt I could call someone to share the evening with, making the time pass in a pleasant, enjoyable way. Then the night. Well, as I said, we should let nature take care of itself or words to that effect, but somehow I had allowed the argument Serena and I had on the telephone over the Eaton Square home to get inside my head and mess things up. So I went to my club and took a room there. I ended up chatting to Oliver Ronda, the Member of Parliament for some obscure part of the United Kingdom, with whom I played rugby at Cambridge when we were both there and a considerable bit younger. We put the world to rights before I turned in, leaving him in the company of another person I knew, but cannot recall the name of.

It came as a bolt out of the blue at breakfast to find a sealed note had been left with the desk steward from the Director of the American Department of National Intelligence, a Mr Howard James Fredrick Mercer II. Would I please call him at the address on the card? It was urgent! The number was not for the embassy, which for many reasons I knew by heart. It was for the American Ambassador, at Winfield House, in the centre of Regent's Park. Mercer's note had been left at my club an hour before I had risen. He was an early bird, for sure, as it was a little past seven o'clock in the morning. It crossed my mind to wonder if a similar message had been left at the Chester Square address, but then I wondered why he would know of that address?

We met an hour or so later the same morning at the restaurant in the Inner Circle of Regent's Park. Although it was a short walk from the American ambassador's residence, I thought Mercer would arrive by the usual American showy motor vehicle cavalcade of at least four, or more, blue-and-red-light-flashing, noisy cars. I pictured the staff trying to pacify the elderly customers at the quiet, very old-fashioned restaurant as they fainted in shock from it all. But I had not allowed for my habit of incorrect assessments. It had not changed. I was wrong. Mercer had walked. What's more, he was in a buoyant mood, unlike the first time we had met.

"How's our old Kathy keeping nowadays, your lordship? I make it a habit of keeping up with our Russian friends as much as I can. You're looking in fine fettle, I must say," he said, as he extended a hand in greeting.

I shook his hand and signalled to a waitress we were ready to order. I thought he wouldn't be, but I was ravenous, having taken only tea with toast at the club, not wishing to dull my appetite. I did not allow a response to his puerile question concerning Katherine to spoil the occasion, but just as I decided not to answer, I remember thinking how he had a bit of a subdued crush on her the last time the three of us met, in her luxurious apartment in New York.

"I remember so clearly your final remark to the lady you speak of, Jimmy. Can you remember what you said?"

"I haven't got a solitary, Harry, old bean," he replied, in a pronounced, sarcastic English tone.

"I'll take an English tea, Miss, please, and I've already eaten with the ambassador this morning, so I won't require a menu." He returned the menu to the waitress. I noted the ambassadorial comment, as did no doubt at least two of the other diners, along with our waitress.

"The reason why I remember what you said is that I wish I'd thought it myself. You said, 'May your future be one of broad-painted strokes of respectability.' I thought it to be very charming and very unlike you."

The middle-aged waitress wore a deadpan expression, being accustomed to so many diners over the years that not a lot would cause her any distress.

"I'll have a full English, please," I said as I, too, handed her my menu.

"A full English? Aren't you English enough, Harry? I would have thought being a lord would make you a full enough Englishman," an excited Mercer asked in a loud, agitated voice, losing the sarcastic English inflection in favour of his native New York accent, causing the diner with her back to us on the table nearest, to turn around to see what the disturbance was all about. The waitress had adopted a slight smile to the edges of her deepened expression and decided to enter the exchange.

"It's the breakfast, sir, the full English. It's on the menu. Very hearty and popular. Here it is, sir. Would you like to order one as well?" she suggested, handing Mercer an open menu with her finger pointing to the selection of a Full English Breakfast, along with the full list of its contents underneath. Jimmy was genuinely smiling at the menu-holding waitress as he slowly shook his head in self-denial.

I'm sure I glimpsed the lady opposite, who had

turned around and previously appeared startled, smile to her friend who also was smiling. It maybe strange to foreigners how the British laugh at themselves, but to me I find it reassuring how we as a race find humour in most things we come across, never afraid to find all manner of things harmlessly amusing.

Mercer was very smartly dressed, in a dark blue suit and a white shirt, with a yellow-and-blue striped tie. His shoes were of the highly polished variety and his hair, what there was of it, neat and tidy. He was almost bald now, whereas before when we'd met, he still had some white hair. I was smiling to myself as I knew his age to be fifty-six, getting it from a phone call to the station officer at Thames House, thereby avoiding the need for an estimate, and getting it wrong.

The heavy, black-rimmed glasses he wore were the same, or at least very similar, which, as he polished them in a deliberate manner, clearly showed his small, brown-coloured, pinched eyes to be most certainly the same. The other thing that had not altered was his physique. He still appeared to be underfed and weak. I dare not think of him in the clutches of an energetic woman, I'm afraid he would disintegrate. His annoying impatience had not changed, either. His voice quietened to a fading whisper, as he explained his purpose.

"I know you are aware of a Russian agent I used

to run when in the CIA, codenamed Vagabond. You also know his real name: Alexi Vasilyev. I'm aware he has informed you, through the detainee you have in Scotland, that he wishes to defect, wanting you to be the one in overall control of his defection. There is also another Russian national that wants to jump ship. His name is Valery Agapov."

He stopped speaking to assess how much his declaration had affected me. His eyes darted from one of my eyes to the other. I hoped I showed no reaction. However, inside I wondered how he knew, as there were no directional microphones anywhere near Gardie House. I did not say a word. I had no need to!

"Don't trouble yourself wondering how I know. Vagabond was following my department's instructions, first to tell Agapov how much he wants to defect, and then get that message to you. Hmm, the tea's very good. I couldn't trust the coffee. Let's see where this all began, Harry, shall we?"

Again there was the examination and yes, I was intrigued, but I had learned the last time we met not to encourage him with speculation. Just allow the dialogue to proceed with him setting the tempo.

"Your buddy, this Viscount Bottomly. What a name that is to walk around with! Thankfully, that's his problem, not mine."

No, I would not rise to his bait, although I did worry about what was to come. The first jolt to my friendship with Winston Bottomly was when Gerald

Neil mentioned the gambling debt; after that, it was downhill all the way. Wherever the Director of American National Intelligence was going with his denunciation, it would not be the start of the end to my friendship with Bottomly, but it could well be the ending of the end, of that I was, thankfully, aware.

"He helped us with one or two little difficulties we had during the troubles between the South Africans and every mercenary the Russians could give an automatic Kalashnikov rifle to. Anyhow, this Bottomly struck up a relationship with this Russian called Valery Agapov, way back when the South Africans were having a spot more bother than they needed. The UK had abandoned them, as had we and the whole of Western society, who branded them odious and repulsive depending on which politician was asked. But, at the time, they were the only ones in that part of the world standing up against communism.

"The Russians wanted Angola as bright a red-coloured communist state as was possible. If they could have established a base there, they would have secured their stretched supply lines, allowing them to push on and take over Namibia, Zambia, all parts north until they could link hands with the Al-Qaeda group we've identified in the Congo.

"If those two countries fell under the Russian influence, the nightmare could become the truth with the rest of southern and middle Africa painted red again. Not this time as British territory. It would have been fully Russian. It really wouldn't have taken much for them to achieve that. In one of those ten-year plans the Soviets were so fond of, the complete continent of Africa would be blood-red communist, apart, that is, from South Africa. But only if the Whites held onto power.

"Do you know something, Harry? I could get used to your tea if I was over here for any amount of time. I can still taste the tea we had at your little place in Yorkshire, with your butler serving it in the summerhouse that day you told me to keep my hands well clear of anything of yours. Joseph was your butler's name, was it not? Still there, is he?"

"It is, yes, and thank you. He is still with me, Jimmy. I shall pass on your regards."

Was I in the company of the same man? I couldn't believe it. He was polite, where before he was the complete opposite. He liked walking and liked tea. Could I possibly begin to like him? We must see, I vowed.

"The day I was at your place, I remember you saying how much you hoped we never met again. Well, we have. I'm hoping we can get on better than the last time. We have work to do together, Harry. It's important work, but first, let me not forget my manners and personally thank you for your discovery of the Russian spy, 'Lionel'. I can't remember if I did add my thanks to the millions you must have had.

Time may have moved on from those Cold War days, but knowing 'Lionel's' real name helped my men in the intelligence agencies a whole lot. Now, the two of us have another problem to solve. If you've finished that breakfast of yours, it's a lovely day for a walk and I have a story to tell you that might take a while."

Winston Bottomly and Valery Agapov had been exchanging information ever since the Russian invasion of Afghanistan on Christmas Eve 1979. "The whole issue of Afghanistan is complicated," said Mercer, or he used very similar words.

Great Britain had problems with Russia back when India was part of the British Raj and the area has attracted interest from not only the countries mentioned, but China has flexed its muscles and of course there's Pakistan and Iran, who have obvious interests over who's in charge. I was thankful we did not dwell on that part of the world for long.

Mercer never commented on the rights or wrongs of previous American operations inside Afghanistan, or on the legitimacy of them. The terrorist atrocities on September 11th had given them enough reason to go in. Whether it was the real motive or not, it was the Al-Qaeda-inspired attack on their country that was used as the reason to enter Afghanistan and then stay while trying to establish a stable government. I was given to understand by Bottomly, he had the same wish—stability for South Africa.

Presumably he had stability in mind when he orchestrated the trading of weapons from America through Israel to the AWB. He told Agapov the details of that deal, arguing that no matter what weapons the Russians put into the hands of the Cubans engaged in the Angolan war, the Americans would not only match it, they would exceed its killing power. Those weapons arrived and when they did, the South African military put them to good use, causing the ragbag army of what the AWB called 'terrorists' to eventually scatter to all parts of Africa.

In regards to the intelligence aspect of the war, at first Agapov contented himself with the small snippets Bottomly was prepared to impart. Valery's problem was he knew nothing about the political players inside Angola or Namibia, but in time he met the man who did. Bottomly organised the introduction of Valery Agapov to Sabah Al Salim. The friendship the two men struck up was a thin affair, based on the one thing the Russians were good at—disruption. With that disruption in mind, Valery wanted to install a communist regime, whereas Sabah wanted to install an ever-growing money chain from the minerals to be found in both Angola and Namibia. The monetary value of the deal Sabah and Valery signed favoured both men, but that was not the only interest they shared.

According to Jimmy Mercer, the relationship between Sabah Al Salim and Winston Bottomly was, and is, far stronger. Not only do they share the love of money, they share the love of women, gambling, and power. Those passions held the same intimacy for Valery. However, it was the obscene accumulation of vast sums of money that gave Valery Agapov the greatest satisfaction.

Listening to the account of the accumulation of money made me wonder if the reason Gerald Neil allowed Bottomly to amass such a large debt was because somehow he knew the extent of Winston's true wealth? I quickly dismissed that as the nonsense it must be, returning to hear what Mercer had to say, intrigued by the scope of what he knew; and I didn't.

Sabah was a financier, rather than the banker he'd been depicted to be in other places. He fitted in with the others in this story including Judith's father Edwin, who, according to Mercer's departmental files, had dealings with Sabah Al Salim and other named monetary speculators, several of whom I was aware of. Sabah had, allegedly, many unscrupulous dealings, all of which centred around his idealisation of money, and it was there we were heading. As I already knew, Sabah Al Salim was not his original name, however, I did not know his birth name with its real significance to the story; it was Ali Babak Rostam Farid.

Ali Babak Rostam Farid's family's roots could, and Mercer's department had done so, be traced as far back in time to Darius I. I had no idea who Darius I was, and I certainly didn't want a history lesson, but

Mercer wanted to explain some points. Darius was more commonly known as Darius the Great, the third Persian King of Kings, dating from 522 BC to 486 BC. According to the American research, this King Darius had many wealthy disciples who each constructed powerful, self-perpetuating empires which existed to this day.

His income came from the legitimate ancient monetary systems spread around his empire, including forms of government revenues, that were still in existence and were fully operational. Most of the revenues generated by the ancient avenues of income were, apparently, easy to trace and delve into. Sabah kept all the generated dividend, diverting it into accounts named from derivatives of his birth name. Back in Washington, the employee Mercer had delegated to follow the trail left by the money had unearthed three hundred and fifteen consolidated bank accounts scattered around the world and he was still counting.

One of my previous speculations was true. Mercer confirmed it was Sabah who convinced Bottomly to murder Samantha Bond. The information I had discovered about her earlier life was accurate, leading to her falling into Salim's grasp. Mercer was ambivalent about exactly when it was Sabah considered changing Samantha's role in life, but he was unequivocal about why it was. There was a nasty sting to his words when he explained it was my acceptance of Winston's offer to attend his shoot that impacted on the ultimate decision. I protested, telling him how Sir Leonard Miles was to take my role as the witness to it being an accident before I had accepted the offer, but it counted for nothing.

In inimitable American fashion, Mercer dismissed the British government's Solicitor General's admission in a succinct way; he called him a liar and me naive. When I asked if it was Sabah Al Salim who persuaded Bottomly to propose marriage to the woman he murdered, he admitted he didn't know, but disregarded the question I posed about who had initiated it by saying it was unimportant.

We had been walking for quite some time, which did nothing positive for my knee, which was beginning to ache. I remember thinking the bench we were slowly approaching, nestling under the shadow of spreading branches from what looked to be an ancient oak tree, seemed to be a great place to sit. Mercer must have read my mind. As we sat, I withdrew my hip flask, which we shared, as the explanation continued with the pain in my knee lessening with each swallow.

I listened intently to the complex reason he tendered as to why the murder of Samantha Burns was so pivotal to the overall scenario. It started with Liam Gibson, Gerald Neil and the island of Samothrace. The same place Judith kept wanting to tell me about and I kept wanting to buy time before I heard her. Why was that, I wondered?

Mercer's theory—because that's all it was, a theory—was that somehow Liam Gibson knew Gerald Neil had property on the island of Samothrace. He put forward no concrete evidence to show how Liam knew, but it could have come about through any number of general conversations he had with Bottomly who knew Gerald very well; remarkably well, if the size of his debt was any measurement.

Mercer maintained Gibson spent time researching the island and it was during his research he found it was not reputable archaeologists digging on the island who discovered the missing porcelain fingers Meadows had mentioned; the team responsible for the excavations had no qualifications at all. They were English, so the reports said, but other than that nothing was known.

Further research was impossible as the five men responsible for the digging were all dead. According to the reports, it looked as though they had all been murdered in various manners in different places around the world.

Mercer put forward yet another unsupported hypothesis, this time one that suggested Liam Gibson believed Gerald Neil knew about the dig because of his questionable past. Yes, it was true he had a criminal record, but it was years old, happening when he was a juvenile. The truth was he was a storyteller and the more colourful the story, the better for those listening, followed by the stronger the possibility they would return to his club.

Liam listened to Bottomly retelling some of Gerald Neil's colourful tales and who knows why, but he believed them. Perhaps Liam knew one or more of the murdered men and just knew, or suspected, there must be something vastly valuable hidden on the island. He reasoned if that was true, it meant Gerald Neil had a good idea where, as well as what it was. He waited for a chance to 'ask' him.

As I think I have already mentioned, Mercer's Department of National Intelligence outranked all of the other intelligence agencies in America and as such, it required the man I referred to as Jimmy to report to his President three times a week in peacetime, more so if the need arose in 'other' times. One of the 'other' occasions arose when Alexi Vasilyev, under his code name of Vagabond, contacted Mercer with a story about a bank.

This new secret bank, so Vagabond said, was configured in such a way that the deposited money was kept secret from other investors. Depositors in this new bank included the terrorist groups of Al-Qaeda and ISIS along with smaller groupings in the Middle East, but also money from clearing banks held short-term as well as long-term. Like the bank I had discovered in Panama, it also held misappropriated funds from the American Defence budget, with, in all probability, diverted allocated money to intelligence agencies.

Vagabond knew of the bank because some his departments were running agents in ISIS as well as inside other organisations, several of whom boasted how their money was banked side by side with money from the American CIA.

Mercer approached his President, asking for permission to extend the FBI's existing programme of tracking certain foreign nationals' telephone conversations on landlines, to cellular phones. Vagabond had heard the word Samothrace mentioned and had recommended Mercer concentrate resources there. The extract history function on his department's vast ability for internet searches was engaged which, amongst others, pinged the name of Liam Gibson.

First Gibson's phones were targeted, quickly followed by everyone he called, then those they called, with the system spreading like bees when looking for a new home, and the huge government IBM machines logged them all.

It was unclear as to whether Gibson telephoned Bottomly when Gerald Neil arrived at Devonish House for the annual shoot, or if it was a rehearsed plan put into action when Gerald arrived late on Friday. Jimmy Mercer chose the second scenario for his theory, but it would work either way.

As I thought back to the time in question, I could

recall Winston Bottomly taking a telephone call on the Friday night, when he appeared concerned and agitated. Was it just that part that was rehearsed? If Mercer was correct about Gibson torturing Gerald Neil in order to reveal something about the island, it was obvious Gerald had not divulged a thing, as the CIA had detailed two teams of four agents to the island, carrying Liam Gibson's photograph in their hands.

Now came the time when Jimmy Mercer's true interest kicked in. He was still speculating, but nevertheless he had my attention. During one of Bottomly and Valery Agapov's regular meetings, Bottomly mentions the island to his Russian contact. Valery Agapov's Directorate Q organisation knows about the bank as he reports to his superior Alexi Vasilyev, telling him in confidence how he knows most of the account holders. The conversation went something like this:

"Under another name that I occasionally use, I am a very close friend of the high-ranking American CIA officer in charge of the keys to the bank, Alexi. What, will I tell you his name? Of course not. I'll keep it safe in case I need it sometime in the future. I will tell you the bank's name: it's part of a company called The Pegasus Mercantile Company. My contact in London, the South African one you know of, told me the name of a Greek island: Samothrace. He clammed up after that. I know nothing else, sir."

Back in Washington D.C., Mercer's computer machinery is watching for anything to do with the word Samothrace, other than being part of an ancient area of the world known as the Levant. These extraordinary computers inside his department are calibrated in such a sensitive manner that if even the minutest amount of interest is shown in a particular area, or topic, or a specific word is used, an alert will sound on the bank of screens corresponding to the individual analytical display. It gives Mercer an edge to counter-terrorism. It also gave him an extra pair of eyes on any abnormal activity touching on Samothrace.

The red flashing alert on the main DNI screen was repeated in the office of the same man who had traced Sabah Al Salim's Persian family history he would rather not have been traced. The flashing light on both computer screens was triggered by a laptop owned by Sabah Al Salim, who was by now not only listed as one of the King of Kings of Persia, but also as a terrorist financial supporter who served various of their number with his expertise in accumulating money.

As soon as the laptop was opened, a red light started to flash in the office of the American Intelligence officer who had already gathered valuable information on several terrorist organisations. There was another light flashing on a mainframe computer. This time it was the one in the penthouse apartment in Abu Dhabi, owned by Sabah Al Salim.

He instantly knew then that one or more American Intelligence Agencies were looking at him. "Perhaps," he said to the man he was entertaining, "if they look long and hard, they will find the bank that we both want to keep away from the world's eyes."

"Maybe," Sabah's guest replied, " now would be a good time to find another place as secure as the present one."

And that's roughly where Samantha had the unfortunate luck to come in! How's that, you're asking? Well, here goes, I'll tell it in Mercer's words.

"In just general conversation, Bottomly told Sabah Al Salim he's hosting a 'Glorious Twelfth' shoot which the 'famous' government banker and spy, the English gentleman Lord Harry Paterson, is attending. He's famous not only because he cracked open a Russian spy ring in London, but he safely extracted a Russian born English master double spy from the heart of Russia, Sabah."

And there you have it. Sabah hears that the Paterson family are bankers, or, "Okay," Mercer says, when I raise a hand in protest, "used to be bankers for the British Government, but he's still a lord and still a spy.

"Sabah has two options. One, with you leading the investigations he can find out how close you're getting to the bank he's concerned with and two, he knows there's something suspicious about the island of Samothrace. What it is he doesn't know, but you might solve it if you're as good as what Bottomly says. Sabah sends in Samantha Burns to tie your hands to the sound of both triggers being pulled on a Purdey shotgun, which are heard to resonate from computers screens in Washington D.C. to the state of Virginia and across to the Russian embassy in London before travelling on to Moscow. Good luck with it all, Harry. I'll be at the end of a phone."

CHAPTER NINE
DEATH MUST COME

My education did not end under the branches of that oak tree in Regent's Park. When my hip flask was empty, we carried on walking, with Mercer telling me more of what he wanted.

"I won't apologise for offering your name up to Valery Agapov. It was done so he'll believe his defection will go as smoothly as possible. It's just that I'd like what he knows of this Pegasus Mercantile Company and I'd like it before he decides to leave."

I voiced my worries over the possibility of Alexi Vasilyev holding grudges and wanting revenge for the devastating injuries he incurred when my great-grandfather's son Paulo attempted to kill him, but Mercer would have none of it. He insisted that Alexi had changed from being "a bit headstrong," as he put it, to being "more of a cuddly bear nowadays," he declared.

"Anyhow," he expressed, in a voice I'm sure could be heard in the garden of the Ambassador's house, half a mile away. Luckily for the nearby squawking parakeets, his voice was calmer when he continued—"After they're gone, you won't be bumping shoulders with either of them anytime soon, will you?"

I thought it would be useless to comment so I left it there. Another thing Mercer wanted that I decided not to commit myself on, was total control with the defection, not wanting London engaged more than necessary. Vasilyev's request of me being in charge meant nothing to Mercer—"he's my agent, and my mark. I'm handling it," was his response when I asked what he meant by 'necessary'.

He agreed that Jerry Furley would need to know the specifics, but drew the line at him, saying he didn't trust any government-appointed official such as a Solicitor General, who 'lied', or a chief civil servant who served a prime minister, who, as he put it, "My president tells lies to so why wouldn't your guy?" I had no answer.

We reached the road that ran around Regent's Park and Mercer stopped walking and spoke into a microphone he had in the cuff of his shirt. Within a few seconds, a huge car arrived with two more of his protection team in a second vehicle of a similar nature. I commented on the size of cars he used and wondered why, if he wanted to keep his presence in the country a secret, there was the need for this kind of ostentatious vehicle. He shrugged his shoulders and replied they were both Cadillacs used by the President, who sent them over for Mercer's use whilst he was in Europe.

"I told the President about the ride you gave me in your Rolls Royce when I was last over here, Harry, so he sent these two monsters over so as not to be outdone by anything you had.

"Back home, these things are called 'Beasts'. Can you believe the doors weigh the same as the doors on a Boeing 757 aircraft? These ones have five inches of bulletproof glass all the way round. I'm off to Germany in a couple of days and taking the cars with me, so I've rechristened them Black Moons. I thought the name reflected me—kind of mysterious. What do you think?" He was laughing as he asked, but I felt he meant it.

* * *

I didn't mention Judith and how she wanted to tell me about the island, and again I had no idea why that place seemed to play such an important part in my life. I had never heard of the place before Gerald Neil told me he moored one of his yachts there, having a villa built on the island, next to where he grew his own grapes to make his own labelled wine.

There must be more to the place than that. There was certainly something about the island of Samothrace that had a hold over me.

Although having no direct effect on the island of Samothrace that I could think of, the two vitally important British bases of Akrotiri and Dhekelia on the island of Cyprus had not warranted a comment or observation from Mercer. I found that strange, as the influence their positions have on any targeted terrorist groups is immense. The intelligence this over-the-horizon technique provided had demonstrated its worth so many times by curtailing several terrorist plans before they could be become a major problem. I knew of two such instances. If I knew of them, I figured Mercer must know of substantially more.

The radar coverage those two bases give to British, American and NATO 'eyes', cover an area stretching from the northern extremes of the Russian Federation bordering Kazakhstan, to, in the east, areas of China still designated as top secret to prying drone eyes. The range covers areas of Syria, Iraq, Iran, Afghanistan, Pakistan and the western side of India.

There was a similar installation at the American base in Djibouti that covered an area from roughly Burma to Guinea in Western Africa. I knew of a third site on the British Overseas Territory of Ascension Island in the South Atlantic and it would not come as a shock to find another further south on the

Falkland Islands, allowing the two to cover the whole of South America and Africa, including the South Atlantic to the Indian Ocean. These detector sites are not confined to Cyprus or the bases I've identified, but it would be indiscreet of me to name more.

I did not gain this knowledge from any part of my military service. It came from an intelligence briefing I was invited to attend at Beaulieu Palace in Hampshire, England, last year when my personal clearance level was upgraded from CTC—handling sensitive data or working with unrestricted access to certain government or commercial establishments—to DV. The highest level of security clearance.

Without these extraordinary radar sites, code-named Mace One, Mace Two, in the Cyprus case, knowledge of terrorist movement, as well as to some extent their objectives, would be crucially decreased. Of course, not only terrorists are covered by these bases. Military exercises, or simple troop movements by the Russians, who do not as yet have this capability, are constantly monitored.

With that coverage in mind, I wondered why it was Mercer had chosen not to speak of it. Nor did he speak of Syrian aggression against the Kurdish people along the Turkish border. For the moment, Russia had entered the war on the side of the Syrian president's military intervention against ISIS and Daesh, but how long that support would last was anyone's guess.

My knowledge of the unrest in the Middle East was not as extensive as I would have liked, but Jerry Furley had all the information I needed, so by the time I began to leave London for the return to Shetlands, I appreciated the situation far better than before. In fact, I would go as far as to say I had the semblance of an idea of how important the island of Samothrace was to the area of the Mediterranean, with the Dardanelles Straits the only way in and out of the Black Sea.

With a clearer mind than I had enjoyed for a long time, I was waiting in the boarding lounge for a return flight to Aberdeen when my mobile phone rang. I had already answered quite a few SMS messages from Serena and taken about seven or eight of her calls in the taxi to the City airport, so I was annoyed when it rang yet again, as my curt, "Hello, yes, what do you want this time?" gave testament to. I was, as I admit, abrupt and abrasive, but considering how the previous conversations had gone, it was quite understandable. However, it wasn't my irascible Serena this time, it was Bottomly.

Knowing he was mixed up in the mess Mercer and I had been speaking of, I'd pushed him to the back of my mind so I consciously held myself in check when we spoke. He had arrived in London and was staying for a few days at an address in Chelsea. If all went to plan, he said in what seemed to be a well-rehearsed, deliberate voice, he was returning to South

Africa in three or four days' time. He added how much he hoped to see me whilst he was in the UK.

I had arranged to call on George and Sophie at Eaton Square, but after explaining my delay was inevitable, I turned the cab around and met Bottomly in the restaurant at the Chelsea Harbour Hotel, half an hour or so later.

The first thing I mentioned on seeing him, was the diverted shipment of Chinese weapons from South Africa to the harbour at Walvis Bay, on the Atlantic coast of Namibia. Although not specifically addressed, the cargo was destined for the so-called 'Tam Terras', an idiom for tame terrorists, who held the capital city of Windhoek. I wanted to know if that shipment had arrived at a South African port yet and if the cargo manifest had been altered with the ship's documentation following suit.

With an undisguised grin on his face, he told me the ship had docked at the port I'd mentioned, with the cargo being safely delivered to a site on the southern reaches of the Namibian capital, he added, with a distressing smile to his face.

"Oh yes, Harry, the ship's manifest was certainly changed. What's more, I registered it myself with the Maritime Archives of Lloyds of London's Register of Shipping. I've made sure everything can be found very easily, even for the Chinese," he chuckled, before starting off on another of his practised tirades of insults at the ANC government first, then in no particular order that I can recall, the British government, the White House, plus Americans in general.

I had the chance to make a quick reflection on his overall honesty when I asked if it was more fulfilling for him to have a relationship with a Russian meteorologist, or for Valery Agapov to air his communist views to a South African fascist? But he never answered. Looking back on it now, I doubt he even noticed my sarcasm.

It was going to be a long haul trying hard not to show my true feelings about him and Liam Gibson, together with the AWB fascists they both supported, but in order to get away from the subject somewhat, I went off on a parallel to the proposed takeover.

"By the way, I've spoken to Charles Oswald Wallace, the man with the Prime Minister's ear, about your proposal. I sounded him out on the possibility of Great Britain and South Africa renewing political ties. I mentioned South Africa coming back into the fold as an associate member of the Commonwealth. I obviously mentioned the Cape Town agreement along with the returning minority rule. The last part, the anticipated return of apartheid, he was, as you would expect, none too optimistic about.

"But I put it to him in much the same way as you explained the proposals to me, plus I went out on a limb a bit. I hope you don't mind. I said you could arrange for all, if not all, then most, of the cobalt production to be exported to the UK. He said that to successfully get it through parliament, he would need an appreciable price concession.

"I also said I had great faith in you being able to deliver on your statement of indigenous Black South Africans being at your side when the ANC was removed. After I told him you would include ethnic minorities inside the inclusive South African government, he changed his initial antipathy towards the proposals.

"He's promised to address the subject with the Prime Minister at the end of this week when foreign affairs are usually discussed. At least Wallace seemed sold on the idea. He said it may not come immediately, but he was confident the PM would go along with it, in principle. You know what the civil service is like. It usually takes them years to decide what tea bags to buy for Portcullis House."

I was pleased there was to be no dispute over the cobalt arrangement. I was equally pleased at being able to persuade him to give me the name of the contact he had inside the upper echelons of the Inter-Services Intelligence agency of Pakistan. He wrote the name down for me and as soon as I had the chance I phoned Furley, giving him the name.

I let Bottomly ramble on about one or two things, simply prodding him in the direction I wanted him to speak now and again. One of those directions I wanted him to enlarge upon was the Black Vault illegals I was told were operating in Afghanistan, Iraq, and Iran. 'Black Vault' was a Russian label they gave to a selection of individuals for training as 'in place intelligence covert supply'.

The usual ways of selecting a person to spy on their own country included: financial inducements involving various amounts of money; political persuasion, i.e. dissatisfaction with the ruling government, helping to bring it down; blackmail because of sexual indiscretion; or, something that happens more and more I find in society, emotional dependence, by that I mean—falling in love. The label of Black Vault was used as the gathered intelligence went into a Vault of sorts, first the mind, then somewhere more secure, and the art of spying was often referred to as a Black art.

Bottomly had first-hand knowledge of a number of these Black Vault chosen agents who had infiltrated the Taliban in Afghanistan and ISIS in the same country. I told him London was interested in the Cuban militia in Angola. He confirmed what Alice had told me, but he'd heard from Liam Gibson how his group had captured two Cubans from a prisoner-securing mission. Gibson's group had turned the Cubans by offering money.

Unfortunately, one was killed in an operation when neither of them were able to withdraw. As far as Bottomly knew, there was still one illegal inside the Cuban militia.

He mentioned the name of General du Preez,

but when I pressed him for more detailed information of what was discussed he clammed up, but despite his refusal, I persevered along the lines of my previous lie.

"I almost forgot something. I had a communication from the Foreign and Commonwealth Office before coming here. I told them how you and the General had met in London a little while ago and they asked if the next time you have a meeting with him, you would tell me. I could then arrange for someone to attend as a representative of the government. They could open a line of communication with your General."

Having already mentioned his name, he asked if it was Charles Oswald Wallace who I was speaking to. "No, it wasn't," I replied, "but Wallace had put me in touch with another official, this time at the Home Office."

Once again, Bottomly asked if the attending official would at any time be Wallace. At that, I was sure I sensed animosity towards the Wallace name, so as I thought there might be an opportunity.

"I met with Valery Agapov in London recently over a cup of coffee. Part of our conversation turned to a certain mutual friend of yours, a Sergei Ivanov. Would you like to tell me about him?" Bottomly didn't look very surprised!

"I've spoken to him on numerous occasions in my role with South African intelligence. I think it was he who taught me how to down so much booze without falling over drunk. We had a lot of time together in London, spending several nights enjoying the feminine company at Gerald Neil's club. He knew Gerald and he knew Samantha.

"There's something he told me about British intelligence I've been holding onto in case I needed to barter to get a better position over the ANC business, but we seem to be getting along fine with that. I need you to get me a one-to-one with the British PM at a time that suits me and I'll tell him what Ivanov said. I'm not yet in a position to know for sure when it will be the most beneficial time for me, but when I know, I'll contact you to set it up. Agreed, Harry?"

"Tell me what you know and I'll contact London today. If what you have is as good as you think, then I can assure you the meeting will be made. You have my word on that, and you know what my word counts for."

It worked! Bottomly told me how one night, after consuming many bottles of red wine, mixed with the usual vodka, Sergei Ivanov told a story about a group intelligence briefing held at the Russian embassy in London, where Valery Agapov was boasting how the Russian military had discovered a way to deflect the British radar system installed on Cyprus.

"According to Agapov, the Russians were constructing a jamming system at the Syrian naval base, opposite the island of Cyprus, to deflect radar beams from the RAF bases. Agapov had heard from an unnamed source that instead of sending pulses of radio waves towards an object, the British system sent a cluster of electronic resistant homing head signals to selected orbiting satellites, chosen by a Cybernetic Command desk in London, from where the radar beacons were manoeuvred. The beams would be bounced from these satellites at targets above the normal horizon.

"The targets for these satellites were determined by current events, but Agapov's 'informed' source said the United States Army Cyber Command, at Fort Gordon in Georgia, were co-partners with the British as operational controllers. Agapov went on to say, it was Fort Gordon who correlated the military intelligence, not the British."

I wondered if Jerry Furley might be behind that decision, otherwise the first port of call for the military intelligence report would be the same place as day-to-day information, the office of Charles Oswald Wallace.

Apparently Sergei Ivanov did not know any further details, nor was he certain of any exact dateline; even so, he was absolutely sure Russian intelligence would have feet on the ground in Cyprus, looking to see how the radar worked.

This naval base in Syria was news to me, so I started to dig around for information, messaging Jerry for all he had. Later, as I read the report he'd sent, I could see the connection between the island of Samothrace and the island of Cyprus becoming more obvious, but I wanted to steer clear of Cyprus with its Russian connotations so I changed the subject, asking Bottomly once more if he knew Sabah Al Salim.

Perhaps it was the tone of voice I used, or maybe I wore an expression I was unaware I had, but his mood immediately changed. From being politely sociable, chatting of secret radar bases, he became angrily jingoistic, citing the bloodshed we had both seen on gruesome battlefields around the world.

"Until now, what you and I have seen will count for nothing. What will happen in my country will overshadow the genocide in the Balkans, or anything in Afghanistan, added to the blooded footprints in Iraq. The dead will number close to the total of the two World Wars.

"Never again will the sons and daughters of White-skinned pioneers of the South African veldt, those who developed the South African economy, be subjected to the insatiable Black man's hunger for absolute power. White-skinned South Africans have had to sit back, watching Blacks abuse all we had built, preserved, or managed to defend. I speak for thousands of us and say we've had enough!

"Why should we pander to the greed and gluttony of the few who stuff their bellies full, laughing at the poverty of their fellow Black-skinned people who are suffering, whilst blaming us? We intend to rule the country for the many, but first, death and blood must come. There must at first be a cleansing of the selfish.

"When the last droplet of blood has been spilled, not only the people of my South Africa but all the African nations and beyond will have to judge and choose sides. Mark my words, there will be a revolution throughout Africa, lasting for many years and it will be the Black man who leads that revolt against the tyranny of his fellow ruling Black."

I was struggling to find the right response to his insanity. The one vision I could not get rid of was that of Hitler addressing the obsequious masses in Berlin, with the swastika-emblazoned flags flying in the wind before the slaughter began. I didn't want to get dragged into that discussion.

"That's all well and good, but you haven't answered my question. Do you know Sabah Al Salim, Winston?" I was steaming, but hoped I was able to hide my anger.

"Yes, I know Sabah. I know him very well. It's his money behind what we're planning." Mercer was right, so were my instincts.

"What's more, he, with others like him, have undertaken to fund the first year's programme of the next government of South Africa, allowing what we have in mind to be completed in full. After all that has been achieved, come and ask me if it worked."

I admit I'd had enough. I should have pressed

him about Sabah Al Salim having a connection to the Syrian base at Tartus. Possibly it was he who was scheming to negate the radar stations opposite, but I didn't ask. Nor did he hold back!

"So, you've not put it together yet, Harry, have you? Is the great London hope floundering in the shallows? Come on, man, use a bit of imagination, please. Sabah and I want Russian money, but for Agapov it's more than that. I want British influence switched around to us, then maybe, just maybe I'll be finished with Agapov." He had not finished here with his reproach, but I couldn't put up with any more of this rubbish.

"You're being stupid. You're acting as if your age is the same as your shoe size. None of what you said will ever happen. But I'm not staying to argue with you. It's impossible to argue with a fool, as a fool will never change his opinion. And you're the biggest fool I've come across, Bottomly."

I made my excuses after his all-conquering decree, which made me feel nauseous, not a comfortable feeling for a taxi ride across town to face George, where the over-brewed tea would not only be waiting, but seething to explode after the three-hour delay.

I had used the excuse of having to see Serena later and not wishing to smell of alcohol to not only leave as soon as I could, but also to refuse a drink. This left him to finish the bottle of fine white wine on the table himself. As he'd already made a decent effort to empty it, I couldn't see him having much trouble.

It was not a lie about seeing Serena, but I didn't have to see her today. She was in England, having arrived the day before yesterday from Portugal. She was with Breno, staying with a school friend of hers living in the small hamlet of Goddards Green, West Sussex. I'd met her friend once, some time ago now, when Serena and I, with Breno, had driven out to see her on our way to Brighton for some reason. She seemed a nice person who had a great gallop layout for the horses she trained and bred. I hazarded an educated guess that Breno would prefer to stay in Sussex, riding horses, rather than travel into urban, smelly London to see his ageing father.

Later that day, Jerry confirmed what I'd hoped to be the truth; the four British agents inside Afghanistan and Pakistan had been withdrawn from their assignments, with the last one of them on his way back to the UK.

After my meeting with Serena, who did nothing to compose my nerves, I needed to see Judith and hear more of what Valery Agapov had told her.

CHAPTER TEN

GEORGE AND SOPHIE

I had not noticed the days flashing past, spent delving into secrets, until now. It may have been due to the fact of Serena leaving England for Portugal and Breno returning to Switzerland for his final term at junior school. I was delighted to spend what little time I had available in London with my son. My wife was a different matter. She shouted, she screamed and she cried, all tactics employed to persuade me not to sell the house in London, until she was willing to forgo any wish of using it.

As much as I disliked London, I had no plans of selling the house the family had owned since Lord Maudlin Paterson purchased it in the years between the two World Wars for a reason I can only imagine; but without sullying his memory I cannot offer liaisons of a sexual nature as the only purpose. As far as I was concerned, I was prepared to offer it to Serena to occupy whenever the need arose. The only objections I would have of her using it would be if she was involved with another man and wished to stay there. Until that happened, I could use my club if our requirements clashed.

I wanted Breno to spend time with me on the home estate at Harrogate, where we could ride out together and perhaps pursue other country sports. Somewhat naively, I told myself once this government assignment was ended there would be plenty of opportunities to spend time in Yorkshire. That was what I told him before I left the house in Chester Square, more in hope than expectation.

My meeting with Bottomly had raised issues that required my verbal report to Jerry Furley, so I had no choice but to alter my plans of calling on George and Sophie at Eaton Square, and report directly to him all I had learned with Bottomly. As Serena, with Breno beside her, was finally leaving our London home, fate played another hand in whatever destiny was in store for me. I took a call on my mobile telephone that I certainly did not expect, one that required another change of plan, making a visit to Eaton Square a priority.

George sounded cheerful on the phone but, knowing his voice as well as I did, I thought I detected a problem. Unfortunately I was right, however

I did not discover what it was from him. I had to wait until Sophie told me.

Over the relatively short time I had known Sophie, I had nothing but admiration for the lady. I hope that statement does not appear condescending, nor, I hope, am I being audacious when I say she was 'good' for George. When my father was murdered, George needed someone who could depend on him in a like manner that Elliot had.

As head of the family, I gave George a lease on the Eaton Square home to run for as long he lived. After his marriage, I included Sophie in that arrangement. I made no consultation with others of the Paterson clan to assess their feelings on the matter. I assumed they would not agree with me, but having not put it to the test, I could not offer any concrete evidence to my conclusion. The case for my part would rest on supposition based on years of knowledge of their behaviour anywhere near money.

When the topic did arise, on the day of Elliot's entombment, I was proven correct in my assumption. I had not made the settlement with George through any sense of duty, I made it through a sense of love. I had come to love George as the blood relative he was. His true existence was kept from his legal family to save my great-grandfather Maudlin's blushes over an illegitimate birth.

Mrs Squires, the live-in cook at Eaton Square when Elliot was there, was now quite elderly. After serving meals for the family in London for the whole of her working life, I had made provision for her to move into a new home on the estate at Harrogate some years back. She now lived in a house next door to the one where Joseph lived with Mrs Franks. As was her wont, she would occasionally visit The Hall with Mrs Franks, wandering into the kitchen to keep her hand in, as it were. The nights at The Hall when the two of them served their individual meat pies were occasions I expressly looked forward to and I have first-hand knowledge of invitations to the dinner being a sought-after commodity. As I understood things, apart from the cook, with the solitary house-maid-cum-housekeeper, the huge house at 16 Eaton Square housed only George and Sophie.

Even allowing for the household changes, or perhaps because of them, I was told George helped out every day in the kitchen, also helping to keep the house. After her marriage, Sophie continued her work as the head librarian for the Royal Borough of Kensington and Chelsea, meaning George had a grave need to occupy his mind for the hours she was away. That was the problem he was hiding, the one Sophie referred to when we spoke on the telephone. Overall, I came to the conclusion I was being irresponsible by leaving him to find an occupation without direct help, but it wasn't easy.

I had employed an estate manager ever since Elliot moved permanently to London, leaving me to divide my time between the estate at Harrogate, the chemical company I represented, and the intelligence service. Amongst his many duties aside from the livestock and arable farming, he took care of the vast amount of paperwork a business such as mine generates, but I could not think of any other way of helping George than to incorporate him into the estate. He had, quite simply, too much time on his hands. To help to fill it, I created a role for him as the estate's bookkeeper.

I explained the situation with my estate manager, having no wish that he should think I lacked trust in him. He understood, sending invoices, etc. by email, then receipts of income in the form of rents from tenanted farmers, sale of livestock, revenue from the different crops under cultivation, both in open field as well as under cover, along with the origins of other saleable items. These were sent every month for George to assemble, then, when required, calculate the various payable taxes.

Overall, I came to the conclusion that I was being irresponsible by leaving him to find occupation without my direct help.

It was a pleasant day so walked the short distance from Chester Square to George and Sophie's home, thoroughly engrossed in thoughts of how wrong I had been about Bottomly. I had known him for virtually all of my life and had never once suspected him of being a diehard activist, let alone the drunken gambler he'd become. Having now admitted to making that error, it opened the door to the distinct possibility of being wrong about everyone, but I drew the line at George and Sophie.

* * *

Over tea, served in the first floor sitting room, I asked Sophie to examine all she could find about the island of Samothrace. I explained some of what I'd been doing, without breaching any trust. I included the part where I was about to travel to the island of Bressay in the Shetlands to interview a traitor. It was then she came up with her idea. It was the idea I hoped she would have thought of.

"Why don't you take George with you, Harry?" she suggested with a teacup in hand, looking directly at her virtuous husband. "You would absolutely love a trip to Scotland, wouldn't you, dear?" He, like me, was caught off guard for a moment.

Along similar lines to George, I had learned Sophie never did anything without a reason. No matter that I couldn't see any inducement to be officious, it did not mean there was none. At the moment when I was about to give up on my mental search for a possibility, George perked up, but his bright, cheerful face belied the indecisive, timid character he normally was. If I had any doubt, it was shown in his question of, was I certain I wanted him to come? Sophie offered her inspiring words of encouragement alongside my own, so as we were finishing our tea, his mood had changed considerably.

If desire to visit Scotland could be measured by the size of human smiles, then the one on George's face, when once again I confirmed my wish for his company, would have been in the running for the gold medal, as the widest and most radiant. Then followed another surprise.

"Are we driving there?" he asked, as he flung wide the door of the sitting room, on his way to pack his bags, thus leaving me a mite disordered as the thought had not crossed my mind. My reply was simply a puzzled look. George took control.

"The car is fuelled to the brim, as it always is when I leave it. I always fill it up at the petrol station in Ebury Bridge Road, before I park it in the underground garage. I can't remember when Sophie and I last went anywhere in it. To be honest with you, it could do with a drive to Shetland, and to be truthful, so could I."

I'm sure I've told you, but if not, then I will now —my normal instinct would tell me to distrust, vehemently, anyone who used aphorisms, such as 'to be truthful', 'quite honestly', 'to tell the truth', or a comparable phrase, but not so with George. I made special exemptions where George was concerned, because not only did I know I could trust him unconditionally, but both of his expressions were common in his normal speech. What I had not given any thought to was his keen suggestion of driving all the way there.

The next flight from City airport was over four hours away, by which time we could be well into the journey if we drove. My contemplation was broken by Sophie's voice coming from somewhere on the floor above us. I had not noticed her leaving the room.

"As the crow flies, it's roughly seven hundred and eighty miles from here to Bressay, so not only can you not drive across the water between Scotland and Shetland, you should stop overnight somewhere. If you two idiots are going to drive most of the way, which I must say is stupid, then whilst I'm researching that Greek island of yours, Harry, I'll find a hotel for you to stay. By the time you get away it will be midday, therefore I would suggest Edinburgh, from where you can catch a flight to Shetland tomorrow after breakfast. Which reminds me. Please make sure George has an adequate meal both tonight and tomorrow morning. Lately, he's developed a tendency to pick at meals. No good for him, or Cook."

"It's eleven o'clock now," she declared, and instinctively I checked my watch. I shouldn't have bothered; she was absolutely correct.

"If it was George and me going, I would be looking to park up for the night around seven o'clock. Shower, then change for dinner at eight, in bed before turning into pumpkins at midnight. What do you think? Scrummy dinner and full breakfast, then sit back and fly? Good plan, do you agree?"

With the magnetic enthusiasm from George and Sophie, I suggested the one hotel I knew of in that part of the world; the Balmoral, in Edinburgh.

* * *

It didn't take long for George to pack and safely stow his bag away, then, with him behind the wheel, the two of us set off for the Scottish capital where, to my chagrin, I had found a liking for Scotland far beyond just its ability to distil the drink I'd enjoyed since first finding it when at university. For years, I had relied on the opinion I had of Scottish people based on the few Scots I had come across in an army uniform, or drunk in pubs. They were, I thought, a race of people to steer clear of unless you were looking for an argument.

The last time I came across an aggressive Scotsman was when Serena and I were still in love. Her brand of clothing was establishing itself in the wallets of the upper-class, high-end fashion outlets at a rapidity that had surprised us both. Our surprise was not because it wasn't fashionable, no, that was not in question; it was a case of a new brand breaking through the invisible barriers erected by the buying public, who affixed some sort of magical quality to the established, expensive labels.

We had visited Dundee and Aberdeen, where all went smoothly without any traumas, and it wasn't until the show reached Glasgow that my prejudice proved to be right. Although nobody in the least bit sane would call me fashionable, I was given the front-end role of the fashion show. Although I was at the rear of the viewing public, it was still called the front end. It was a simple task, whereby I had to be somewhere in front of the 'runway' to some, and to others the 'catwalk'.

Both words are used to describe the elevated platform where the models walk along in their inimitable way, to display the clothes of the designer. In this case, designed by my wife and her chief designer, the cow-loving Tanta. In the other places we'd visited, I'd had very little to deal with, perhaps an enquiry or three but nothing of note, but in Glasgow the situation changed.

There were two men hovering by a door that led from where the show was being hosted to another part of the hotel, both of whom were obviously the worse for drink. As the first model, the one who had the honour of opening the show, normally the designer's pick, made her entrance along the runway, one of the men made a disparaging remark about her figure, as the other chap chose that precise moment to reach for two glasses from the tray of champagne flutes one of the waitresses was carrying towards the invited guests. His unsteady hand caused the tray to fall to the carpeted floor.

Quite a few heads turned our way. It was just the kind of awkward situation I did not want. I asked them both to leave, politely. The one who had been the most abusive used some more expletives to explain they were not moving and it should be me who would find it better to go, or be visiting a hospital.

He swung a fist that missed my head by miles, leaving him open for me to hit him in the throat. I didn't hit him hard. If I had, then he could have died. I just wanted to disable him. It worked. He grasped at his windpipe, desperately trying to breathe. When doubled over in pain, he fell to the ground onto the upturned drinks tray, causing any unbroken glasses to break and any already broken to shred further into a mass of glass shards.

The man whose fault it was for the fallen tray, threw a punch at me whilst I was looking at the man on the ground lying in the glass splinters.

Unfortunately for the punch-throwing individual, the movement of my head away from the direction of his fist, meant his hand hit a rather solid part of the wall behind me, which broke all four knuckles of his right hand. To make matters worse, he dislocated his thumb. Of course, I'd had nothing to do with that.

As his screams of pain were dying down, two hotel security men arrived. One of them was trained in first aid which he administered to both drunks, concentrating more on the one with the breathing difficulties as he also had deep cuts on his hands, with the distinct possibility of cuts elsewhere.

I spent most of the remaining time of Serena's show explaining to the local police what had happened. It was immediately after my time with them that I found the people in the hotel who had seen the show, and those who had not, to be selflessly compassionate and caring when offering assistance. I was humbled by the people I went on to meet. That humbling sensation was on my mind when I remembered the first phone call I had taken on leaving the house in Chester Square, on the way to Sophie and George.

I answered my ringing mobile phone expecting it to be one of any number of female friends who were missing my scintillating company. Have I told you how highly I regard myself? No, you say? Well, I will leave that for another day, as we have more to cover before I can indulge you with my ego. The call was not from someone I could have anticipated; it was from Valery Agapov.

My first response was to question how he came by my telephone number, but I got as far as the bit where I asked, "How did you..." and I stopped in mid-sentence. What was the point in asking? He had it. Instead of that mindless enquiry, I tried a more relevant one—"What do you want?"

The answer contained ominous undertones.

"Alexi Vasilyev wants to meet with George Northcliffe."

My first thought was what if George had heard of Alexi Vasilyev from his father Paulo, and the two of them had discussed Paulo's plan to rid himself of Alexi? How about in any of the conversations the two of them had whilst Paulo was still alive and living in luxury in Knightsbridge? How would George feel about meeting the target who had survived? Would he be worried or not, I wondered? A game of chess can exhaust conversations. Politics and espionage were never topics Paulo and I discussed, but with George things could have been different.

The drive to Scotland passed comfortably, without incident, with George and me chatting amicably, but I found no suitable opportunity to mention Agapov's phone call. During the times when the easy, gentle conversation faded away to silence, I had the opportunity to think of the times George spent with my father. Inevitably, I recalled the distressing telephone call telling me of missing bank money, followed shortly by Elliot's subsequent murder.

I've never asked George how he felt when alone with his thoughts. Regrets came next into the silence. I had regrets when thinking I'd done enough for him and Sophie, then remembered how I had ignored them both. I could not hide myself behind any saintly thoughts of, if I had visited more, it might have been seen as interference. I could not say to myself, or anyone else come to that, that I had consciously stayed away so as not to be seen as an old interfering lord of the manor. No, I was selfish in not visiting, thinking of only me. I vowed to change.

'Change' was a subject on George's mind, too. He wanted more to do, he said, almost as many times as we saw a motorway sign with an arrow pointing upwards towards the dark sky, with the threatening words of—THE NORTH. He said it again just as I was thinking of the Pegasus Mercantile Company. With little hope of discovering more names than I already knew, I asked him to investigate the company's financial structure to see if names of personnel came up.

George had many strengths; dependability and determination being just two, and a third forte of his came from an Open University accounting course he took after my father's death. With comfortable ease he passed all his examinations.

We left the hotel in Edinburgh after breakfast in time to catch the flight Sophie had booked from Edinburgh to Sumburgh Airport, without any mention of the phone call I'd been deliberately avoiding. After landing, we took a taxi the length of the early-autumnal-covered island to Lerwick. I had telephoned Mrs Tate, the photographer and MI5 home casual, before we arrived at Lerwick, asking for recommendations of a hotel for George.

With the increased garrison strength at Gardie, I could not ask for an extra billet; in any case, George was thrilled to be left on Shetland. In the end, he had good reason to be. Mrs Tate offered her home along with time spent with her husband formatting his newspaper. I was thrilled as George jumped at the chance of meeting real people and turning his hand to something new.

" I shall watch how Mr Tate goes about doing this newspaper of his, then, if I think it's something I could enjoy doing, I might ask Sophie to help me set up a local Eaton Square magazine. We could put the machinery in the cellar. What do you think? I can fit that in with the paperwork from the estate with no trouble. It could be good for us both."

I smiled heartily at that thought, wanting him to succeed. Whilst I was waiting for the ferry to set sail I explained the details of a crucial task I wanted him to do for me. I handed him a photograph of Valery Agapov, asking him to look through the newspaper's catalogues of photos the Tates would have, to see if Agapov had visited the island more times than the one occasion I knew of.

In my document case, I had a photograph of

Alexi Vasilyev dressed in full army uniform of the Colonel General he was. I hoped by showing it to George I would find a moment to mention the sensitive phone call, so, as a throwaway remark, I asked him to keep a lookout for his face turning up in Mrs Tate's photograph catalogue.

His reaction on hearing his name and seeing the photograph was not the one I expected. Instead of asking if he was, therefore, alive, he asked if Vasilyev would want revenge on any member of Paulo's family? I told him the truth by saying I wasn't sure, but I told him it was highly unlikely as both he and Valery Agapov wanted to defect. I added, I was the one who would be handling both of those defections. I was about to mention the phone call, but George beat me to it.

"Remember I'm new to this, Harry, I've never been to see someone defecting, only I was wondering if they want to defect inside Russian territory or over here? Obviously I can't leave Sophie, she would be lost without me. But I'd love to help if you would allow me. If you're pushed, I'm sure she would let me go abroad to help you out, although I've no idea where to find my passport," he stated, with an edginess to his voice, then he immediately had a change of mind.

"That's silly of me. Sophie would know where the passport is, of course. I'll call her."

I agreed with him about Sophie's competence but

not completely about Russia. Instead, I offered my belief that Agapov would swap sides in London, or some other point on British soil. With Alexi, I wasn't sure. He pressed me about Vasilyev, and I thought the nervousness in his voice was still there. I confessed I did not have a complete picture with regard to his situation, saying only that I imagined it would take place somewhere in Europe. I told him wherever it was, I would need time to assess the suitability of his choice. If it was safe for George to help, then I would welcome his assistance.

"Then I shall bookmark it as a 'must do', Harry. I shall look forward to it."

Perhaps, I was mistaken. What I'd believed to be nerves or indecisiveness on his part were nothing but excitement. Certainly, any fear I thought I'd detected in George's voice had disappeared when the chance to be involved came along. Had I been concentrating better, I would have seen how wrong I was. Before a military mission, I've known the hands of experienced soldiers to shake, but when the mission began, where they were part of the action, the adrenaline would kick in, making them as calm as the serenity of death when it settles on a face plagued by acute pain.

The phlegmatic approach adopted by my friend gave me the opportunity to tell the truth at last. However, I reasoned by doing so, it could leave him believing it was the motive behind his invitation. That may have been the naked truth, but my version of the truth lay in the fact of my forgetfulness. I had forgotten about George, and it's there the truth could be found. Paulo had forgotten he had a son. I had forgotten I had a friend.

I made a silent promise to myself—as far as I was able, I would not allow George to discover my selfish forgetfulness.

On my arrival at Gardie House, Judith was sitting on the grass with her back against one of the trees in the garden, reading a book which was opened on her lap. She said she was expecting me, having overheard news of my arrival when passing close to two of the sentries, adding how she had heard I had not come alone. Another topic of conversation held between ratings on sentry duty was, apparently, my impending arrival at Lerwick, accompanied by another man.

My companion was, she confidently told me, none other than George Northcliffe. My obvious question was—what made her think it was George who was with me? To that, she had a ready-constructed reply, citing a remarkable memory which was more than capable of storing George's appearance, gait, and characteristics.

She enquired after his health and I was able to say he was well, as, indeed, was his wife, Sophie. She was unaware he was married and had no idea of where Sophie had come from. That impairment did not stop her from passing a comment on each participant. "On balance," she volunteered, "George would appear to be a fine candidate, and anyone marrying him must have been born with extremely good judgement."

For a split second or two, I considered telling George he had Judith's unequivocal endorsement, but split seconds equate to hours when more important things happen, overshadowing the irrelevant.

Once we got the conversation past the marriage point, I thought she was in a pensive mood, certainly nostalgic and somewhat regretful, but it was more than just that. For an unfathomable reason, her thoughts were absorbed by London, mentioning her house quite near Clapham Common and the dog she had there, which wasn't hers at all but belonged to her late husband, as did the house. Her late husband had been a Major in the army's Explosive Ordinance Disposal and Search Regiment. Sadly, he died on active service in Afghanistan.

I was not being uncharitable, I expressed my sympathy when she had told me of his passing, but that was then; now, I was silently laughing as I remembered my inane attempt to lure her to my bed when I stayed for that single night at the Clapham home.

I wasn't being as clever as I thought. I must have shown some sign of my amusement as she enquired what caused such levity. I hid nothing. I told her all I remembered, which made us both laugh, recalling her terse refusal causing my embarrassed face. Despite her obvious longing to reminisce, I directed her thoughts to the here and now, mentioning the sacred word of Samothrace. She closed the book she had been reading, showing me the front cover—*A View On Greek Mythology*, by a Professor Pullbright.

"I've had plenty of time to research that island of yours, Harry. I'm hoping to safeguard my transfer to warmer climes, with what I know. Mind you, I have something far more valuable than an island to trade, but more of that later," she declared tantalisingly.

I told her I had not heard of any discussion on clemency, adding that if the information was good, I would put forward her request to MI6 and the Home Office, but there was no guarantee of the outcome. The political situation was not new to her, she said rather melancholically, with a somewhat piteous acceptance of future decisions taken by the 'others' in the abstract chain of mercy.

Despite this plaintive mood, nothing would stop her from her disclosures.

"This book's been good. I've been learning how, according to Greek mythology, Nike, the daughter of Ares, the Greek god of war, along with Pegasus, the winged horse of Victory who was raised by the Muses at Mount Helicon, actually set up home on the island of Samothrace.

"But if it's not your cup of tea, this mythology thing, I'm not going to throw that stuff at you. Mind you, if I don't teach you, then you'll never know how the rivers came into being, or how the women on the island of Lemnos killed all the single men there after their husbands went off to fight in the Battle of the Titans. And that is how the Pegasus company is connected to the island. But you're looking worried, why's that?"

"I followed, well, I sort of followed, what you were saying about the mythological connection, but so far there's nothing concrete to put the Pegasus Mercantile Company on the island of Samothrace. Unless the people who run the banking side of the company are devotees of ancient Greek mythology and dance around some sacrifice, every full moon.

"I do believe I'm right and there's a Pegasus star constellation as well. Let alone—no, don't stop me—Pegasus is the emblem of the British parachute regiment, so perhaps it was founded by someone from there, eh? Or maybe they're star watchers? Ah, that's it, isn't it?"

"Now you're being plain stupid, Harry. There really is nothing changed about you, is there? You're still playing the role of the village idiot and getting away with it. How on earth do you work for British Intelligence?"

After taking a deep breath then exhaling loudly, to make sure I could hear her displeasure, she carried on in the same vein of insults. Only this time there was a distinct look of contempt on her face instead of her previous studious appearance.

"In the island's port town of Kamariotissa, there are two blue-painted, three-storeyed houses that are attached to one another. They run parallel to the sea, standing at the far western end of the promenade. There are no more buildings after those two, just mountains rising up to the sky, with the houses looking as though they are built into them. For all intents and purposes they appear to be two separate homes, but they're not.

"It is one enormous house, inside which there is all you need to know about the Pegasus company. Every name ever to be associated with it, every transaction it has ever been involved in, every deposit and every withdrawal inside, or generated by the whole money chain that makes up the Pegasus corporation."

I guessed that by giving prominence to the word 'whole,' by extension, it was meant to convey a sense of huge, but having quite a bit of knowledge myself on the banking world, I already knew what the word 'whole' meant, so what was the bloody point? I asked, using those same words.

"Please try not to be so rude, Mr Williamson, and do wait until I'm finished before posing your cretinous, unhelpful questions."

Yet another loud intake of air, then the theatrical

exhaling of breath before she judged I had been scolded enough and carried on.

"Underneath this extended building there is a basement running the whole length and breadth of it. Part was detonated from under the actual mountain. I'm told there are files dating back to April '53 and the early days of Dwight D. Eisenhower's presidency. That's when the idea was devised to siphon away money from its lawful government destinations.

"The paper files down in the basement account for every single dollar that was misappropriated from the American defence budget, going back to April '53. Everything is numbered, index-card-linked in a library-like catalogue system that takes up the space of what would be a sizeable sitting room, floor to ceiling. I was once told how they would be installing a modern way of registration, but unless someone has made a start since you had me locked up, then it will not have changed.

"I was told there are separate rooms full up with identical index card filing systems for each executive branch of the federal government for syphoning away funds, going back to the Cuban Crisis. The Korean War, the Vietnam one, the invasions of Iraq and Afghanistan, the original trouble in Iran. Each has its own room with its own card filing system to account for the displaced money."

"I can't believe all that came from Professor Pullbright's book. Where else did you stumble over that knowledge?"

"If you need me to tell you, then you're not the man I used to know.

Where do you think?

I thought I detected a weakness, one I hoped I could exploit.

"If it came from Valery Agapov, then why did he tell you and not tell me on the day of, or before, the time he wants for his defection?"

Almost instantly, her face drained of its normal, healthy colour, leaving a chalky-white haze. Her lips tightened, changing from a shade of faded pink to a pending stormy grey. I had taken her by surprise, but that was not the only emotion she displayed. She was angry. I was right about a weakness.

"I wonder why he didn't tell you he wanted to change sides, Miss Fields? My, my, how remiss on his part. Tut, tut. If I were you, I'd tear him off a strip or two next time he pops his head through the fence. What was it you called me, was it a cretin? Hmm, I would leave you my handkerchief to wipe your tears away, if I carried one."

I could look beyond her anger and sense how lonely she was. If she knew of her old lover being exchanged for an American pilot, it's possible she would know he was living in a modern apartment in the centre of Moscow, with all probability of having some dacha in the countryside and a boat on the Sea of Azov. Then along comes a potential new lover who betrays her by not telling her his plans to get far away.

"Have you never been scared they will be coming to kill you, now you're on your own, Judith?" I asked with genuine concern.

"It's not my time to die, Harry. But I've been worried about that ever since Agapov told me he knew something else about the island. If I live long enough, perhaps I'll tell you what he said."

CHAPTER ELEVEN
NOW WE ARE SIX

Before George and I left for Scotland, Jerry Furley sent me all the intelligence reports he had on Russian movements in and around the port of Tartus, on the Syrian coast, including interesting arrivals at the nearby Hmeimim military air base. Unable to fall asleep as quickly as I had done in the Edinburgh hotel suite, I found plenty of time to read it.

My security clearance allowed me to read of how British intelligence had an active covert cell operating in Syria with an 'elite illegal' operative working inside the ruling political Ba'ath Party. The secret intelligence service had also acquired access to another operative inside Daesh, ISIS, who wasn't designated as any kind of illegal. I would have liked to have asked why he wasn't included in what was referred to as the J-list, but I thought I might know why he wasn't on it, no matter what name it went by. I thought the Daesh illegal operative would be Sabah Al Salim, who at this stage, I thought, was playing everyone.

Included in the classified account I was reading was a report from the 'elite illegal' who had attended an invitation dinner for high ranking Syrian government officials given by the Commander-in-Chief of the Russian Mediterranean Fleet, enjoying their anchorage at the port of Tartus.

When the meal finished, whilst the invited guests, accompanied by their hosts, were enjoying their after-dinner treats of dancing women, troops from the rebel Syrian Democratic Force launched a mortar attack on the outer reaches of the base, allowing the SIS agent time to photograph a series of scaled drawings she found conveniently spread out on a table inside an office attached to the Russian base commander's private quarters.

The images in the photographs, which had not been shared with any other agency, ended their journey on Jerry's desk. There was no appendage detailing casualties, or who organised the affair. Whoever put it together did so with great precision. What's more, our 'elite illegal' escaped undetected and, just as importantly, unharmed. I was mulling over in my mind the complexity of such an operation when the lie I'd told George came to the forefront of my mind. I managed to ignore it, but for how long I wasn't sure. I jammed my mind full of the details of the last briefing, hoping to quieten the accusations that kept hitting me between the eyes.

The construction drawings showed the configuration of what were referred to, after translation, as a three-sided, solid-state, optically aspect phased radar, which when the site becomes fully functional, would be used to reverse the high resistance beams, or any conventional microwave beams, emanating from the two RAF bases on the island of Cyprus.

The written premise at the end of the photographed report concluded that the deflected pattern of beams would then be aimed at a rotating laser geo-dynamics satellite. It then came to the important part. This satellite would, when launched, be able to render invalid the images shown on the screens in the NATO monitoring stations.

Jerry Furley added a note saying there was no previous mention of any type of laser geo-dynamics satellite he could find in other accounts, or a mention from any other agency. He did, however, find something of great interest which could well be a hidden clue.

There was a signed accompaniment to the written report, one that I found not only interesting, but immensely significant. I would normally be bored silly reading anything stated to be A Professional Deduction, but this one was different. The 'professional' who made the deduction was in charge of a department I'd never heard of called, the Home Office Forensic.

I studied every detail it was possible to unearth on this graphology expert in the Forensic Document Department, but other than the normal university entries, I hit a brick wall. I turned to an old army friend of mine who was in a position to inquire into any sensitive areas regarding personnel I'd stumble across. I needed to know exactly who this Professor Doyle was and how competent he was in his field.

The information passed on to me quoted him as being a hugely respected authority on the subject of how systematic analysis of the way words and letters are formed in one's normal handwriting, can reveal traits of a person's character. In other words, the way we write can be analysed to reveal our innermost personality, as well as being distinctive in style in much the same way as fingerprints are unique. It was, so I read, accepted inside the British intelligence community as another form of DNA.

In the document I was reading on the port of Tartus, Professor Doyle had compared two other signed documents by the person he suspected of having drafted the record of the communication. He concluded all three had been written by the same man: a Colonel General Alexi Vasilyev.

If Doyle's deduction was correct, and there were plenty of ethical academic findings to say it was, then it was perfectly feasible to suggest the Americans already knew, word for word, what Jerry was trying to keep from them.

If I were to be asked where my preference would lie, either tell or not, I would have to say I came down on the side of absolute secrecy, i.e. not to share the conclusions Professor Doyle arrived at with any sections of MI6, nor with heads of departments within the secret intelligence service. It was not that I suspected a traitor inside any of the organisations again, it was only my absurd insecurities pounding away inside my head.

On the strength of the report I was studying, Jerry Furley had contacted the government's Skynet Satellite Communications, via his opposite number at the Ministry of Defence, who had sent orders for an orbiting satellite to be redirected over an area of interest inside Kazakhstan, an area known to be used by the Russians for satellite launches. The first pass over the relevant zone revealed a rocket capable of carrying a satellite at the usual Baikonur cosmodrome. A projectile was on a launch pad, awaiting its payload.

The conclusion drawn from this, I read in the handwritten synopsis attached to the report, was the Russians seemed to have the capability of ending the advantage the NATO alliance had enjoyed with the beyond-the-horizon radar on Cyprus. It did not mean, so the author to the report added, the Russians know how to construct their own advanced radar system, but as a proviso it went on to say, *it will not be long before they understand how to make one.* There was no commitment in the document to any operational timescale nor any alternative action proposed.

There was a private coded message from Jerry Furley delivered separately along with details of its deciphering, which could have been harder to crack than the body of the message. The subject heading on the electronic PDF contained just four letters—NWAS, and the body of the message consisted of a series of numbers with just two inserted letters—D&A, which I knew stood for 'down and across'. It was a one-time pad code. The hardest encryption technique to crack unless you knew where the 'down and across' numbers will apply.

Here's another confession I must share with you before we can go any further. I share a personal secret with Jerry Isaac Furley, one that only the two of us know. We are both admirers of the author A.A. Milne, and belong to the Friends of A.A. Milne Society. Generally, if we were passing messages between the two of us that needed to be kept secret, we would use books of Milne's for our encryption. I therefore knew, beyond doubt, the 'N.W.A.S.' stood for one thing and one thing only—*Now We Are Six*, A. A. Milne's second book of verse for young readers, featuring the timeless, beloved Winnie-the-Pooh and friends. The book, looked upon a different way, is for children who don't want to be older than six years of age.

Using page and line numbers in the book I had in the library section on my phone, I deciphered Jerry's coded message well before we arrived for the ferry crossing from Lerwick, so it would be right to say I was in a fairly reflective mood as George spoke and reminded me once more of a lie I had told.

"My love of boats goes back to when I was young and growing up with my mother. We had never been on one, but I'd seen pictures of boats. It was with one of those pictures I formed my relationship with them. Not long ago, I suggested to Sophie we take a cruise as a holiday. To me, it wasn't the destination that was important. What was, was being onboard a boat, but my idea was no good. Sophie told me she hated boats."

As he turned his head away from me I heard a tiny, mournful sigh. My first thought was he was on the edge of crying, but luckily he didn't. I use the word 'luckily' because at that moment, I was about to leave by boarding the ferry, meaning he would have been left alone, at the terminal. I wouldn't like to have left him in such an emotional mess before he found his way back to the Tates' home. It was an ugly thought; the one of leaving him that concentrated my mind on the lie I had told George and Sophie. I decided to 'jump ship', metaphorically speaking to tell him more of what I knew about Alexi Vasilyev.

* * *

It was a blissful September with the warm days spreading into warm nights. George and I found a quiet pub garden for my moment of truth. I had no more than three hours before the last ferry to Bressay. However, in an emergency, I could call the guard at Gardie and request one of the two boats that were either tied up or circling the island to pick me up, but I wasn't going to try that route unless I really had no other choice.

The same expression George had on his face when I spoke of the two Russians' defections was there again. This time, I needed nobody to kick me on the shins to remind me of how wrong I could be. If I had learned anything of George, then it should be just how enigmatic he could be. He was a difficult man to judge, never having had what I would call a 'normal' upbringing, nor a subsequent life that could be interpreted by reading facial expressions.

For the first years of his life, he lived alone with his mother, whom Paulo, with Maudlin's help, had managed to smuggle into London during a visit of Premier Nikita Khrushchev, leader of the Soviet Union to Great Britain. When his mother died, Maudlin moved the young George, aged fourteen, to live and grow up in The Hall at Harrogate, telling his wife, along with the rest of the Patersons, that he was the abandoned son of a close friend who had no living relatives.

Only Maudlin's wife, then later Elliot when Maudlin was dying, knew the true history of George. George suspected his past was not straightforward, but it was not until he met his father in Switzerland, just a few years ago, that he discovered the real facts. If that meeting had not taken place, I doubt George would know of his real father and the relationship he has with the Paterson ancestry.

When Elliot died, I transferred a sum of money into the personal account George held in the private bank of Annie's. Together, we went to open a high street bank account, then for the first time in his life he had a cheque book and debit card.

Paulo left a considerable estate when he passed away. He had invested his money wisely, dating back to when he was rising through the KGB ranks, then moving through the Politburo. He needed money to buy himself the favours that accelerated his climb. The majority of his funding came from Maudlin and Annie's! The ownership of property was not encouraged in Soviet Russia, but with the help his money was able to buy, he invested in property beyond the boundary of the Soviet Union.

He had his apartment in Switzerland together with the one in London, which were gifted to his son

George and daughter Katherine, on his death. Before Paulo's passing, George had found a friend first, then a lover, then a wife in Sophie, who, although having no need to work in regard to money, wanted to keep busy.

George was never the type to sit and watch TV all day, nor could he be left alone to twiddle his fingers. On the days of the week that Sophie worked, George went with her. The other four days, apart from the bookkeeping for the estate which he busied himself with, they spent time together gardening, window shopping or reading books. They often compared the books they'd read, commenting on them in the three book clubs the pair belong to. Of course, Sophie also found time to write her novels, inviting George to offer his advice.

With these antecedents in my mind, I told him outright how Alexi Vasilyev wanted to meet. Before he could reply, I added my own thoughts of the man and how my mind was working with a view to dealing directly with him. The long and short of it all was, I wanted him at my side when I met with Alexi.

To start with, I told him I did not believe Valery Agapov was going to defect. I believed Alexi Vasilyev wanted to defect because his time was coming to the inevitable end anyone in his position must reach. However, with a man as powerful as he was, I found it impossible to believe it would be allowed to happen. The most crucial element about both men was the extent of knowledge they had of the Russian intelligence reach, but in Alexi Vasilyev's case, it was said his disfigurements had curtailed his ability to be useful anywhere other than at a desk, therefore the Russians would have to keep him on a short leash to avoid him leaving Russia.

In years gone by, Agapov would most likely have been shot for just saying the word 'defect', let alone before he was in the act of changing allegiances. In this case, it should surely be Valery's fate; but no, he was still very much alive and that could only mean it must be Vasilyev's hand keeping Agapov alive. With Vasilyev's split allegiance between America and Russia, came a split loyalty between the freedom from Russian bureaucracy he so wanted and the betrayal of Agapov's trust which, when he was relocated, he didn't need. Or did he? Was he, I silently wondered, working along a different line nobody had thought of?

With the Cold War ended and the differences between East and Western ideology 'fought' more and more on the 'electronic' front, shootings, or other acts of murder conducted in a sovereign country, could be considered as an act of war, or at least an act deserving extreme sanctions from a host of countries. So I couldn't see Alexi Vasilyev being stupid enough to want to kill anyone, but I had been known to be wrong in the past. Not wishing to be overdramatic, but the death of my friend George Northcliffe was not something to be contemplated.

No doubt Agapov would be made to disappear when his use was said to have expired, after the departure of Vasilyev, but when would that be and how was it to happen? With Vasilyev having sent Agapov to fill Judith Meadows' head with more than enough Greek mythology to confuse the island issue for idiots like me, I wouldn't be surprised if Gerald Neil's Russian-friendly croupier went missing as well. But why, I asked, concoct such a tangled scheme simply to eliminate a traitor whose traitorous behaviour must have been known for quite some time? There was more to it than just that.

From the little I had been able to learn about Vasilyev, I thought he was a long way from the type of person who acted on impulse alone. Whether or not he was always the same, or circumstances had changed him, I marked him down to be a thoughtful, premeditated man, calculating every step of his journey to avoid any electrically charged door handles, or other traps. One of the problems I had, was where did Alexi see the end of his journey? Was it in the West, on a farm in Northern America, or somewhere in a higher position in the East, where perhaps his power would be, or could become, absolute?

The handwritten notes attached to the construction details of the port of Tartus, were not meant to conceal Alexi Vasilyev's participation in its configuration; he had left his handwriting on them for me to find. I had Alexi served on a plate sitting next to

Valery Agapov; all I needed was—what? I told George I had missed something, but what was it?

I left him at the door to Mr and Mrs Tate's home, knowing he would phone Sophie as soon as he was alone. I asked him to find out from her all she had discovered about the island, as well as any new information. I promised to meet with him as soon as possible the next day, after seeing Judith. I then managed to catch the last ferry, arriving back at Gardie House with many thoughts to keep me company as I slept.

CHAPTER TWELVE
THE CAYMAN ISLANDS

It was not only Sophie I'd asked to research SAVAK, the Iranian secret intelligence service Sabah Al Salim's father was in charge of when Iran was under the rule of the last Shah; she had plenty of other work I'd asked her to undertake. I had put her in touch with the sections on the counter-intelligence floor at Vauxhall who specialised in Middle Eastern affairs. I knew this was going to be a difficult task for Sophie, coming up against many solid walls or places of misinformation, which the Vauxhall departments could circumnavigate.

I thought it obvious it would have been the family's wealth that protected him and his son, Ali Babak Rostam Farid, from the carnage of liberation the incoming Ayatollah Khomeini brought with him. But after hearing the scale of Sabah, or Rostam Farid's, wealth from Jimmy Mercer, I wondered if Sophie could be successful in linking any money of the last Shah of Iran to Farid's money inside the Pegasus Bank?

I already knew something of the intelligence service named SAVAK, but owing to Sophie's diligence I was able to see how it was instituted through a combination of the offices of the Shah and the American CIA. The Shah was an avid supporter of his intelligence bureau, in the horrific ways and means it adopted to crush all who opposed his rule.

It was not until 1969, when Richard Nixon was elected President of America, that the United States finally agreed to sever all contact with those Iranians opposed to the Shah's regime, a concession Iran had been seeking since 1958. The often very anti-American tone of the Iranian press was ignored because the Shah supported the U.S. in the Vietnam War and likewise, the Americans ignored the Shah's power when he raised oil prices, despite the fact it cost many American consumers more at the petrol pumps.

Until the Shah's manipulation of the cost of crude oil directly through his presidency of OPEC, Organisation of Petroleum Exporting Countries, his reign in Iran was very much in the interests of America and Great Britain, but from that date in 1969, things started to change. Instead of Iran being dependent on the West for so much of its needs, the

West became dependent on the oil supply from the OPEC nations, and especially its largest supplier at the time: Iran. During the last years of his regime, the Shah's government became more autocratic, with pictures of him, or members of his family, extending from the beginning of film showings in public theatres, to billboards along the main thoroughfares, together with being shown in people's homes on their television screens.

European royalty appeared in Tehran as guests of the Shah, but his courtship did not end at the gates of palaces. He was pursued for money elsewhere. In a televised speech in January 1975, he excelled in explaining why he was lending Harold Wilson's British Labour government a sum equal to one billion U.S. dollars. Another country he was 'honoured' to declare he 'helped' was France, under Valéry Giscard d'Estaing.

He proclaimed how he had known the dark hours when Iranians were obliged to pass under the tutelage of foreign powers, one of them being the British Empire. However, with the wealth from his inflated oil prices, he said his nation of Iran was willing to render monetary assistance to his equal of Great Britain with pleasure. Iran, he added, belonged to this new world and as such, he could not allow any of his new European friends to collapse economically. As Britain had often dominated Iran in the past, the change in roles was greatly gratifying to the Shah.

This almost dictatorial approach to government with a passion to curb the influence of several of the old elite factions of Iran, worried Sabah's father with his ancient Persian roots. He believed the Shah's actions threatened to destroy the Byzantine financial structure created to protect his son. He was not the only high-ranking member of the intelligence community who was deeply concerned by the unlimited power being wielded by the Shah.

It was during this time that the Shah decided to make a massive investment in his military strength as well as the construction of many nuclear facilities, to the bitter resentment of the Israelis.

By 1977, Iran was considered to be the fifth strongest nation in the world. He announced the days of foreign exploitation of his country were over, making broadcasted statements such as—*nobody can dictate to us, and nobody can wave a finger at us because we will wave ten fingers back.*

Iran started to considerably interfere in the foreign relationships of other countries following the lines of CIA objectives. By clandestine means, they provided funds and equipment for uprisings in Iraq, as well as giving military support to the Sultan of Oman, strategically placed on the edge of the Persian Gulf. A rebellion against the Sultan was put down, in part by forces from Great Britain's Special Air Services, the SAS. The overall actions in the region promoted the CIA to conclude that because of oil reserves, Iran was set for growth and stability of government for as far as they could see.

The earliest embers of discontent towards the Shah's reign were seen following on from the death of the Ayatollah Khomeini's son Mostafa, when a few hundred militant anti-Shah students demonstrated in the capital of Tehran. In the first month of 1978, a newspaper article was published attacking Ruhollah Khomeini, who was in exile in Iraq. It referred to him as a homosexual drug addict, who was a British spy. It went on to claim he was an Indian, not an Iranian. The next day, protests against the article began in the holy city of Qom, a traditional centre of opposition to the Shah's dynasty.

According to Sophie, by the latter end of 1978, the deepening unrest and opposition to the Shah's reign erupted in widespread demonstrations and rioting. The Shah realised the level of violence used by SAVAK to crush the rebellion had failed. He was left with no choice. With his family around him, he abdicated the throne on the 16 January 1979, first fleeing to the Bahamas.

Only a very few of the Shah's court knew he had been diagnosed with chronic lymphocytic leukaemia. By the middle of 1978, it was so severe that he spent the whole summer at the royal retreat on the Caspian Sea, where two prominent French cancer doctors tried to ease his pain by prescribing a drug that was known to cause depression and to impair one's thinking.

One of those who knew the seriousness of his condition, together with the nature of the treatment, was Sabah's father. Another person to know was an American, who the Shah instructed Sabah's father to tell of his condition. The American who was told was a serving CIA officer, according to the records that were found, stationed in an unlisted field office in Sarasota, Florida.

At first, it was counter-intelligence at Vauxhall who found this man, then, following my instructions, they notified Sophie. It was mainly intuition she was relying on, but I trusted that. It was her opinion he'd been the notional head of the Pegasus Mercantile Company.

She used the words 'notional head' as she was unable to trace his participation in the company beyond the year of 1981 when, at the age of fifty-six, he met a very mysterious death in the sugarcane fields on the island of Grande-Terre at the French resort of Guadeloupe. The case was still open, with no person on any suspect list.

His name first appeared on an invoice shown in an editorial in the *Daily Pan-American News*, published in Mexico City. It itemised a hotel bill for the Shah of Iran when he temporarily stayed at the México Reforma Hotel. The article castigated the Shah for squandering so much money whilst, not a mile away, there were so many attempting to survive whilst living in abject poverty.

The report in the newspaper was about how the Shah, when banished from Iran and not having a permanent home, wanted his suite of rooms at the hotel extended into the next suite on the same floor. The hotel agreed to the alteration if the Shah paid for it to be done, and then, if he decided to move from the México Reforma, either because his application for residency in Mexico was refused or for any other reason, everything was to be returned to its original condition at his expense.

The invoice, for $167,000, was dated 16th of May 1979, and carried the name of the managing director of the company—The Pegasus Mercantile Company. I sent the name off to Jimmy Mercer who messaged me back as soon as he was able. The man's name was known to Mercer, but not only the Jimmy Mercer I was dealing with. The name, Frank Parker, was also known by Jimmy's father, Rudi Mercer.

* * *

Despite decades of pervasive surveillance by SAVAK, working closely with the experts of the CIA, the extent of public opposition to the Shah and his sudden departure came as a considerable surprise to both the British and US intelligence community. As late as 28th September 1978, the U.S. Defence Intelligence Agency, a branch of the CIA, reported the Shah being expected to remain in power for at least the next ten years. Part of that report, the part with the time prognosis, was written by the same CIA officer who was found face-down on the sugarcane estate; one Frank Parker.

Even though the Shah's period in exile was short as a span of time, the number of countries he travelled to, who subsequently refused his request to settle, was immense. All that proved once more, if it was needed to be proven, that friends bought by money were worthless friends.

The 1979 Islamic revolution that led to the toppling of the Shah, was believed by many and reported by some, to have been a British-backed uprising. One of those who believed it was the Shah himself, who was convinced until the day he died, in Egypt in July 1980. Sophie asked me if it was true and I smiled as I replied I didn't know. She said she didn't believe me, and I smiled even more.

When the new government of Iran finally stopped the ritual bloodletting so commonly used by revolutionaries to repress oppression, it kept a few of the senior officers from inside the corridors of the hitherto despised SAVAK, who had sensed the oncoming change, to create a new tyranny in the shape of the Ministry of Intelligence and National Security of Iran, or SAVAMA for short.

The prime concern of this new institution was to

infiltrate the proliferation of fanatical left-wing student groups that were calling for military support from Soviet Russia for their cause. Sabah Al Salim's father presented the case privately to the new ruler, Ayatollah Ruhollah Khomeini, that there was nobody better placed for this role than his own anonymous son, already enrolled in his first year at the University of Tehran. It could be reliably assumed, so Sophie speculated, that Sabah's father would have 'invested' some funds for the Ayatollah into an account in the banking side of Pegasus, whilst enjoying his private audience. If only we could look into the accounts, she said, to which I added my own hopes.

While she was waiting, she said laughingly she had located several banks in Iran once owned by the Shah which were transferred on his death to the Islamic State, along with other banks throughout the world he was using alongside leading members of his family. Most of these banks were in North America, with more in Mexico City and others in the Bahamas, where at one time he tried to buy an island.

She managed to trace a list of an exceedingly large amount of incredibly valuable art work said to be owned by Empress Farah Diba, the widow of the last Shah of Iran, Mohammad Reza Pahlavi. Most of it was on display in three world-renowned museums.

It would be an estimate, of course, as nobody could be sure of the Shah's worth, but Sophie had unearthed estimates dated back as far as the early

1970s, so she was reasonably placed to form an opinion. Her guess was in excess of fifty billion US dollars, to which she added, she was being modest. No matter which way it was looked at, it was a sizeable amount of money even for an ancient Persian King. As I replaced the secure telephone receiver in Captain Lloyd's office, I wondered how much Sabah Al Salim could be worth.

The initials F.P., belonging to the agent Frank Parker Sophie had come across, kept cropping up in the research conducted on the CIA's role in the city of Panama, from the counter-intelligence floor at Vauxhall. They could find no direct interference by the CIA into the existing Panama banking system, but several accounts in different banks carried the names of people who miraculously had those same F.P. initials.

Another meaningful discovery made at Vauxhall, this time through the Financial Terrorist Index, was the creation of a major financial corporation called the Cayman Island Corporation, that now had fingers spreading out into many other fiscal pies. It had taken several weeks to discover how the corporation was generated by the State Governor who, simply but fraudulently, converted three otherwise unknown investment companies in the British Sovereign Overseas Territory into one single vast conglomerate. It was opened in 1980 in the name of a Cayman Island resident—Frank Parker.

After one month of the Cayman Island Corporation being in operation, the State Governor resigned his position, leaving Grand Cayman for an undisclosed destination, presumably somewhere in Venezuela after his chartered aircraft landed at the capital of Caracas, from where Sophie was unable to track him further. When I finished speaking to Sophie, it was Jimmy Mercer who next had my ear.

CHAPTER THIRTEEN

CHAPTER TWELVE+ONE

BANKING

I was delighted Judith had met with Valery Agapov twice as many times as I thought. My delight extended into how George had dovetailed with his wife into my new detective company when he uncovered another photograph of Agapov ready to board the ferry at Lerwick, taken the day after I left Gardie. I knew Judith had no choice but to cooperate, even so, the lure of the predominately English-speaking Ottawa district, in Canada, was a benefit. She assured me she had been working as well as anyone could, trying hard to secure the name of the head of the Pegasus Bank from Valery Agapov.

I had arranged for Captain Lloyd to give Judith a mobile phone, one that could be monitored by the Ministry of Defence. She was then instructed to arrange for Agapov to visit. It was an idea I'd asked

Jerry about, whose only comment was that I inform the commanding officer of the base. There was only one number she could call from her phone, Agapov's number, with each call being recorded.

As far back as our meeting in St James's Park, I had considered asking Valery about the bank myself, making confiding in me a condition of granting him the asylum he wanted, but there was something not right in what Judith told me when I confronted her with the first photograph of his visit.

Judith had said the same man who organised the successful assassination of Colette in Paris, had arranged for something to be picked up by her before she left this country for France. She was to collect some material from a usual drop-off point outside Kenwood House, on Hampstead Heath. This was something she had only done on rare occasions so was looking forward to it. Whatever this material was, it was left there by Agapov after Page Boucher had provided some logistical information to the Russian, unaware of its purpose.

Agapov was curious. The man arranging it for him had told Valery his 'top operator, a woman' would collect it. It was a mistake, of course, saying it was woman who would do the collecting. As soon as he'd said it, he realised what he'd done, but it was too late. He toyed with the idea of saying nothing to Meadows, then toyed with the idea of telling her. If he said nothing, then if Meadows was to see Agapov, she would assume she was blown. She would act as protocol dictated, and with it went the whole mission. In a confused state, it could take her as far as thinking there was a chance of those involved in the operation being caught, or worse; killed.

If he went the other way of telling her, she might have a visitor at the dead-letter pick-up. What harm would it cause? Yes, he would lose face for making a mistake and having to admit it, but everyone was on the same team, were they not? So it wasn't such a big mistake, was it? He paced his office, three floors below the top floor where he often pictured himself sitting in a smart, bespoke chair of his choice, looking at the panoramic view of the Thames and beyond. But, if he was really successful, as Moscow envisaged, it would not be just the Thames he would be able to view. If he was promoted to becoming controller of MI6, his office would look out onto Parliament itself. He would have all the keys to all the locked doors along the tunnel to Westminster, together with the codes to pass through the guarded security gates. Of course for that to happen, his treacherous side must never be discovered. He opted for losing face.

Agapov was unaware that day of being looked for by Judith until it was too late. He thought he had concealed himself well, in order to see the woman who was coming to collect the small sheet of folded, lined, coded paper he'd left behind the loose yellow brick, one course down from the top of the inside wall that was directly next to the left-hand-side pillar, leading into the lawned front entrance of Kenwood House, on Hampstead Heath. The sign on the door advertised a free event, *Friends of Kenwood Society Spring Art Show, Open to All.*

He was obscured from view by a large chestnut tree in the shrubbery that Monday in April, watching carefully as a meagre number of avid art enthusiasts passed through the gates. He was looking for the one that stood out from the dedicated folk who had braved the cold, bleak east wind, cutting through the bones of anyone exposed to it.

There she was, a size zero woman dressed as a—what? What was she? Was she a shop mannequin in that short coat that wouldn't keep a cat warm? Was she a fashion model, he wondered, who did a bit of intel work on the quiet for some extra cash money? Or was she a wannabe film-star, doing a 'run-through' in fashionable Hampstead, hoping to be spotted? He didn't know what, but she stood out enough to stay in his memory for four solid years before he saw her again.

Not long after that, I ruined it all by revealing her to be not only a spy but an assassin as well. Valery already knew these facts. He found them out as soon as he 'looked her up' on the embassy computer files. So, as attested by history, he was attracted even more deeply. Whereas he wanted her to be the tough spy, killing when ordered without a thought, he wanted her to be another kind of woman, too.

They had met, Judith confined in me; met and drunk wine in an intimate wine bar Agapov said he'd often used, just off the main road in Notting Hill Gate. It was not that first night, although she was tempted, but later in their relationship, when she invited him to her apartment where—"Well, Harry, you wouldn't expect a lady to tell you how she took her lover's breath away, now would you?" she told me, with as straight a face as she could manage. Don't ask me how I felt, because I don't know. I knew it was a strange relationship I had with her, but I ploughed on after telling myself Agapov had engineered whatever it was they had going.

So I wanted Judith to tell me the name of the man Valery Agapov, as Yuri Bogdan, regularly met to discuss the liquidity of the Pegasus vaults in the port town of Kamariotissa, on the island of Samothrace. As an addition, I wanted to know why it was that Yuri Bogdan met the head of the bank and not Valery Agapov? Without thinking there could be anything wrong, I asked her how the conversation about Valery's proposed defection went, if in fact it had been raised.

It had been spoken of, she said, but not in a beneficial way to either of them. Judith had lost her temper and Agapov was thankful for the hasty intervention of an armed rating who'd heard the noisy commotion on the telephone. There was more talking to be done.

* * *

I was singularly happy there were many miles of water between me and Howard James Fredrick Mercer II inside his office at the White House, next to his President, as he shouted his disbelief down the transatlantic phone line, with his voice being transferred to the specially secured phone line initiated into my headphones from Jerry Furley at the Vauxhall Box.

When he finished his tirade against the combined worldly injustice he'd found in his life, the moment of silence shared by Jerry and me felt as deeply quiet as he had been excessively loud.

The man who Valery had identified was indeed a senior high-ranking officer inside the CIA, stationed in their headquarters at Langley, in McLean, Virginia, but it wasn't his rank that had Mercer spitting bullets down the phone connection, it was the fact this man spoke to Mercer at least five times a week on briefing matters before Jimmy presented the concise intelligence information to the President.

Jerry Furley could not be certain what were the full range of duties this senior CIA officer was engaged in, so it shouldn't surprise anyone when I say I had no idea either, but putting all humour aside, unfortunately for all of us Jimmy Mercer could not categorically say what were his principal responsibilities; if indeed this man was engaged in concerns of his department or occupied all of his time in the bank's affairs.

One thing the two of us were certain of after a rough translation of the more discernible parts of Jimmy Mercer's verbal onslaught, was that one of the four CIA officers stationed on the island of Samothrace, had recognised Liam Gibson's face from the photographs that had been distributed between them. The officer had carried out his orders and successfully followed Liam to one of the 'front doors' of the two blue attached houses making up the Pegasus Mercantile Company.

With his back to the agent, Gibson entered the seven correct digits into the combination lock on the code-protected door. After that procedure, but without trying the door handle, he swiped his proximity card through the reader access system. It was then he opened the door, quickly disappearing inside the building. He reappeared after a short period of approximately twelve minutes. When he came out he was carrying a blue coloured fabric bag in one hand with what the agent guessed was money inside. One would assume it to be quite a reasonable guess in the circumstances.

During a short break when I thought Mercer was taking more breath into his lungs ready for a second onslaught, I asked what I knew was a loaded question, however, I never anticipated all of his reply. My question was about the number of American CIA officers on the island. "Was it true," I asked, "there were only four CIA agents on the island and not, as I'd been told, more, masquerading as a company of American surveyors?"

For a moment he stalled with an answer. A fraction of a second later, when he'd had time to think of a suitable one, he agreed with my speculation about having more people on the island, but he did not say why they were there. There was another strange thing about his reaction. Instead of asking me why I thought he was having the island surveyed, he said, rather than asked, that he wanted me to meet Alexi Vasilyev in two days' time in Warsaw, Poland. There was a suite of rooms booked for me in the Raffle Europejski Hotel on Krakowskie Przedmieście, but it was not there where I was to meet him. The address for this monumental occasion was to be texted to me later—in code!

It was easy to sense his hostility, but I was unsure whether it was me causing the ill feeling or the previous business about the internal head of the Pegasus

Bank. I decided not to hedge my bets; instead, I'd jump in with both feet. I asked if Alexi Vasilyev would be expected to know anything about the future of the Lockheed Martin SR-72, the hypersonic aircraft presently using the RAF bases on Cyprus. I thought I could feel the heat from what must have been an embarrassed Mercer, as the only reply I got was in the form of an order—"I want you inside the Ambassador's residence in Regent's Park by three o'clock this afternoon, Paterson. And, seriously, don't be late!"

The quality of the curses he chose to use was, it must be said, enlightening, even so I considered it to be alarmingly offensive, finding no trouble within myself to tell him so. After I quietly told him he was a buffoon who should have found out where I was, on the Isle of Shetland, before telling me what to do, I told him to stop being so impolite. One thing was certain, and that was the Americans were not monitoring my movements. I then suggested I should either meet him tomorrow or some other time.

Unknown to me, my old friend Sir Rupert Draycott, who I'd asked to use his Special Branch connections to assist me in research, was married to a Greek woman whose family had a home on Samothrace which was available for his, or their, use at any time either wanted. He was also a lover of all things

Greek, for which I learned he was called a Philhellene. Yet another lesson came when he told me of a saying credited to the German philosopher Friedrich Nietzsche—'The Greeks have never been overestimated.'

Draycott arrived on the island at roughly the same time as did the team of eight Americans. They came in two 'People Carriers' whereas Rupert came by foot and borrowed a car from his Greek family. The party of Americans could all be, so Rupert reported, CIA officers, but there was no way he could tell without asking. Being the resourceful man he was, he found a way to ask.

The company of Americans were billeted in some apartments near the Archaeological Museum on the island, with most days spent driving, then walking, around the far western edge of the island, where on a map it looked as though there is a long breakwater. The area was mostly level, being subdivided into small farms, or what we would call smallholdings, of between one and ten acres. The majority of the company regularly used a nightclub near the area they were 'surveying', which was called The Rebel Club.

Rupert didn't go into the nightclub himself, using age as his excuse. Instead, he got a niece to do all his 'work' inside the club for him. It didn't take her long to find out what we wanted to know as she went with two girlfriends, and all three girls spoke reasonable

English. The Americans were very talkative. They were on the island to survey the area for a viability report before an airstrip could be built for the Greek government, who must have plans for redevelopment, they said.

Rupert's niece got a photo of the group which was sent to Jerry. Four of the six men in her photograph were accredited CIA officers. From facial recognition at the IOMS facility, the other two in the photo, together with the two who remained in their apartment, were identified as engineering contractors used by the National Security Agency. Some of the faces were last identified in Iraq, surveying a construction of a military complex that included a runway.

I eventually met Jimmy Mercer in the ambassador's residence in Regents Park the day after arriving back in London from Shetland. Having left George's car in the garage of the Balmoral Hotel in Edinburgh, when we flew off to Shetland, was a great idea, but driving home from Scotland was a different matter. I could have left George to drive back on his own, which in all probability would have meant I could have arrived at Mercer's meeting far quicker if I caught a plane, but I just could not leave George on his own to do that. The meeting was important, but George was more so.

I said goodbye to George, who was standing next to his wife under the portico of number 16 Eaton

Square, stealing the odd glance at the same security camera that captured the then black-hooded, unrecognisable Judith Meadows as she drilled out the lock before entering and murdering my father. With so many memories of bad times, I vowed I would do all I could to ensure the future would hold only memories of good.

Judith's future was no longer in my hands. It was in the early stages of being developed by the three Home Office agencies whose task it was to first manufacture a name to fit inside a workable legend that would enable her to live peacefully wherever she had chosen. The final place of residence would not be known by those agencies. As far as I was concerned, our meetings were finished, with my recommendation being that she be allowed to live in Ottawa, as she wished.

It could be said I shouldn't know where she was going, but I did know. I knew the person responsible had chosen a destination called Carleton Place, a town in Eastern Ontario, Canada, in Lanark County, about twenty-eight miles west of downtown Ottawa, as her eventual home. Nobody at that stage other than me knew who was to live there. The extent of the main plans was to be known by three people only: Jerry Furley, Jimmy Mercer, and me.

I still did not fully trust Judith. I could not trust her not to contact Vasilyev with a mind on retribution. Her freedom made the possibility of not only Vasilyev wanting revenge on the Patersons, but Judith being in a position to execute any revenge she wanted. Wasn't it Paulo who was to blame for Alexi's disfigurement, as well as being the primary person of the Paterson lineage to blame for Judith's incarceration, allied to the fact she had lost her lover to Moscow?

I had a real fear for the safety for everyone around me. For Serena with Breno, for George and Sophie, as well as for Katherine and Luca. No matter what Alexi said about his love for Katherine, she was a starting point for any thoughts he had on retaliation on my line of the Patersons; plus he was a well-practised liar.

There was one stipulation I did make. I was to be consulted on areas of suitability for Judith's final settlement. Although it had to be chosen with a great deal of care, I wanted it close to Halls Mills and the home of Christopher Metsos, the man behind the Russian illegals programme that had been destroyed by the FBI in 2010. I had an operation in mind that involved Metsos and Meadows, but it was for the future. For now, it was to be put in a back pocket and maybe taken out again later.

I played it over in my mind, with logic telling me I was right. I had approached the situation carefully, but with the next step I proposed, I was not being cautious. Others could say I was careless in showing a side of me I had no need of showing, but that would be what others would say, not me.

I asked Judith if she would object to me knowing where she was to be relocated. She asked if I had an idea of where it would be. I gave her an honest answer.

I told her I wanted her permission to ask the team of people responsible for its exact location. I was hoping she would agree because she felt I had feelings towards her, but knowing exactly where she was to be resettled would be my insurance.

I wanted her to believe I was still in love with her. It was important to me not to have to look over my shoulder for the rest of my life, not only for my safety, but for all of those I've listed. My problem was in finding a way where that would be possible. I thought I had the seed of an idea. However, for a part of it to work, I would need Judith's cooperation.

We had been fortunate inasmuch as there was no ferry leaving the island to Greece until the day after Liam Gibson had been apprehended by the CIA coming out of the Pegasus building carrying a bag, presumed to be full of money. When I was able to interrupt Jimmy Mercer's verbal onslaught, I managed to get him to instruct his agents to keep Gibson out of sight until I was ready. To his question of why, I told him I'd tell him later.

You see, whilst the experts in all the departments affiliated to MI6 were busy examining the areas where American intelligence and ours might be overlapping, I gave Sophie comprehensive access to all the declassified documents I could get my hands on to do with the operation to assassinate the French Colette in Paris. Sophie was allowed usage of an IOMS unit stationed in Greenwich, South London, and quickly found Judith's Achilles heel.

When the spy I discovered working inside British intelligence was given all the assurances he needed before being settled into his new place of Russian residence, he asked to see the money he had accumulated for his treason. He was introduced to Yuri Bogdan, who of course he knew was Valery Agapov. Valery's double identity was not a concern for him. He was only concerned with seeing the money his treachery had amassed inside the Pegasus Bank. Yuri Bogdan had an advantage only one other enjoyed. The other person was the CIA officer Valery Agapov had exposed to Judith Meadows, and the advantage the two shared was to have unlimited access to the vaults of the Pegasus Bank.

Agapov arranged a visit to the bank for the English traitor, who first made a request to clear a deposit box he held in a bank in Maidstone, Kent. He wanted that done before he left England. It could require the use of a diplomatic pouch to carry the contents from a safety deposit box through airport scrutiny to another deposit box on the island, but not this time. The departure of a traitor from UK shores was one the British government had no wish to impede, especially as the contents of the box was just a letter. Valery's consent carried one proviso; he wanted to know what was in that letter.

CHAPTER FOURTEEN

POLAND

The instructions had arrived from Jimmy Mercer. I was to meet with Alexi Vasilyev in the Desa Unicum Auction House at the northern end of a park called the Ujazdowski, then walk him through to the American Embassy at 29/31 Aleje Ujazdowskie, just the other side of this park, whenever he was ready to go. Mercer repeated his instruction of Vasilyev being in absolute charge of the timing to this operation. He expected him to be appropriately protected.

Those instructions were not the only written orders contained in the coded email from Jimmy; the rest followed much of what Jerry Furley had told me when we were in Aberdeen for the extended lunch. Both men were senior officers in their respected intelligence services, as was Vasilyev in Russia. The fundamental message they were both saying was to think of Alexi Vasilyev as a top-ranking official and as such, expect top-quality security to be present everywhere he goes.

* * *

I knew Vasilyev was Polish. What I had not known was he was born on the same street as the American Embassy, eighteen years after the embassy was re-established at the end of WWII. As soon as I was able, I contacted the British Embassy in Warsaw, arranging to meet with the MI6 station head the day following my arrival. I had thought long and hard about the day I was to meet Alexi without actually knowing where it was to take place. Now, despite knowing, I was none the wiser regarding how to handle it.

Despite my misgivings, the head of operations at the Warsaw embassy was supremely composed when I told him what was to take place on his home ground. I sensed nothing but self-control and expertise. He assured me all assistance needed would be forthcoming, firmly reasserting his station's capability even though no defections had taken place, as he put it, on his watch. I was thankful he didn't ask if I had handled any before.

By now, you are probably aware that I'm not good at analysing myself, or at finding faults. I'm not about to change that defect any time soon, so I'm stuck with making the decisions affecting me based purely on impulse. With that in mind, I'm sure it will come as no surprise to find I invited Katherine to meet with me in the same hotel I was to stay in. I knew it was dangerous for many reasons, but blame my inherent risk-taking.

Luca was away at school for the time I needed her and I thought she could distract me much better than reading a book. I thought I was fully aware of just how much affection Alexi Vasilyev had for Katherine. I might have been right about his feelings, nevertheless I was wrong about hers.

I was correct about how important the intelligence Alexi was bringing with him was. For one thing, he immediately gave up the name of the American serviceman who had been monitoring radio traffic emanating from the Iraqi military base at Al-Qa'im, before he defected to ISIS. The encryption he developed was the most dominant topic being spoken about in London. I guessed the same was true in most of Jimmy Mercer's intelligence units.

He was a highly valuable target, thought to be the creator of this so-called one-way compression function of converting data into code. He was the man we had followed to a military complex, still available to the terrorists, at Ar Raqqah, with Sabah Al Salim and a deputy leader of the Syrian arm of ISIS, a person named Abu Ala al-Mulard, along with a man named Abu Saleh Al-Sabaid who was yet another deputy leader of the military arm identified at the site.

I needed Alexi's help to confirm the Syrian Colonel I'd seen leaving the same complex was indeed Hafez al-Rifaaz, plus I would need his much informed opinion on what he was doing there.

There was, of course, much more wanted by the Americans, which no doubt Vagabond could supply, but from our viewpoint the position of Cyprus, with the new installations opposite at Tartus, was at the top of any list I imagined we would have.

If I was right about the defensive screen being constructed in the naval port, it would follow that the British RAF Sovereign Base Areas would be declared redundant. If that scenario was true, the second part of the hypothesis I had sent to Furley could become a reality, with the surveyors on Samothrace implementing Mercer's plans to build runways.

Jimmy Mercer's timetable for my meeting with Alexi coincided with the time President Putin ordered a major reshuffle of Russia's top two security services. In essence, Alexi was to become one of the first of Russia's elitist spymasters when Putin merged the Foreign Intelligence Service with the Federal Security Service, making a new Ministry of State Security. An agency of the same name was a precursor to the KGB, during Stalin's tenure as head of the Soviet Union.

Although it was, perhaps, not an ideal time to defect because of the timing of the merger, it was, for another reason, precisely perfect. Alexi's mother had died five years after he was born, making this year the fiftieth anniversary of her passing and, in two days' time, the exact date, fifty years past.

It gave him a worthy reason to leave his positions in Russia's SVR and FSB. He also had a valid reason to be in the Desa Unicum auction house. He was a well-known collector of a specific Spanish sculptor named Eduardo Chillida, whose famous bronze work of art called *San Cristobal*, was on sale at the auction rooms. It was in those rooms where our first 'meeting' was to take place.

Alexi's research had been correct. It was the first of two viewing days, with the premises moderately busy on the day we were to see each other, without speaking. Eduardo Chillida was renowned for his large municipal works of art, some huge in size, with the vast majority of his work only suitable for display outside in the fresh air. The *San Cristobal* piece was one of the few he'd created that was small enough to go inside a dwelling. Alexi's collection of this man's work included a few of his smaller sculptures as well as paintings, making him famous in the illustrious sphere of government circles he moved in.

* * *

Although it was still September, with the weather quite mild, the wearing of a coat was a requirement most had adopted, as was the wearing of hats of one description or another. In one of his messages, Alexi had said he would be without any head-covering whilst in Poland. The reason he gave could well have been the truth, as he said it was for showing respect to his dead mother. I thought it could have been for another reason; one involving his escape.

In case you're worried, none of his messages were sent directly to me. They were addressed to Ms. Sophie Prosser, Central Library, Royal Borough of Kensington and Chelsea, 12 Phillimore Walk, London W8. They were disguised as requests for precise information on the whereabouts of specific prints, paintings, and various other contemporary compositions of Chillida, found in London. As I said, all the messages were coded, giving Sophie and George plenty of work and experience to decipher.

* * *

I would say at least eighty percent of the left-hand side of his face was scarred beyond recognition. On that side of his face, the skin had a stark-white effect, as if bleached, travelling from his chin through where an ear would be expected to be, but wasn't. The same distinct colouring carried on into his hairline, where the hair was burnt away to the very top of his head. I'm not overstating anything in telling you he was a grotesque sight, causing the hair on the back of my neck to stand on end.

I gave no thought to any other injury he may have suffered. What I could see was enough for me to re-engage with the worry I had about his need for revenge that he might be contemplating. Even allowing for the death of the man who caused those injuries, if I was him, I would want to kill any person connected to that man, very slowly, inflicting the most agony I was able to inflict.

With a great effort I averted my eyes, but it didn't improve any sense of benevolence I felt towards him or this defection job, which I now thought would be impossible! *How can I get him to the embassy before his escort notices him missing, if that's the speed he walks?* Those were my thoughts after settling down from the shock of his appearance. Yes, I knew he had trouble walking, but how did the man expect to get away if he was virtually rooted to the spot? Perhaps, a wheelchair would be the answer. If not, then kill the guards? No! I might get caught and the prisons in Poland haven't any Michelin Stars, let alone bottles of Jura.

I had been hypnotised by his demanding walking ability, preferring to use two stout walking sticks for support rather than ask for help from either of the two burly aides he had with him. One, the larger of the two aides, was in front, with the other one walking ever so slightly more slowly behind. Their presence obviously made our private meeting much more difficult to arrange. I hoped he had used the time he'd had to devise a plan we could use to our advantage.

In Mercer's first instructions, he'd made mention in a metaphorical way the possibility of holding Vasilyev's hand and walking him the short distance from the auction rooms to the American embassy. In reality, the embassy's front gates were about five hundred yards away, which in my estimation would need at least ten, if not fifteen minutes for Alexi to walk such a distance. One thing was certain—walking wasn't an option. I would need vehicles to set up the defection. I had an embassy-issued burner phone which I used to message the British embassy station officer, arranging to meet later at the hotel. I had enough things to think about for a while.

When Furley was in Aberdeen, we had discussed many things, one of which was the security Alexi's presence would generate from both the Russian embassy in Warsaw, as well as special security from the Poles themselves; to that, I had to add the two close escorts I'd seen with him. There was a driver when they pulled into the hotel, but he had not stayed. I thought he might have been an embassy driver.

Strangely, I had not seen any medical aid with Vasilyev, but perhaps they were coming later.

When I'd met with the Warsaw station head, he'd given me a folder of photographs of the Russian foot soldiers working out of their embassy. Up until this point, I hadn't seen any. According to Harvey Burgess, the MI6 head of station in Warsaw, the Polish security would be harder to spot as they generally operated well away from sight. The ABW, as they were called, had operatives everywhere in the capital, most of whom would never be suspected.

I broached the subject of the Russian presence in Warsaw with Valery Agapov before coming here, listening to his opinion that they wouldn't be a problem. He called them Lazy Ivans, interested in imported Russian vodka, cocaine, money and girls. Nothing else, he said. I found this too simplistic to be taken as absolute truth. However, the conversation we were having at that time was loose and irrelevant to the situation, so I encouraged his conjecture. He said Vasilyev was lucky. I asked him what made him say that, considering the man's physical condition. It was his reply that made me take notice.

"He's going over in his home town. Warsaw was where he grew up and he made his friends. Some of those friends will still be there. There's one thing about life that never changes and that's the past. Polish people hate Russians, my lord. If Vasilyev's protection detail are Russians, nobody will notice if they oversleep one day, or if they accidentally fall down the lift shaft. It would be easy enough for me to find out if they're Russian or Polish, for a friend, Mr Paterson, sir."

I replied how a friend would be willing to place a premium on such a favour, placing the supplier in a commanding position if negotiations had to be conducted at a later stage.

I followed that up by asking if Alexi had confessed to having specific friends in Warsaw and if so, had he given the addresses or occupation of any? "Only one," Valery replied. I asked if he'd told him this friend's occupation or address? His reply was again interesting.

"Alexi never tells anyone anything without a reason. He didn't tell me about his friend's occupation or his address. He didn't tell me if he's short or tall, or whether he liked girls or boys. He didn't tell me shit! But he did have a huge smile on his distorted face when he told me his friend would help him escape if he asked him. He added, his friend would die for him if he asked. But no. He didn't tell me if he'd asked him to do either."

* * *

I followed the message directives Alexi had sent to Sophie, and made my way towards a spot inside the auction rooms where he said he would be able to see me, as well as my being able to get a clear view of his party of three; near the door to the auctioneers office where the crowd would be at its thinnest. As instructed, I was using a black walking stick, similar to his own, and wearing a sky-blue silk scarf.

He walked with his head down, eyes looking at the uncovered floorboards, showing no interest in his surroundings. When he neared where I stood, his head rose from its bowed position. It was then he saw me, but there was only the merest hint of recognition on his face, one that, if you were not expecting to see one, you wouldn't.

As his escort moved around the natural curvature of the wall-cabinets containing some of the valuable items to be sold, Alexi stopped. At that point his rear protection, with his attention elsewhere, unwittingly walked marginally in front, before realising what he'd done. When there was a faint gap between Vasilyev and this protection officer, a screwed-up cigarette packet smoothly slipped to the floor from Alexi's left hand, which instead of holding the walking stick by its handle, he held suspended by its strap. The noise of a crowded room full of anticipatory people, plus the sound of Alexi's stick striking the floor, covered the commonplace sound of its fall, yet to me, it sounded as loud as a metal hammer falling to the solid ground.

Somehow, I was controlling an intense impulse to look him in the eyes as he passed no more than three or four steps in front of where I stood. In spite of the compulsion growing stronger with each movement he made to close the gap, I did exercise restraint. What's more, I managed to edge my way towards the fallen packet, daring not to look away while they walked past.

When I was happy nobody was watching, I picked the thing up. It was an empty Dunhill International packet. I laughed very quietly, one part of me admiring his scrutiny of my habits and another part, worried by the same study.

I had no idea what to expect inside the packet, or from him when we met. However, there was another surprise to come. Inside the discarded packet was a USB flash drive that, after reading what was on it, made me wish the ground would open up and swallow me.

The evening before all that occurred in the auction house, I watched from my balcony on the fifth floor of the hotel, as the Russian diplomatic Mercedes-Benz SUV pulled into the car park of the Raffle Europejski Hotel from Chopin airport, carrying Alexi with the same two protection officers, along with all their luggage. When I went down in the elevator, I saw the shorter of the two men I'd seen at the auction preview, standing alone at the receptionist desk talking to the concierge. By the amiability the two men shared, it appeared as though they knew each other. The second man I'd seen in the Desa Unicum rooms was at Alexi's side as he painfully made his way into the hotel bar area. I was quietly satisfied I had not left all the arrangements for his defection to him alone. I had a couple of surprises in store for him.

Katherine greeted him as though there was nothing wrong with his broken body, he being the long-lost lover she had been waiting for all these years. It shocked me. I had always known the affair I'd had with her was just for mutual convenience, with the continuance of our relationship, without any physicality, being for Luca's sake.

To my shame, the special connection I had with Luca crossed my mind as I stared at the intensity of Katherine and Alexi's embrace. Selfishly, I wondered what might happen with the affinity I shared with my son if the two people I was staring at got together in any form of partnership. Those confusing thoughts were far from conducive to the moment.

Even though I had a crystal clear interest in their caress, I couldn't help feeling embarrassed by looking, so, as if I'd been caught doing something wrong, I hastily turned away, picking up a magazine from the table in front of me, then settling into a hotel foyer chair before starting to skim through the pages without reading a word.

I wanted to know what was happening, but the

only way I could manage that was by messaging a member of the embassy team who was closer to them, but there was nobody close enough to overhear.

This was where I was about to gamble and where the second surprise came in. George had come with me. He had flown into Warsaw from Paris, not from London where I had come from. There was no reason to believe any of the four directly involved intelligence agencies, ours, the Russians, the Poles, or the Americans, would know who he was, but even so I didn't want to take any unnecessary risks. His inclusion was not only a gamble in the sense of his inexperience, it was dangerous if Alexi did want revenge.

My first guess was that he wouldn't be so stupid, but just in case, I was armed, as was each member of the embassy team. Everyone involved also had two-way radio communication with the fifth member of my team, who was listening to the proceedings from her hotel room.

It was Katherine who introduced George to Vasilyev. I was seated behind him so I cannot say whether he was overcome by her expressive greeting, or he was tired from exertion of the journey, but what I can say is he paid no attention to George, other than making a rudimentary shake of his proffered hand.

CHAPTER FIFTEEN
COLONEL OBORKA

Shortly after breakfast on the second day in Warsaw, Alexi Vasilyev, with one of his protection officers seated next to him and the other behind the steering wheel of a Russian embassy vehicle, drove away from the hotel heading north to the Powązki Cemetery, where once again he paid homage to his mother.

The Russia analysts' desks on the seventh floor at Vauxhall found a record of five previous visits he'd made to this cemetery on this exact date each year. They were also able to validate the story of his mother's death being precisely fifty years ago, to this very day.

Nevertheless, this day differed in ways unknown to the analysts. The first difference came when a small procession of robed clerics, gently swinging scented thuribles, followed by a handful of elderly mourners, approached the flower-decorated family mausoleum.

Since the collapse of Soviet Russia in 1991, the whole of the seventh floor at Vauxhall had evolved into specialist networks, bridging small and large units with the relatively new IOMS programme, thereby providing the connection into every face recognition apparatus available worldwide. The terminology I used of every apparatus available, meant it was not restricted to this country.

The unrolled IOMS practice, working in tandem with the cyber security so relevant to the intelligence industry, had identified one of Alexi's protection team from the Home Security photography in New York as soon as he arrived in Warsaw. It was Colonel Dimitri Georgievich Oborka. Oborka's arrival, then subsequent travel to the Russian embassy, had alerted all the facial recognition posts.

After a short period of time, the complete history of the journeys he made when in America was despatched to me as well as those 'desks' on the seventh floor. The photographic file showed him meeting Katherine, who would have been quickly identified by Jimmy Mercer, but perhaps not yet by those at Vauxhall.

As far as I was aware, nobody at Vauxhall knew of Alexi Vasilyev's habit of using anagrams, such as the surname of Oborka, but to me the full circle of Vasilyev's communication to Katherine, the one that led me to Judith Meadows, along with the island of Samothrace, a would-be strategic key to the Dardanelles and the Black Sea beyond, was completed.

On the USB flash drive was Alexi's authentic plan of escape. It was not to take place in any auction rooms, as Mercer believed. The more I looked at this plan, the more I preferred it to the plan Jimmy had told me about, but even so, it scared the proverbial out of me.

* * *

Alexi waited with his head bowed in front of the mausoleum as the religious procession passed, embracing each of the followers before adding the European fraternal kiss on a cheek. When the procession had moved away, with everyone having been kissed, he put one foot painfully in front of the other, until at last he entered the grey, stone-built, unexceptional building, a short way from the family crypt. He was expected there. It was, so my Polish driver companion told me, the local government office where a maintenance fee for the various burial chambers would have to be paid when due.

It was usual practice for local councils to charge a fee, which, if not paid for any length of time, meant the council could sell the plot to a family of someone who needed to be buried.

I was inside an unmarked British embassy white

Ford van that had been intricately modified with covert listening devices, as well as having recording and surveillance equipment added with no outward sign of remodelling. It was driven by one of the local team, a female, who had picked me up after I left Ujazdowski Park, meeting up with one of the agents sent from London in a street called Johna Lennona. He had been checking I had not been followed. We had made our way to the cemetery without incident and we were now watching and listening to the proceedings from inside the rear of the vehicle.

Alexi's two protection officers were standing either side of the local government's office door when suddenly, Colonel Dimitri Georgievich Oborka became agitated after looking at his watch. Alexi had been inside for no more than a minute or two, nonetheless Oborka was gesticulating wildly, seemingly without any reason, unless, like me, you had read the script of the escape plan. What should happen next, did!

On the directional microphone in the re-fashioned vehicle, we heard Oborka ordering his fellow officer to enter the government office to ascertain what was going on in there.

"What on earth has happened to the General? He's been gone too long to simply pay a fee. If he's defected, or worse, if he's speaking to spies, we'll be shot! You must remember what I said to you last night about his recent behaviour. You go in and I'll stand guard out here in case there are other collaborators around," was what Oborka said.

From inside the building, we could hear Alexi Vasilyev verbally castigate the protection officer for entering. He could then be clearly heard to repeatedly hit the man with one of his sticks whilst shouting, "How dare you suspect this gentleman of wrongdoing! "Expect to be transferred immediately. Go, before I change my mind and have you shot!" The officer's voice was shaking in the microphone as he tried his best to justify what had happened by demonstrating how Oborka was acting before he was ordered to check his General's wellbeing.

For those who did not know Alexi's detailed plans, the tension coming through the microphone was indeed alarming, but of course I did know his plans; but even so, I was not ready for what I next heard. It was the unmistakable *spat*, *spat*, two distinct shots from a suppressed firearm. What I didn't know at that stage was—who had shot who? The next thing we heard was the instruction I was waiting for, in more ways than one! "Come now!" The order was in Alexi's voice.

Within seconds, we were outside the building with both Oborka and Alexi Vasilyev about to climb through the side door of this unregistered British embassy vehicle. Being unregistered meant it wouldn't arouse any interest from Russian, or Polish embassy, vehicle watchers, but that had a sting in its tail. It also meant anyone found inside could not claim any diplomatic immunity.

"What the hell happened, Alexi? Who did you shoot?" I shouted my questions in Russian as Oborka was giving him a final shove through the door.

"Stop worrying. Everything's in hand. I killed my guard, but the people inside are my Polack friends, they will take care of everything. You would never have agreed to it. I won't be missed by anyone at the embassy for hours, by which time everything inside will be cleaned away. There are plenty of holes out here where an extra body can eventually be hidden."

Following Vasilyev's plan, I had placed two other 'teams' in the cemetery, able to monitor the entrances, with another two outside on the route he had mapped out for us to take to the American embassy. Apart from those precautions, his plan requested one Polish female agent, whom he named, walking nearby in the cemetery at the time he entered the office. With intricate precision, he had instructed this agent "to make her way into the outer office as soon as the way was clear".

I had no need to ask the reason for this specification, since he gave the reason in the flash drive.

When the police arrived, she was to say she was there for the same reason as Alexi, to pay the maintenance fee on a family grave, that of her late husband. All this was true. In the bag she was carrying was the money, the equivalent Polish złoty of £60 sterling, the cost of a year's maintenance fee.

The two stories, hers together with that of the government cemetery official, were pivotal to Vasilyev's safe defection. It would be exactly as it happened, only without any mention of shots fired or heard, or dead bodies. As far as the woman and the official were concerned, neither saw the reprimanded protection officer after he left the building. However, very soon after Vasilyev left the building they heard a powerful car pull up outside, followed by the sound of screeching tyres. Both would say they assumed Alexi Vasilyev must have called the Russian embassy for a car. They had no idea what happened to his remaining protection officer.

"As soon as someone asks how long the woman had been in the offices, then that's the time to confess."

It is the affair the two were having that is their disclosure of truth. Her husband was dead, she told them, as was his wife. He went on to add how nobody was being hurt by the affair. Just the same, he had two married children who did not approve of this liaison, and he was a coward wanting a quiet life as well as what the affair offered. All of that was the truth and easily checked.

The day after the investigation started, the police would receive two anonymous calls, from untraceable telephones. The callers would say how two shots were softly heard coming from a part of the cemetery near the east gate. The direct way back to the hotel for someone having to hobble!

What was not mentioned in this plan was the fate of the lone fee-paying woman. If, as I surmised, the man in the office with her was the man whom Valery Agapov had referred to as Vasilyev's friend who would not stand in the way of his escape, it left the woman standing in the open as a loose end. I hadn't suddenly developed a squeamish streak, nevertheless I wanted to know the fate of this woman, whom I judged to be a dangerous detail as yet unsettled.

I had no need to worry. The woman was Alexi Vasilyev's secret Polish sister. The different surnames meant nothing; what did, was the secret she and the government official shared. Her relationship with Alexi Vasilyev was a secret until that moment in the back of the embassy van, known by only those three.

* * *

There was no mention that I heard in Alexi's escape plan, as laid out on the memory stick, as to why his personal secretary, Colonel Oborka, would suddenly raise doubts in the dead protection officer's mind about General Vasilyev's loyalty, outside the government office. That question was answered by one of my street officers, who had overheard something on the first evening at the hotel.

My street officer's name is not important; what he overheard is. Colonel Dimitri Georgievich Oborka, with the other man, now dead, whose name we didn't know, were having an in-depth conversation the first night everyone arrived. It was what Oborka referred to when he said, "You must remember what I said to you last night."

They were sitting at a table in the hotel bar area when one of the two pairs of operatives from London entered. My first pair sat at the table next to where Oborka was sitting with his colleague. As they did so, my man politely said 'good evening' in Polish.

Oborka returned the greeting, then immediately apologised profusely for not being able speak any language other than his native Russian, with a slight splattering of Polish. He then ended the conversation by turning back to his comrade. A little time after this, their voices became raised and my man, who could speak Russian fluently with Polish as a second language, could hear and understand what was being said.

Oborka was trying to impress on his friend how much his boss, the Colonel General, was not trusted in Moscow and how the two of them did not want to 'go down' because of him. On the other hand, if they were diligent, there may be a possibility of catching him passing on information to a possible spy! And then, said Oborka, he was sure they would be considerably well rewarded.

" How do I know we will be rewarded well? I know because I delivered a coded letter from the General to a woman in New York. I'm trusting you with my life here, but we both can earn good money if we're clever. The General gave me seventy-five thousand roubles for taking the letter to New York. Not only that, but he paid for me to go first-class on an aeroplane, as well as to stay in a suite in a five-star hotel. That was all too much for me to turn down."

An unerring journey started that night for the protection officer, with doubts of Vasilyev's honour feeding the growing greed which prematurely ended this officer's life. But it wasn't just his fate that was bothering me.

Immediately after being told of the conversation, I called Harvey Burgess, the station officer in Warsaw. On my instructions, he contacted his Polish counterpart, who in turn instigated a scan on the telephone records at our hotel, looking for calls made from the room the dead protection officer was then occupying.

* * *

As we waited in the rear of the converted van for Alexi Vasilyev to emerge from the government offices inside the cemetery, my phone had vibrated three times; regrettably, none of those calls were from Burgess, but the fourth one was. There had been a solitary call made from the room of the dead FSB agent.

CHAPTER SIXTEEN

A CHANGE OF PLAN

Howard James Fredrick Mercer II, better known to me as Jimmy, was waiting in the ambassador's office in the American Embassy on Aleje Ujazdowskie, Warsaw. He was smoking his fourth cigar of the morning as a trolley, laden with various salads, wraps, buns and bagels for a cold brunch, was wheeled in by a uniformed Marine. Even allowing for Jimmy Mercer's inherent impatience, this morning his agitation was badly affecting his country's ambassador. Who tried again to get rid of him with his disconcerted nerves!

"Thank all those in the kitchens for me, please," the ambassador announced to the Marine in his polished Texas drawl, as he was about to leave. As the door to his office closed behind the soldier, he rose from his desk chair, reaching for a turkey wrap, his favourite mid-morning snack.

"I don't think anyone's coming," he declared, hesitating on taking a bite before adding further advice. "It could be time for you to call it a day, Mr Director-General."

* * *

When I'd informed Jerry Furley of Alexi Vasilyev's wish not only to defect, but wanting me to coordinate it, he was positively drooling at the mouth at the thought of a Q&A session with him. Even so, I did not tell him of Alexi's secret plan as dictated on what was left in the discarded cigarette packet. I thought the overall situation could be used to our benefit and his exuberance could be an untapped bonus.

I reminded Jerry that, as an American double agent, Alexi's first duty would be to defect to them, not us. I hoped he'd thought of it; nevertheless, as I told him, his previous eagerness was replaced by the phlegmatic look of detachment, making him resemble a man I pictured as being used to disappointment, whereas Mercer, I knew, was not akin to disenchantment.

My phone was showing six unanswered calls from Jimmy Mercer that I blamed on the job's requirement of silence. When he told me he'd heard that excuse a million times, I tried using the attraction

Katherine was having for Vasilyev overriding Vanguard's obligation, citing my million pointless attempts to intervene.

I made things sound more thrilling by adding how my constant efforts to persuade Vasilyev to answer the call of duty were being ignored. Alexi kept stating he would allow his heart to overrule responsibility, and follow love, rather than defect to America.

At one stage, I said, he threatened to remain in Russia, taking up his role within the new Ministry of State Security if his defection to Great Britain was refused or obstructed by American agitation. He was serious when he said he would stay in Russia, keeping the secrets he was to share with the West to die with him, which was the ending to that threat. He said he would be willing to trade what he knew of the United States with the Russian de-briefers, in order to stay alive.

Jimmy screamed the now normal, foul-mouthed obscenities along the restored telephone signal at me in which, from the parts I managed to interpret, he reminded me how Katherine did not reside in England, but did have an apartment in New York, where, if his information was correct, Vasilyev had sent a certain Colonel Dimitri Georgievich Oborka to contact her.

I admitted that was the case, nevertheless I impressed upon him how, as the mother of my son Luca, Katherine had permanent residence with me at The

Hall in Yorkshire anytime she wanted. He was not overwhelmed by any of it, but I'm sure I heard Furley, inside his Vauxhall office, singing *God Save The Queen* when I arrived at the British embassy in Warsaw with Alexi Vasilyev willing to trade everything he was asked for a welcome from Katherine. As far as Jimmy went, he was parked up for a future slot in time.

When I had Alexi to myself, I mentioned the handwriting forensic expert who had examined the notes about Tartus I'd seen photographed and, without me asking for anything, he gave over a fairly comprehensive list of objectives the Russians had in mind for the Syrian naval base. I know I'm shamefully immodest, but even so, he praised my ingenuity in using such a person. As I say, I did like it when he said he thought I was good. Was that praise before the chop? I had no one to ask.

On the list he gave, he included the equipment on the site for the future blocking of the two stations on Cyprus. He gave the names of five South African illegal agents working in the Middle East that I'd heard mention of somewhere. Four were in Iran and one in Saudi Arabia. There was also an active American illegal, he told me, placed in an elevated position in the Iranian military. The details would make splendid reading in Vauxhall. In the back of my mind was the British operative we had in Iran. Of course I never mentioned him, but even so, it crossed my mind how pleased Furley would be with the information on all those placements.

There was more. The Iranians knew what this person was doing, but had decided to leave him in place. At first, this had worried Alexi as he couldn't see a clear reason for not exposing him. From what Vasilyev had seen, there was ample evidence for a genuine trial without the 'show trial' label such events are normally called by the Western press.

He knew some of the leaked intelligence was pure misinformation to deceive, or at best was scurrilous. Some were loaded statistics on proposed output from a particular nuclear power plant that appeared, on first read, legitimate, but from research he conducted, it went too far with mindless detail to be considered bona fide material to be passed on to any interested governments.

Vasilyev could do nothing about this episode of detail being passed to the American CIA, as it was on that very day he returned to his apartment to be electrocuted, almost to death. Despite his injuries, one of the first things he did when he was on his way to recovery was to ask Jimmy Mercer where the detailed information was passed on to inside the CIA. The answer Mercer received was ambiguous.

It said the intelligence had never left Iran. It was, according to Mercer's research study, redirected to a leading administrator inside SAVAMA. Being very careful, Alexi made skilful enquiries inside Moscow to find what he could on the Iranian Intelligence Ministry. He was told by one who was then a superior, to keep his nose out of things of no concern to him.

During a communication Alexi Vasilyev had with Valery Agapov, the name of Sabah Al Salim was mentioned by Agapov, who knew of Vasilyev's enquiries in Moscow. Valery was most insistent his friend should stop any more searching questions about Al Salim. He told Vasilyev a story.

He had seen Sabah's name in an embassy message to the Head of Station in London. Valery was, as we know, an inquisitive person, leading him to have contacts all over the diplomatic world. One was in the Iranian embassy in London. The head of Moscow Station in London, Mikhail Sidorov, asked Agapov to get in touch with his man requesting all he knew of the head of SAVAMA. Vasilyev thought Moscow had asked Sidorov knowing exactly the situation in London. They hoped to get more information because of Agapov's connections. If it all went wrong in any way, well, Agapov was an easy option to lose.

Agapov told how he could hear the tangible fear in his Iranian contact's voice when he spoke of SAVAMA being coordinated with the National Intelligence of Iran. He had Valery juddering slightly until the man was named: it was Sabah Al Salim.

When I met with Jerry Furley in Aberdeen, he told how one of the Iran desks at Vauxhall had identified the South African agent who was inside this ISIS group. They had also been able to lift some intelligence on the position of who headed up the Ministry of Intelligence and National Security of Iran now the two services had merged; they added their confirmation of it being Sabah Al Salim, but I wanted Alexi to tell me he knew the name for a different reason.

Agapov had repeated Sabah's name to Alexi, adding how he knew the man socially. His offer to introduce Alexi to Sabah was accepted. When they met, the main topic of conversation the three of them had was set squarely on the Pegasus Bank.

Until we reached this point in our conversation, it had been more Alexi Vasilyev telling me things, than me having to ask. That changed when I asked if he'd heard Agapov mention the name of the CIA agent who he dealt with at the bank. He shook his head, indicating he didn't know.

One part of me wanted to leave it there. I told myself it was best for both of us to leave further questioning to later. We were both mentally tired from the assiduousness of the day, anything more could confuse the memory by overlapping people with places. Overall, I thought leaving the debrief to later would benefit me more. I'm not sure what, but something changed inside me, pressing me to plough on in discovering multifarious issues I knew nothing about.

* * *

My world as an effective agent of British intelligence was, as our friends in American would say, on the up-slope, but my life as a single man who had fathered two children, was a complete and utter shambolic disaster. As I sat in the soundproofed underground room playing back the recordings of what Vasilyev knew of the world, I started to wonder where my place in it would be after the infinitesimal subtleties of espionage had finished with me. I was caught up in thoughts of myself when the single desk telephone pinged red on its console.

On telling Alexi what was said on the phone about having to leave in a short period of time, he told me what was perhaps the real gem amongst the intelligence he'd given up in the first hour we'd had together. It was the location of the American serviceman everyone back home, as well as across the sea, was talking about. Not only was this the man presumed to be the one responsible for the in-line encryption process giving headaches to all concerned, he was also the same one who, after changing sides to ISIS, was now their prisoner, being held under the sentence of death.

I judged this information was too 'hot' to keep to ourselves, let alone just me. I phoned Section 9 at Vauxhall first, but immediately I finished with them I called Jimmy Mercer, where I was met with shrills of gratitude as he was thankful, albeit, he said, for small mercies.

It must have been his mention of mercy when, for one of those few illogical moments in time when thoughts decide to venture away from the logical line, my immediate thoughts centred on what Paulo had loosely called the Russian Mafia, when he wanted his nemesis Alexi Vasilyev dead.

If that pseudo society was still surviving, could the Count, Viscount Bottomly, be its Capo Dei Capi? Not too far removed from logic, do you think?

CHAPTER SEVENTEEN
OBLIVION

One piece of personal satisfaction came my way before we managed to smuggle Vasilyev from Warsaw to first London, then on to Hampshire, was that I'd hit the jackpot with my identification of Colonel Hafez al-Rifaaz. Vasilyev confirmed it was him in the photograph Sir Leonard had shown me. What's more, he confirmed the place as Ar Raqqah, as well as identifying the other two as being the American code inventor with Sabah Al Salim.

I had also been correct in assuming he was not a simple army Colonel. He was, in fact, a highly-placed intelligence officer in a part of the Syrian Military Intelligence Division known as the Mukhabarat, an organisation which was suspected of having connections with many different radical or terrorist groups, depending on your viewpoint.

It had taken me a day or two, after seeing the photograph, before I could, hand on heart, identify him to Section 9. Much to my incredulity, my single identification was not enough to set in motion what was to ultimately happen. Service protocol dictated they had to wait for at least one other definite recognition. With Vasilyev being positive about who it was, a positional sighting was requested from RAF Cyprus as well as from other operational missions over Syria.

Information from an IOMS unit, sited at RAF Al Udeid in Qatar, illustrated how Colonel Hafez al-Rifaaz was the main instigator of torture of the civilian relatives of ISIS fighters in the Al Hol internment camp, inside Syria. He was housed in the capital of the area, a place called Al-Hasakah. It was confirmed by a ground operative unit, how twice a week, with military punctuality, the Colonel travelled to the camp in a motorised column of four heavily protected personnel carriers from Al-Hasakah, along the desert roads.

On the first day, when Alexi Vasilyev began his debrief at Beaulieu, a remotely guided Reaper Drone, controlled by a senior naval rating onboard a ship which was part of the HMS Queen Elizabeth battle group, sailing in the Mediterranean, blasted his personal carrier, the second from the last in the cavalcade, to oblivion.

* * *

In a similar span of time, GCHQ traced the call which Harvey Burgess, Warsaw station head, had discovered to have been made from hotel room number 854, occupied by Alexi Vasilyev's dead protection officer. It was made to an office address in the city of Cherepovets, about four hundred kilometres north of Moscow. The address was unlisted on any intelligence register Jerry Furley could find.

The small one-man office, on the shores of the lake made by the Rybinsk Reservoir, was surrounded by water from tributaries of the mighty Volga River. The story of the mysterious, maybe sinister, phone call did not end in the beautiful manner that this man's office perhaps deserved, nor did it end well for certain people, but not necessarily in the way you're thinking.

The business conducted from the office was owned by the elder brother of the man Vasilyev had shot dead. Through the necessity this story deserved, I have drowned you in difficult to pronounce names and places. I do not wish to overburden you in that regard if I can avoid it, so for the sake of clarity I shall refer to the dead man as Mr A. Mr A's elder brother was, by profession, a computer programmer. Equally important he was, by birth, Mr A's only sibling.

We cannot be completely sure what Mr A said to his brother. It could have been a conversation about the weather in Warsaw, or it could have been about everything Colonel Dimitri Georgievich Oborka said after a couple of drinks had loosened his tongue in the warm, cordial atmosphere of the hotel bar. What could not be denied was that Mr A's brother was a liability to both Oborka and Vasilyev's long-term wellbeing, especially so if Mr A's brother suspected foul play had ended his brother's life.

* * *

Since Vasilyev and Oborka's temporary housing in Hampshire, I had exchanged quite a few telephone calls with Jimmy Mercer; in contrast, when those two were with me in Warsaw, Jimmy and I had seldom spoken. Nevertheless, there was one call in particular I remember making, and that was the one I promised I would make when I had the address of this man in his office on the shore of the Rybinsk Reservoir; Mr A's brother. In addition, I'd promised the full conversation Oborka had with the dead man.

Oborka was candid when I asked him. He explained how he meant no disrespect to his Colonel General, nor doubts of his loyalty, it was merely the product of too much vodka mixed with too much luxury, neither of which, he said, was he accustomed to. He was expansive in describing how the pleasant atmosphere had adversely affected him. Later, he said, he tried to apologise for being a fool.

Before we ended this acknowledgement of his faults, he expressed his undying love for the Colonel

General, accompanied by a vow sworn upon his honour never to repeat anything like it again. I told Dimitri Oborka if he never wanted his beloved Colonel General to know of this slip of decorum, he would have to submit to being an American puppet for eternity. He was to do exactly what they told him to do, when they told him to do it. Then, when I asked him what it was they asked of him, he was to tell me, only me, until I told him otherwise.

I was able to fulfil the promise I made to Mercer, including sending him a copy of Oborka's statement, with the commitment he made to America in writing, signed and witnessed. I did not tell him about the verbal agreement I made with Oborka, although I expect he would have suspected such a thing to have happened.

At around the same time, I confirmed Alexi Vasilyev's involvement with the AWB in South Africa to Jerry Furley, also how he had knowledge of the bank on Samothrace. There was also the possibly of him knowing the American plans for the island, although I hadn't spoken with him of those.

Vasilyev's knowledge of the AWB was extensive. He was able to name the entire twelve who comprised the total membership of what was named The War Council, as well as the position and roles of both

Liam Gibson and Viscount Winston Bottomly. I found his undeniable respect for both men to be thoroughly insulting, before I realised it was their organisational skills he respected.

This admiration Alexi had seemed to stretch to all things South African, as he extended his commendation to what I had referred to as the club called Broederbond. And the more the name stayed in the forefront of my mind, the theory I had of a pseudo mafia theme running through what I had investigated so far remained a strong prospect.

Vasilyev had been to a meeting of this 'club' when he stayed with the 'Count', who, by this time, he'd confirmed was Bottomly. I asked him where the two of them had stayed. Before answering, he looked at me as though I was a toddler on the verge of bawling my eyes out for losing a toy.

"On his estate, my lord. Do you not know it? Oh dear. I thought you two were old school friends. It's a few miles from the town of Upington, in the North Cape, a beautiful setting. The main house is a huge mansion of a place, I'd say almost the size of your Buckingham Palace, sited on the banks of the Orange River, a marvellous spot. I actually saw hippos when I was there. It was magical."

Whilst he stayed with Bottomly, he had great delight in telling me, he was introduced to his fellow Russian, Sergei Ivanov, finding a shared interest between his Special Activities Division and Ivanov's

Search and Destroy team's activities in Southern Africa. Apparently, Winston took the two Russians out to hunt lions! I didn't comment, but I did when he said he could supply the obscured location of the military weapons as well as the biological stock held by the AWB, as he'd hidden a global positional finder in the lining of his luggage. Why didn't I suspect he would do something like that!

There was another revelation I felt uncomfortable with. He asked what I thought of the photograph the Count had.

* * *

In Warsaw, there was plenty to think of, other than photographs. One would be the auction house engagement Alexi Vasilyev had with Colonel Dimitri Georgievich Oborka alongside. When we were in the back of the Ford van coming away from the cemetery and Vasilyev said it would be hours before he would missed by his embassy, I thought he was wrong. He had come to Warsaw to attend the auction which was due to begin roughly ninety minutes after the shooting. That was where I thought the two of them would be first missed. I was wrong, but almost right.

The government's official at the cemetery had followed Alexi's licentious telephoned orders of 'staying the distance, as it were' with his sister, before telephoning the police to report the Russian embassy vehicle being outside his office doors..

The Polish police arrived to interview the official, who introduced them to the person who had 'distracted' his attention for almost the entire ninety minutes, but not quite. When the pocket books appeared, the two lovers stuck to the story they had rehearsed, repeating it to the local police officers, who, when satisfied, were about to discharge Alexi's sister from the scene, then allowing the lucky, or unlucky official, depending on your individual points of view, to return to his work, when three men waving Agency for Polish Internal Security identification cards arrived.

The one in charge was, in fact, the man Valery Agapov had made mention of, in not standing in Vasilyev's way. He wasn't wrong. Everything that could be done to slow down the investigation by the Russians was done. And done rigorously!

CHAPTER EIGHTEEN
DELAY

Lack of progress was a subject not only on the Russian ambassador's mind, it was central to Jimmy Mercer's thinking as well. It was easier for Jimmy to work out where Vagabond had gone, presumably with this Colonel Oborka, but until he could speak to anyone at the British embassy it was pure speculation on his part.

The American ambassador had used the words 'agitated', and then 'troubled', when describing Mercer's mood to his secretary who had advocated walking to the British embassy when, for the hundredth time, the Polish phone companies, or specifically those in the Warsaw area, apologised for the lack of any telephone signal emanating from, or to, his embassy.

The company's representative was cursing, having relied only on satellites without having land cables as a backup. Mercer shouted at him how the satellites were his and they were not to blame, someone was shutting them out. He knew how good the British technicians at GCHQ, Cheltenham, England were at disrupting communications by using a channel of radio-transmitted signals from satellites targeted at sectors such as government departments, embassies, consulates and military installations with pinpoint accuracy. It was developed for NATO as a defence mechanism to stop any Russian cyberattacks, but now he discovered how it had a double edge.

The CIA head of station explained to Jimmy how a walk to the British embassy compound could alert the Russians to a difficulty happening in real time, as opposed to the current Director-General of the American Department of National Intelligence out for an autumnal stroll in the Polish sunshine. He reminded the Director-General that as far as he and his staff were aware, nobody other than a few handpicked agents, not even the ambassador, had been given prior knowledge of his visit.

"So why spook them by going for a walk, sir?" he asked, but never received a spoken answer, just a look of moody irritation.

Another thing the American ambassador was not told until the last minute, was news of the defection.

He was able to deny all knowledge of it without the need to lie. Mercer, on the other hand, could not deny knowing of it. However, he was unable to tell the whole truth, because he was unaware of all the truth.

Perhaps that was the reason, perhaps not, but whatever it was, nobody had a definitive answer to the question of why Jimmy had quietened down. Possibly he had simply run out of bluster by the time he was smuggled out of Warsaw in an army Humvee for the one hundred-plus-kilometre drive to the 32nd Air Force base at Lask in Poland.

It was not so much the thought of the journey that occupied Jimmy's mind, it was more the wording he was to use in the report to his President when he got there...

Mr President, sir, he imagined beginning, in a magisterial voice that, after the first two phrases, changed ever so slightly into a more imperious one. With the 'all eyes in Warsaw' bit, he had a touch of arrogance.

Then, with the last sentence, he attached a hint of humility to his voice in order to finish the matter—or so he hoped. *After taking all things into consideration, and after consultations with my officers on the ground, in order to get this Russian safely out of Poland I thought it was better to get the British to handle his extraction. All eyes in Warsaw were on us when his people discovered him gone. I have a spe-*

cialist team ready to fly out to retrieve him from England whenever I think we should, sir.

* * *

The ability to trade was uppermost in Colonel Oborka's mind on the plane to Andrews Air Base, in Washington D.C. He had stayed long enough with the 'handlers' at Beaulieu before the transfer to RAF Brize Norton for his American adventure. From the handlers' point of view, as with mine, it had been a critical element of his persuasion to understand the significance Mr A's brother had on his future.

Our leverage came from the fact that Mr A's brother, ensconced in the city of Cherepovets, did not know his brother was dead. Jerry Furley had no fixed idea how to use Mr A's brother, but one suggestion I made was to apply his computer programming skills to hack into systems that, perhaps being nearer to our eventual targets, could be advantageous to some degree. The young 'scruffy' man that Judith made mention of could be just the type to be able to help with ideas. I reminded myself to make sure Jerry knew about him.

The Director-General of the American Department of National Intelligence might have several names, but one of them was not 'fool'. Jimmy Mercer was nobody's fool, there was a good possibility he would know we had Colonel Dimitri Oborka in our back pocket; nonetheless, the Colonel was a valuable commodity, one that a clever man such as Jimmy could aim back at us if he played him in that way. I didn't believe Oborka was likely to turn on us with the threat of vengeful anger coming from a resourceful man such as Alexi Vasilyev aimed at him if he did.

* * *

I had flown back to the UK by the time Jerry Furley had promised Alexi Vasilyev unrestricted access to his funds in the Pegasus Bank, but I was not present at their location. Also promised to Alexi was the choice of relocation points in any country within the fifty-four members of the political association known as the British Commonwealth of Nations.

Jerry informed him how Colonel Oborka had elected to go to America before finally deciding on where to settle. America had struck a chord in his heart when contacting Katherine. At that stage, Katherine had escaped being mentioned to me by Jerry. I had not contacted her, nor she me.

Despite that last statement being the truth, it would be a lie to suggest I had not thought of her. I would have been an idiot not to. I had also thought of the consequences Alexi's new identity would bring to my life with Luca in mind. A new life would bring a whole lot of complications, not only to my son's life, but also affecting the same list of names as before.

I had been with him when he broached the subject of how secret his ultimate place of refuge would be. He said his principal concern was, if his location was completely secret, how would he ever meet with Katherine, or Katyerena, as he now called her?

When he and I were alone in the basement of the embassy in Warsaw, talking of the Balkans and our different roles in that European conflict, he asked if he would be allowed to meet with her before leaving for wherever it was he would go? I answered I would try my best to arrange for a meeting, which he seemed to accept. He then asked a loaded question with a heavy tone of ridicule to his voice.

"If you were able to tell me the truth, would it make you happy if I was never to speak with the mother of your son Luca ever again?"

I tried my best not to give a straight answer. I said that despite being uncertain about their relationship, having seen Katherine greet him in the hotel I could see she had strong feelings for him. My own feelings for her were, as I said, ambivalent. Before I had completely done with the subject, I went on to say how I would be unequivocal in my dislike of him having any influence over my son's life, so much so, I would not agree to any request of custody that included him.

He hadn't finished, either. He had one more

question. "By the greeting you mentioned, you must know she loves me and I love her, do you not?"

Again, I dodged giving a direct answer. Instead, I asked a question with a veiled threat to it. How could he feel safe from Russian retribution, I asked, if his whereabouts could be traced, or, worst, tortured from Katherine? Without bothering to answer my sensible question, he asked a purely speculative one, which I should have ignored by walking out of the room.

"If Judith chooses to live in Canada, would you look for her if you didn't know her location? Or, if you did know, which I expect you do, will you knock on her door one day?"

Was the destination of Canada just an educated guess, with other defecting spies settling in that country? Was it? Despite the fact I wanted to ask, I was wary I had already shown enough of my emotions towards her. He had found a weakness in my hesitation. There was a follow-up question, one perhaps holding more danger and difficulties to face.

"You haven't asked me about the photograph yet, Harry. Why is that? Could it be you know who is in it?"

This photograph Alexi was frantic to tell me about, was the one I thought I knew, or at least had an idea, who was in it. One party I'm pretty sure was Valery Agapov and the other, well, at this moment I won't say. Before I volunteered my guess at an answer, I wanted answers to other mysteries.

One of those 'issues' Alexi Vasilyev and I discussed, when he was in my custody in Warsaw, was that of him knowing how Viscount Bottomly was known as the 'Count' in the circles they moved in, where actual names were not necessarily used.

One of the circles must include the wealthy who banked in the Pegasus on the island of Samothrace. The next question to be answered could be done at home. Did he know if Judith's father had withdrawn all his funds from Pegasus? If so, was the bank still connected to Judith Meadows? Alexi knew of Meadows. His knowledge of her was not exclusive to the bank. All the same, it seemed the island was of great significance to not only both of them, but many others too.

* * *

I can't recall exactly where my questioning was heading, but it certainly was not going anywhere near where his question came from. He asked me why I thought the British prisoner held in the Shetland Isles on charges of treason and murder, was still alive.

Once again, I had not anticipated his question which had caught me off-guard, because of course he must know about her role with the traitor in London working for Russia. If he did not have first-hand knowledge, then he would most definitely have heard of her from Valery Agapov.

At first sight, she was a major liability to Russian intelligence. Not only did she know the sexual orientation of the traitor when he was inside British intelligence, she would know some of his contacts. She might also know the methods used for communication. The codes he and his 'friends' used, along with the tradecraft they employed at the time, would also be under threat. As would the addresses of the safe houses they may have needed. All of those precious details could have been traded with the British for her freedom, unbeknown to the Russians.

It was a reasonable assumption that Russian procedure was much the same as our own; i.e. when an operative was blown, protocol would demand that all, or any, systems connected to her/him should be changed, immediately. That statement was particularly true if there could be something she knew that would be dynamite in British hands, if it could be prised from her. The only certain way of making sure nothing was given away, would be to end her life. So, yes, I had wondered why she was still alive, and I was still wondering even though I had increased her guards.

Because Vasilyev was engaged in hunting the British agent Paulo Sergeyovitch Korovin, working inside his own intelligence service, he knew the Russians had an agent deeply embedded in British intelligence. But he did not know his, or her, position. Nor did he have a name; that I was sure of.

After the KGB was disbanded, it was succeeded by the Foreign Intelligence Service where Alexi's previous commander, Valentin Antopolov, became the overall head of all the intelligence services inside Russia. One day, Alexi was called into Valentin Antopolov's Lubyanka office to see a deciphered message from the London agent who was known to his Russian Control as *шеврон*, or Chevron in English.

The message spoke of an assassination Chevron was left with no choice but to authorise. It was of a Russian agent known to British intelligence as Colette. Her assassination was essential, he said, because he felt his position was in imminent danger of discovery by this Colette tripping over him.

He'd had a crazy idea one moment whilst bored, of becoming her handler in a sting operation on a British aristocrat with South African roots. Chevron thought that by running this Colette, he could successfully turn the aristocrat into not only working for Russia, but Colette could become his controlling officer. What's more, he added near the end of his message, he could manage to do all that without ever having to meet with either of them.

Chevron was aware of how dangerous it would be and how important his position was. Even so, he thought the intelligence Colette could tap into would develop into the whereabouts of the South African arsenal. If it worked, it would be a huge triumph for Russia and another medal on Antopolov's chest. But

Antopolov was far from being excited, he was furiously angry, shouting his obscenities at the walls of his office rather than to anyone in particular. As soon as his anger calmed he messaged London to put an end to the nonsense, thereby restoring Chevron's concentration to his original role.

Not long after, Valentin Antopolov showed Alexi the whole message he received from Chevron, drawing his attention to the ending. Vasilyev remembered it well. It detailed how Chevron had instructed Meadows to return the weapon used in the assassination, a Glock pistol, including used cartridge cases, to the British Embassy in Paris after making sure all inside the bookshop named Librairie Ducard on Rue Saint-Eloi were dead. The directive was 'idiotic', according to Valentin Antopolov, but that was before he had read Chevron's detailed reasons.

Following existing convention, duplicated in the emailed orders from Chevron's office, the gun was returned from Paris to the Foreign and Commonwealth Office in London, from where Chevron collected it. The years he'd spent in concealment had taught him how to be furtive in the normal things in life, as well as those considered to be of a clandestine nature, if indeed there was a difference.

His late father had a multitude of friends in the diplomatic corps, many of whom he'd met. One of those was, as his official title would have it, the Turkish High Commissar to Cyprus in Great

Britain. The Turkish High Commission was a short walk away from Chevron's office in St James's Square. It was no trouble to carry the small secure box to his friend who, a few hours later, passed it to Valery Agapov, without any name being mentioned. Agapov did as Chevron instructed; depositing the gun in the vault at the Pegasus Bank on Samothrace.

Valentin Antopolov's anger had slowly been replaced by exasperation, as he and the silent Alexi read further on into what Chevron had to say. The gun, according to the message, gave the Russian government a means of affecting European affairs. An English subject, he named her in full, had murdered two French nationals on French soil whilst engaged in covert action authorised by the British government.

If ever the murder was to be published in the French newspapers, it would cause a huge rift between the British and the Europeans, one Russia might be able to utilise. And that, according to Alexi Vasilyev, was why Judith Meadows was still alive.

After listening, I was certain of at least two things. Alexi did not know I had increased the naval presence on Bressay, and his lack of knowledge meant Agapov had not told him. Perhaps neither man was included in all of each other's thoughts. There was one other thing, of course; I wanted to know how the Russians thought they could connect the gun to first, the murders, and then to Judith Meadows.

Alexi had his answer waiting for me, as the last letter 's' of Meadows left my lips.

"On the day of leaving your country, the British traitor we called Chevron was taken from prison to a bank a short way from London, where he was met by a delegation from the Russian embassy. He entered the bank, under British guard, and was allowed to take away the contents of a safe deposit box he had there. It was an unopened envelope taken from the box that, as Chevron boarded his flight to Russia, he gave to Valery Agapov."

Following Chevron's instructions, Agapov opened the envelope as the plane took off for Russia. Inside was the signed, detailed record given to Judith Meadows on the day preceding the assassination, setting out her orders. Alongside that was the operation completion mandate, again signed by Judith Meadows. The document contained the specifics of her operation.

Both numbered documents carry the British Government classification seal of confidentiality. Contained in the envelope is proof beyond any doubt of what took place in Librairie Ducard on the Rue Saint-Eloi, in Paris, France, and who the murderer was. As if for good measure, the role her father played in the every day life of Her Majesty was also detailed in an enclosed letter.

Having heard all of that, I wondered if I was mistaken in assuming Agapov and Vasilyev did not share all the details of their individual conducted operations.

* * *

I asked Vasilyev outright if he knew Valery Agapov wanted to defect to Great Britain as he had successfully managed. I read the apathetic look on Alexi's face to be false. To my mind, he didn't know. I thought the reason he'd given me as to why Meadows was still alive was equally false. Of course, it was more a feeling than a certainty. My analysis was, Alexi wanted Meadows alive for one specific reason. In order to be certain about the theory I held, I needed an honest answer from a man of whom I had no idea as to the true value he put on honesty. There again, why would he be any different to the rest of us, as truth was a convention rarely seen in this business.

By allowing the conversation with Vasilyev to go off on a different line, there was no time remaining to discuss the photograph he'd mentioned before his journey to the UK began.

* * *

I was required to travel by a different route in order to eventually arrive at the same destination as Alexi, but first, I was needed to go to the city of Alexandroupoli, on mainland Greece, where Viscount Bottomly was being held in a police cell, not far from the military hospital where Liam Gibson was being treated. Gibson had required emergency treatment on the island where he'd been shot, before being transferred to Alexandroupoli by police launch. For my journey from Warsaw to Athens I travelled alone, but I had company for the final leg to Alexandroupoli, where I was met in my hotel by the disguised figure of Jimmy Mercer II.

CHAPTER NINETEEN
BOATS

Before being arrested, Viscount Winston Bottomly had been waiting in the port area of Alexandroupoli, on mainland Greece. It had taken him an hour or so to get from the Alexandroupolis Airport into the port area, the traffic being heavy at the time of day on that road. He had seen Gibson's three-month-old Learjet in a hanger on the periphery of the airport. He checked it had been refuelled for the two-stop journey home to South Africa. The return flight plan had been lodged ready for early next morning.

He confirmed Gibson had paid the usual customs officers, who had discharged the remuneration in the normal manner. Next, he took a taxi from the airport to the port, selecting a favourable wooden bench to sit and wait on; then, with the aid of his binoculars, he scanned the horizon until he could see the boat, but he could not see Liam Gibson anywhere outside on the decking.

Strange, he thought, for it was a warm, balmy evening, one on which Bottomly did not expect Gibson to be inside the ferry. Liam was not one to shelter inside the musty-smelling superstructure that was built without any thought of air-conditioning. At least that's how it was the last time Bots had travelled on it, roughly two weeks ago, after landing at the International Airport in Athens then taking a connecting flight here and finally, a taxi ride to his hotel. Today was to be different. Gibson had what Bottomly wanted. Then there was to be the hard work of lifting sizeable amounts of boxes onto the boats to be air-freighted back to South Africa, but that was for others to handle, not him or Liam. They had no need to dirty their hands in that way.

Tonight, he arrived at the bench early, walking approximately two miles from his hotel past the restaurant he and Gibson had eaten at, drinking a few glasses of Ouzo to wash down the lamb. It had been well cooked but... it wasn't like back home, was it? No, he mouthed silently in fond memory, moments before he felt a forceful tap on his shoulder, followed by a curt inquiry of "Mr Bottomly?", spoken in a Greek island accent. Seconds ago, he was being nostalgic and the next... what, exactly?

He was shaken. He had probably felt his phone vibrate with Gibson messaging him, but, no, wait a moment. That's not right. Neither is the fact that there's no boat at the terminal. Who's this, and where did he come from? His confused thoughts held no logic.

As if he was controlled by wires from a puppeteer's hands, he turned his head towards his 'touched' shoulder, then slowly raised his eyes to see his abuser. He noticed the dark blue uniform first, then, after lifting his head, the face. It was one that could do with a shave, and probably a wash too, he thought, still utterly oblivious to what was happening.

From the tap Winston felt on his shoulder, to the consciousness of who stood beside him, was no more than two seconds, but to the Count it was like a lifetime being lived backwards. A customs police officer was the culprit; even so, it could just as well have been a member of the Pontifical Swiss Guard, only the Swiss Guard would not normally be expected to be so tanned in colour.

In broken English, he was informed there was "nothing serious to worry about". Just a problem with the transit log issued to the yacht that was moored in the harbour. Bottomly explained the yacht was no longer his. He'd sold it earlier in the year, he said, looking out to sea again through the binoculars.

"No matter, Mr Bottomly. We know you sold it. The new owner renewed all the licences to run from the day of the sale, but the 'permit for transit' was due to be renewed two days before the sale date. Therefore those two days are your responsibility. Come with us, please, sir. It shouldn't take long."

He had faced the excessive bureaucracy of the port authorities before over inconsequential matters, so he offered to pay there and then, with an additional amount of money for the expected incentive to forget such trivialities. He opened a pocket in his money belt, pulling a quantity of English money from it.

"There," he said. "Take it. It must be at least five hundred pounds sterling," he announced, with the disdain and contempt the English use to address natives who dared to speak the English language incorrectly.

It takes years of experience to recognise that with some people, there's no chance of bribing them. With others, the opposite is true, there's every chance. The uniformed official was one of the first type of person, which Bottomly thought to be very odd, as he'd found all Greeks, in both high and low positions, to be open to monetary persuasion. Sadly, he knew this was not the case as the officer placed a hand under his armpit, gently lifting him up from where he sat. Without thought, he glanced out to sea where there was still no sign of the ferry that was now an hour overdue.

"Do you know why the ferry from Samothrace is so late, officer?" he asked.

"There was an incident at the harbour, with gunfire being heard. All I know is an American was injured."

* * *

It was a gruelling flight from Durban. Two stops for fuel before the airport at Alexandroupolis. The first in Tanzania and the other in the Sudan at Khartoum, where he had stayed the night. For insurance purposes, it was meant to be a two-pilot journey, but who needed insurance now and again, he thought as he sipped his Greek beer, this was going to be a one-off flight. In the engrossed mood he was in, he admitted to himself that a bit over fourteen hours was a long journey in the air on your own. A smile lit up his craggy face as his thoughts widened onto the aircraft he'd flown. It was a sweet little thing, he thought, if you ignored the cost at a little over two and half million dollars. He smiled as he remembered signing the unremarkable slip of paper from the transfer machine!

He was seated at the bar of the Kamariotissa Hotel, waiting for the hour of the ferry, when two Americans dressed in grey suits sat on the plain wood barstools either side of him. The one to his left announced they were CIA agents. He produced his badge before asking Liam for the parcel on the bar next to his bottled beer to be handed over. Gibson picked up the bottle of Greek beer, but instead of drinking from it, he smashed it into the side of the agent's head. The force, although considerable enough to knock him from the stool, did not force him to fall to the floor. Next, he attempted to hit the other CIA man with the same bottle, but this one had time to fight back, with both men falling in a heap, grappling with each other. Gibson's training was slow to kick in. He had spent too long paying others to do what he could have done at one time with one hand tied behind his back, for free.

The agent who had taken the first blow had recovered sufficiently to pull his issued sidearm from its holster, under his jacket.

"Hold it right there, bud!" he shouted, pointing it at Gibson who was about to land another blow into the second officer's face. With his left hand, Gibson reached inside the jacket of the man beneath him and in one movement; unclipping, then pulling this officer's gun free.

The man on the ground reacted quickly, shouting as loudly as he was able, "Gun!" at about the same time as Gibson had the weapon levelled at his standing colleague. That CIA agent fired his pointed gun at Gibson.

The round hit Liam in the upper arm, missing the 'widow-maker's artery' by no more than an inch, to clip a rib before it lodged against his shoulder blade.

* * *

I was told it had been a long time since Mercer had been an active agent for any agency under an American intelligence umbrella, but it didn't show. For a start, he was suitably dressed. Gone was the American equivalent to Savile Row suits, his usual attire. He wasn't quite as scruffy as I, but he was most certainly more of a casually dressed holidaymaker than the wealthy American government employee, in suit, collar and tie, that he was.

Whereas Mercer resembled the holidaymaker, enjoying the warm autumn sun, strolling on the shores of the Thracian Sea, possibly in town for a boating holiday, the three men trailing along a few yards behind, looked exactly what they were—his security team drawn from the ranks of the heavily-built CIA, leaving the imagination to work overtime to decipher the conflicting information swirling around the mind.

When it all settled, his explanation, given to the receptionist at The Lighthouse of Alexandroupoli Hotel, that he was visiting the place to view a boat he was buying and that his three friends here would oversee its transference to his home in America, sounded plausible, even allowing for the accentuated New Yorker dialect. It caused Jerry Furley to ask me if Jimmy really did come from the East Coast. Although I could answer his question, I did not.

The journey from Athens, an overcrowded city that was suffocating in over 100 degrees of heat, to Alexandroupoli, was undertaken in one of the few private jets H.M. Government keep for special occasions, or for the use of special people. This was certainly a special occasion and Jerry Furley was a special person. I was included simply because I was there. Furley had never met Mercer, and Jerry thought it best if I was to introduce the pair to one another. They had spoken on the transatlantic telephone link often enough which, if one did not know better, one could think had been tuned to carry only expletives rather than civil speech. No matter; during the flight Furley explained how some of the question and answer sessions he'd been able to have with Vasilyev had progressed.

Alexi had identified three CIA agents in photographs, linked to Bottomly's AWB South African command. He also supplied some more of the names of the actual command set-up, those seldom associated so conclusively. He first identified the code name the Russians attributed to a high-ranking FBI officer, who worked closely with a named member of ISIS. Next, he was able to name and identify the FBI man, and the member of ISIS he contacted, both from IOMS facial images.

Valery Agapov's defection was spoken of, with the name of Meadows cropping up several times throughout the conversation. Was she right, Furley had asked, about her assumption he would know the names of the Russians having banking accounts in London, as well as property under fictitious names? Alexi Vasilyev was vague, so Jerry Furley reported.

"He'd certainly lost most of his assertiveness. I'd say his reply was faltering. He said he thought he would know, but any confidence seemed to have drained from him, for some reason."

Once they were all back home here in the UK, the bargaining Jimmy Mercer, with Furley, had to conduct with Viscount Bottomly and Liam Gibson was to be way above where my pay grade could ever be. My use was confined to the introductory stage, shake hands, provide some documents, then move aside to catch a separate plane home. That plane was to take me to London but not, unfortunately, all the way home to Yorkshire, for at least a while. I had stayed in touch with Joseph and on occasions I had spoken to my estate manager, both of whom had only the regular kind of news to report. There was nothing at home to worry me.

Any worry I might have, plus any bargaining I had to do, would be with Bottomly. I needed to know if he was willing to accept the defeat of his AWB plans for a South African takeover. I then needed the photograph everyone wanted me to get hold of. Or did I have that wrong, and they didn't want me to know anything about it?

* * *

Before leaving Athens, I followed my instructions and arranged to meet with Valery Agapov in London. He was another person about whom I'd voiced my doubts over the value he placed on his own honesty. A major doubt I had about Agapov was his desire to defect. As far as I could remember, two people had told me Agapov wanted to defect: Bottomly was the first, then Meadows, who added a warning of danger without any adequate detail other than the voiced opinion, 'he knows a lot of people'. I had guessed that must be true, but as yet, I'd heard nothing about defection from Agapov. No, for all the praise he layered on me for arranging Russian defections whilst he was counselling Vasilyev, he had not asked for himself.

My aversion to London is not for its architecture, which I could love if it was not overrun with folk speaking as if they were trying to imitate the multiplicity of languages spoken at the Tower of Babel for some thespian role in theatre-land. My avid dislike was because of the stink from diesel engines, the London double-decker bus being the main culprit.

Flanders and Swann, a Music Hall comedy singing duo of the late 1950s, sang a song my mother was known to sing along to, of which the following lyrics were part: *The big six-wheeler, scarlet-painted, London Transport, diesel-engined, ninety-seven horse-power omnibus.*

It had reeked in the 1950s, and the passing of almost seventy years had not brought an end to the engine emitting its characteristic disgusting, foul stink. There was no hope of them stopping until all were electrified, at which time my opinion might change, that's if I were still alive. With that in mind and a stink of it in my nostrils, I could have regretted yielding to Agapov's choice of rendezvous. At least I did not have to wait for him. He was seated on the terrace, at a table with his back to Tower Bridge, facing the only entrance, in the Chop House Bar and Grill at Butler's Wharf on the south side of the River Thames.

One of the things I wanted to address was the document he'd looked at after it was taken from a bank in Kent, before he deposited it in the Pegasus Bank on the island. It didn't take long, as the version Agapov gave me confirmed Alexi Vasilyev had it almost word perfect. It was indeed Judith's signed completion of the assassination of a French agent in Paris. Just the same, there were discrepancies from what I understood to be a completion statement.

On the one Agapov had seen, it not only comprised of what I'd expect to find, it also had numbers that caused Valery Agapov to take a second look. So much so that, being the kind of man he was, he took a photograph of it. I was grateful for Russian competence.

Apart from the date of the document, as well as

the date of the operation, there were also two sets of numbers with a couple of letters coupled on. I couldn't understand why they were there, as I presumed them to be Judith's National Insurance number along with her date of birth. I also took a photo so as to confirm my suspicions, later.

Personally speaking, I don't mind people speculating on what I've done or haven't done in the secret service, as it can, in the right circumstances, be inspirational and seductive, but I draw the line at those below my level of security clearance knowing beyond doubt what my history has been. It was absolutely clear from this document what was done on the particular date and who did it.

Apart from the realistic theory Alexi had placed on it, I wondered if Valery Agapov had any idea why it had been kept. He had! His idea was along the same lines as Alexi's, except his use was not limited to the extortion of money from nations. He thought a single person could be the final target.

That was precisely my line of thinking, but when I asked Agapov if he had any idea who that person may be, he said he hadn't thought about it. If he had placed the gun in the bank, which clearly he had, then he most certainly must have wondered why it was there, which clearly again he had, so why on earth would I believe he had not thought about who Judith was going to assassinate with it?

I was at the point I had made mention of to you

—can I trust this man to tell me the truth? There was a way I could try to find out. You see, I thought I knew why the gun was kept and I thought Vasilyev may have told Valery.

There was no guarantee he would have told him, or anyone else, as there was nothing suggesting it; on the contrary, wasn't Alexi Vasilyev the master of concealment? Wasn't he the next master double-spy who'd eluded capture? I was having a go at 'tilting at windmills', merely waiting to see what happened.

Having twisted the contents of my mind inside out, there were questions I needed to ask. One was, who was in the photograph that kept raising its head? I asked and he admitted it was him with a woman, but as much as I asked him who she was, he would not tell. He said Bottomly did not know, either. That was strange, as I had not asked if Winston knew who she was. Someone knew, but who?

The next question I asked was one I did not know the answer to. I asked Agapov who had the photograph now, thinking there was only one person who could have it. But he did not confirm the name I had in my head.

He had been honest with his admission of being one of the two subjects in the photo. He had not lied about knowing who had it now, so should I accept he really doesn't know Bottomly has the photograph? I thought it could only be Bottomly. Who else was there? Was I wrong, do you think?

CHAPTER TWENTY
PICKERING'S

After I had fully recovered from indulging in the sheer luxury senior government ministers enjoy when on board the jet from Athens, I asked Furley to have the interrogators at Beaulieu get Vasilyev to open up about any relationship he had with the FBI officers he had already mentioned.

I wanted to know if it was he who had intimated the need for an English army officer with a unique understanding of several African languages, especially in regards to the fatuous requirement the FBI asked for—a better understanding of a region of the world where Afrikaans was spoken. I stressed they should look for anything unusual about Alexi Vasilyev's mannerisms when he replied. I believed he would lie and deny he had made any request like that. By the time the request was made, Winston Bottomly had served his time in Iraq and his liaison with the French Colette was finished.

I had continued to ask myself why Alexi Vasilyev moved a piece on his chessboard when it seemed he had complete control of it. Why have Bottomly running a risk when there was absolutely no need? Could it be another lapse on his part, like his previous ones of not changing both first and last name, or was he showing me something like the signatures on the documents at Tartus? I remembered Agapov saying how Vasilyev never did something without having a reason.

It had been Valery Agapov who had first told Judith Meadows of Canada, with the whereabouts of Metsos, in the suburbs of Ottawa, even suggesting she was to go there to be resettled. Would that be where Gibson was to take the gun she'd used in Paris? Could that be connected to when Vasilyev was resettled? Somehow one being used to hide the other? No. life's not that straightforward. Is it?

Alexi told me himself the words his boss Valentin Antopolov had said to him when they were in his illustrious office and Antopolov was beside himself with rage after reading a dispatch from Moscow's number one operative.

He had shouted at Alexi. "Get this Colette woman away from Chevron," he had ordered. Was it an order to a man unaware of one agent about to blow the cover of another vastly valuable agent? Am I to believe the intelligence service inside Russia is so ineffective that an eventual head of its most prestigious organisations does not know the whereabouts of its operatives?

Yes, that could be true; or, it could be true he did know her. If I had to bet, then I would place my money on him knowing of her, wanting her to stumble on the name of Chevron. Without showing his hand was in play, Alexi wanted Colette to draw Chevron out from under his Moscow cover, thereby making the unmasking of the great ghost of Paulo Sergeyovitch Korovin easier for him to step forward, accepting the acclaim. But, no, there's no ambiguity about Valentin Antopolov's command of 'get her away', is there?

Wait a minute. How was Colette close, I asked myself? She was a million miles away from discovering Chevron, she was not even in the same book, let alone on the same page. She was far away from Alexi Vasilyev, simply listening to Bottomly and reporting to—ah! Who? Nobody was there. There was no Jackson, according to Furley. Bottomly never went to Beaulieu to learn his tradecraft or listen to the name of Henry Liddell's daughter. Not even the lure of playing with the Latin names for second or third could tempt him. The story was as illusionary as *Alice in Wonderland.*

So someone, or something, panicked Chevron enough for him to reveal his fear of detection to Moscow. Quite some step! Maybe he was just getting tired of the secrecy of living two lives. How did panic suddenly hit him, a composed man such as he was? Was Bottomly to blame somehow? Did Chevron know of Bottomly before Colette came knocking at his Vauxhall door? Although I've got nothing to link the two, Chevron must have known them, otherwise why want to be Colette's control?

I was still trying to piece things together in my mind using chess pieces as an analogy. It had been speculation on my part putting Sergei Ivanov as part of Valery Agapov's Directorate Q; it mattered not, as he was most certainly a major part of Recces, the South African Special Forces Brigade. Ivanov, Bottomly, Agapov all knew one another. Add one missing part of Alexi Vasilyev, and we had all the connection I needed. But it still left the question of who was ruffling Vasilyev enough for him to make a move?

It wasn't Judith. She told me about suspecting Alexi Vasilyev of being a double agent way back in Switzerland when we met with Paulo. The span of time dictated she knew about him before she killed Colette. I drew down the Colette file again to check the date she was assassinated. I also pulled up a report I'd asked for some time back, on when Valery Agapov had travelled to Kuwait on a diplomatic passport in the name of Yuri Bogdan. He made the journey at the end of July. I hadn't made any connection about that journey, I just needed reminding of it and reminding myself how nowhere had I put Sabah Al Salim into this puzzle.

Jerry contacted me to say Beaulieu had been in touch that very morning. Vasilyev knew nothing of a FBI request for a translator of South African languages. At least, that's what he said, but the lead senior interrogator, a retired Vice-Admiral I had met socially several times at council meetings and the like, who lived fairly close to The Hall in Harrogate, thought he was lying.

It was a strong word to use about an espionage agent being debriefed prior to full defection. I knew this Vice-Admiral was a very experienced interrogator as well as being experienced in the art of debriefing agents. Normally these agents would be friendly. The interview had been filmed, then sent on to me for my views on Alexi's reaction.

I watched the file, but came to no conclusion over his behaviour. Sure, perhaps he did hesitate slightly longer than would be normal for a thoroughly focused answer, but no more than slightly.

I was staring at the blank computer screen when, in my mind's eye, all I could see was Serena sitting inside her aircraft with a cocktail in one hand and an oversized order book in the other. I drafted an email to Charles Oswald Wallace requesting the executive jet to be stocked with my forty-year-old Jura single malt, adding the appendage of *especially if you want me to make use of the jet otherwise I won't,* but I didn't send it, neither did I delete it. I kept it as a draft—just in case it became my regular mode of transport. I laughed at myself. I then laughed again. This time at finding time in this perfidious undertaking to find time to laugh.

* * *

Jerry Furley told me the American private jet was ten times more luxurious than the British one we'd travelled in from Athens, but it was when the jet was refuelling whilst still flying, that really sold it to him as his mode of future flying. He said he wanted to be American if he could believe in reincarnation.

I did wonder, though, if he was suffering from a personality disorder when he decided to stay British, because of the two fighter jets flying as their armed escort. It was a bit over the top, he said, nevertheless it did bring a smile to his face. His smile was not as large as the one plastered across my face when I eventually finished reading Viscount Bottomly's answers to the list of questions I had outlined and given to Jerry.

When I was in America, at Bottomly's Aunt Alice's place in Maryland, she found it easy to speak to me about her nephew. She was worried about how far he had progressed down the road to what she called fanaticism. She quoted part of a speech she'd heard

Winston give to the AWB, in South Africa. The manner of his delivery greatly resembled Hitler's infamous antisemitism, with his own extreme of racial prejudice.

His prophecies of another reign of White Supremacists, with a revised system of apartheid being reintroduced, was laughed at by the Blacks within the ruling ANC. As was his announcement at the end of his address, that one day he would become the leader of the ruling political party in South Africa. Their mocking stopped when they heard that would not be the ANC. They would be cast aside, to be remembered as just another failed political party.

She covered more facts about Bottomly than I would ever have been able to discover had I not bothered to visit her. Another innocent uncovering happened during my further education into her brand of what she called whisky. It was when she mentioned how the Bottomly clan had three homes in South Africa, and not just the one I thought they had. I had heard of the vast estate in the Northern Cape, to the south-west of Upington, near Hartebeest Vlakte, but I had never heard of it being not far from a place called Augrabies.

Another of these homes was close to where Liam Gibson lived in Durban, with the third being in a place unmarked on any conventional map. The nearest point would be a place called Boomrivier, eighty or so kilometres from Hartebeest Vlakte. Although each of the names of those places were evocative as well as being atmospheric in so many ways, they sent shivers up my back, but at that time I did not realise why.

Some interesting facts for my list of questions came about when Alice expanded on Winston's membership of the Afrikaner Nationalists' secret society, called Broederbond. I knew he couldn't be just a name on a list; what I didn't realise, though, was how, according to Alice, he was actually worshiped in the society. That was the word she used, as if it was a church, and he was their god.

Carrying on in the same vein, she told how, by the time of my visit to Hagerstown, he was the unchallenged leader of the AWB. This was the man I knew in England, the one whose side I had rushed to, to administer aid at the scene of such tragedy, on the occasion of his Glorious Twelfth shoot on his English estate. The same one I knew in the Regiment of Guards in areas of armed conflict, as well as at home, or on ceremonial duties. The one I knew socially, was not this man I had come across in America, as told to me by his close relative.

There were graphic parallels Alice drew, between Nazi antisemitism and the Broederbond's idea of the Afrikaner being the 'chosen people'. The rules of the society set out to defend the right of Afrikaners to speak the language, or unite to fight off foreign influences that come from Black people or Jews. There was even a mention of the pernicious influence English-speaking settlers had on South Africa, although that remark, according to the smiling Alice, did not include me, or any of Winston's present or future friends.

From what Bottomly had already told me, I took it that the reference to English-speaking people having an adverse effect on South Africa was no longer the case, with Winston's wish of closer ties to Great Britain. Despite what I'd heard from him, Alice was able to paint lifelike, vivid pictures of the proposed mass slaughter Bottomly was championing alongside his pals of the far-right. She said she hoped I would be able to stop him!

I listened carefully to the story she wanted me to know, picking my way across the history of racism in South Africa. How the ANC was banned in 1960 then, with the elections of 1994, they formed the government, but what she gave me formed the basis for the questionnaire I prepared for Jerry Furley and the Vice-Admiral to ask Bottomly.

According to Alice, Viscount Bottomly's ultimate aim was the complete annihilation of the indigenous Black African race in South Africa. His AWB would be removing them from the southern half of Namibia, Botswana, Mozambique, and Zimbabwe. All those removed would be relocated in Zambia. His plan would take years, she said, but he and those close to him were resigned to its fulfilment.

* * *

Although I accepted her sincerity to be real, I found her announcement impossible to believe, as it was not the kind of thing someone as educated as Bottomly would say. She said he had planned it all out and was to be financed through the Pegasus Bank, a company which, as we've discovered, had affiliations with, of all people the murdered Hugh Pickering.

Bottomly's connection to the Pegasus Bank had moved upwards from being just an investor, to where he was one of those who decide who can, and who cannot, hold a deposit in the bank. Pegasus was not a regular cheque-book bank. It is where one's surplus cash is kept. If a withdrawal is ever needed from an account holder who does not wish to close their account, then the money would be withdrawn from the respectable City of London bank, the one with the name of Pickering's Private Investment Bank above the door, in Finsbury Circus, EC2.

Small world, eh? Well, it was made even smaller with an additional name I was familiar with, who Alice mentioned as one more of the Viscount's original financiers: Sabah Al Salim. I felt it grow even smaller as I considered the name of Hugh Pickering allied with Alexi Vasilyev. It was Pickering's past association with anonymous agents of the CIA that I had first worried about. Would Valery Agapov's impending defection impact badly on Vasilyev through

Agapov's banking connection with the CIA? What had I been thinking?

What if the CIA officer at the top of the Pegasus Mercantile Company knew of Vagabond? Thank goodness Jimmy Mercer knew the name, as I would think it highly likely he had been working up a suitable legend for his Russian Vagabond agent ever since he was made aware of the existence of a bank. I had another thing on my mind, of seemingly less importance. I had given Vasilyev my word that I would ask Katherine whether or not she wanted to see him before he selected a place to be resettled.

When I departed for home, I was still under the impression Jerry Furley was none the wiser about the CIA officer at the top of the Pegasus tree. If that had changed I wasn't told, but, as I think I've informed you, as high as my security clearance was, it wasn't yet at their dizzy heights. In other words, I might never know the name, unless someone higher than I decided I needed to know.

One thing I did need to know, apparently, was that the Russian Embassy in Warsaw had been on a Red Alert status when Alexi never returned from his visit to the cemetery. They had notification of his non-appearance at the auction, which on its own would have been a worry, but when the Polish police eventually notified them about the Russian vehicle apparently abandoned outside the Government Remittance Office, near the East Gate entrance of the

Powązki Cemetery, it became an emergency of the highest nature. All three Russians who had departed more than six hours earlier from the Raffle Europejski Hotel that morning had disappeared.

GCHQ had restored the ability to send and receive signalling messages from the embassies in the Warsaw area, with the British Embassy being, in the ambassador's words, bombarded with acrimonious accusations of abduction from the Russians. I imagined the American embassy must have been the same, but Mercer never told me if that was the case. The Polish government was accused of collaborating with Western imperialists in the illegal abduction of three legitimate officials of the Russian Federation in an act of contrition whilst in a holy place. Heady stuff, I thought, without offering a suitable explanation, nor evidence to confuse or seduce.

For another inexplicable reason, I suddenly wondered if Alexi Vasilyev would be able to live without the restraints he was accustomed to in the secret world in which he lived? Could he feel comfortable not dealing with the pressures his role in Russian intelligence had placed on him? How would he feel about George and me, if Katherine decided not to see him again? Now, there was a question I wouldn't want to answer.

As I thought of Warsaw, I remembered how Katherine had greeted Vasilyev. But then a black cloud entered my memory when recalling his discourteous dismissal of George without a word, when George had offered a hand in salutation. What did that impudent manner indicate?

Ordinarily, from anyone other than Vasilyev it could be ignored, but not from him. As I'd heard it, everything he did he did for a reason. My thoughts had not rationalised themselves enough to deal with that sort of conduct. I decided it was best left alone for now, as any action he intended was not going to happen right now, and the present felt good to me.

* * *

Ever since knowing of it, I had been working on the assumption Vasilyev had made a mistake when initiating the request from the FBI for an Afrikaans-speaking English military officer. It wasn't his mistake. It was my biggest mistake, to date. My mistake was a failure to take a careful look at the timing. I was way off target.

Bottomly had run across Colette in Iraq in early 2003. He had met Rachel at her analyst's desks in the underground facility hidden in New Mexico, some time around 2012. The statement made by Valentin Antopolov about Colette was made back in the 2003 timeline. I realised any dependence on it for the here and now would not be relevant.

As soon as I had a chance I saw George, to share Jerry's news with him about Jimmy Mercer confirming his government's commitment to build a runway on the island of Samothrace. Once the whole base was completed, it was to be signed over to the RAF, with a dedicated usage clause inserted in favour of the US air force. The RAF would install, then have direct control over, the over-the-horizon radar.

I learned later that the British Government's QinetiQ research facilities had developed what they called an electronic array of active, solid state scanned beams, which enhance the capabilities of the new installation on a superior location than Cyprus. But not only did Samothrace offer a better site for what was called 'targeted' radar, it was also a place for potential control over the whole Dardanelles.

The American decision to build on Samothrace gave rise to a point Judith had told me before I met Alexi Vasilyev in Warsaw. It was something Valery Agapov had told her. Agapov alleged Vasilyev was playing tricks, his words, over some construction works Agapov did not fully elaborate on. The only thing I could think of was the Tartus construction site. But why would Agapov want to prevaricate when Judith asked him where this site was?

I think I may have stumbled on the 'why' and the 'where'. Vasilyev was delaying work on Tartus because he was aware of the need to move the Pegasus Bank from the island of Samothrace. He was deliberately delaying the construction to allow as much time as possible for moving the money, without raising too much suspicion. But that alone threw up so many unanswered questions it would become a whole new ball game, as they say somewhere.

* * *

George had beaten me home by two days, so, with Sophie by his side, he had been checking through the questionnaires I'd prepared for Winston, as well as Gibson, to answer. Another task I'd asked Sophie to perform was to trace any movement of money deposited in accounts in either Judith's name or the name of her father, Edwin Meadows. It would probably be a waste of time trying to trace where it originated, but why not try to find it, she'd said, when I thought I was talking to myself.

Amongst many things, I'd asked Sophie to look into the relationship between Bottomly and Gerald Neil, the scope of which I was unaware of, until Gerald's son Ryan Neil told me. Apparently, it was born in the mouth of a disaster, a tragic one for nineteen sailors, but thankfully not for either Gerald's father or Bottomly's.

The two men were amongst three hundred other yacht crews taking part in the biannual Fastnet Race in 1979. The yachts set off in fair weather, but by the third day they were just two of the one hundred and twenty-five other sailors who were forced to abandon their boats, due to the severity of the violent storm that hit the spread-out race, midway between Land's End and Fastnet.

The two men were luckily rescued by the Irish coastguard, launched from Dunmore East, in County Waterford, where they were treated in the local hospital. That's where the previous simple acquaintance they'd shared through their love of yachting grew into a friendship due to a sailing disaster. None of that I knew, and although I couldn't see its relevance to anything I was doing, I put it in my over-stocked memory bank in the 'just in case' box.

I told George how Jerry Furley had been busy taking calls from America and South Africa about the two who'd been detained in Greece. There had been plenty of calls about Bottomly, who was proving popular with a few British Members of Parliament. When I mentioned Parliament, George said he wasn't at all surprised, as when he was helping Sophie with the research of the Fastnet Race he discovered Gerald Neil's father, Oliver Neil, had sold his munitions business immediately after the racing accident, to become an advisor to Margaret Thatcher's three-month-old government.

He became a Member of Parliament in the 1992 election. He kept his seat throughout the Socialist years of Blair, then Brown, to find a position in the cabinet when the Conservative Party returned under David Cameron.

Oliver Humphrey Neil retired from politics when he became ill in 2017, dying the same year. Winston's father had died earlier that year and it was reported in many newspapers how people who knew both men, said the unexpected death of Winston's father had contributed as much to Oliver's death as his own illness had done.

As I listened to George telling me the story, I seriously wished I'd known of the close friendship the two men had shared, as I think it might have explained some of the odd behaviour Winston exhibited, specifically with the gambling debt being allowed to climb so high. I had never believed Gerald when he said it was an employee's mistake that allowed Winston to exceed a limit Gerald had told nobody of.

George wanted me to stay with him and Sophie in Eaton Square, but I was looking forward to solitude with time to think about everything that had taken place in the past few days—or was it weeks? I have forgotten how long this has taken—had been feverish at times, which a short period of quiet would do no harm to endure.

* * *

I had poured my first Jura of the evening when Jimmy Mercer called to tell me how, although his President thanked me for helping with the defections of Alexi Vasilyev and Dimitri Oborka, he could not do that publicly. If he did, it could show he had prior knowledge of the event.

Even allowing for the slight disappointment, I was delighted to know how the President of the United States had personally thanked me for my work in discovering what the Russians intended to do at the Mediterranean base in Tartus, on the Syrian coast. I did tell him how I explained it wasn't just me, but he wouldn't listen.

Jerry Furley called, telling me he'd heard from Charles Wallace, saying how Viscount Bottomly was to lose the hereditary title, as well as his United Kingdom passport being forfeited. His UK bank account was to be frozen, along with any other assets his family had in Great Britain, which were to be taken from him. Needless to say, the South African authorities were closely following what actions were taken by the government in London, but had already frozen his bank accounts.

He was to face trial in this country, which, like Judith Meadows' trial, would be held in camera. I thought of another similarity he might share with Meadows, which was that he could serve his sentence at Gardie House, in the Shetlands. When, of course, it eventually became vacant.

It was decided Liam Gibson had committed no crime the UK government felt necessary to prosecute, nor any crime where the Americans would become involved. There was no substance that could be used from the statement Gibson was alleged to have made in Kuwait, where he boasted about visiting two people in England a friend wanted him to kill.

The fact that his face was recognised on the route Hugh Pickering would have been transported along, on his way to Primrose Hill and his death, was to be held on file. It was circumstantial evidence at best, as he would have known, but it wasn't finished there.

* * *

Jerry Furley had been included in a conversation Jimmy Mercer had with Liam Gibson. Mercer wanted an assault to be made on the central Iranian radar centre the AWB had planned to mount on Israel's behalf, brought forward to within the next ten days. It was a mission Israel had also asked America to help with, but Liam's proximity made him an ideal candidate. Once inside the control complex, the AWB unit were to take the whole system down to allow time for Israeli aircraft to obliterate it.

Gibson, with his team from the AWB, would be given the codes to enter the building along with the codes to enter the computer room, as well as the procedure required to stop the radial programming of the existing algorithm runtime. Israeli High Command would be made aware of the raid and would run their attack whilst monitoring the situation.

In return for complete cooperation, Furley heard Mercer say, he and his department would turn a blind eye to Gibson's withdrawal of deposits held in the Pegasus Bank. All of this was, he said, without his President's knowledge.

* * *

From nowhere, I felt a chill. I was in the first-floor sitting room at Chester Square, on the soft sofa across from one of the bow windows at the front of the house. I was alone, but very comfortable. I had loads of reading to do as well as a huge amount of computer work to wade through. With the Scotch decanter next to me and glass in hand, I welcomed the peace and quiet and being able to smoke without complaint. It was as I lit a cigarette that my neck felt chilled. I stopped what I was doing to rub it. It wasn't the kind of chill one was able to rub away, it was deep inside.

I had been set up, and it was then, as I rubbed at the delusional chill, that I grasped what I'd missed.

There was one question not on the list I'd prepared for Jerry Furley to ask. It was the one where I already had half of the answer. The question concerned the photograph with Agapov in it. Who was he with?

CHAPTER TWENTY-ONE
SKYROS

I saw Alexi Vasilyev's defection as real enough. I even expected most of the intelligence he gave over to be valuable. I told Jimmy Mercer about Alexi's habit of giving Russian assets to us by not changing all of their identity, like, for example, Christopher Metsos. Then, when Alexi Vasilyev wanted to show the man to us for some reason I've yet to discover, he oversees his new legend, leaving him exposed by changing his name to Christopher Signalman. I explained to him how it had been the same with Katherine.

I got another commendation from Jimmy Mercer about the unearthing of Pavel Kapustin, aka Christopher Signalman. My section at Vauxhall had passed on the information of his whereabouts to the FBI, who had, with the Canadian's government's permission, started a watching brief. They had an unexpected sighting of a known member of ISIS, who they successfully followed to a cell of terrorists in Ottawa, who the Canadians took over, now having them under constant observation, both static and mobile. Could one of them be the man Alexi Vasilyev had referred to as a veritable prize on my sleeve, in his message to Katherine?

With suspicions firmly to the fore of my mind, I considered Vasilyev's main reason to be in the 'West' was a selfish need of revenge. This revenge he was after was not an eye-for-an-eye kind of thing. It was more subtle than that. To understand his direction in life, we must try to understand the man. From the day of his electrocution, he was no longer any use as a covert agent, which was his first love.

His value, since the electrical incident, was in administration, where he would never admit to it, but he was exceptionally good. He would never allow himself to become attached to anything he managed since Paulo had intervened in his life.

I further believe that, had I not walked into Samantha's life in August, Alexi would have defected to America, using the same method of deception he used in Warsaw on the same day. It was logical to think that. He decided to first go to Great Britain because of George and me. His scheme of using Judith, with the gun Gibson retrieved from the Pegasus vaults, to assassinate both of us, was to be coordinated from wherever he was resettled. That was my firm belief.

From the conversation we'd had, reinforced by the tapes from the debrief at Beaulieu, I was of the opinion that he thought his confinement in an office was a form of punishment brought upon him by my family. By looking into any number of mirrors, either deliberately or accidentally, every day of his life, he was reminded of how Paulo had taken away so much of him.

I had no idea what effect the amount of electrical current that passed through his body could have on his sexual capability, nor was I about to ask. Nor, it was fair to say, did I really know what he looked like before becoming so grotesquely disfigured, but when I asked myself if I would want revenge, then I answered, yes, in a big way I would. What's more, nobody would stand in my way.

I believed he'd had no choice but to accept his appearance as the obstacle that stood in his way to returning to the intelligence community as an effective spy. But for a man like him, there was no quiet acceptance. In my opinion, his ultimate aim was now to influence the political proceedings in certain parts of the world. To do that effectively, he needed money, heaps of money, along with a central base. What made me think that was what he wanted?

Well, Agapov more or less told me. He mentioned how he and Vasilyev's primary interests were in South African politics. Their natural allies were in the ANC, along with the rebels that could be found in nations from Angola eastwards and northwards, covering almost a third of the continent of Africa. How could they help the ANC achieve the freedom they wanted, when Bottomly with his bloodthirsty AWB intended their annihilation? The only way I could think of was buy more guns, more ammunition and more means to kill.

I went out on a limb a couple of times before I was in Warsaw, with one of those times being very rewarding and that was when I asked Agapov what he knew of Liam Gibson. I had half an idea the two knew each other. Maybe it was just in passing, or his name being mentioned by Winston Bottomly, or it could have been through the communist party. I was right. Valery Agapov did know Gibson and quite well at that!

Sir Rupert Draycott's assumption of Agapov having known Bottomly since the Russians invaded Afghanistan, over forty years ago, had proved to be correct. The Viscount had found a listening ear to the snippets of intelligence he could get from the British Ministry of Defence. He got his information either through friends employed inside the MOD or through his connections in Military Intelligence, MI5. And a grateful Russian named Valery Agapov was the beneficiary.

Agapov petitioned his superiors to be stationed

permanently in London as the embassy's meteorologist. In return, he promised Viscount Bottomly would in time lead the Russian intelligence service to riches in Africa that would otherwise be beyond their reach. He promoted his wonder catchment, as he called him, to the not so intelligent code name of Count.

Agapov met Gibson in London when Liam was in England on leave from covering Bottomly. Funnily enough Agapov had found him through his friendship with Bottomly. He saw mileage in the cultivation of them both. However, it almost blew up in his face, as it were.

Valery Agapov told how he was with Gibson in a pub in Ladbroke Grove one Saturday lunchtime, probably talking about the weather in the world in general, when mention was made of the Viscount and the AWB. It was mainly about how far to the right the AWB views were developing.

Valery was not shy. Outright, he asked Gibson how he could keep his friendship with Bottomly when his true communist convictions clashed so dramatically with the fascist leanings of the South African, Afrikaner Weerstandsbeweging.

Agapov alleged the bomb Bottomly's butler found on the doorstep of Devonish House after the inquest into Samantha's death, was made by Gibson. I was astonished to learn of that. Stupidly, I asked what had changed in the two men's relationship since then. The answer was staring at me from the island—

it was money, rooms full of it, literally from floor to ceiling. From being made aware of the amount of money, Gibson's political philosophy changed, overnight.

With all that money deposited in the bank of the Pegasus Mercantile Company on my mind, I made arrangements to meet with Sabah Al Salim, through his half-brother Shaikh Al-Sabah who I met in Boodles for lunch. My friend was well, having won a considerable amount of money, in the higher end of a six figure range, on a wager he'd made with Gerald Neil's son Ryan. I supposed it was being a bit grouchy of me, but I couldn't help wondering if Ryan Neil would have a nightclub called Crocketts for much longer.

Sabah was to be in London at the weekend, which left me with three days to visit Judith Meadows up in the Shetlands, as well as see what Sophie had discovered about the monetary movements from the Pegasus Bank. Sophie had been working with the counter-intelligence arm of MI5 in conjunction with the anti-terrorism unit at Scotland Yard's Special Branch office. Sir Rupert Draycott was also at the end of a phone, he'd told her.

She was excited to report how she had been working in an office of the anti-corruption section of the Bank of England. Although the banking arm of the Pegasus Bank was far beyond the regulations of the City of London, its financial dealings fell within a remit of a part of the Bank of England. Meadows had moved money from his deposits in Pegasus into the private City bank of Pickering's. The movement of such a large amount of money had flagged up on computer screens in international counter-terrorism departments around the world. In itself, the movement of money was nothing to take special note of, but the amount made it so; it was £375,000,000 sterling.

I genuinely believed I had finished with Judith Meadows, or Fields as she was known in the Shetlands, but sadly for us both, I hadn't. She was waiting for me, in a bad temper! She was upset I'd taken so long to see her since my return from Poland. How was Valery, she asked, to which I'm sure I screwed my face up in surprise at her question. I replied he was fine, with the feeling of holes being chiselled into my forehead by her eyes, to gauge the truth of my remark.

She made no comment, which made me think I had not given away any act of astonishment on my part. Why Agapov and not Vasilyev? Whilst I was thinking of why she'd asked that question, she answered my unasked question as if it was either stage-managed, or one or both of us was telepathic.

"I asked because I didn't know if he'd defected?

As you know, I thought Alexi would go over, but I wasn't sure Agapov would like to go to America."

I told her Alexi Vasilyev had elected to go first to Britain, while he weighed his options by talking to the same people that she had once spoken to. I was reminding myself not to mention Gibson nor any gun. She shrugged, then looked skywards before delivering her told-you-so moment.

"When I told you Vasilyev was an arsehole, perhaps you didn't understand what being a powerful, cataclysmic arsehole meant. You know he was an American double agent, Harry. He stole secrets from them and the Russians. I'm betting at least one CIA asset and one from the FSB, or whatever Putin is calling the KGB nowadays, is looking for him right now. Both of them having 'strictly personal' reasons. I would bet on both them wanting to rip his head off, as a way of execution. I told you they will be after you and I will be right. Carry a gun with you from now on—old sport, and keep an eye out for suicidal grouse!" Her sarcasm was impossible to miss.

I broached the subject of her father's huge transfer of money from Samothrace into Pickering's. I asked if she had any idea what he wanted it for. After I'd listened to her futile attempts at being funny, like buy her freedom, or get me some lessons at RADA, the royal academy of dramatic art for a role on the stage as an actor, she said she didn't know, "unless he thought the bank on the island was closing down".

"What makes you think that?" I asked.

Although it was a sensible answer given all the circumstances, without the missing knowledge, it was a strange answer for a guess. Then came the next surprise.

The closure of the whole Mercantile Company was mooted as far back as the time she was with both her parents, staying for the first time with the Bottomlys, on the South African estate. She was, she thought, about twelve years of age, sitting around a pool with many adults. None, other than her parents and Winston, were memorable.

The adults were engaged in a dispiriting conversation, inasmuch as they were speaking of leaving an island she'd had no chance to visit. Her spirits rose on hearing of an alternative. An island she could pronounce without as much difficulty as the first island they'd mentioned. The island they were moving to was Skyros, further south than in the Aegean Sea and closer to Athens.

"Daddy, Daddy," she'd pleaded, "can we go there, before that too is dispensed with?"

I asked her if, in her opinion, the company was going to reopen on Skyros? To which civil question I got a rather rude shouted reply of, "How the hell would I know, you idiot. I haven't spoken with any family for years."

I was going to shout his name back at her, reminding her who was to blame for the state of affairs, but it was pointless. I feared it would be a hollow expression to reassert my dwindling authority, but I tried.

"Did the shit Agapov ever tell you who he was with in the photograph he gave to Winston Bottomly, around the time Bottomly shot his fiancée?"

I'm not sure what made me ask the question, but it had returned and found the box in my memory, where it would normally go, only to find it overflowing. There was no other course of action, but to ask.

"You are an odd person, Harry. That must be the question you have been dying to ask since you first came to the island to find me. Why didn't you ask Agapov, or perhaps you have, and now you're trying to catch me out?"

I stared back into those large, hazelnut-shaped, green eyes of hers, not flinching or moving a fraction of an inch away from holding her critical, steady stare. Who on earth did she think she was? I lost my patience with her!

"It's a simple enough question, Judith, nothing more. If you don't, or can't, answer it, then don't, but don't give me a hard time over it. I'm here to ask questions, not to answer any of yours. I could still send you to the UK post at the North Pole, if you're not careful."

"I was told it was the wife of the prime minister's personal secretary. Stella Wallace. I'm sorry, Harry. I didn't mean to upset you. I thought you might be up for a game."

Two conflicting emotions overcame me. First, I thought I was fortunate to be sitting, not standing, when I heard who the woman in the photograph was, otherwise I might faint, and secondly, I thought how irascible I'd been when I scolded her. What would I have done had she not told me? All I could think of was COW's wife.

I had never met the woman so I had no idea what she looked like, but I used to play a game in my head where I would imagine what a lady's husband might look like, or, perhaps it's more correct to say, I used to imagine what a chap's girlfriend looked like on hearing he had one.

Some men are destined to have an appeal to women, as in plural, likewise some women have an appeal to men, in plural. There is, as someone said, someone for everyone, or similar words were used, but it's my opinion that's an oversimplification of a complicated business. For some, man or woman, there is nobody. Somehow or other, that brought my attention back to Judith's revelation.

'Surprised' is an overused word in the English language. To me, 'astonished' was a soft word carrying no element of shock. I thought 'flabbergasted' to be a great word, but even for me it was too old-fashioned.

I'm going to say the feeling I got when she told

me was the same as being knocked over backwards in a rugby tackle, when hit by a shoulder driven hard into your midriff, driving all the wind from your lungs through an uncontrollable gaping mouth.

That's how I greeted the news of Charles Oswald Wallace, having a wife. I felt sorry for Valery Agapov, but that wasn't the point, was it?

CHAPTER TWENTY-TWO
TRUCKS

I had walked to the ferry terminal with the purpose of catching the first boat sailing from the island that morning to Lerwick, then taking the familiar ride across Shetland for the first leg of the two-flight journey to London, but I must have left the forceful part of my resolve lying next to the small amount of belongings still in my quarters.

By the time I had walked all the way back, Judith was in the garden at Gardie House. The sun was shining, but I cannot say all was right in the world. She had no idea where I'd been, nor what was on my mind. I said nothing of my plans. The previous afternoon and evening we had spent in predicting where we thought the Pegasus Bank could be rebuilt when it moved from Samothrace.

With the help of the map the Royal Navy had

provided, which was laid out on the table in front of us, the island of Skyros was deemed to be a possible site for the commercial offices of the Mercantile Company, but if the move had to be completed fairly urgently, then the construction of vaults that were large enough and secure enough to hold the amount of physical money, along with the paper index files Judith expected the bank must hold, would take at least a year, if not more.

However, there was an existing underground site already holding enough large equipment to supply an army. Logic was demanding the bank to be sited on the Bottomly's estate, at the same place as the South African army munitions. We worked on the logistics of transportation. I say 'we', meaning Judith and I.

Someone, I'm not sure which one of us, offered the opinion that the best way to shift the contents of the vaults on Samothrace to South Africa would be by boat to either Durban or Cape Town, depending on what was the best route to the part of the Bottomly estate being used.

"If it was left to me," I offered, "I would fly the load from Durban to Upington, but either Bottomly or Gibson would know better than I."

It was Sophie who solved the riddle for us. She called me when I was in the garden with Judith. I mentioned our dilemma to her and she reminded me how Sabah Al Salim was a named director of a shipping company with its registered offices in the Iranian port of Chabahar.

As usual, Sophie's research was thorough and exhaustive. Although the port was in Iran on the Gulf of Oman, it was operated under an Indian licence, which, according to the studies she was able to complete, indicated a measure of either inefficiency or a tendency to turn a blind eye to matters, as the port had exercised 'wayward' regulatory control over many of its vessels.

The port authorities had been prosecuted by the International Maritime Organisation on three occasions recently, for failing to adequately certify ships' equipment and crew. Not one of those listed ships was registered to the Persis Shipping Company, the one having a strong association with Sabah Al Salim.

I wondered if we could assume cargo loaded onto Sabah's ships was not regulated as cargo on other ships would be? If so, could any arrangement Sabah may have be transferred to other ports, in particular the ones in South Africa? Hopefully, I could find that out soon.

Following on closely to the news of the American investment in a runway on Samothrace, came news of further construction on the island. This time it was to be at the port of Kamariotissa, where a deep water terminal, to take ocean-going vessels, or OGV's, was to commence in approximately one year's time. The building work would conceivably be too late to move the money by an OGV. But if a loading out at sea was out of the question, then a ship from the Persis Shipping Company could dock at the Greek port of Alexandroupoli, where some hired fishing boats, taking their time so as not to be noticed, could ferry the load from the vaults at Samothrace. Whilst Judith and I were speaking of various modes of transport, my mobile phone rang. I excused myself to take the call.

It was the Vice-Admiral who was in charge of the interrogation at Beaulieu. He said Alexi Vasilyev confirmed what we thought. He was deliberately slowing the fabrication of the Tartus site to facilitate Valery Agapov's wish of shifting the money from the Pegasus bank.

The usefulness of this news was not in the confirmation of the theory we were all working on, it proved something different to me. To me, it showed beyond doubt the idea that had been growing in my mind ever since Judith said she'd not heard of Agapov's intent to defect.

* * *

With my mind engaged on making an effort to ignore the consequences and repercussions of the confirmation of Valery Agapov's importance in the Russian hierarchy, I was considering the predictions we were making about Sabah Al Salim ships. Then came another jolt to the growing circle of acquaintances. Judith was expanding on her conjecture of why her father was moving his money.

His money was connected, in a way, to the photograph of Mrs Wallace. Edwin Meadows was a close friend of Sabah Al Salim, but his friendship, or his acquaintanceship, did not end there. He was also a close friend of Charles Oswald Wallace, who Judith had met on quite a few occasions, to her distaste if going by her screwed-up face, at the mention of his name, was anything to go by.

She was fast becoming a fount of information. The obvious link even I could make between her father and Wallace, was through money, which came from the investment opportunities Edwin had recommended down through many years of friendship and Sabah's shrewd acquisitions.

Judith had heard her father admit to some fortuitous investments someone who was 'connected' had mentioned over a brandy in a club somewhere, following a delicious lunch or dinner, and as she was speaking, I was imagining being there, enjoying the occasion. That type of unlawful trading was widespread for a considerable time until it was broadcast on news channels, labelled as insider dealings, a catchphrase newspapers loved, becoming the news pariah of Fleet Street.

I mentioned how Wallace came to have Oswald as his middle name. She hadn't known of the family's close connection to Oswald Mosley, who was a member of the British Parliament before becoming leader of the British Union of Fascists seven years before the start of WWII. Her father, she said, was an outspoken supporter of the racial segregation in South Africa which she passionately opposed. It was through the sharing of the same political ideals that Edwin Meadows, Charles Oswald Wallace and Winston Bottomly all came to know each other.

It was then, through the financial advice Edwin Meadows gave them, that they came to have considerable deposits in the Pegasus Bank. Another who benefitted by listening to advice from Meadows senior was the man the Russians called Chevron, although he had now moved his money.

Through the anti-corruption department of C9, working with the regulative arm of The Bank of England, money was discovered being moved from the bank on Samothrace into, first, Pickering's Private Investment Bank, then some of it was moved into a part of the world we all thought would become important.

Several million dollars were transferred from Pickering's bank in London into the Athens headquarters branch of the Bank of Greece. All it would require, in order to be physically moved, would be a truck load of dollar bills coming from the head office, to the branch of the bank in the port city of Alexandroupoli. It could then be moved to the dock to be loaded onto the ship to South Africa. All I could do was guess as to how many truck journeys it would require.

I believed Judith when she said she had no inkling of any arrangement made with anyone to do with the gun Liam Gibson had retrieved from its Pegasus concealment. Her assumption was the gun had been sent back to London to be replaced in the registry. She could throw no light on why that would not be. I had spoken to Sophie about it and all she could think of was its eventual use to cause embarrassment between Britain and France in a sensitive part of the world where ISIS is a problem. That would be in Iraq, or Iran. I was unsure.

Total, the giant French energy company, had recently signed a huge billion-dollar deal with Iran. If the Paris assassination could be shown as a ruinous rift between two Western allies, could that rift fuel more Muslim unrest in the region? Could it be enough to threaten the security of Western investments in that part of the Middle East and beyond? Could that small spark be the same as the assassination of Archduke Ferdinand of Austria in Sarajevo? That murder led directly to the millions who died in World War I. Could Judith's gun spark the death of millions more?

* * *

I had to assume the missing photograph of Agapov was as licentious as I was imagining. To imagine anything less would be ineffectual at best. I would be equally incompetent if I was to ignore the potential disaster with the water supply to the town of Rustenburg. But it would be my secondary knowledge of the platinum-group of metals, iridium, palladium, along with the rhodium found at a mine outside the town that would attract the most interest from Western governments. Could the two be addressed as one? I thought they could.

In various preparations, either together or separately, iridium, palladium and rhodium are essential in the building of nuclear weapons. These weapons could be manufactured by an established country, one registered by the Nuclear Regulatory Commission, or as a so-called dirty bomb, by a terrorist organisation. Whichever way, I figured Jimmy Mercer needed to know. Nobody wanted ISIS to get hold of it, especially if they could get hold of any of the discarded South African parts of nuclear weapons to use in places where they thought they were making a difference.

I'm not a political animal, not in the sense of closely following what's happening in the world at large. Some would say I should take more interest, but to them I would say, as an entity of one, I cannot make a direct difference. If I work with others, then I can help to change things. That's if, indeed, things needed changing. By working with the Director General of the American Department of National Intelligence, I might be able to help. That was my train of thought when my mobile phone rang; it was Jerry Furley.

The American army officer who developed the encryption system everyone in communications was jumping up and down about, had been traced and captured. He was the one who had been monitoring radio signals before going over to ISIS, who then held him captive because of a perceived insult against Daesh. When captured, he was with Abu Ala al-Mulard, a deputy leader of ISIS we had identified through images from an IOMS unit, being at Ar Raqqah together. Abu Ala al-Mulard was also in custody.

One concern I'd had when Abu Ala al-Mulard was first identified as travelling with the American, was why Sabah Al Salim was with them in the back of the truck when he could have found a more comfortable place to meet? The answer came when they were interrogated. According to both men, there had never been three in the back of the truck. There was only the two of them! The third, Sabah, had only met them when they were near the Ar Raqqah complex.

The American communication expert had shown Abu Ala al-Mulard how the encryption was accomplished, then sold him the technique behind the process. They maintained they were the only two who knew how to put it all together, then how to decipher the coded material in whatever form of communication it came in.

I didn't enquire how it happened, but shortly after the CIA agent in charge of the interrogation was certain he understood the encoding process sufficiently well to show others how it was done, both men in captivity were declared dead. Going back to what I said about my non-interest in global politics, as always, I blindly accepted the American intelligence agencies' unspoken capabilities of providing death certificates claiming both men died of heart attacks.

There would be no resurrection for either or both of those two men by any proclamation of an injustice having occurred from me. The only way I could make an impression would be to ask the other man who I'd seen coming from the back of that truck in Ar Raqqah, if he wanted to stay alive.

CHAPTER TWENTY-THREE
LONDON

As arranged, I met with Sabah Al Salim in my club at a quarter past one for lunch. Well, to be truthful, I was a little late and hugely embarrassed by it. "I'm so sorry! I only had a mile or so to travel, but the cab driver found the most awful traffic imaginable. I never thought London could be this busy."

"Don't worry, Lord Paterson. It's a pleasure to meet you. I'm honoured by your hospitality."

He was smiling as I accepted his extended hand in greeting. His grip was strong and purposeful. He continued to speak as we shook hands.

"I think London is so crowded because of this on-coming pandemic. People are stocking up on perish-ables, in case, or should I say, as will happen, this country follows others in creating areas of lockdowns. It will be especially true in big city centres such as

London. I've heard there will be an announcement in a few days' time. It's my understanding something will be done this coming month. Anyway, that's what I've heard. I'm making travel arrangements based on that and I would strongly advise you to do the same. We are probably enjoying the last few months of freedom."

I go through life making mental notes about everyone I meet. Because of that, Sabah's half-brother, Shaikh Al Sabah, did not escape my analysis. It was partially because of those mental notes that the first thing I noticed was how much taller Sabah was than his half-brother. He must have been a good four or five inches taller. The two shared the same mother. They shared the same hair colouring, as well as the colouring of their eyes. They differed facially, with Sabah having an angular face to Shaikh's round, cherubic shape. I would have said Sabah was the older of the two, but, as you are aware, my ability to estimate a person's age was not improved by any of the social categorisations I practised.

If pushed, I would estimate his age at the early to middle sixties mark. I think my inability to judge the age of someone is partially because of the facial products people apply, together with the degrees of cosmetic surgery money can buy. He was smartly dressed as would be expected of a man of money, apart from myself of course. But then one must accept some oddities in life. An old saying I've heard more than once—never disappoint someone by the tie you're wearing.

I know I've explained some of the elements of Sabah's early life leading to his role in the secret intelligence community of Iran, so I was surprised this meeting was taking place. I say surprised, because although the position he held in his own country was equivalent to Jimmy Mercer's in America, Jimmy could lose his job on the whim of his President, but only divine providence could unseat Sabah Al Salim.

Even though neither he nor I expected any divine appearance in London, his presence on the streets could present an element of danger from mere mortals. The deterrent to danger was more extensive than I'd imagined it would be. There was the three-man team who were occupying the table beside our own, as well as the lone person standing close to the white-stone columns, at the entrance to the club. Perhaps, he was leaning casually against the black, wrought-iron railings, smoking a cigarette.

The driver of Sabah's car, a black Rolls Royce, had been lucky to find an unoccupied parking bay outside the club. The same luck did not quite apply to the driver of the transport for his team of 'minders', who was parked behind on a yellow line, waiting in a silver Range Rover. His diplomatic immunity would save him from parking tickets.

I had notified Sir Leonard Miles of the meeting, leaving him to arrange for the two MI5 protection officers seated at a table next to one of the doors of the club restaurant. Lunch was to cost me a fortune, but at least I was not expected to pay for any of the watching Military Intelligence contingent outside in St James's Street.

I did not know how true his prediction of a forthcoming lockdown would be, but he would have contacts everywhere, including in Whitehall. As I was thinking of the power and influence this man had, one thing Winston's aunt told me was rattling around inside my head. It was when she told how the organisation in South Africa, the AWB, ran guns to a Black APLA party, who then used those weapons for a massacre of other Blacks in a church named after a Saint—St James's. I wondered if Sabah had either supplied the guns or shipped them to South Africa, or was he responsible for both shipping and supplying?

We started off speaking of Samantha, or Charlotte Marchand, a person we both knew, although his knowledge was far more extensive than mine. He was open about her early life in Kuwait, living with her grandparents on his estate after her father had died in Sabah's employment. I had been told how the last Iraqi, the one who had killed Christopher Burns, had died in hospital from his wounds, but his wounds were described at the scene in one paramedic's journal as minimal, not life-threatening. So what happened? I asked.

He never tried to dodge the straight answer by a false declaration of not knowing, or never being told, as if he never was when controlling his vast empire. The man was interrogated by a section of his bodyguards who knew Samantha's father well, liking and respecting him. At the end of his questioning, when they had all the information they wanted about who organised the assassination attempt, his throat was cut open. It was a quick and relatively painless death compared to how it might have ended.

One surprising aspect of the affair I had not known, was how the filming of this man's death was watched by Samantha Burns when she was living in the apartment Sabah had provided in the Grosvenor House Hotel.

It was not only death we spoke of over a good lunch served with fine wines and brandy. Each question I asked was, luckily, recorded, as the heady combination was not conducive to having a reliable memory. One question I do remember asking was about his knowledge of Hugh Pickering. He laughed in an accusatory manner, as if he was shaming me.

"Surely you want to know about a bank, not this man, Lord Paterson. The man is unimportant, as essentially is his bank of Pickering's. It is no more than a convenient drop-off point, similar to the places where Amazon leave parcels to be collected later.

"I know you have people looking at the geographic footprint of my shipping company and soon,

I expect, my airfreight company. I'm flattered someone such as yourself would bother to have an interest in me. You are welcome to look as I have nothing to hide. But I suspect your true interest is with the bank, at the port of Kamariotissa on the island of Samothrace. It is perfectly legitimate as I'm sure your enquiries have shown.

"Nonetheless, as a person from a banking family I would expect you to know how those who deposit money in the bank expect privacy. I'm also aware of your searches into Viscount Bottomly's connection to the bank, as well as the connection of the Russian, Valery Agapov. I would prefer it if Agapov was not one of your..." he hesitated for a moment searching for the right words to use, before starting with "... persons of interest. I am both confounded and disappointed by your enquiries into Viscount Bottomly. I would have thought one of the last things you would want to do is upset the people around the Count, as you're aware Viscount Bottomly is known. He is a well-respected man within the circle of friends he has."

When he finally stopped speaking, I thought I would try to add substance to our hypothesis. I asked why there was a necessity to move the money from the bank on Samothrace to the Bottomly family's estate, using his ships? Why not transfer it all into the Pickering's private bank, which the CIA owned?

Our working theory was right. The money was

being moved to Winston's family's estate in South Africa using ships from Sabah Al Salim's shipping company. Pickering's had been considered, but rejected for the reasons I had thought of—'insufficient' room. The bank's safe was too small. We were correct about the quantity of money being huge.

He had accepted my invitation not to threaten but to investigate. He wanted to know how much we knew. But why was that? I wondered. Just as I thought we had finished, Sabah made a surprising comment as he and his 'minders' made to leave Boodles. One neither I, nor anyone else, had seen coming.

"Was I correct in assuming you would welcome another prize to wear on your sleeve, your Lordship? A veritable one, as you English say? There's no need to look so puzzled. I knew of the communication that was safely delivered to a lady in New York. It made pleasant reading. I will be in this country until around six this evening. I'm leaving to get well ahead of any restrictions your government may see fit to install, and believe me they will. All private flights as well as commercial airlines will be grounded. I need to be in America for business shortly. If you decide you need the prize the message referred to, you should be able to reach me on this number."

He passed a shiny black business card across the table with a telephone number embossed in gold on the front of it. There was no name. On the reverse side of the card, which he'd quickly shown, was a single, handwritten word—*StoneGhost*. I knew what the word referred to, but I had no idea how Sabah would know of what I understood to be a highly classified secret.

His three protection men had risen from their table and were at the opposite side of the exit doors leading to the first floor flight of stairs, before Sabah had made his final goodbye. Apparently, he had been waiting for the moment when they were all out of earshot. He spoke to me in a soft voice.

"I find myself at a time for change. I want to work closely with your SIS, but in particular I want to work with you, Lord Paterson. We have a lot in common. I want you to be my case officer. Please, call me on the number on that card before I leave." He picked up the card from the table, this time handing it to me.

I walked down the stairs with him in silent deliberation, keeping what I thought to be a respectable distance. His minders were in front, reaching the pavement just as the driver, who was waiting on the pavement edge, placed his chauffeur's hat on his head and the protection officer, who in my imagination had been waiting outside the club smoking cigarettes, held open the rear nearside door of the richly polished car.

As Sabah got into the rear of the vehicle I was standing under the club's outside canopy a few feet away from the pavement. I saw the rear nearside door close behind him and his 'door-holding' loyal officer climb in the front of the Rolls to take his seat alongside the driver, who was now behind the steering wheel. The remaining three of his private protection entourage were walking towards the silver Range Rover, where the driver was waiting.

What happened next took everyone by absolute surprise. As the Rolls Royce car went to pull away from the kerb, a motorcycle with a passenger on the pillion seat pulled alongside the car. The passenger on the bike produced an automatic weapon, opening fire at point-blank range at first the rear, then the front side windows of the car, turning around once on the motorbike to fire at the other guards who were almost inside the Range Rover. There was one of his team outside the silver car with a weapon pointing at the motorcycle. I presumed it was because he had fired at the motorcycle that the pillion passenger had turned his attention away from Sabah's vehicle.

Although I had served in areas of hostility, and I was used to hearing guns fired at both a distance, or guns fired from my hand, I still hesitated for a micro-second before I pulled my own gun. I had a clear shot, so in order to save life, I fired just once. The gunman had turned to face towards the Range Rover leaving me with, as I said, a clear line of fire. I saw my shot hit him in the chest, causing him to fall from the bike onto the road surface, hitting his helmeted head hard onto the tarmac surface. Above all the other noise, I clearly heard his helmet hit the road.

There was silence for a second, before the harsh screech from a spinning wheel of the motorcycle, making a crazy dash for safety without a passenger. He was left lying alone on the road, in a blood defining silhouette of death.

Sabah's guard in the front seat of the car was leaning forward with his head towards the windscreen which, with the small amount of glass remaining in the side window, was covered in a mixture of blood and human remains. What was left of his head was lying against the dashboard. I did not open the door.

I quickly looked at the fallen pillion rider, picking up his gun from the road. I made the weapon safe as I checked his pulse at his exposed neck. There was no sign of life. That was not the same with the driver of the Rolls.

At first, I did not think that could possibly be the case, as he was slumped against the door on his side of the vehicle, not moving. Although most of the gunfire was aimed at the Rolls, resulting in both offside windows, front and rear, being completely devoid of glass, the wound to the side of the driver's head was not fatal, nor was the wound to his shoulder. He was able to move, but I advised him to stay where he was. I could already hear sirens.

When I had looked at the front-seated guard, I had seen Sabah lying face down on the floor of the car, behind the front seating. The glass partition his model of vehicle was fitted with, had been completely shot away. He was covered in glass, but, at that stage, I could not see any wound, or blood. As I'd moved around the car I asked if he was hit.

He had been shot in the upper arm with a little blood flowing from the wound. Both the entry and exit wounds were open, with neither showing any tissue damage that I could see. There was no apparent damage to any bone. There was a tear to his suit jacket as well as his shirt, but again he was lucky, as I could not see any material missing from either garment to suggest there could be any inside the wound.

He had been very lucky. That wasn't the same for everyone. Two passing pedestrians had been hit. They were both on the pavement, ahead of the Rolls, north towards Piccadilly. The first, a man, was hit somewhere in the back. He was bleeding profusely, but had a woman with him who looked calm, knowing what to do. Another woman was standing nearby using her phone. When I shouted if she was calling an ambulance, she replied she was. Another voice, that of a man, said he was calling the police.

The sirens I'd heard had been joined by others, and the noise was getting closer.

The second civilian was a young woman, shot in the head. I judged her to be dead from her injury at the scene. Later, at the post-mortem examination, it was determined both those shots had come from the gun fired by the Iranian protection officer from the silver Range Rover. He was not authorised to carry firearms on the streets of London.

Although the driver had survived the glancing wound to his head, he had been badly injured by the shot to the shoulder. He survived the scene but never drove another vehicle for the rest of his life. On the day itself, he could only remember the noise. When I visited him some two or three months later, when he was convalescing at home, he could not remember anything else.

His injury and treatment did not stop on the day he was discharged from hospital. For several years, he suffered attacks of anxiety and bouts depression due to the traumatic experience which he always found painful to speak about. It was said by the health professionals I spoke to, he would never fully recover. Sabah Al Salim paid for the private treatment he underwent in therapy sessions for his anxiety, but there's no amount of money able to treat that.

He was not a young man, but neither was he old. He had no pension plan nor sickness benefit to provide any income. Those two facts together could have caused his anxiety to worsen. Here again, Sabah stepped forward with his generosity. He paid the man a monthly salary equivalent to the one he was earning before the tragic event. When a sum of money was settled on him from the Criminal Injuries Compensation, it was never taken into account by Sabah, who continued to pay the salary for the eight years it took the man to reach the age of retirement at sixty-five. I thought it to be a tremendous gesture.

The pedestrian who was shot in the back was not as seriously injured as he could have been. The soft-pointed bullet had missed his spinal column, his liver and spleen, lodging just above his stomach from the rear entry point. After two operations, followed by a long period of hospitalisation, of more than three months, he was discharged into the care of his wife at home. I never kept in touch after he left the hospital. I didn't think it right.

The bullet that killed the pillion passenger with the automatic weapon came from my gun, a Glock 17. In front of two police officers present at the scene, I counted sixteen nine-millimetre shells remaining in the gun. It meant one shell had been fired. If you're worried about the legality of me carrying a weapon on British soil, then don't. Despite the fact I'm not James Bond, nor trying to be, I can assure you I am authorised to carry weapons by an edict issued by the Ministry of Defence.

Eventually, when the newspapers had stopped

accusing every government from Angola to Russia of being responsible for the attack, and the bullets proved beyond all shadow of doubt who had fired which shells, there was no claim of responsibility, either of a real nature or imaginary, made to the British government.

CHAPTER TWENTY-FOUR

A PLAN

Sabah was treated at the scene for the injury he sustained, rather than take the paramedic's advice of travelling in the back of the ambulance to a nearby hospital. He was insistent, saying if he couldn't be treated where he was, he'd seek treatment in the Iranian embassy. It was judged best to stitch the wound at the scene rather than not, so after an injection of local anaesthetic accompanied by an injection of antibiotics, the wounds were cleaned and butterfly stitches applied to the entry and exit wound.

Both his vehicles were left at the murder scene for the police to decide when to release them, as obviously they formed part of the investigations as well as having a dead body in one. So it was in a newly arrived embassy car that I travelled with Sabah to his apartment at 199 Knightsbridge, where it could be said this all started.

It felt somewhat strange to enter the place where Page Boucher, the French agent, along with the woman whose name I'm ashamed to admit I had forgotten, were murdered such a short time ago.

As we were leaving St James's Street, I asked if he wanted to stay at Chester Square in order to wash and change his clothing, but no, was his terse reply. He was already staying at 199, having clothes at the address. I asked why he hadn't sold the place considering what had happened there, but as soon as I'd asked, it felt rude of me, making me apologise for being so crass.

"No need," he'd said. "In the circumstances, it was a perfectly reasonable question."

We left two of his minders at the scene with the police, to whom I'd given one of my cards with numbers to contact in Westminster, in order to answer any questions they wanted to ask. One of the protection team who was inside Boodles went with the driver of the Rolls to hospital, as did the other driver, simply to be checked over. I had informed Jerry Furley at Vauxhall, who called military intelligence at the Ministry of Defence building on Millbank under whose jurisdiction any incident on UK soil involving people such as I would fall. Apparently, they had already been informed.

The two MI5 personnel who had been inside

Boodles from the Ministry of Defence, were now following us in their car. The duty officer at Thames House had promised six operatives as static guards for 199 Knightsbridge.

The number equates to two agents outside the building, two on the same floor as apartment number 75 and two inside the apartment itself. It was adequate.

We left the embassy driver with Sabah's minder at the front entrance to the block as I travelled in the lift with him to the 'cleaned' apartment. The Iranian embassy had provided a professional company to clean the scene. I learned the two bodies were cremated. I imagined the company was in constant use by the Iranians, but perhaps not often in London. I did wonder how Page Boucher's relations would take the news of there being no body to grieve over and how his death would, or had been, imparted to them? What about the woman whose name I couldn't remember? How would her death be told?

Making small talk to pass the time, I'd asked if this cleaning company had travelled far, to which he replied they'd come from France. He then offered some information I really did not know what to do with. He said the company was used wherever and whenever an Iranian intelligence agent could be implicated in any way, no matter how small, in something illegal, but that wasn't all that worried me.

Apparently, after ten days had passed from attending to the scene at apartment 75, 199 Knightsbridge, all three of the clean-up team were assassinated at the cleaning company's headquarters address in Lyon, France. Whoever the perpetrators of this act were, they were still at large.

Again, he expressed his desire to work with British Intelligence. Whether that assassination was part of the reason he didn't say. When I indicated a need to be quiet, by holding a finger across my lips, he said the apartment was routinely swept free of any listening devices so although our conversation was brief owing to the circumstances, he spoke openly of his willingness to cooperate in all fields, when able.

I asked him what he knew of StoneGhost, which was the code name of a communication network. The subject matter, normally military, was shared with selected national intelligence agencies between the United States, the United Kingdom, Canada, New Zealand, as well as Australia.

Originally, StoneGhost differed from the more commonly known FiveEyes agreement, in only one way. It did not carry any Interlinked Top-Secret information. But due to a successful defence strategy against a cyber attack on the infrastructure of the signal, from a known Russian injection point on the FiveEyes report in Canada, StoneGhost now linked the intelligence communities of the United States, the United Kingdom, Canada, New Zealand and Australia at one level higher—at a Top-Secret/Special Classified level. It also carried a significant anti insurgent response, not seen in FiveEyes.

It wasn't only I who was worried about what Sabah knew of it; Jerry Furley was almost ready to jump from his lofty position at The Box into the River Thames and drown.

* * *

Following Home Office protocol, The Special Investigation Department of the Ministry of Defence was in charge at the scene, outside Boodles.

* * *

Away from St James's, counter-intelligence desks from every department of the UK Border Force to the specialist departments of Scotland Yard, were checking reams of photographic recognition against the obscured facials of a motorcyclist from the two street cameras on the corner of Piccadilly and St James's Street. The full facial of the dead pillion passenger, the one I had taken when he was lying on the ground, had been successfully identified. A copy of the dead man's face, with his name, was sent through to my phone.

It was the only piece of information at this early stage that was available to the authorities. I had calls from each of the investigating teams, as well as from

Sir Leonard, asking if Sabah Al Salim had any idea who the shooter was, or if there was anyone he could think of wanting him dead.

Sabah had never heard of the dead motorcycle rider. He had people of his own who would be investigating, trying to discover a connection, but in the meantime he was safe. As far as the names of people wanting him dead went, he said he would need the side of a London bus to write their names on as there were probably so many, but off the top of his head he could not think of anyone being that brazen.

With the audacity of this attempt on his life in mind, I quickly devised a plan in my head that involved the moving of the target, as the secret service agents who protect the President of America say in moments such as this.

My plan had none of the apparatus available to the Americans, but I thought I could improvise, with help from George. My phone was switched off as I needed the time to think, not answer calls that kept coming. I'll deal with all that later, I told myself, as the plan had not been finalised when I called his number.

George was roughly the same build as Sabah, and any difference could be covered over by a well-placed hat or a longer coat than a jacket. My idea was for

George, disguised as Sabah, to travel to the airfield outside Guildford where Sabah was expected. If my friend was okay with everything, then a short flight in the Iranian's private aircraft would throw anyone following Sabah off the track.

I was explaining what was still formulating in my brain to Sabah, when I wondered if Sophie might object to me putting her husband in danger. I knew George wouldn't worry, in fact the more danger, the more excited he would be. But caution prevailed. Hastily, I arranged for the duty officer at Millbank to lay on a police escort, as well as some motorcycle outriders for the journey to the airfield, outside. I hoped that would soothe any worries Sophie might have.

My plan was simple—it amounted to when George, disguised as Sabah, was in the air, Sabah and I would travel to my address in Chester Square where he should be safe until whoever it was behind the assassination attempt was found, either by his own men, or by the British authorities with him and me helping. I would have preferred to use Harrogate but that was too far to go.

Both he and George agreed to the plan. So, after George made a quick stop at 199 Knightsbridge, entering by the rear door then exiting using the front entrance wearing one of Sabah's coats and a suitable hat, he set off, travelling in the same car we'd used from the embassy, for the journey to Guildford and a waiting plane.

I waited for my nerves to settle down before making our next move.

* * *

Sabah Al Salim was in normal times a gregarious man. However, he had to curtail his convivial feelings now he was about to deceive all those close to him, who had already been deprived of their phones. I was taking no chances with anyone, including his own intelligence community, in case they were behind the attempt on his life.

I told nobody at Thames House or the Iranian embassy where we were going, simply excusing ourselves from his protection officers by saying we were going to meet with Sir Leonard Miles who had called me soon after the Ministry of Defence arrived on the scene in St James's. It was plausible, and as far as I could see they accepted it as the truth, but it was dangerous if someone did not believe it.

All I told Sir Leonard was that Sabah was safe. I had to think fast when Sir Leonard followed up his first question of how I was feeling after shooting the pillion passenger on the motorbike, with one concerning Sabah Al Salim's next move. I said he would not change his plans, and was already in the air on his way to Budapest for a meeting.

I filled it out a bit by saying I'd advised caution with the bullet wound, but he was convinced painkillers would suffice. Sir Leonard seemed to accept my hastily contrived answer before the paternal side of his nature kicked in with advice to seek professional help if I suffered any trauma from the incident. I assured him I would take his advice, which I'm sure he didn't believe.

Sabah and I left 199 Knightsbridge by foot from the rear of the building to Lancelot Place, taking special care not to be followed. Once there, we walked briskly out to Brompton Road where we jumped into a cab that had stopped at the traffic lights, taking it to the completely empty Chester Square home. Nobody followed us.

* * *

Jerry Furley was alone, waiting inside a car parked further along on the opposite side of the square, when we arrived. Sabah immediately called his embassy to say he was on his way to Budapest. We knew he would be missed, as would I; nevertheless, it would give him a chance to focus his mind and give Jerry and me a chance to fully understand what it was he wanted, as well as how he knew of StoneGhost.

One thing he didn't need was information on Viscount Winston Bottomly and Valery Agapov. He probably knew them both far better than we did. He had stayed on the Bottomly estate in South Africa with Liam Gibson. He had also seen the weaponry held underground in an area he could mark on an ordnance survey map. One thing up until now Sabah had not mentioned was the defection in Warsaw. That did not mean he didn't know of it.

When Jerry Furley learned of the previous impregnability of the Iranian Directorate being brushed aside with aplomb, it caused him to laugh in satisfaction, but he was the same as I in not understanding what Sabah wanted from us in return for whatever he had to trade.

I had probably a million questions to ask and where to start was a concern, but as you must know by now I'm not one to procrastinate or worry unduly about causing offence; however, with Sabah there was a case for being more circumspect with my attitude. With the word 'prudence' in mind, I jumped in ahead of Jerry. I began cautiously.

"From an overhead satellite picture, I saw you with an American communications officer at Ar Raqqah alongside Colonel Hafez al-Rifaaz, whom I understand to be a highly-placed intelligence officer in a part of the Syrian Military Intelligence Division known as the Mukhabarat. By now, the American military has got to them both, but what they don't know is who else this young communications officer spoke to about his encryption methods, other than you and the Colonel? Incidentally, let me tell you, when I was asked if I recognised you from the image we had, I denied that I did."

Sabah was laughing as he asked if I thought the CIA could be behind the assassination attempt, but he had a point. "Do you think they are trying to wipe away all those outside the agency who they think might know how to use it? Or do you think that's too far-fetched even for them, Harry?"

He knew how the formula worked, to not only break but how to write the cybernetic encryption applied to the email that had people in London and Langley jumping up and down like demented rabbits. Although I was not guilty of jumping up and down, I certainly counted myself amongst those having no knowledge of what volumetric spears were, let alone multiple layered analytic engines. But, were we saved because Sabah Al Salim knew, or were we lost forever?

So that was where we began the debriefing session that was to continue into the early hours of the next day. I had some food delivered from the local restaurant, which was nothing unusual, and I moderated my drinking which was unusual. Jerry fell in with the revised behaviour to suit Sabah's religious beliefs, but in other respects we did not hold off.

I wanted to keep the atmosphere light, certainly not mentioning Vasilyev, so I spoke of his late cousin, Sheikh Talib Habbad. I imagined Jerry Furley knew the name, but if not, I didn't think it was important.

With what I hoped was an encouraging smile, I asked if he knew who had killed his cousin."Yes," he replied. "I had him killed. I had to. He was discovered passing on secrets to the French."

The well-liked cousin was found to be passing on Iranian classified secret material to the Frenchman, Page Boucher. It was Samantha who had told Sabah about his treacherous relative. Jerry was ignoring me. Until he asked what happened after his cousin was killed. Apparently, Page Boucher was in Sabah Al Salim's pocket from then on, as he too was exposed by Samantha Burns to be selling French secrets to the Syrians, as well as to the Lebanese.

With the tape recorder of Jerry's mobile recording device working overtime, Sabah explained some of the implications to the one-way trade Boucher was operating with the Syrians. The grouping of Hizballah, ISIS, Hamas and the Abdullah Azzam Brigades, all benefitted in some ways from what Page Boucher supplied, but overall it was Hizballah who benefitted the most, with the Iranian cousin's contributions taken into account. Sabah went on to confirm Iran provided monetary aid to Hizballah, with a proportion of it finding its way into an account in the Pegasus bank.

As far as Jerry was aware, none of what Sabah said was known to MI6. He wanted it all recorded on computer files, so he left the two of us speaking without being able to connect the attempt on Sabah life to anything in his life-threatening existence. One of the only matters we could agree on was that everything has a price, including death, with perhaps revenge having the highest value in a market where the devil is the supreme ruler.

Before we could finish, I decided to return the conversation to our shared vocation; the gathering of knowledge held secretly. He said he had not heard of any illegal British agents operating inside Pakistan, India or any in Afghanistan, but he was aware of one in Iran. He knew of the same number, but with a different name, operating in Iraq. He had an agent, who he named, inside the Daesh group of ISIS operating in South Africa.

His agent was working in the South African Ministry of Defence. It was when the South Africans met with their opposite numbers in the Defence Ministry of the Iranian government, that the illegal inside the Iranian Ministry was identified. Not only did that meeting have Alexi Vasilyev very jumpy, Sabah Al Salim was, too.

A similar anxious experience was felt over the military command of ISIS. There was one person whom the facial identification department of Section 9 at Vauxhall was confident of knowing with a strong degree of certainty. It was another deputy military leader inside ISIS; one Abu Saleh Al-Sabaid, whom I'm sure I mentioned being recorded by an IOMS unit as also being at Ar Raqqah. He wasn't an illegal of course, but the officer below him in rank was.

This officer had been successfully nurtured by

Sabah Al Salim over several years of patient, solid, intelligence work. There was an occasion which led him to disclose his superior officer's, Abu Saleh Al-Sabaid's, sexual orientation. He carried on with his story to tell how it manifested itself in a less than discreet manner. Abu Saleh Al-Sabaid's indiscretion allowed Sabah Al Salim to recruit and secure him for, as he said 'the good of Iran', without his subordinate knowing. It meant they were spying on each other.

Between the two of them, Iran was supplied with top-grade insights into the hierarchy of ISIS, along with not only, under certain circumstances, future targets, but the methods they employed to get inside other countries' networks. Women were specifically recruited for this work. He said he could supply details of names, along with the addresses they used, when his wound had stopped throbbing. I offered the use of my private, London doctor which he thought might be a good idea. It was too late to call, but he agreed with my suggestion to call later that morning.

We moved on to how Jimmy Mercer had come by the codes to the Iranian radar command centre. Sabah was hesitant, and it wasn't to do with his wound, that was not troubling him. I asked what was the matter, to which he replied, somewhat curiously, "Would you mind if I answered that a bit later, as it's quite involved." Having no option but to agree, I waited for him to move the conversation along. This he did, but in a direction I was not completely happy with.

He did apparently know something of Alexi Vasilyev's defection. He knew he was thinking about it. That had come from, of all people, Agapov, but he did not know it had already happened. I knew Agapov was a talkative chap but I didn't know he was that loose-lipped.

I glossed over my thoughts on Valery Agapov, not wishing to get bogged down in any of the details, but it had certainly surprised me to learn he would give away information as sensitive as a fellow Russian's thoughts on defection. I shouldn't have been surprised, should I?

It wouldn't normally matter, the fact of Sabah knowing or not knowing; what did matter to him and matter a great deal, was Agapov's other great revelation of the day, that of Alexi Vasilyev being an American double agent. Could the fact of him being a double agent rebound on Sabah?

Why? Because through the thorough application of his practised hand, he had, over years, propelled a known American illegal into a very senior position as the personal secretary to the highest-ranking officer in solitary command of the Iranian Army. She was there for Sabah to have an extra pair of eyes on the military.

Years ago, so he said, he was informed that the woman was working for the Americans by an anonymous CIA agent using tradecraft employed by agents of his own SAVAMA. Everything was going well until he heard Agapov declare Vasilyev was an agent for the American government. That's when he started to be worried about what could happen if it had been Vasilyev who originally placed this illegal?

The information crossing this woman's desk that could be of some interest to the Americans, would concern the Iran-Iraqi war, along with the differences between the Shia and Sunni Moslems. It was radical information, but not security-threatening. It would be worse if Vasilyev knew it was Sabah who was now 'running' the illegal. Sabah might be approached by the CIA, the approach could be fatal—for him!

Added to all that worry was what Valery Agapov had said of the positions Alexi Vasilyev held in the modern day Russian SVR. The whole package made Sabah apprehensive about Vasilyev. He was disturbed enough to make him realise he was in desperate need of friends.

If Vasilyev was operating this female illegal, she could quite reasonably expect to be executed for being engaged in espionage. But Sabah was not operating her, he only knew of her! However, he would have a huge problem proving it was not detrimental to the State. All he wanted to know from her was what the military were planning in regards to possible regime changes. He didn't need to know what Vasilyev knew. This was where Jimmy Mercer and the codes came in.

For some time, Sabah had been watching two of the most senior ranking officers of the Iranian armed services, whom he suspected of plotting against him. Five months ago, an army Colonel came to him claiming he'd overheard a group of officers, including the two Sabah least trusted, praising the constitution of a new intelligence service one of Sabah's nemeses was proposing.

The Colonel feared for his life if he was to be named in any prosecution. Both these officers were too highly placed in the military order for unsubstantiated allegations to impact. The Colonel said he had been ignored for promotion and wanted simple recognition.

In spite of Sabah's might and influence, he felt the Iranian military were too powerful for him to mount an attack on its hierarchical structure. He needed to devise a clever plan to destabilise the armed forces by discrediting those two senior officers, thereby sending a signal to them all in the armed services—disloyalty would not be tolerated, instead it would be severely punished.

If he was successful with his machinations, two potential problems would be dealt with simultaneously. However, all was not as simple as he hoped it would be. Despite trying as hard as he could to concoct a viable proposal, where someone other than the American illegal would be held accountable for the leak, he couldn't. Then, as if by providence, along came news from Agapov—Vasilyev, the double agent, was to defect.

Could he be devious enough to use Alexi Vasilyev's position as a double agent to his advantage? He thought and thought and thought. Eventually coming up with a strategy devised around a message giving details of the location of a stock of weapon-producing uranium-235.

Using the same encryption process the American communication officer had shown Sabah, he was able to route the message through an IP address that, if you knew how to do it, and Sabah now did, could be traced to a Syrian Colonel serving on President Bashar al-Assad's staff in the army headquarters in Damascus.

The signal gave the map reference to the place where the unregistered stock was kept. The message went on to say, if the negotiations were concluded successfully, the uranium would be shipped to Chabahar Port, in the Gulf of Oman. The same Iranian port Sabah used for his own benefit. This port, along with Sabah's shipping company, had been used countless times before when dealing with a valuable cargo where any cash would be divided up.

The communication was intercepted by the signals centre of SAVAMA's command. First, the body of the message was decoded. It then went directly to Sabah's deck. The precise details of location and product being offered had to be decoded by him. He then acted as he would whenever a chance of extra remuneration arose for the inner circle of specially chosen government influencers.

Following respective spheres of procedure, he forwarded it to the head of the Navy. The Admiral would provide a ship, ostensibly on manoeuvres, to act as a guarantor of safe passage for Sabah's freighter. Employing protocol previously used, Sabah sent notification of prospective measures to the heads of the Justice department, Defence and Armed Forces Logistics department, as well as the Economic Affairs and Finance departments.

Not one word of the signal would go anywhere near the American illegal working from the headquarters of the army. From then on, Sabah had to be extremely vigilant with the precautions he took. All his time-practised customs were adhered to when any contract of cash value was on offer involving the shipping of cargo.

He double-checked everything, then, after checking again, made sure all the necessary in-house emails were sent to those who would normally profit from the distribution of cash.

His own Persis Shipping Company was the perpetually used company of choice. The company not only supplied the ship with crew, but also all the bonus payments to those normally involved in like operations. The money divided would not be paid until completion, as per protocol.

Instructions were put in motion for the manifest of the ship to register a container of 'Drilling Machinery' to be loaded from the port of Durban, South Africa. Persis Shipping had a vessel in the North Atlantic calling at the port of Nouakchott, Mauritania on the western coast of Africa. It was picking up cargo for Madagascar. The captain of the *Derafsh*, the designated ship, was notified of the diversion to South Africa; it was just another cargo shipment to him.

Nothing of harmful calibre was ever recorded in the Persis Company ledgers for future discovery. Anything that would normally be deemed unfavourable, was recorded in a set of specially prepared copied manifest books. Under these circumstances, a cargo of radioactive uranium-235, the origin of which was questionable, would be classified as an unfavourable cargo.

All these measures were put in place for the inevitable enquiry Sabah anticipated. They mirrored exactly what would occur if such a cargo really existed, necessitating the special arrangements that would be made at the Iranian end.

After the impromptu approach was concluded to his satisfaction, his thoughts turned to a subject closer to his heart; one of revenge. He wanted the two military officers his irritation was fixed on, to be executed without formality. If they were dishonourably discharged, it left them alive, able to seek their own revenge. The two concerned were: a Major-General of the Islamic Revolutionary Guard Corps, Ground Forces, with the same Fleet Admiral of the Islamic Revolutionary Guard Corps to whom his signal was delivered.

He started composing a dispatch founded squarely on sincere humanitarian concerns over this forthcoming cargo. Copies of the initial communication itemising the shipment were forwarded on to both men at the beginning of the weekend, when their mail boxes were not being constantly monitored by any secretary.

On the pretext of it being an exercise, measuring the different rates of response to different degrees of alerts, he instructed some junior communication cadets to create, then send, messages about the combined armed services' level of readiness to face a land, sea and air invasion, to the head of the air force, the head of the army, and the head of the navy. They should be sent at differing times of day to reflect what could be the emerging intensity of battle. He gave an outline to what should be included in the early messages, leaving the ones that could follow to the cadets' imaginations. Create a complete War Games scenario against one, then two, attackers, he suggested. His idea was to fill the General's and Admiral's mailboxes with so much signal traffic that the messages sent by Sabah about the cargo were buried.

He set about his task to not only write the message, but disguise where it originated. When happy he had the text as he wanted, he drove himself to the Amir Al-Momenin University, an Islamic Revolutionary military College, where he found an office to send his public-spirited message. But his target audience at that stage was not any of the newspapers where it was destined to be printed, nor any of the news broadcast stations. No, first it went as one half of a bargaining chip.

In exchange for the codes allowing access into the Iranian radar control centre that Sabah Al Salim gave to Jimmy Mercer, Jimmy arranged to have Sabah's carefully worded message re-routed around the billions of untraceable algorithms in the computers as the Director of National Intelligence had absolute control over at the Pentagon. For good luck, he sent the message around a further billion or so algorithms at the computer complex inside the Virginia headquarters of the U.S. Department of Defence.

When Jimmy Mercer was satisfied the IP address of the originator of the message, winging its way to the editor at the Washington Post, was without doubt a certain Major-General of the Islamic Revolutionary Guard Corps, Ground Forces named Abbas Afzali, the message was sent.

Embedded into the text of the email was the Major-General's full name with rank. His electronic signature was proudly displayed alongside the signature of Karim Nader Hosseini, Fleet Admiral of the Islamic Revolutionary Guard Corps.

That weekend, the article appeared in a prominent online newspaper, as well as making it onto the same newspaper's print version, which had a small distribution network, mainly in the Middle East. By the first editions of the following day, it was carried by all the major European newspapers as well as being broadcast on a wide variety of televised news channels, ranging from Africa News, to Sky News, to the BBC, to CNN, to the Al Jazeera news outlet. The translated version read—

> *To our utmost disgust, we find the country we have both served for the majority of our lives to be procuring perilous weapon grade uranium to help construct a nuclear bomb. It is our combined opinion the government of Iran is pushing our country towards being the creators of an end of the world sequence of events. The world is dangerous enough without our beloved country having governments wanting nuclear weapons of such desolation.*

To this statement was added the official stamps of office the two philanthropic military companions occupied. Unfortunately, neither the General nor the Admiral were aware they'd signed the documents, when away from their offices at home with their families.

In order to corroborate this evidence of sedition, an email was formulated by an officer on Jimmy Mercer's national cybersecurity staff, who sent it to the second-in-command of the Revolutionary Guards, a Brigadier-General. In the message, Vasilyev praised his boss, the Major-General Abbas Afzali, for the way his Islamic Revolutionary Guard Corps had conducted themselves in a recent action taken to repel a combined incursion force of American and Iraqi military, on the Iran Iraqi border.

Nothing demonic in that, you think? Well, it wouldn't be except it was dated in March last year and addressed from Alexi Vasilyev's offices on Moscow's Ulitsa Kuznetsky, but Alexi never sent it!

It was there ready to be found when the Iranian government instructed Sabah Al Salim's national counter-intelligence offices of SAVAMA to examine the case of treason against the General and the Admiral. Neither the commander of the Islamic Revolutionary Guard Corps, nor the Admiral of the Navy, were able to defend themselves against the shocking attacks on their integrity and loyalty.

The two thorns that had been inside Sabah's shoes were removed by bullets from a firing squad three days after the article appeared, by which time Alexi Vasilyev was in protective custody in America, unaware of what was happening in Iran.

On the same day as the execution, Liam Gibson's team of selected experts, using the codes provided, gained entry to the Iranian radar monitoring station. A few seconds after they were inside the building, the radar located a solitary Israeli F-35 stealth fighter jet less than twenty miles from the Iranian border. There was also the faint trace of what was suspected to be a Boeing 707, a refuelling aircraft. As a message was about to be sent to the Air Defence Command, all the screens in the radar monitoring centre went dark as the Command Centre lost all power.

Roughly two minutes later, a large building on the same site as the Bushehr Nuclear Power Plant, next to the calm waters of the Persian Gulf, was wiped from the face of this earth.

The captain onboard the *Derafsh* was cabled by the manager of Sabah's Persis Shipping, telling him of the need to cancel the load from Durban. Every email sent to the parties concerned in the division of funds from the cargo were informed of the cancelation, but mysteriously, whoever it was who had sent the original order for the cargo could not be found.

Before Sabah had finished his business with me, he mentioned how Alexi Vasilyev had been obstructing the move of the bank from Samothrace by delaying the progress of the construction works at Tartus. He said Vasilyev had just one objective—to extract money from the trustees of the bank. His motive relied on keeping the RAF radar installation on Cyprus for as long as possible.

I didn't pass comment. But my thoughts turned to silently ask if something had taken precedence over money in Alexi's mind for him to decide to jump now, or did he think he could still pull the strings of Tartus from a safe place in America?

If the Russian signal defences were erected quickly, the radar installations on Cyprus were redundant, making the transfer of the radar equipment to the island of Samothrace more urgent. This would, of course, necessitate leaving the runway on Cyprus open for operational use until the one on Samothrace was constructed. He was somewhat perplexed, he said, by the statement he'd heard the head of the American intelligence community make. Apparently, he said the Americans would hand over the facilities, along with the runway on Samothrace, when completed, to the RAF for use. Great Britain would have two airstrips available in the eastern edge of the Mediterranean.

"Why would you need two?" he asked. To which, in that moment of time, I had no answer.

* * *

Before I could find sleep, I had to address what had been rolling through my mind ever since I spoke to the first police officer on the scene at St James's Street. Of course, I knew of the occasion when Judith Meadows was part of a team sent from MI6 and the CIA to take Sabah's life, and although it had crossed my mind to tell him about it, I had not mentioned it. I had a voice message from Gardie House from Captain William Lloyd. My absence had been noticed. Apparently, Miss Fields was missing me. There were still things to cover so I needed to find time to visit.

CHAPTER TWENTY-FIVE

THE BANK OF FIRST CHOICE

It was over breakfast the following morning that Sabah announced that after all, he would not be staying until the assassin was found. My doctor was due this morning at eleven, but even news of his arrival would not stop him from returning to his apartment. He had been thinking of nothing else but the attempt on his life. The name of the man I'd shot came through whilst we were still at Knightsbridge, and Sabah had been phoning all his contacts ever since then to track down the name, without success.

Jerry Furley had returned to Chester Square as Sabah excused himself to retire to bed, taking some paracetamols with him for pain relief. The two of us caught up a little on drinking my whisky whilst discussing the list of people we could think of who might have wanted revenge on Sabah Al Salim for one reason or another. No matter how hard we looked, the shooter did not seem to be one of them.

His name was Phillip Adams, aged twenty-two, with quite a record of being a violent transgressor involving assault of various criminal degrees one might expect to be recorded against a person willing to kill another human seemingly without a motive, other than what could only be money.

His father, along with additional members with the same family name, had connections to a known South London gang noted for armed robberies, as well as violent crime involving aggression of one sort or another, but there was nothing associated to Iranian politics or the Middle East.

The circumstances of the executions of the two senior military officers who had caused so much antagonism for Sabah, had caused no hostile comments to appear in Iranian newspaper other than what could be expected from anti-authoritarians. The Admiral's name brought forward no utterance from any anarchists, but for the full Major-General it was a thoroughly different matter. The news reports had been intercepted by GCHQ, to be verified, then forwarded on to Jerry Furley.

Evidently the General was a man who had seen action in Syria. His name was noted by a reporter at a press conference as having had been mentioned by the Russian 'advisors' in their war against ISIS as a formidable tactician. He was referred to more than once as a far-sighted, yet guarded man, who was walking in his father's footsteps. It surely wasn't beyond imagination there could be someone in the General's family who wanted revenge, but he had only been dead for a matter of days.

There was a dedicated section of the Ministry of Defence who dealt exclusively with ancestry. The tracing of relatives. They had been looking into Phillip Adams for some hours before being notified of the General. From a pragmatic point of view, it would seem more likely to be a revenge attack from a relative of the General's than anything to do with Adams. The search widened.

* * *

We had briefly broached the subject of why he wanted to work with British intelligence, saying all I wanted was a brief summary of what he expected without going into too many incidentals. He admitted it was his worries about the agent inside the Iranian military being known by Vasilyev that had tipped him over to us. He could not turn to the Americans because, he alleged, Vasilyev as well as Mercer may well have issues with him as head of the Ministry of Intelligence and National Security of Iran. I told him I could understand his position.

He claimed Jimmy Mercer had changed his

ideals when confronted with the vast enormity of the holdings on deposit in the banking arm of the Pegasus Mercantile Company. Sabah's alleged personal deposit amounted to several billion dollars. Yes, billions! After I poured a reviving Jura for myself, he volunteered his approximation of Winston's deposit at ten to fifteen billion.

When I said I'd heard from someone about Bottomly's share in the bank being more than his own holdings, he said that whoever told me would be correct if he, or she, never knew all of the accounts he held under his index of miscellaneous pseudonyms.

The need for those names was twofold: oppression and jealousy. His aliases had been created from his Persian roots, as well as using his name at birth, and that's how I came to know Jimmy Mercer was telling me the truth during the time we had spent together in London's Regent's Park.

Before I said goodbye to Sabah that morning when he returned to his apartment, I asked him outright if he had told Jimmy Mercer about the Pegasus Bank being moved onto Bottomly's estate. If he had, how did Mercer react? He told me Mercer had not liked the idea. However, Sabah was insistent. I accepted his assurances over Jimmy Mercer holding no deposits in the bank of Pegasus.

That was not the reason for his dislike. I suspected it was because if the bank was to stay on Samothrace, he could, to some extent, monitor who had a stake in it despite most transactions being conducted online, or through transfers beginning at Pickering's Bank where he already had elaborate scanners available to the American fiscal departments.

When I eventually got around to speaking to Mercer, he used the example of catching Gibson with the gun only because of the physical presence on the island of the CIA. He was right, of course, but why not, I suggested, work with what he'd got to keep the bank where it was? He knew the name of who it was inside his intelligence community holding the keys of the Pegasus Bank. He actually had one of those favourite American words, leverage, on the situation.

I told him as far as I was aware, Sabah Al Salim would raise no objection to leaving the bank where it was for now, provided the source of his money was not examined further.

Mercer's primary interest was in the terrorist groups who used the facilities of the Pegasus Mercantile Company. They were able to clean the money they deposited in the bank by using the various legitimate arms of the company. He wanted to keep close to the bank, in order to know what these groups were thinking. As far as I could see, the effective control of the bank would be in his hands if he played his cards right, persuading the CIA officer to postpone the move.

If all went as it should, then Jimmy Mercer could tell his president that the Director-General of the American Department of National Intelligence, was now the executor of the Pegasus Bank.

"It wouldn't just be me as an executor, Harry. Whatever control I had on the bank business, I want you to have the same. I'm sure your Prime Minister would love to know how we manage the bank of first choice for your regular terrorist groups."

I chose not to comment on his speculation. Trying to curb my imagination running away with itself when it came to keeping such a thing as he proposed secret, was becoming a losing battle. I considered announcing I would become tea-total, unless he admitted he was away with the fairies. Nevertheless, I did find enough energy to comment on Alexi Vasilyev's delaying tactics at the Tartus site, saying if the Russians were not aware of his strategy, it could still work.

I recommended the CIA looked for someone else to take over that course of action, to which Mercer asked if I was going to put my name forward for the role. I laughed, then said I thought the Syrian government might complain. We spoke more about Bottomly, which put the photograph back in my mind. I didn't want Jimmy to know anything about it, but even so I would need the physical item at some stage. It was something I had no choice about.

Another no choice option for me was to visit Shetland and Miss Fields, as she's known, on the island of Bressay. With Sabah Al Salim wanting to work closely with me, the very last thing I needed was for him to be killed whilst I sat back in comparative comfort for a journey I was becoming bored with.

* * *

The aftermath of the assassination attempt in St James's Street, London, had been seen on the television screens at Gardie House. There was one television set in the library where Judith had seen it all, but luckily my name was not mentioned. That wasn't the case for the premeditated victim of the attempted assassination, Sabah Al Salim, nor the dead Phillip Adams, who was revealed as the assailant.

She was outside in the garden at Gardie where I asked her if she knew Adams. She didn't. Her kind of logic led her to ask, in an accusing fashion, if it was me who'd shot him. I was taken aback by her question, but admitted to myself that throughout our conversations, particularly the ones at The Hall, her line of logical thinking was impressive.

I confessed, and was almost knocked over again by her response. She actually asked if I was okay. Adding how she knew what it took to kill someone.

Of course she did. *You're an idiot, Harry,* I told myself. If I needed proof of my stupidity, it was there in her admission.

It was as I was about to light my first cigarette since arriving on the island when I had a flash of déjà vu, or whatever it's called when a past memory flashes across your mind. I was with Judy, as I referred to her then, in, I think, Paulo's hotel suite in Switzerland, when she said she'd found something in the conversation the three of us were having, and was off to find a telephone to call the permanent First Secretary to the Foreign and Commonwealth Office in London, Sir David Haig.

The call she made was about what Paulo Sergeyovitch Korovin had said when he'd been put in charge of the repatriation of all the state-owned Russian assets at the time the Federation of Soviet States was abolished. He thought his job would centre on military equipment, which he did have to deal with, but that wasn't the only part of his remit.

In the portfolio he was given, there were several laboratories where equipment needed to be retrieved, along with an enormous amount of, what was itemised as stock. The laboratories and the stock were bundled as one, with the same coding of Pasha. It was that name that was pushing my memory into top gear, remembering it all as if it had just been said.

Paulo's first line of enquiry indicated that the laboratories were strictly commercial, operating for profit in supplying the markets that Russia dominated in several African countries, along with some of Russia's neighbours in Europe, as well as the emerging markets of Brazil and India, where they were exporting large amounts of normal pharmaceuticals.

As he made tentative investigations into the stock held at those sites, he came up with what he expected —conventional medicines and vaccines, along with mainstream research, all again under the same code name of Pasha. Nothing was divided into any A or B listings.

He was intrigued, but when he tried to look deeper he was blocked out of the system. Even he at his high level of clearance could not access the data. The only thing he could testify to was that there had been regular shipments of unspecified material, simply classified as 'pharmaceutical compounds' to the very volatile Middle Eastern countries of Iran, Iraq, Syria, and Lebanon. He put this together with his knowledge of those regions, and came up with biological weapons as being an explanation. That's what I presumed had upset Judith Meadows.

As my mind cleared of that moment in my past, I was reminded of something I had been thinking of earlier concerning Aunt Alice's account of Viscount Bottomly's racial prejudice. The extent of how extreme he was with it. He was so fanatical, or so she said, he frightened her. It was as I was thinking of him, that I thought of the bank.

If Sabah was taken out of the workings of the Pegasus bank, then Agapov, wearing his Yuri Bogdan label, would have much more authority over its day-to-day operations. The same would apply, of course, about the Count, Viscount Winston Bottomly. He didn't know the CIA would arrest him with Liam Gibson. So, even with the arrest, it was feasible that a two-man team from Gibson's specials could have been prepared for the assassination attempt on Sabah's life. I excused myself from Judith and made a call.

Jimmy Mercer had beaten me to it. He'd asked Gibson if either he or the Count were implicated in the attack as soon as he'd heard of the attempt on Sabah Al Salim's life. They were not. Mercer was sure the answer he got from them both was the truth. How he recognised the truth was for him to say, but I thought I might have trouble with it. What about Agapov? Now, there was a possibility. All of a sudden my mind was going everywhere. It might sound stupid, I know, but I needed something to stabilise it.

I had missed calls from Katherine as well as from Serena, and neither had left a message, which meant I had no idea why they'd called. I hoped it was to find out how I was, yet there was one part of me that doubted it would not be without some complaint from Serena about accommodation, or from Katherine, some agonising over Vasilyev. I decided I was in the wrong mood to call. It would be better to leave them both until later. The redirection I'd found had not stopped my mind from wandering. There was more to come as my mind wandered onto topics I thought I'd dealt with.

Whatever it was that panicked Chevron it was powerful enough for him to reveal his fear of detection to Moscow. Quite some step after his years inside our system and, if he played his cards right, many more years to come! He must have experienced other close situations than just the one Colette apparently presented. Surely? No, it was not her. I was certain of it. But going back over those times, there was never someone for Bottomly to report to. There was no evidence of there being a man called Jackson. No evidence of Bottomly ever going to Beaulieu to learn his tradecraft. Why did he take the risk of saying he had done so?

Was it Bottomly who frightened Chevron? Could it have been his clumsiness over this Colette? His disregard of standardised protocol? As of yet, I had discovered nothing to link Chevron and Bottomly and it would stay that way, unless a big IF, in Capital Letters, came strolling along my way.

Could it be, I asked myself, markets in Africa, where the biological weapons from Russia were being exported to. Was it Bottomly's AWB, in South

Africa, who were inadvertently rocking Chevron's boat? Was it a home team's own goal with the exported 'pharmaceutical compounds' that pushed Chevron over the edge enough to take on Colette and shepherd this Count elsewhere? If that was true, then I thought it was time to catch someone else.

CHAPTER TWENTY-SIX
DEMENTIA

I had returned a few of those unanswered calls I've mentioned, including the one made by Katherine. I was delighted to discover she had indeed phoned to enquire into my well-being. After I had assured her I was perfectly okay, the next few moments were pleasurably spent catching up with the past and just chatting of easier times in both our lives.

Without effort our conversation drifted onto Luca, but despite the cordiality of it all I had the unenviable task of asking if she wanted to see Alexi Vasilyev before he was relocated. Again, she showed a side of herself I thought she possessed, but was never completely sure until this day. She asked how I would feel about another man having an input and, to some degree, an influence over Luca's upbringing?

I gave the only answer I could. I said I would regret not being with my son, but the fault for that was mine. Perhaps, had I tried harder, the two of us could have developed into something more than what we had both settled for. I added how I thought she must genuinely love Alexi. Here again, I expressed my regrets, as well as my doubts this time, about how Luca would react to Vasilyev's mutilated condition.

Would he grow used to it, accepting Alexi's appearance as one would accept anyone's outward appearance, or would our son be embarrassed, or provoked, if he suffered ridicule from ignorant children of his own age? I added how, although we all dream of living in a utopian paradise, it's not to be found on this earth.

The consideration of Luca's mocking peers heaping shame upon him, were issues she would have to address if she wanted a lasting relationship with them both. I left it there, I said, as Vasilyev's injuries were not my own, nor were Luca's feelings. As I closed the call I felt utterly lonely. I think it was loneliness behind the reason I thought of the next person.

I hadn't thought of Serena for quite some time, but although I did need to return her calls, I couldn't think of anything to say. She was in control of her everyday and business life, without any need of me. That was also true with Breno. In his life, she was directing his academic studies commendably, alongside the skills he had since birth with horses, which were increasing daily. Her handprint on his life was admirable and, in lots of ways; I envied them.

A sinking moment of regret came over me. I was on the deck of an enormous boat, surrounded by shipping containers all being lashed by mammoth waves. I was keeping upright by hanging onto a rope, but my grip gave way meaning I was about to be swept overboard when the next wave crashed into the boat. It was Judith's hand that pulled me back from my nightmare as I saw her reach out into the surging sea from the shoreline, whisking me ashore through some kind of magic, to be sitting opposite her in the garden at Gardie.

I shook the feeling of malaise away as quickly as I could, drawing just a passing comment from Judith who asked if the journey to the island had been especially tiring as I looked in need of sleep. I thanked her for the concern, adding, without, I hoped, any ominous tone, how it was time for our final question and answer session, with a lot hanging in the balance.

To myself, I wondered where her version of the truth would take me? Would I be as certain as Jimmy Mercer had been with Bottomly and Gibson, or would I be left to doubt her? I wondered aloud if the catalyst could have been in Switzerland, when we were both there? I excused myself for a second time, explaining how I needed to make one more telephone call before we could begin. She smiled, as would matron at boarding school when one had a slight chill and wanted a day off lessons, with matron knowing exactly what you were doing, but was... indulgent.

* * *

I called Jerry Furley, then waited nervously for him to return the call. Even allowing for the fact it had not taken long in measurable time on a clock face for him to call back, it felt like years of my life had flown past without my memory assembling a single record of it.

As I dialled the number Furley had given me, I wondered if this strange agitation I felt might have been an everyday event for the once permanent first secretary to the Foreign and Commonwealth Office, Sir David Haig. He was, so Judith had informed me at the time, a relative of the infamous 'Butcher Haig', or Douglas Haig, 1st Earl Haig of World War I notoriety. Yet, having displayed that amount of knowledge, she never did get around to saying how the two men were related. That was the subject with which I opened our telephone conversation, asking what relationship he had to the Field Marshal of the First World War. There was a motive behind the question.

Sir David had been retired from public life for almost eight years, he told me, but he could still clearly recall both me and Judith Meadows and also the name of man now referred to as Chevron, but the awkward thing was, he added, he could not remember what relationship he had with the 1st Earl Haig.

With abject sincerity, he declared he had the onset of dementia, adding quickly, before I could even think of a suitable reply, that he was perfectly able to remember clearly everything there was about Judith Meadows, a one-time British intelligence operative. He could also remember the conversation he had just had with the current head of MI6, with all being authenticated by a phone call to the headquarters of the Secret Intelligence Service, Vauxhall. His clarity was the reason behind my question. I hoped he was right.

I asked him if anything strange or even plain odd had happened after Judith Meadows, with Chevron, was arrested for treason. Specifically about any pharmaceuticals his department had notice of being exported by the Russian Federation. He hesitated for what seemed a lifetime, making my fears about him not being able to remember what the date was becoming more real with every breath I took, when suddenly I swear I could hear his jaw moving with the deliberate enunciation of each word as though his life depended on it.

"I could not possibly forget, Lord Paterson. The day after your man was flown out to Poland, for the Americans' exchange, I think he went over the border at Mażucie, into Russian Kaliningrad, I had a call from the Hellenic Greek Minister of the Interior, to give him his full title. His name was Vasso something."

The line went quiet before Sir David apologised for forgetting the man's surname, causing me to stifle a laugh. There was me sweating on him remembering anything and all he'd forgotten was, what he said was a difficult to pronounce Greek surname. The silence didn't last for long."This Greek Minister, Vasso someone, said he'd heard from the Port Commissioner on the island of Samothrace, in the Thracian Sea, to say the port police had reason to search a British-registered yacht.

"During the search of the yacht, a quantity of glass laboratory slides, all thankfully in hermetic sealed containers, was discovered. The slides were covered in an unknown white substance which was obviously not cocaine. The port authorities sent the unopened containers to the nearest laboratories, which were at the General University Hospital on the mainland at Alexandroupolis. On examination, they were found to contain spores of Bacillus Anthracis. And I'm sure you know what that is."

I replied I knew the substance to be every terrorist's dream, and the whole of civilisation's nightmare —anthrax. He finished this part of our conversation by saying he didn't have much more to do with it, other than he notified the Ministry of Defence at Porton Down. He then had another telephone call on the subject later that day.

This time it was about Greece, rather than from Greece. A Special Branch inquiry into this anthrax was directed to his department from the Home Office. The Home Office official wanted to give Sir David what he called a 'heads-up' on a person they thought Sir David might know. His name was Sir Arthur Birch, who David said he knew very well. He was the chief civil servant at the Department for International Development. Which was, in fact, a branch of the Foreign and Commonwealth Office.

"Sir Arthur Birch told the police officer from the Ministry of Defence who went to interview him, that he had a property in Greece on the island of Samothrace, outside a village called Alonia."

I was on the verge of complimenting Sir David on his powers of memory, but any words I may have wanted to use vanished as soon I opened my mouth to reply with something I thought important, only to find no word would form on my tongue. Eventually, it came to me.

"It was on Alonia where Gerald Neil told me he had his estate!"

* * *

The yacht on which the spores had been found was owned by Sir Arthur, but he seldom used it, he said, owing to an accident he had whilst driving in the 24-hour Le Mans car race of 1998. The sting to this story came when all was investigated and the name of one of Sir Arthur's two co-drivers for the race was disclosed—it was the real name of Chevron.

It had been Chevron who had chartered the captain with a two-man crew to sail Sir Arthur Birch's yacht and load the sealed cargo from a building with the Greek lettering for Scientific Research at a place on the Gallipoli peninsula called Cape Helles. Chevron had made those arrangements eleven days before his arrest.

When he was interviewed the chartered yacht captain agreed with the investigating authorities, thinking it to be slightly suspicious, but "what wasn't, in the waters of the Aegean?" he answered, smiling at the inquisitive port police officer, quickly adding, "but it was an English gentleman who had arranged it."

Sir David spoke to Birch, asking for his thoughts on how something so deadly as anthrax had come to be on his yacht. He said he knew Chevron's father, Sir Raymond, who had a seat on the board at Smith-Kline Beecham, and indeed knew his son had some sort of dealings there. He presumed Chevron's laboratory, that he'd allowed to be built on a part of his property on Samothrace, was something to do with research conducted away from, as he put it, 'corporate eyes'.

The Ministry of Defence sent a Chief Superintendent with a Sergeant to carry his bags, to fly out to

Greece, with a forensic unit from Porton Down. On arrival, the party was met by Greek police who ferried them, with their equipment, to the island.

The examination of Chevron's not insignificant laboratory, as well as the four wooden outbuildings, took six days in total, with the slides of bacteria cells securely packaged and flown back to Porton Down for safe, secure eradication.

By this time of course, Sir David added, Chevron was gone, so he thought it to be a needless burden on everyone concerned to cause Sir Arthur any further embarrassment by moving the case along to the Intelligence Services. He said he hoped I was well, then hung up. I didn't have the time, nor the heart, to explain to him how things had changed!

I was thankful for his ability to remember so much detail, having come across such a memory once before. It was Sophie with her Hyperthymesia, her exceptional memory. I hoped both of them would escape dementia in later life.

Forgetfulness happens to us all, as in this case. If Chevron had indeed been linked with research into fentanyl when I came across him, then surely that would have been investigated by someone after I was stood down from his case. The investigation I was concerned with did not lead me to suspect he would have a research laboratory on the island of Samothrace. It wasn't long before I found out this was the secret Judith wanted so much to tell me about. But I wanted the other secret that maybe she knew.

"When you went to the Bottomly estate with the rest of your family, Judith, when you were a child of ten or twelve, I think you said, did our man Chevron accompany you?"

We were seated under a tall, spreading sycamore tree that was ever so gently swaying in the breeze. There was a tray of two teacups, milk jug with teapot and hot water jug under a cosy, on a normal-sized, round, metal garden table, painted in the best navy grey colour one could find.

The crockery was a real surprise, as it was of the dainty kind, not the more usual heavy mug sort that only comes in depressing shades of pretend colour. Our cups came on saucers, all covered with the same matching pattern of butterflies, with bespoke room for the little finger to be extended, as propriety dictated. I had thrown the question at her as she had decided to be 'mother' without any argument coming from my side of the table.

"Yes, he was there then. As he was every time I went out to South Africa with Father. He mostly came with us, or was there before we arrived. I'm surprised you never saw a photograph of the two of them together."

"Did you ever overhear them speaking of any pharmaceuticals at all? I don't mean paracetamols or the like, but deadly bacteria spores more likely?"

"No, I bloody well did not! No! Are you suggesting either of those two men would have anything to do with bacteria, or biological warfare? How about what do I know of bioterrorism? Hmm, want me to draw you a picture, do you? Do you imagine I might know the best spot for Sarin on the London underground? Of course I do not, nor did anyone I know speak of such atrocities, Harry. I'm so disappointed you could think it!"

Now I had Judith's truth—I've got no doubt anywhere in my body that she believed anything else could be possible. My truth was different. The facts fitted my truth, not hers.

* * *

I had to tell her some of my distressing truth. I told her how I thought Chevron had plans to use her to assassinate someone important, using the gun he had concealed on the island. The same gun she had used to murder in Paris. A British-trained killer murdering a Frenchman as well as a Frenchwoman on French soil. How about if the gun she used was subsequently used to kill a Muslim? Someone who believed and trusted the Western world? How about if she was discovered, as was Chevron's plan, literally holding the gun? Yes, I calmly told her protestations, I knew the target she was to be aimed at, and yes, I knew how the gun was to be delivered. And yes, I knew why it had to be this gun.

What I didn't know, I told her, was how would she look upon Chevron once all that had happened. Would she still have any love for him?

"Hmm?" I used her trade-mark exclamation to reflect my distaste for a liar, especially a lonely one so accustomed to telling lies that the truth becomes impossible to see.

CHAPTER TWENTY-SEVEN

WHO'S DIGGING FOR OIL?

Judith had been allotted a destination. I was at Gardie House when the notification came through to me, in code. It took me almost thirty minutes to decode it, after which it was put through the Ministry of Defence secure shredder in Captain William Lloyd's office.

Together we looked the destination up on Google maps—on the shore line of Bragg Creek, near the Elbow River hamlet. It wasn't far, about ten miles we guessed, from the centre of the oil-rich town of Calgary with its skyscraper office blocks, designer shops with plush restaurants and bars, as well as the Calgary Stampede, its massive July rodeo.

The so-called Canadian oil capital was a mere two hundred kilometres from the American border. Nor was she far from like-minded, sympathetic Russians. One, surprise, surprise, being Christopher Metsos, now Signalman. No longer to be found at The Signals Sandwich Bar, Halls Mills. I didn't tell her the news of Metsos yet, I wanted her mind working on the chemical industry.

Finally, I had what I wanted in place to begin the further debrief I needed with her.

"I want to go back to Switzerland and find the letter Paulo put into George's jacket pocket the night he met his father for the first time. From what I can remember, George never saw it until the following morning, when he was packing to come home. He told you of it and that's when you told me about it.

"In this letter, Paulo claimed the chemical company I was working for was a cover for a wider operation, set up to enhance, as well as avert attention away from, what he called; major undercover operations. Unbeknown to us at the time, he was also telling us how Chevron was following Russia's thinking into how to absorb the impact biotechnology would make on the pharmaceutical industry. Not only for the profitable commercial manufacture of antibiotics, hormones and the like, but for the inclusion of bioweapons.

"Paulo went further. Alleging how two Russian placements inside a British company had, before they were discovered by MI5, been instrumental in propelling the British chemical industry to achieve a level of excellence other governments could only look on with envy. Because of the country's position, it became easy for these two to convince the government of the day into taking over the company I eventually joined.

"The Russian placements went further in this enterprise, advising the use of private funding to conceal any official involvement from public audit companies that were answerable to Parliament. The purpose of this was to disguise the perceived heavy hand of centralisation.

"If I remember correctly, he went on to say the real purpose of the takeover was not to deceive political commentators, it was to pass onto interested parties in Russia the direction the company was taking with biological fuels, such as ethanol and biodiesel, being developed in what was fast becoming the leading company in those fields in the world.

"The work my laboratory was concerned with was the evolution of a relatively new synthetic biofuel production using everyday waste such as garbage, animal fats, alongside spent cooking oil, to produce useable liquid fuels which was not only unique, but innovative as well. We had people willing to push the edges of any preconceived ideas, coming up with a new plastic compound which was both pliable yet solid in the same composites. But Russia wanted all this. They wanted the trade copyright to the intellectual work in order to shut it down so that Europe was dependent on Russia's own fossil fuels.

"My present day thinking is along the lines of—before Chevron was stopped, then exchanged, he passed on the process of production of this new plastic to Winston Bottomly, who directly funded the set-up he had on the island of Samothrace you were going to tell me about sometime before you went off to Canada."

"Bloody hell! Do you still blame someone other than yourself for all of your shortcomings, H? I mean to say, how many times have you asked me about the sodding island? Hmm, none? Is that about the score? You have never asked me!"

"I'll ignore your tantrum. Writing it off as juvenile excitement. Did you two talk about the properties of fentanyl into the small hours? How it works for pain? Or did you mix it with heroin for the trip of your life? Were those the topics of fireside conversations? What did the Turkish orphan want with a laboratory up in the hills of Samothrace, Judy?"

She was seated with her eyes pointing skywards into the swaying leaves of the sycamore tree, as she took one more of my cigarettes, having finished the five packets of her brand I'd brought her just the other day. The exact day, I had forgotten. Momentarily, I wished I had Sir David Haig's powers of memory, then, just as quickly as that thought entered my mind, so it went when I thought of all the bad memories I would be forced to confront rather than forget.

No, not remembering the precise day I gave her the cigarettes was not important, nor was her smoking my cigarettes important as long as I had enough, I thought, watching her exhaled smoke fight its way clear of the overhanging leaves still on the branches, waiting for their autumn drop.

She spoke before I had stopped day-dreaming. I was not ready for her to begin and far from ready for the depth of her reply.

"A short time before I was recruited, which if you remember correctly happened after my husband Tony was blown up in Afghanistan in 2001, there was a series of special units set up in Russia by one of the departments Valery Agapov was to inherit later on in his illustrious career. Of course, back then nobody told a little old nothing like me anything about special units, until, that is, I was recruited into the MI9 'kill squad' on our side that I told you about.

"I'm rather liking the American pseudonym of Chevron, so I'll play along, using the name. He met me soon after the aborted mission in Iraq to eliminate Sabah Al Salim. Incidentally, I know how the adrenalin was pumping through my veins after that operation, so I'm guessing you're still high from what happened in London." I shook my head to indicate I was fine.

"Okay, I guess we're all different. I will carry on

then." It was said as an objective rather than an enquiry. I nodded adding a very quiet "okay."

"He met me in his favourite place to conduct anything covert to do with The Box. The Vauxhall Tavern, in Harleyford Road in the one-way at Vauxhall Cross. That was when I heard of MI9, the name given to the units. He said he wanted to give them something in the future, but didn't say what that was. In the meantime, he wanted me to travel to meet up with a female operative from one of these American SCO15 units at a place called Beltsville, Maryland, America.

"This was where the headquarters of a highly classified department known as the Special Collection Service, or SCO, could be found. I was to make myself known to this woman, then pass on whatever it was he wanted me to take. I was to hang around waiting until she was ready to pass on to me whatever it was to come back. There was a national park nearby where I was to 'accidentally' meet this woman.

"It all sounds innocent enough, doesn't it? Routine recon, then a handover, nothing unusual apart from what he wanted me to take. It was one strip of ten, white-coloured tablets in blister pack form. It had one missing. They were about the same size and appearance as normal paracetamols. As the printing on the back attested to. *Paracetamol*, stamped diagonally across it. The missing tablet was, so he said, to confuse any customs officer into believing they were ordinary headache tablets and I'd taken one."

I went to say something, but was not allowed. She had sensed it.

"Let me finish before you say anything, please. I'm determined to get rid of it all. The American NSA, National Security Agency, is more complex, as well as more intricate, but is on a par to being the equivalent of GCHQ in many ways. The programme they, with the CIA, initiated under the umbrella of this SCO at Beltsville, was to insert eavesdropping equipment in difficult-to-reach places, such as foreign embassies, communications centres, along with unfriendly foreign government installations.

"They were also working on being able to close out communications from given sites such as the ones I've mentioned. The Americans coded it F6. Chevron wanted to know how all that was achieved, not only for Russia. He wanted to share some with the SIS, not for any patriotic reasons, Harry, so don't look so smug. It was purely egotistic.

"According to him, if he gave the Vauxhall top-floor gannets some snippets of intel, he said it would propel, not only his name, but mine as well up the invisible rungs on the ladder to a seat among the greedy on the top floor.

"Everything went smoothly with me giving over the blister pack to this woman, who I met again two days later when she gave a similar strip to me. This time two more of the tablets were missing. I can't be sure if it was the same strip, but it looked the same. The handover was simplicity itself. It was like two old friends meeting up when she came into the coffee shop I was seated in. She breezed over, with the usual rich, American style effervescence, saying, "Hi there, I'm glad to see you again so soon. That headache of mine went on its own. Here, I never used any of those pills you gave me. I think I was just a bit dehydrated and that's what brought it on."

"Chevron didn't tell me what, or if he did send anything over to the handlers on the top floor at Vauxhall, but I know my name was put forward onto the register for more decent jobs after that one. I never did get around to asking what that blister pack was, but I don't think it takes a lot of working out, does it?"

There was a pause, during which time I simply stared back at her piecing gaze, imagining her in the library in The Hall with her legs tucked under her spread-out figure, cushion on lap with fingers drumming on her notebook waiting for me to speak, but it was not I who broke the silence this time, it was she.

"I'm a terrible spy, H, aren't I?"

Despite not answering, I did bite hard onto my jaw, pulling in the line of my cheek as a kind of recognition to her honesty in answering some awkward questions in the difficult situation she found herself in. Stupidly, I hoped the gesture didn't go unnoticed.

* * *

Chevron had discovered a new way of passing on secrets on microfilm, or codes of some description, contained in a substance that resembled a common tablet. It was something I knew nothing about. I checked with Furley to find out if he knew of this practice. No, was the answer to my question. I had more luck with my enquiry into any intelligence coming away from the complex at Beltsville, Maryland, as well as knowing of the American department called SCO His answer was a yes to both these questions.

GCHQ was able to use part of the information that came out of the NSA/CIA operation to assist the defection we conducted in Warsaw. It shut down the communications from sensitive outlets for the time we needed. Two units from this 'SCO' were known to have penetrated a Ukrainian communications set-up, before Crimea was invaded by Russian forces in 2014.

Some of the operations were actively tracked from what was called the American Office of Tailored Access Operations, yet another American highly classified communications and cyber-warfare intelligence-gathering unit of the NSA, the National Security Agency. Apparently, this agency had taken over the SCO.

When Furley received the information he immediately red-flagged the identification letters to the combined counter-terrorism and counter-intelligence desks in the UK. Furley's action initiated a call from an officer at The Office of Tailored Access Operations, the OTAO. The OIC told Furley one unit of Russian opposition had survived the decommissioning exercise conducted in Ukraine, only to meet a similar end later that year. He would not go into details. As far as the officer in command of the OTAO at Fort Meade was concerned, his operations had encountered—squat, as a way of defence.

Jerry Furley contacted me saying he knew nothing of these specialist units other what he been told minutes ago, when his red flag raised a response. Instead of being pleased, he sounded acutely concerned over what he'd heard. It came from a message the IOMS units at Greenwich had intercepted when tracing communications from a meeting of Daesh leaders to an IPS account with the same identification as one attributed to this SCO. The odd and worrying thing about this was its date—a week ago.

After all was deciphered, it originated from Recces Command Centre CO. Sergei Ivanov. It carried details of an S/D team—Search and Destroy—which had taken possession of a quantity of what was referred to as 'Hazardous Material'. It was collected from two sites in the Northern Cape Province, being transported on two lorries making their way to Pier 1, Container Terminal, Port Durban. There were four containers on these two articulated lorries, all four going to different destinations.

When I was in Hagerstown, Maryland with Alice, she'd told me of a top secret plant the last White supremacist governments had constructed, that held over one hundred tons of weaponised Sarin gas. There was another plant where lethal chemical gases were kept alongside other biological weapons. Both these sites were underground somewhere in the Veld. When the ANC took power in South Africa, these two sites were said to have been destroyed under a project called Project Coast.

I told Jerry he was right to worry, but worry on its own did nothing constructive. I suggested we needed to know where those containers went. He had beaten me to it, having desks working on a trace!

* * *

Even though I had no news of a positive note I telephoned Sabah Al Salim.

There had been no identification from the host of street-traffic photographs taken by the cameras the motorcyclist had driven past, but the bike had at least been found. It was abandoned, parked tidily in a marked motorcycle bay, in the road leading to the Embankment from Trafalgar Square, where, guess what, there was no camera.

I slept uneasily that night, mainly because of

what I'd learned from Judith as well as from Furley. It felt very much as if there was a sword hanging over our heads. I had not enjoyed my Jura nightcap, as throughout life I was never able to find solace in whisky when I was bereft of comfort elsewhere. Jura was a drink to enjoy when happy, not a drink in which to look for happiness.

With all that melancholy aside, I had found a good motive for Chevron to have his laboratory on Samothrace, where he could work on his blister tablets in privacy. I couldn't help but admire the ingenuity that must have gone into discovering how to ferret away a microchip of a secret document inside a tablet resembling something one would take for an ordinary headache, using the exact synthetic compound I invented.

That alone gave rise to the obvious wish of developing more of this method of passing secrets sooner, but life is never easy when you want it to be. There was another thing this new knowledge gave rise to and that was the work involved in the re-examination of procedure that always takes place when anything secret could have been lost erroneously. Even though the best minds in the intelligence industry were to be engaged in an extensive re-examination, the extent of possible lost material was limitless.

CHAPTER TWENTY-EIGHT

AGAPOV

It didn't take a qualified therapist to diagnosis the agitation mixed with fear in Valery Agapov's voice. He had a slight shake to the hand holding the cigarette I'd just given him that he'd had difficulty in lighting, but the hand holding his glass of whisky was as steady as mine.

"My CIA contact at Pegasus is dead. His body was fished out of Lake Anna, Virginia yesterday. It was covered in detail on the six o'clock CNN news. He was shot in the head but I found out later from my contacts he'd been tortured. That wasn't common knowledge. I had to ask a friend in the Washington mortuary, who asked at the Orange County Morgue to find that out. I would say it was Al Salim's work. Has he said anything to you about it?"

"No, he hasn't and I doubt it was him. He's been

ducking bullets himself. I wondered if that had something to do with you, Valery? Perhaps an elimination policy?"

He denied it and I've got to say, rightly or wrongly, at the time I believed him. The body of the CIA man was dragged out of the lake around the same time as Sabah was fired at; the difference in time would not favour a reprisal attack from Agapov. The more I thought about the attack on Sabah the more I was coming around to think it came from someone unconnected to the intelligence community.

I had left Judith Meadows to think about her time in Canada, returning to London overnight on a sleeper train from Edinburgh. Indispensable sleep deserted me yet again, so much so that despite an invigorating shower on the train, I still felt exhausted when alighting in London. The ferry, taxi ride, flight to Aberdeen, then train to catch the sleeper, had taken a heavy toll on my aching body, but I think it was my brain that ached the most. Someone was going around killing people, or at least trying, and I had no idea who that was.

Agapov, as Yuri Bogdan, had gone through all his usual security agenda when contacting his CIA link, only to be spooked by a series of 'clicking noises' on the telephone landline he used. He never kept to the same pattern when dealing with Pegasus matters. He was, after all, a top class Russian agent in the field for fast approaching forty years, not one to make mistakes too readily, or easily. He always used a different landline to call from, some were in the vicinity of the Russian embassy and some not. He'd always watched for followers, seeing none. He had looked out for anything unusual along one of many chosen routes, noticing none.

He would change the way he'd leave Notting Hill, using the underground, bus, cab, or walk but he's human, so even he could have made a mistake. He was positive he hadn't. He'd checked what he'd done three times, going over and over, coming up clean each time. Nothing could account for those clicks he'd heard, no mistakes with them, though. He deduced it could only mean the CIA end of the phone line was tapped.

"What was the name of your CIA man at the Pegasus bank, Valery? It doesn't matter now if I know what it was. I never got around to asking Jimmy Mercer. By the way, I call him plain Jimmy, but his full name is far longer than that."

Of course, he knew who Jimmy was. Of course, he would know about the laboratory on Samothrace, but I couldn't be absolutely sure he did know about it. As he was lighting another nerve-soothing cigarette, I was torn between asking him now about the laboratory, or leaving it for a while longer to see where his conversation might lead. I came down on the 'leave it for now' side.

"He said to call him Parker. Apparently it was a tradition that the agency operative in charge of the bank was always named Parker. He said he had chosen his name to be Finch Parker. Said it could be used either way round: Parker Finch, or his way round, Finch Parker. It wasn't he who was clever with the name. It was the person who started the game with the name of Parker, but he did recognise how versatile the name could be. Passing the Pegasus torch down was not a complicated affair, the opposite was true.

"The retiring Parker simply passed the position down to his number two, which in this case would be me, but normally he would have voluntarily retired. He had told me of one other Parker who was 'retired' early, but that was a long time ago. I thought this one was safe. Anyhow, the one in charge should have selected a successor from his friends or colleagues. Like-thinking ones, obviously."

With the smoking cigarette balanced between index and middle finger, his elbow on the table surface, arm pointed upwards, he moved the still shaking palm of his hand towards his mouth, inhaling deeply.

"He came out with it in conversation once, he was not a real hard drinker in the way you or I am. Drinking is a weakness of Parker's. I mean was, don't I? He was stationed at the Americans' Fort Meade, but you would not be able to guess what unit or department he was attached to, in a million years, Lord Paterson."

I was aware of there being somewhere between fifty to a hundred different parts of the United States military, or departments connected to the military, in one way or another at Fort Meade, Maryland. I had been there. I'd been to a part called the McGill Training Center. I had been travelling around America for about four weeks or so in the early '90s, doing studies for the Foreign Office. I looked in at most of the main headquarter buildings and from I saw, I'd say it ranged from space communications to cyber command centres. So, being the non-gambling person I am, I did not wager a bet on the outcome of Finch Parker's detachment, or anything of Finch Parker's come to that, but any deficiency did not stop me admiring the complexity of the thinking behind selecting Parker as the name of the one in charge.

It was the potent combination of drink mixed with pride that forced Parker to declare he was part of the brass section of the US Army Field Band. He had gone on to say, apart from the pleasure that blowing a trumpet on a stage in the band gave him, he enjoyed the overseas tours to wherever American troops were stationed. The ability to roam the world doing what he enjoyed so immensely, was just one aspect of this Field Band posting. Another high up on his personal list of satisfaction, was the opportunity to identify places for investment which otherwise he might not be aware of.

Agapov had opened the door for me to ask if this Parker chap had found any investment opportunities throughout his travels, but if he had, Agapov was keeping deathly quiet about them. I thought it about time to spread my search.

"Why did you not defect at the same time as Alexi Vasilyev? It would have been a lot easier if you had done it then, than what you're doing now, waiting to see who's coming out on top. Is that what you are after, Valery?"

"Who mentioned defection to you? It wasn't me. No, you're going down the wrong road with that. I'm perfectly happy here in London, predicting the weather and talking to intelligent people like yourself. Why on earth would I defect? I can understand Vasilyev wanting a new life. He lived a dangerous life as a double agent, plus his life in the field was finished, but I would think his life is still in peril. He cannot hide his broken body caused by that other dangerous double agent you smuggled out of Russia.

"You're making a habit of helping Russian traitors, my lord. It might be wise for you to watch your back. But I'm getting melodramatic. Perhaps all is not lost with Vasilyev. If he has the plastic surgery I hear is good in the West to cover his face sufficiently well, then who knows, it could work.

"What would work better for him would be to be

married to the traitor's daughter, the mother of your son, Katherine, is her name. There would be nobody alive who could think that woman's husband could be the traitor Vasilyev, but to be a hundred percent sure, they go live in the North Pole. Then he might survive. For him, defection is death. Staying alive is death. He will have no life. For me, defection? No! Not for me. Your source is mistaken, my lord." His hand was no longer shaking.

Intriguing. Don't you think? The title he chose of 'my lord', to close his denial. It was said in such a contemptuous manner, it seemed as if I had been his lifetime enemy and he had been waiting for this chance to roll the insult from his tongue towards my face. Was it supposed to hurt me? Perhaps it was. Maybe I was meant to react in a medieval fashion, challenging him to a duel. Perhaps, not. Let me see.

"Indulge me for a moment, Valery, if you would be so kind." He made no protest, or comment, so I continued.

"I know we have discussed your colleague Sergei Ivanov before, but I would like to tackle something about the man once again. I'm sure there will be details of what I'm about to say filed inside your Directorate Q, but I'm hoping you would be able to help me without waiting to look there."

Again, there was no comment or complaint, just a blank face staring back at me. I pressed on.

"A little while ago, Sergei was commanding a

team of the Recces Search and Destroy officers in South Africa when, far from destroying something, his orders were changed to preserve first, then transport, four containers on the back of two lorries to the Port of Durban—where they were sent to? Now there's my problem, Valery.

"Where did they go? At the moment we've lost them at the port, but that situation won't last. We have a special unit deep down in the bowels of Vauxhall just starting to look for these containers. Could you help us with this? Only it's rather urgent, as we have very good cause to believe inside each of those containers was a biological weapon, or maybe some kind of virus similar to, but probably more deadly than, the one that is starting to travel around the world from China, as we speak.

"There's something you should take into account whilst you have a chance to search your memory. A department at the Ministry of Defence from Porton Down, plus a section from QinetiQ, both subsections of the British Government I'm totally sure you're up to date with, are sending forensic teams to a village called Alonia, on the island of Samothrace.

"It was at this same place a Russian spy you knew as Chevron used a laboratory to produce blister packs of tablets in which was passed stolen intelligence. We are not interested in that product at the moment, nor are we interested in the document you took Chevron to collect. What we are interested in is something far more deadly. We believe he produced weaponised anthrax in this lab in either military form as an artillery shell, or as a civilian-released virus, or as an aimed explosive.

"As you can appreciate, this is serious stuff, which we're taking very seriously indeed. If all of this is true, then the sanctions imposed on your country will be massive. Impossible to visualise, the whole world acting as one. There will be no support for Russia, as it seems enormously likely that we can level the blame at your door. However, if you can help, then, well, you know the game. Quid pro quo, and all that. I'm sure there's something we can do in return. Perhaps declare Sergei Ivanov to be a demented terrorist!"

I hadn't moved an inch but the difference I felt inside was as though I had moved from a hard, upright, wooden chair into a soft-covered, luxury one where I was lying backwards having my knee massaged. It should have been a moment to celebrate, with him dangling from my fishing hook, waiting for me to fetch the net closer, but as Agapov began to speak it became clear life wasn't going to be that simple.

* * *

I had always suspected Alexi Vasilyev's motive to defect was never a straightforward change of lifestyle, but although I suspected his reasons could have been murderous, I was never sure who he wanted to murder the most in retribution for his life-changing injuries. I had managed to get my hands on a photograph of him taken before Paulo trampled on his life in such a noxious manner. I had tried to turn my mind away from the truth his disfigurement had filled my eyes with that first time, and last time, I saw him. I thought his was a truth I could turn my mind from, until Valery Agapov closed the door, leaving me nowhere to run.

My excuse could be found in the affection Katherine had showered upon him. Her warmth of greeting had drawn me deep into a denial of the wretchedness he had to wear every day of his life simply because my great-grandfather's illegitimate son was chasing his dream of escaping from all things Russian.

I think I knew all along it would be Katherine, followed by George, who would be his first targets. And then, although Agapov did not get this far along the list, my son Luca, with Sophie.

Vasilyev's sights for his protracted revenge had an escalating sequence of murders centred around Maudlin and Paulo. Mother then son. Wife, then husband. For probably eight years, he had been thinking of how to exact his reprisal, ever since the moment that his hand touched the door handle to his apartment in Moscow, sending him crashing to the floor, then onto a hospital bed. And I'd asked the mother of my son if she wanted to see him again before winging his way near to the same place as Meadows was to go, Carleton Place.

My mind missed a gear as a shudder ran through my imagination. I was in the hard, solid chair, only this time I was at my first school, the Ashville Preparatory School, just beyond one set of gates to the Paterson estate. I was sitting at my desk, listening to a lesson on how to pay attention to more subjects than one at the same time. Somewhere, I had lost my concentration, which in this case meant I had missed something important.

CHAPTER TWENTY-NINE

WHAT WAS MISSED?

I started with Metsos, real name Pavel Kapustin. He had been many things in his professional life, but when he left Russia he was the essential banker. He used twenty or more aliases throughout those banking years, all of which I had listed in a nice fat file. It had been transferred, then set out in writing, by Sophie from the file I'd read first in the office on the floor below Jerry's. Some I had memorised. One was easy, the coded name his funding operation in America was given, Ghost Stories. Another of those remembered facts, he was Ukrainian.

It was after Judith Meadows' mention of his name that I read up on him and the Ghost Stories the FBI had coded his operation. She told me where in Canada he was, and how Vasilyev had given him the new life-legend of Signalman with a fresh food business near the place he lived, without obeying the first rule of identity change—all names must be changed. Christopher Metsos was eventually arrested by the FBI, but he escaped to become Christopher Signalman with a new fresh food delicatessen but still visible and wanted by the FBI. A silly schoolboy mistake?

I had never run an extensive check with Vauxhall before today about him, because I had no reason to. Why should I have checked? It was not something I cared much about then, but I do care now.

Christopher Metsos could no longer be found living in the Halls Mills suburb of the Canadian By-Ward Market, spelled with a capital W in the middle, but his name was still above the sandwich-cum-delicatessen shop in the upbeat market found there. The trouble was, the shop had not opened for about two weeks by the time the Canadian part of the team I had been allocated enquired.

Nobody had seen him since around the time Section 9 contacted the Canadian Security Intelligence Service, who in turn contacted the Canadian Ottawa State Police, who knocked on the door at his last known address in Halls Mills. When the door remained closed, the two police officers drove the short distance to his sandwich-cum-delicatessen shop where, according to his three staff members, he should have been.

"He left about an hour ago," said one, a Miss Elizabeth Hawkins, who lived quite near the shop.

"He was certainly in a hurry," Miss Ellen Ivery voluntarily told them, while Mrs Jane Hawkins, the mother of the younger Elizabeth, who was serving the solitary customer, agreed with the other two by fiercely nodding her head, not wishing to speak in case she lost mental count of the customer's bill.

Section 9 wanted to know what was my concern about Metsos, to which I had no real answer other than the hair on the back of my neck was bristling with excitement.

As I understood matters Metsos was the run-around stooge funding an illegals cell operating in North America. The FBI had been following him for months, before arresting him financing what they estimated to be at least a dozen operatives, by the amount of the money he was carrying. The only charge they could nail on him was failing to register as an agent of a foreign government; Russia.

There was a connection running through this, but where was it and who was involved? Was it as simple as what was staring me in the face—money? It could be. Judith had adopted a nonchalant attitude towards the close proximity of Metsos to where she was first to go, which did not change in the slightest when she found her place of rest had been changed. At the time, I had accepted her response as authentic, but now I wasn't so sure.

I was anticipating his arrest, but not his absconding again. Was that supposed to happen, I wondered? Was Meadows playing me? Could she conceivably be cooperating with Vasilyev at this early stage in some obtuse way? I had spun her a pack of lies, as I'm sure you worked out, but had she also been lying to me, and I had missed all her lies? Was Metsos meant to run as Meadows arrived? Surely they were meant to meet? But why? Where? What for? My head was buzzing with the emptiness. It started to hurt.

Katherine called. I had several missed calls from her with no messages, so I'd assumed her calls were not vital. For that reason, I had not transferred her to the 'important' box inside that dark, shadowy area called my mind. That was another mistake of mine as it was indeed a crucial call.

She had thought long and hard about my offer of seeing Vasilyev before he left for a secret location, coming down on the side of no, not to see him before he was relocated. Nor did she want any knowledge of where he was to go. It had to be a clean break, she said, with the same defiant tone to her voice I'd heard some years ago when Jimmy Mercer, who was then a working operative of the CIA, was asking about her work inside the KGB. She'd offered Jimmy a variety of defiant denials of knowing who the KGB were. At that time, I was sure I was rescuing her from him;

now I was sure she was rescuing herself from Vasilyev.

I've spent a lot of my time reminiscing whilst on this operation; more, I think, than at any time before in my life. Some memories have been good, some bad, but now, as I was doing it again, I enjoyed the smile that spread across my face as I recalled the times Katherine and I had together.

Sooner than I would have liked, I had to go, as I had Sir Arthur Birch on another line returning the call I made to him earlier. I had to take it. It was a despondent sigh that left my lips as I closed the call to Katherine in order to take Sir Arthur's. He'd heard my disappointment.

"Have I interrupted something, old boy? Only I thought it was kind of urgent. At least that's what I was told."

I apologised, blaming it on what it was, "a conversation with a lady friend." It's strange how phrasing a sentence a certain way can elicit a cavalier response. Had I said I was having a conversation with the mother of my son, or I was discussing my son's future, then a mere "Oh, I see," would have been the sort of trite reply I'd expect, but a statement such as the one I'd made carried a degree of understated promiscuity flirting around the edges, so I considered Sir Arthur's response to be no more than tedious and typical.

"Well, good luck to you with that, old boy. It's a bit early in the day for me, but good to see the gearbox of the world is turning over, as it were. What can I do for you?" he said, with a raunchy sparkle to his voice.

My enquiry was along the same lines as Sir David Haig's had been, as well as the Ministry of Defence team who'd visited him. He was now enjoying retirement, apparently sailing off the Amalfi Coast in the Mediterranean. He said he and his wife were near the island of Gallo Lungo, where I'd never been.

I asked him about the anthrax spores and his knowledge of Viscount Winston Bottomly. Apparently, it was Bottomly who built the laboratory complex at Alonia, it was not Chevron as I was led to believe. No, the Viscount had builders on the site for about three or four months. Sir Arthur and Winston met with Chevron at the laboratory complex when all was completed, but most of the business was either conducted in London, or at Sir Arthur's home in a small hamlet in Berkshire called Hyde End, which was about halfway between Bottomly's place in Bath and London.

I learned from the newly opened file on Sir Arthur Birch that the home he and his wife lived in was on the banks of the River Enborne, which for some reason I remember canoeing on when younger. I think it was something to do with when I was in the Guards at Sandhurst. From the Enborne, we went on to the River Kennet, through a couple of canal systems then out to Bristol and a ship back to

Portsmouth. I haven't got a clue why that was, nor can I recall the name of the ship, but it must have been an okay exercise as I'm alive to tell the tale.

I spoke to him briefly about the river, and yes, the Guards do have an annual manoeuvre of some kind running past his back door, as it were. We could only speak briefly because his satellite telephone was intermittently losing its signal. As much as the loss was an inconvenience to me, it was another tragic mistake on an ever-growing list made by Sir Arthur.

Before the signal was lost, we had also spoken of Gerald Neil, who, as his neighbour, he said he knew well. The two of them were indeed speaking about Gerald's wish to purchase some of Sir Arthur's land with the idea of expanding his vineyard, but it was a long way from being a done deal according to Sir Arthur. There were many things to sort out, but luckily, he said, one that didn't need to be addressed was if the extension of land Gerald wanted did not impact on any of the buildings at the site of the laboratory. As far as Sir Arthur was aware, Gerald Neil knew very well Bottomly used the island, not only for somewhere to moor his own boat, but also to do what he called his research work, at the laboratory.

* * *

The recently arrived forensic unit from Porton Down were still working at Alonia, with a revised estimation time on the site being extended to at least six months. The time could alter if the Greek authorities supplied a similar organisation of their own people, but they hadn't got anything remotely close to Porton. There was nothing Jerry could do about it, but at least he had the professionals from Porton Down leading the examination.

One of the reasons why it would take so long was there were trace deposits of many recreational drugs in the outbuildings surrounding the lab as well as inside the laboratory itself, but it was in the larger of the two wooden buildings that the team from our shores made the most disturbing of their discoveries.

Valery Agapov told me of a trapdoor under this wooden building leading to a tunnel, along which was a comprehensive examination area. The door was concealed beneath one of the half-workbenches standing against the wall opposite the entrance door.

One of those two benches that were taking up the whole width of the wall, could be lifted clear by two men. When it was clear, the trapdoor would be found under the neatly stacked empty cardboard boxes. It was down here in the surgically sterile areas where the forensic team would be spending most of their time. None of this area had been discovered when the site was first examined.

There was an ambiguous attachment to the report in which it was unclear how much of this tunnel was newly built, or if it was part of the complex when

Chevron had use of the place. On first examination, they were coming down on the side of it being constructed in the last five years, but in this add-on report, there was one area in particular that appeared to be much older.

The report stressed how one section of this underground construction appeared to be for specialised narcotics. Apparently, there was evidence of small quantities of the higher end of pain relievers such as analgesic and opioids, including fentanyl and morphine. Although what I was reading was a serious matter, there was mention of a more pressing concern. One area they had discovered seemed to have been set aside for the production of something called Black Tar Heroin, of which there was a small amount of deposits detectable on site.

There was a suggestion on the counter-terrorism floor that the enterprise was too small for any of these recreational drugs to find their way onto the European market, let alone the North American. That opinion was shared by the majority. Another opinion shared by all was, whatever the outcome of the forensic team's investigations, we had more information about the site than before, with more discoveries to come the longer the search went on.

* * *

As much as Sir Arthur Birch always praised members of the Greek port authorities to their face, when they weren't looking he expressed his distaste and abhorrence of all things Greek, from food and wine to music and language. Apart from the beautiful weather, there was nothing in that part of the world, be it Greece or Turkey or... no, wait a moment. Yes, he could find some things Italian to his taste, but his repugnance was shown to the fore on his inspection of his yacht after it was restored to his ownership.

After a fastidious examination, accompanied, unfortunately, by a few superficial exhalations of disapproval on finding dust or marks had appeared where none was before it was chartered, he found the charter fee sufficient to cover his displeasure. However, later in his travels he would confess to wishing he had been more industrious in his inspection and less cosmetic, particularly when it concerned the lack of meaningful scrutiny he gave to certain parts of his boat before setting off from Kamariotissa.

With the wonderful wherewithal of hindsight, Sir Arthur regretted being conspicuously neglectful in checking if the scrambling capability for the satellite phone was automatically switched on for whenever it was in use. Unfortunately it wasn't, but it would be reasonable to expect someone in his business to be suspicious and look to see, not only if it was in the working mode, but if any unwanted geographic coordinating system had been added to his boat since it was seized.

Without the scrambler in operation, together with the location signal permanently emitting from his craft, his position had been triangularly traced to a spot forty-seven nautical miles from the same Cape Helles where the previous crew had loaded the slides of anthrax spores.

"It would appear," I said to him in the microphone attached to a transmitter inside the Government Communications Headquarters, commonly referred to as the Doughnut, at Cheltenham in Gloucestershire (his boat was not near the foot of Italy, as he had informed me), "you're in the Aegean Sea, Sir Arthur. You're lying to me," I told him.

Within twenty minutes of replacing the handset of his forsaken telephone, his yacht was apprehended. Once again, his boat was boarded by a company of Greek coastguards from the high-powered patrol boat that had been notified of his position The coastguards piloted the boat for the return journey to the port of Kamariotissa, from where he and his wife were transferred to the mainland, then, acting on instructions from the British Consul, the pair were taken to be held in custody by the police authorities until someone arrived from London. I quite hoped I could get on that party.

* * *

When I learned of their fate I laughed out loud, which embarrassed my host somewhat. I was with Jerry Furley, who sat opposite me looking dumbfounded. I thought it to be very serendipitous, but it was beyond meaningful explanation if, like Jerry, you hadn't lived the life when Chevron was operating in London and Paulo Korovin was trying to stop him from Moscow. I poured two more whiskies from the decanter, always giving full thanks to Vauxhall's limitless budget, lit another cigarette and brought Jerry and myself up to speed.

Sir Arthur's wife, Lady Annabelle Birch, was, on notification from the British Consulate, released from Greek custody on the understanding she would fly home to be detained on arrival at Heathrow. A police officer from the Ministry of Defence eventually attended the Greek holding station where Sir Arthur Birch was being kept, initially to question him over what seemed at the time to be his role in handling illegal substances.

Some days later, after the MOD handed the case over to the secret intelligence service, the SIS, I was sitting with Jerry in his office, able to hear all the questions put to Sir Arthur, and through the wonders of modern science at GCHQ, we could see him answering as well. But where I had mentioned hindsight earlier, to explain how Sir Arthur might have felt at the beginning of his stay with us, it would appear he did not only need to understand a situation after it had occurred; he didn't quite understand the situation as it was unfolding.

With instructions not to hold back on anything, our SIS handler put to him the fact that not only did he have a drug-manufacturing plant at Alonia, the real use for the place was to produce biological weapons to supply terrorist groups including ISIS, Hizballah, Real Irish Republican Army, adding the Japanese Red Army, and the Libyan Islamic Fighting Group, just for luck.

Sir Arthur was told how we had connected Winston Bottomly to the majority of those groups, ergo, by knowledge of him, Sir Arthur Birch was involved. Birch laughed, telling the SIS man where to go.

"Go away, you little man. I know people in high places who will eat you up, then spit you out without even asking for your name. You are really that insignificant."

I interrupted the interview with a written request appearing on the computer screen that only the SIS questioner could see. *Ask him, "What do you know about two shipping containers from Viscount Bottomly's estate in South Africa, carrying biological weapons, possibly weaponised Sarin gas canisters and/or anthrax spores, that have your genetic fingerprints all over them?"*

Perhaps it was his search for an original answer that compelled, the hitherto flamboyant Sir Arthur Birch to fall strangely silent as he stopped stalking the damp room where the interview was being conducted. His disappointment looked somewhat crushing as he sat in the one remaining hard-backed wooden chair, after pulling it away from where it was pushed up tight against the matching wooden table with a deeply carved top, on which sat the overfull ashtray, and a single empty, stained cup that had held our questioner's tea.

On several occasions, Birch had strenuously objected to the smoke in the basement, which gave our man a reason to light more cigarettes than he would normally smoke. Anyone can punish a detainee with the aim of extracting a confession, but pain alone does not necessarily equate to a quality confession. Often pain will just induce any answer for a reprieve from the inflicted pain. Pain and truth are not always cosy bedfellows.

Part of the training to become accepted as an interrogator for the SIS was to learn how to get under the skin of the interviewee in whichever way thought possible. I was privy to one such session of instruction where the hardened instructor took a pee in the corner of the room. If it had been a real scenario, we were told, the interrogator might well have peed somewhere else! It was done to debase the man, to convince him, or her, they meant nothing, not even for the lowest degree of civility.

* * *

Prior to arriving at RAF Brize Norton from Greece, Birch had hardly spoken a single word other than periodically repeating, "You're all in serious trouble." On arrival at the base, a hood was placed over his head, and he was then driven to one of the security service safe houses, this one in Tooting, South London. Once they were safely ensconced in the soundproof basement, the hood was removed, then noisily he waited to be interrogated by trained officers from the National Crime Agency.

I'm somewhat embarrassed to confess I did not know Lady Annabelle Birch. We had never met. Now ordinarily, that confession would not cause any unease to my reputation, but not only were these not ordinary times, she was a spellbinding corporeal beauty. Age in this case is important as it may go to help the understanding of their marriage. Whereas he was rich, ugly, almost seventy and a bore, she was thirty-one, (that was accurate, the result of some research I had done, not one of my guesses) and of a mesmeric exquisiteness that could only be described as divine. As for personality, I could find no fault from our far too brief first encounter.

After her superbly crafted figure requiring, I thought, more appreciation at a later time, the first part of her to hit me was her rich, wide-open, rounded mouth, with her luscious full lips. Her skin appeared unnaturally pale, with some beads of perspiration, looking decidedly out of place, beginning to form on her velvet-smooth forehead, which topped a supreme, heart-shaped face. The eyelids to her radiant, azure blue eyes were lifted high in what I can only describe as fear, and those lustrous eyes were fixed straight back at me, as if afraid to move from my own eyes. Perhaps, I needed to use that fear to our advantage.

Almost immediately, I found there were at least two qualities that Lady Annabelle shared with Serena. The first was the way she wore her blend of perfume; hers was one of coconut and vanilla, and it was as subtle as any my estranged wife would wear. The second likeness was her passionate ability to talk as much as Serena in her early euphoric days, before becoming a diva in the designer fashion industry. In today's world of fashion, she was never flustered by the small changes to her business life that made her what she is today.

When the interview started, we quickly learned how Lady Annabelle's husband, Sir Arthur, had recently spent most of the day on the landline telephone with a Russian he called Yuri, after two words she'd rather not say, but one was 'You', and the other began with an 'F', coming in front of the spoken 'You'. When she was asked where he kept all his bank records, the position in a safe built into the floor of the conservatory, along with its combination, were relinquished without complaint. She, like Agapov, also had her mind on the future, but in her case the consideration was a whole lot easier to solve.

I don't know why I asked her about Christopher Metsos, but ask I did. By the time I introduced his name, I had already established Sir Arthur Birch regularly spent time in South Africa staying at the main —her word, not mine—Bottomly home, with the Orange River at the end of the fenced, ornamental garden. She had stayed there a few times herself where she met a Russian named Yuri Bogden, whose voice she recognised on the phone, as well as an Englishman named Charles Oswald Wallace. That last name came to me as a distinct surprise.

Yes, she knew Metsos, she declared with a heavenly smile on her face, but unfortunately, I had other things on my mind than her delicious smile. Her knowledge of the man Metsos had come in an odd manner.

She and Sir Arthur were staying at the Bottomlys' for a New Year celebration some years ago, unfortunately she could not remember the precise date, when Yuri Bogdan announced that a Russian named Pavel Kapustin was due to arrive. She and her husband were in company with Bottomly, alongside a female whose name she could not recall. Agapov, using the name of Yuri Bogdan, was with another girl from, she thought, the same agency as the one with Bottomly as neither were showing any interest at all in the general conversation, when out of the blue the change of name from Kapustin to Metsos was mentioned, amidst fits of chuckling from both Bottomly as well as the Russian, Yuri Bogdan.

I expect your curiosity is as bad as mine but eventually, I had a chance to ask her why she thought the two females were from an agency specialising in women who kept men company. She recognised the signs, she said, as she had come from one herself when first meeting Sir Arthur.

Four years ago, she'd met Sir Arthur at one of these 'parties', where four people, unknown to each other, play various roles, mostly completely undressed or nearly naked, it matters not. These sorts of 'parties' were, she said, supported by lashings of cocaine and booze with stronger heroin, or the like, if needed. The first 'party' had lasted all weekend and at the end of it, Sir Arthur had proclaimed his love for her.

"You know," she said, "the kind of love that centres on— well, you know." She was blushing.

For a woman more accustomed to the carnal side of life than the vernacular, she appeared to me to be modest, but not in a teasing sense some women pretend to be. No, more withdrawn than coquettish. I thought her to be delightful in all senses of the word, and here, I must add, that opinion was underlined later when I had the chance I'd hoped for, of my further appreciation of her.

Anyway, back to where we were. When the 'party' she was speaking of finished, Sir Arthur paid Annabelle, a 'shed load of money', not for services rendered, but to marry him. "Six figures," she said. "What could a girl do?" she asked. To which I had no answer, other than to ask another question—what happen after the honeymoon?

At first, she said, she and Sir Arthur took several flights on his jet aeroplane to a place she couldn't pronounce on the Greek coast, then trips on her new husband's yacht, from near where they landed, to a place where Sir Arthur said a lot of Turkish and British soldiers and sailors lost their lives in WWI in what was called the Gallipoli campaign.

They were spending time sailing backwards and forwards between the Greek mainland and a place she learned was called Morto Bay, near a spot called Cape Helles. She endured those arduous journeys for roughly a month, stretched out under the sun on the poop deck of the yacht, with, no doubt, Sir Arthur enjoying the view.

When the frequency of flying became less urgent, the social life continued at a rare old pace. She met the Wallaces again and again, partaking in more of those 'parties', also partying with Bottomly, with a different girl each time. Then there were the others, whose faces she managed to identify from MI6 photographs.

She recognised the photo of Samantha Burns, who she did not know was dead. She said from the little she knew of her, she found her to be a lovely, but lonely person. I moved the conversation on to the men she could recognise. Those who had direct dealings with Sir Arthur in either Greece or in England, but solely to do with the cocaine and heroin he was involved with for the last year or so.

We came to an interesting time. The occasion she accompanied Sir Arthur to meet another man, whose name she was never told, on the island of Samothrace. They met away from the coast in the relatively cooler air, at a village named Alonia. It was a name she thought suited the place, as both were beautiful. From the description she gave me, I concluded it to be Chevron, who under no prevailing factors could be described as beautiful, who was now living in Moscow, Russia.

On the same island, she and Sir Arthur once stayed with another Englishman. This one owned a casino, he'd told her, in London. He had taken her out one night down to the harbour for dinner, while her husband was having a business meeting with a couple of the faces she'd picked out from the MI6 data bank. All in all, I thought Lady Annabelle Birch was a dream to interview with the quantity of quality information she volunteered, which helped to whittle down the two index fingers I used for typing.

By the time all these questions were finished, we had the start of a case for treason against a retired top civil servant from the important Department for International Development, a department with high-level representatives in so many places it had the overseas risk assessment desks at the Bank of England, as well as the counter-terrorism at the MOD, MI5 at Thames House, Millbank along with independent divisions of Special Branch, wondering where on earth to start.

The British Home Office were working with those responsible for such things at Vauxhall, making out a case for sedition to be made against Arthur Birch, but as I thought about the evidence against him, combined with those who his wife had identified as a customers of his trade, I couldn't think of him as the one the message originating from Alexi Vasilyev referred to as—becoming a member of a top Security Council, 'who would be a veritable prize on your sleeve, if you needed another one.'

Could the message, first given to Katherine, refer to Sir Arthur Birch? I thought not, but I had escalating history of being wrong.

* * *

Whilst the container vessel was being looked for on the high seas by agencies with specialised equipment, George Northcliffe was sitting beside his wife Sophie, in their home in London. It was a near normal scene for a Wednesday afternoon, but not completely normal. For the last few days, the two of them had been helping to trace the whereabouts of the four hazardous shipping containers that had left Sergei Ivanov's hands, at the port of Durban in South Africa.

It was, I was delighted to learn, George who found the first vital clue to the whereabouts of the containers. Using the shipping container numbers George had been able to get from the team interrogating Bottomly, he located the two containers as having been loaded onto a ship called the *Diniz*, chartered from Sweden's Stockholm Chartering under passage to the Iranian port of Chabahar, where Sabah Al Salim had so much influence.

Using the same method, Sophie found the second ship, called the *Cambis*, a few minutes later. The ship was from Zan Shipping, passaged to Izmir on Turkey's Aegean coast. From here on in, it may have been a whole different story had the ship's transit destinations been the opposite way around.

The tracing of the hazardous containers from the two ports should have been extremely simple, had the necessary labelling been added to the structure of the containers themselves, but unfortunately, this was one of the necessary requirements Valery Agapov had deliberately decided not to incorporate. Regrettably, none of the normal process of notification from the port of delivery had been adhered to, so nobody knew what was in any of the four containers, other than Agapov.

That would have been the truth, had a simple procedure that was said to have been followed had been, but it hadn't.

Winston Bottomly had used the list of itemised stocks of weaponised anthrax his Aunt Alice had drawn up when dealing with the apartheid government of South Africa, to relocate it, all from the secure biological laboratories in which it was stored alongside other biological weapons.

He then organised his own inventory, which he structured in such a way as to register each time any content was withdrawn, but Valery Agapov was able to circumnavigate the security registration, withdrawing all four containers without any convention being breached. Without Agapov's help we were stuck.

That's where we had a bit of luck. The chairman of the British Joint Intelligence Committee, cooperating with the American chairman of the Joint Chiefs of Staff, contacted the Turkish Minister for the Interior asking them to check the records at the port of Izmir. When the port authority checked, they found both containers were still awaiting collection. Neither had been opened, nor, as far as they could see, been approached. That situation changed, dramatically.

They were opened the day after Lady Annabelle Birch arrived in England, ahead of her husband. The first container was a time bomb. Inside was found a quantity of refined cocaine, a quantity of ketamine which can be used as an anaesthetic and, if that wasn't enough, there was a quantity of crystal methamphetamine, a highly addictive stimulant. The three had an estimated street value of over a hundred million pounds sterling. The second container was empty.

I contacted Sabah, who, although having a great deal on his mind, readily agreed to assist. He called his people at the Iranian port of Chabahar and within a few hours we had a destination for both containers that had been delivered to this port. They were transported overland to the Turkish city of Bismil, where one was unloaded. The other one was, as far as anyone could tell, still on the road on the way to another Turkish city, this one called Tekirdağ.

It may have been a coincidence, if you believed in such, as Tekirdağ was about one hundred kilometres from Cape Helles. The same place to which Sir Arthur Birch's yacht paid many visits. This time, we had the Foreign and Commonwealth Office to thank.

Stressing the importance of the operation, the Minister for Foreign Affairs sought the help of the

Secretary General to NATO, who in turn asked the Turkish authorities to check for signs of any biological contamination at the city of Bismil. A team of German technicians wearing anti-chemical protection examined the container at Bismil. There was no trace of any biological pollution. What was found, though, were cases of AK 47 assault rifles. Alongside were cases of ammunition, mines, grenades, as well as other assorted munitions, all of which was said to be destined for the Kurdish tribes engaged with various governments for the establishment of a country to call their own, within the boundaries of the ancient Levant.

The second container was proving difficult to track down. To make things harder for those in charge of tracing the container, it had been unloaded from the first lorry to be loaded on a more common 'flat back' type vehicle, then covered by an off-white tarpaulin.

To apprehend it, three road blocks were set up: the first on the western side of Ankara, the second, fifty kilometres further along, on the road to Bolu and the third, outside the city of Eskişehir, in case the lorry took a different route by staying south of the Sea of Marmara to cross at the Dardanelles Straits, ferrying the cargo to Tekirdağ by boat. All of us needed to be patient and wait.

* * *

Although George was similar to me with his abhorrence of waiting for anything, both he and Sophie were ecstatic over the results of their work so far in finding the culprits in this labyrinth of mystery. I was with them both at number 16 Eaton Square, discussing the need for armed protection in light of Valery Agapov's allegations, when Sophie asked a question I had no answer to, which was; what had now changed in Alexi Vasilyev's life to make the threat more urgent? I would have loved to have stayed trying to find a logical reason for 'why now', but I had somewhere else I had to be.

* * *

Do you know how sometimes, no matter what, you just know the day is not going to be kind? Well, that was exactly how I felt when I found myself sitting on the other side of the table to Valery Agapov. This was not intended to be a 'stroll in the park' type of chat, like the one we had before. To make it appear more hostile for him, I had positioned four Ministry of Defence police officers in uniform in each corner of the medium-sized room, with another standing directly behind him and Jerry Furley sitting directly opposite him.

Valery Agapov was not finding any emotion close to ecstasy flowing through his veins. In fact, it could be said he was feeling decidedly nauseous, fearing his demise might end with a loud bang from a gun fired by someone either to the side, or behind, his head. He requested a glass of water and a cigarette before he felt capable to carry on.

Until now, I have to be fair in saying he'd been good, very good. He had admitted it was he who ordered his subordinate, Sergei Ivanov, to send his Search and Destroy team to take the prepared shipping containers from the sites on the Bottomlys' estate, near Boomrivier, in the Northern Cape Province, then transport them to the port at Durban, undetected. He even confirmed it was he who had arranged to have the canisters removed from Bottomly's secured site. He gave the name of the man who had been paid one thousand South African rand to remove them and then swap them around.

He was able to confirm all the information my home-grown Northcliffe-Prosser investigating team had discovered by using the container numbers Bottomly had then been able to supply. I hoped Agapov would supply the details of the cargo we were yet to uncover, but he was choosing to keep the intelligence he had on that to himself as a bartering tool, he arrogantly declared at the end of his statement, telling us he was an accredited diplomat, therefore he was claiming diplomatic immunity.

I rose from my seat, walked around the table, took the innocuous-looking, thick, paperback novel from where it lay on the seat of the chair opposite mine, the empty one beside Valery, where I'd left it, and hit him twice, fairly hard, around his head. The purpose was to shake him up, not to kill him.

"I hope it hurts, but that's just for starters, old chap. If you choose to remain silent on the contents of the container, which, as a diplomat, is your undeniable right, then I can assure you that gentlemen such as these in this room will take no pleasure whatsoever in seeing you cry as you scream for mercy, but as you know, Valery, there is no mercy to have in this game.

"No matter what process we use, we will eventually discover the contents. You know that to be true! But what if, without touching a hair of your head, we drop you off outside your embassy, with 'traitor' written all over you in big letters? We'll stay close and hold your hand whist kissing you goodbye, that sort of thing. Do you think your lot will believe you never said anything to us? That's, of course, if your lot know about it.

"Maybe they will welcome you home with open arms. Asking you what harm we have done. I don't think they'll do that; more importantly, neither do you. Either way, they'll torture you to find out. Come on, old chap, you have to earn your right to shake the Queen's hand before you can walk through the front door of the thatched cottage next to the salmon stream you so desperately want us to give to you. As well as grant you the right to withdraw your Pegasus hoard."

CHAPTER THIRTY
CAUGHT IN THE HEADLIGHTS

I had an audience. It wasn't in front of the royal family, but I was representing Her Majesty's secret service in front of the next tier down. The man concerned was a very important person. My performance was in front of the Cabinet Secretary and head of the Home Civil Service, who would, until recently, have been Charles Oswald Wallace. Charles had lost his position due to a couple of things. One being the fact he socialised with Sir Arthur Birch, but the main reason he was no longer considered secure was the unacceptable association his wife had with the meteorologist from the Russian embassy What Judith Meadows had told me was true. It had been Charles Wallace's wife, Stella, who had been photographed in what was an 'embarrassing position' with Valery Agapov.

With the power of articulation one would ascribe to a prominent member of the British administration, the new Cabinet Secretary told Valery Agapov Her Majesty's Government considered he had exploited his diplomatic privilege to take advantage of the wife of a senior governmental civil servant. With that in mind, his name was to be removed from the diplomatic list at the Russian embassy, meaning he would be deported to Russia. The Cabinet Secretary said he would make sure a public relations barrage of abuse would be aimed at his bogus status within the embassy, resulting in the ambassador's presence being required at the Foreign Office.

"How would all that play out in the newspapers back home, hmm?" Sir Duncan Fenwick asked, which was my prompt in the performance.

With sincerity, I expressed how Valery Agapov would like to extend his apologies for the awkward situation. He cited his previous exemplary behaviour, blaming what happened on drink, together with a need for affection owing to the loss of so many of his influential friends meeting suspicious deaths. I briefly mentioned the shipping cargo, saying how there was a matter still being investigated in which Agapov was assisting us.

"He is a patriotic man who told me he meant no harm, Sir Duncan. He was simply looking for comfort." I was waiting for the accolades.

It had been George's idea to surround Agapov in

the richness of what's referred to as quintessentially British. Where else could the identifiable quality of that 'Establishment' be found than in the fabric of the centuries of tradition of the Foreign and Commonwealth Office? It had worked better than I could have expected.

Agapov sat motionless, looking ashen-faced, with his sunken eyes fixed firmly on the face of Sir Duncan Fenwick, the newly appointed Cabinet Secretary and Head of the Home Civil Service, who looked as though he had held the post since birth, and what's more absolutely loved every second of it!.

After a brief moment of time, Agapov seemed to sink further down into the soft seat of the green leather chair, and as he did so his head slumped forward, turning to one side to look at me.

We were both sitting in front of the rather imposingly large desk in what was called the Rooms of the Cabinet Secretary. I can't imagine it being simply the majestic surroundings, as grandiose as they were, nor could it be the overpowering sense of occasion, but I have no other way of explaining what happened next. Agapov, it seemed, wanted to sign his own death warrant.

"I cannot return to Russia. There must be another way. We must look."

The following day, Agapov met with Sir Arthur Birch in the Bailey's Hotel, a short walk from South Kensington station. One topic they spoke of was Sir

Arthur's forthcoming appointment to Her Majesty Queen Elizabeth II's Privy Council. He was to become one of her 'token' advisors. On taking his seat on the Privy Council, Birch would be entitled to be called The Right Honourable Sir Arthur Birch. It would appear The Right Honourable Sir Arthur Birch had indeed turned out to be the veritable prize on my sleeve, albeit by default.

Another topic on their agenda, whilst they sat in the hotel's foyer sampling the coffee, was how many surreptitious places the two of them knew where Birch could meet Agapov to pass on the nation's secrets, as well as collecting the Russian assets Agapov could give Birch in exchange.

In return for favours rendered, Sir Arthur was to be 'played back' as a double agent working in Great Britain's interests by suppling Valery Agapov with some information judged not detrimental to NATO, but possibly so to our commercial competitors in Europe. For being allowed to remain in this country as the Russian forecaster of our clement weather, as well as continue to enjoy the benefits of an accredited diplomat, Valery Agapov would supply me, or any other designated representative of Her Majesty's SIS, with intelligence the Russians might not want us to see.

Instead of facing charges related to drug trafficking, or worse, Sir Arthur was required to provide solid assurances never to deal in narcotics of any description. However, his sailing in the Aegean was to continue as though nothing had happened. When the handwritten diaries both he and Lady Annabelle kept were thoroughly scrutinised, there was reference made to a party held on Sir Arthur's boat when moored at Cape Helles last Christmas.

In her diary, Lady Annabelle kept a list of names of the invited guests. Amongst the names were four indigenous Turkish men red-flagged from the recognition data stored at GCHQ. The Turkish National Intelligence Organisation were approached through Special Branch, asking for more information. They wanted to know why Turkish Intelligence had them listed so high on the recognition data. The information we received almost melted the fax machine.

It was decided to use Sir Arthur and Lady Annabelle Birch to open up a line of communication between the Turkish Intelligence and these four Turkish men with an eye to procuring whatever intelligence they could give on the people trafficking they were suspected of controlling by the Turkish and Albanian authorities. Although it was primarily a police matter, the SIS was prepared to help in whatever way they could.

* * *

It had not been Agapov who selected the contents of the stolen canisters. The man who just could not stop surprising me, Viscount Bottomly, had admitted it was he who chose what to load the canisters with. Bottomly arranged with Agapov to use one of Sergei Ivanov's units to pick them up then transport all four to the port at Durban. At no time did he tell Valery Agapov the contents.

From his days in the military, Bottomly knew only too well what could be the cost of life if those gas canisters ended up with any so-called freedom fighters supplied from Cape Helles, the destination of the final container. The flat-back lorry carrying the load was stopped by police on an open stretch of road, a good mile east of the city of Eskişehir, Turkey, where protection from onlookers was provided by trees on both side of the road.

When Bottomly confessed to having prior knowledge of the contents, he was handed over to an 'out-of-house' contractor to be further questioned. With the real threat of physical harm hanging over his head, he confessed to much more than we already knew. Within a few weeks, all of the South African properties owned by the Bottomly family were searched, resulting in the destruction of every weapon, or chemical, that was found. Each registered or suspected member of the AWB was similarly investigated.

Jerry Furley had liaised with Jimmy Mercer from the very beginning when we first knew of these containers. His departments had provided expert advice as well as service where required. It was judged best to use his specialists to deal with the potentially lethal Sarin. Fortunately, there was a unit capable of dealing with the whole situation stationed at a NATO post in Bulgaria.

The American unit exchanged the Sarin canisters for a harmless chemical in similar containers carrying all the correct insignia and signage. There were tracking devices inserted into each canister. Until the contents of the cans were released, any terrorist would believe it was the real gas he or she was purchasing.

From Poole in Dorset, three teams drawn from the Special Boat Service, the SBS, from the Royal Marines, were dispatched to assess the suitability of the Cape Helles site for static reconnaissance to be operated over a prolonged period. The financial viability of this undertaking was to be handled by officials appointed by Jimmy Mercer's office to allow the use of funding from an outside source, notably the Pegasus bank.

One huge consideration left for Jimmy Mercer's decision was what was to become of the Pegasus Mercantile Company, particularly with regards to the bank holding deposits of most of the world's terrorists groups in the Samothrace island's vaults. It seemed as though my family's nemesis of banking would not go away, as my name was put forward to be the theoretical head of a bank. A Parker would be replaced by a

Paterson. As the SIS had a significant hold over one of the bank's trustees, Valery Agapov, all was to stay the same in regards to its structure, which was to be closely monitored from London, alongside Washington. It would not be simple, but stability of the structure was, although ambitious, achievable It was a decision taken by Jerry Furley, in consultation with Mercer, that neither the office of the elected President of America, nor the elected leader of government in London, be told of the Pegasus bank. This decision was not taken lightly, nor with any nefarious motive in mind. It was to enable both occupants of those great offices to truthfully deny knowing of any arrangement about a Pegasus Mercantile Company, or even the existence of one.

I went to see Judith Meadows once more before she was shipped off to pastures new, for her freedom in Canada. The real trouble for Judith was yet to be faced—she could never be free. Completely beyond her control, her movements were not only to be watched, they were, to a great extent, going to be decided upon from London.

I had become fond of my recurring visits to and from Jerry Furley's office, admiring his panoramic views of the seats of government, but I never felt at home discussing Judith Meadows. She was a real dilemma for me. I shared the top-floor opinion that Judith knew far more than she had ever told any interrogation she was subjected to. That included her answers to all the questions I put to her when she was first arrested, then later at Gardie House, on my often visited Scottish island of Bressay.

It was our collective thinking that, after taking a reasonable amount of time to settle into her surroundings in Canada, she would reach out to her old contacts that could be still in operation. In that regard we thought she might well use Agapov, which could be advantageous for both of them.

With help from us, we hoped her infamous reputation would spread to attract interest from the Russian cell we knew was alive in Northern America. We had Agapov available to help her gain entry, as well as open ways into the intricacies of the fairly new FSB, places where he might not for various reasons find it comfortable to go. This would also be a way in which we could check on Agapov's reliability in the intelligence he would be providing.

The aim of the top floor was to develop what was carried over from the old KGB days. The analysts believed the powers of the FSB would eventually be extended to include the collection of intelligence activities in countries that were once members of the now extinct Soviet Union. When the Soviet Union was dissolved, there was a signed agreement not to spy on the countries that left the umbrella grouping, but nobody in the FSB had made such a commitment.

One way of knowing where the FSB were looking was to follow Meadows to get a look inside this Russian cell, as well as the illegals being funded through Metsos. That could be tricky if left to luck, so it was decided the best way to accomplish this was to turn Metsos our way.

Pavel Kapustin had changed his name yet again, this time without any help from Alexi Vasilyev. With financial assurances made on behalf of the acting trustees of the Pegasus Bank, one of which was me, with my work signature on the bank transfer document, Metsos became Richard Belfast, of Calgary, Alberta, Canada. He had shaved his beard, dyed his hair and inserted contact lenses to change his eye colouring. Physically, he had lost three and bit stone in weight to become nearer, what he said was, his optimum fighting weight of twelve stone, ten pounds.

At six foot two inches tall, he made an imposing figure. He was completely unrecognisable from his days as a coffee barista, becoming once more a financial advisor with a plethora of clients. At least, it looked as though he had clients; if appearances were to count for anything, then that's the way it appeared in his office with three telephones on a desk in the centre of a window with a tower of four filing cases on each side. On the walls, could be seen the usual array of framed photographs, pictures and certificates one might expect to find in such an office. The one thing missing from the charade was a secretary for the outer office, where his name and profession was etched into the glass door.

One of Jimmy's departments in Washington had reopened the bankrolling enterprise that had closed when Metsos was apprehended. It was opened for a cluster of five new illegals discovered operating in the North American Continent, inserted in a variety of communication companies by what we in London believed to be a professional Russian cell of three operatives, one a female, working in what was called The Data Intensive Science Company, with registered research premises in the southern San Francisco Bay Area of California, and a headquarters office in Boston, Massachusetts.

Without approaching any of Jimmy Mercer's departments in Washington, we had taken the decision to unleash Valery Agapov to find this cell of three Russian operatives in America. Of course it wasn't our remit, but we felt one person who should have known of these three would have been Alexi Vasilyev, but our information had come from Sabah Al Salim, not Vagabond.

The five illegals were identified using the same classified operation, StoneGhost, mentioned by Sabah Al Salim when I had met him in London. They had all entered America by different means, and by different methods, but all came through

Canada before arriving at their final destinations in California, or, in the case of the one female, in Boston.

Meticulous examinations following stringent lines of inquiry were carried out on qualifications, including levels of education, degree of language skills, scale of academic achievements, with cross-referencing places of birth, parents, religion, etc, done at British IOMS sites, until an overall picture emerged where associations were easier to pinpoint. That done, the only thing delaying the operation, coded Grease Point, was Judith's arrival from England and, fingers crossed, her answering Richard Belfast's local newspaper's advertisement for a secretary.

I had to say my goodbyes to Judith at Gardie, and it was far from an easy time for me. The conflicting emotions I felt had not gone away as I would have hoped. How could I have any feelings bordering on love with the woman who had murdered two members of my family? I had asked myself so many times if those feelings were of love, or was it some middle-aged infatuation with a skeleton? Maybe it was an illness I suffered from?

She was good at playing roles. She was good at being an assassin. That last thought woke my sleeping mind.

CHAPTER THIRTY-ONE
THOUGHTS OF DEATH

I had spoken of the threat Alexi Vasilyev posed for my family, but I had forgotten him. Does that make me irresponsible? Yes, it does, doesn't it? I had a home, with people who rely on me for more than just an income. I found time to go home.

I paid a visit to Bottomly, who was being held in Her Majesty's Prison Wakefield, not far from The Hall at Harrogate. Peter had driven down to London on the morning of the Tuesday, staying at Chester Square until I could get away from Whitehall, then Jerry Furley at Vauxhall. He drove me back to Harrogate on the Wednesday, stopping off at HMP Wakefield, just before lunch.

On my arrival, I had to go through a series of security checks which were as extensive as one would have imagined, but it was after that when my time in

Wakefield became extraordinary, with customs I could never have visualised existing in this century, or in this country.

To be inside a place where the six hundred occupants are the most dangerous criminals in Britain was one thing. The accompanying noise level being something one could expect, but then to be escorted down several flights of winding, metal stairs by two prison wardens, whilst surrounded by only the strange echoing footsteps, to an artificially lit series of corridors containing, one might think, more cells than the solitary one needed by the person I had come to see, was not expected, but was worrying to say the least.

If the noise at the top of those stairs was nothing more than to be regarded as anticipated, then this stagnant, subterranean place made my spirits feel utterly wretched.

Bottomly was kept in solitary confinement, spending twenty-three and a quarter hours each day locked away in his special underground cell beneath the main Wakefield Prison. Not only did he have nothing to do with any inmate, he had nothing to do with any of the staff. Everything, more or less, was done by automation. He was the only human in this huge, medieval dungeon. His only contact with the 'outside' world was through an internal telephone, mounted on one side wall. There was a total of eight visual monitors aimed both inside his cell and along the last corridor the three of us had walked. I spoke to Bottomly through a heavy plastic screen using a telephone handset.

The topic I would have loved to have spoken to him about was why he killed Samantha Burns, but I could not trust there would be no listening devices installed in and around this area for interview. The next thing on my list to discuss was the whereabouts of the photograph of Stella Wallace and Valery Agapov in this compromising position.

He said it was never intended for use in extorting money from Charles Wallace. He also said he wanted it to twist her husband's arm into agreeing to support the establishment of his AWB white supremacist government, after its takeover of South Africa from the democratically elected ANC. The man was certainly an idiot, but not only that, he was a dangerous one.

I told him he was stupid but it seemed senseless to argue. Whoever said you can argue with a wise man, but never argue with a fool, must have come across someone with Bottomly's ideology. It was Winston who had asked to see me, but even so, I had to apply for an Exceptional Authorisation from the Home Office to get inside the prison to see him, and although it's true to say I had arrived feeling somewhere near on top of the world, having fulfilled all

Sir Leonard Miles had asked of me except the retrieval of this photo, my sense of satisfaction never extended as far as Bottomly. Although I left HMP Wakefield knowing where the photograph could be found, I felt no exhilaration with that awareness.

Such is life, I concluded, when dealing with a once friend and colleague waiting to be deported to South Africa to face trial for treason. However, it was his awaiting deportation that he wanted to speak to me about. I made sure he was under no impression I could change the arrangements myself; I did not have that level of influence. Only the Prime Minister could alter the agreement between governments, but I was sure the ANC would love to display the Afrikaner Weerstandsbeweging, with Bottomly at the head, as the architect of a bloody revolution to install a White ruling class once more.

Bottomly had requests. The main one was not to serve his prison sentence in South Africa. His means of negotiation relied on his knowledge of the internal workings of the Pakistan intelligence gathering service, the ISI, the Inter-Services Intelligence. The other carrot he had dangling on a piece of imaginary string was what he knew of the Iranian nuclear programme, although now, after the Israelis had paid a visit, the programme was presumably postponed. I promised to try to get Jerry Furley to intervene with the PM, but I told him not to hold out too much hope.

In return for my help, I wanted to know the real reason behind Liam Gibson's motivation in removing the gun from the security boxes in the Pegasus Bank. What was it going to be used for? I asked, hoping my half-guessed-at answer was wrong.

A sane man would have been shell-shocked at its callousness, but in this business I think any ability to experience sensitivity was driven out of me very early in my colourful career. Valery Agapov had discussed his part in the history of the weapon, with Alexi Vasilyev extolling on how much of a British once-owned mark was there left in its serial number, set alongside the letter retrieved from a Kentish bank. Alexi Vasilyev wanted the gun in the hands of an assassin in order to kill my son, Luca. If his mother, Katherine, died as a consequence, then so be it. Bottomly said he'd heard Vasilyev say he did not care.

A huge part of me was reassured by Katherine's decision not to see Vasilyev before he left Jimmy Mercer's custody; however, the threat to Luca's and her life remained. I had to think of a way to prevent it happening.

I wondered if I was right about Judith Meadows being used as Vasilyev's assassin? I guess it would fit a warped mind such as he must have. By this time, Meadows had been moved from her island in the Shetlands, leaving me with little chance of contacting her before her arrival at Bragg Creek, Calgary, and once there I could not have a presence. It could be feasible to use Richard Belfast to pass on a message, but that might not be as straightforward as it seemed.

At least, I thought, I had time on my side as there now was no gun. The gun had been taken from Liam Gibson, who was released by Mercer to manage the raid on the Iranian radar centre. All had gone well on the mission, so I assumed Gibson was within Mercer's reach. He might be helpful in some way I hadn't yet thought of.

I was about to leave Bottomly's disturbed world of isolation when he threw all my reasoned thoughts into disarray.

"Did Agapov come clean about the pathogen?"

It was not possible to hide my surprise. "What pathogen?" I asked, to which his reply mirrored this attitude he now adopted, of me first, second, and everything else. He wanted his request not to return home to South Africa to be agreed to before he would commit himself to answering any more of my questions. Was he bluffing? I asked myself as I looked at him.

"I will need a lot more than the threat of another virus, Bottomly," I said, with veritable disgust in my voice, through the biggest sneer I could manage on my face. If he noticed, he didn't mention it.

"He has the two: something that's called a paraoxon, used by South African special forces in Namibia before apartheid finished. It's much the same as Sarin. Then there's CR gas, or firegas, as it's called. It was mainly used to debilitate like tear gas, but it causes skin infections. I know it was used in Egypt where several people went blind. Water makes it worse. If it's combined with something called Borepin, it causes a contagious infection leading to death. We used it in Angola whenever we thought it would be best." He was laughing when I left him.

* * *

I had no more than a few hours that afternoon and evening, then a few more after breakfast the following day, to speak with Joseph first, then my housekeeper at The Hall, and finally my estate manager. When Joseph reported all was fine at the house, I almost laughed; my face must have betrayed my innermost thoughts, I guess, as my trusted and loyal butler knew me as well as I knew myself. He asked me outright what was troubling me. I hadn't the heart to burden him.

He was fine, as was his wife, whom I still referred to as Mrs Franks. She has told me more than once how she doesn't mind my error. I have told her I will change, however I do prefer keeping with the tradition. Mrs Squires was well, Joseph told me, with the young kitchen maid being a great help in that department.

From the estate office, not all was well. One of the tenanted farms had at least one case of this newly arrived COVID-19 infection. It was yet another worry for everyone. I asked him to have some notices printed to be put around the house and handed out to the other tenants, warning them of the effects. I started to think of Bottomly's pathogens, just as one of The Hall's landline telephones started ringing. For the first time in an age, Joseph had work to do in front of me. The call was not important but Joseph answering it was. It made me think of my future.

Was it here where, as much as I loved them all, age was catching up on us, or someplace else, maybe abroad, that I should find my own idyllic hideaway? What would I do with them all? What should do I with the estate? I didn't want to sell, but I didn't want to interview a new butler or housekeeper. I hate change. The people I would need to replace shortly had my trust and my respect, and that's not something you find at an interview. I could not see me interviewing for domestic posts. Did I recently write of how I had lost all my sensitivity? I had not lost my past! No, not here, where my character had been born. Oh well, what's more to come, wearily I wondered.

* * *

In the morning, after a hearty breakfast, I said my goodbyes, imploring them all to follow the government's advice about this COVID 19 to the absolute letter, and I set off for the drive back to London with a mask handy to put on if necessary. Jerry Furley telephoned when we nearing the showground, before we had even left Harrogate.

Apparently, working on information Valery Agapov was persuaded to impart, one of the antiterrorism departments at the Ministry Of Defence had discovered a London-based company named Delta G Scientific, that was suspected as acting as a front for the distribution of the pathogens Bottomly had told me about. The company premises were visited by various law enforcement agencies early that morning, finding traces of the chemical Bottomly had mentioned, Borepin, as well as several discarded boxes of unused, square, glass microscope slides. There was nothing else, not even a slip of waste paper. Was that a trace of fear I heard in Jerry's voice?

The general impression was it had been cleared away by a very efficient cleaning company, adept at that sort of thing.

Agapov had been discreetly called to a covert meeting to explain what Bottomly had told me. I was told he looked shocked. Whether it was Bottomly giving up these chemicals that made him nervous, or the existence of these despicable weapons, that were presumably to be aimed at civilians worldwide, was not speculated on. However, he knew of a company with a warehouse that was spoken of as a supply point for the biochemicals to be released on London, at a date yet to be finalised.

I learned how the greatest persuader I had ever come across was used against Valery Agapov. It worked. He was threatened with having all his rights, along with his deposits in the Pegasus bank, withdrawn without any right of appeal or form of redress, unless he directed his attention to the problem of these chemicals. He did so right away.

When he was asked why he had not mentioned the company before when being debriefed in detail, he replied he hadn't taken the threat seriously. In any case, he added, if this Delta G Scientific company was activated, he would then without fail have informed his handler—me. Agapov was to be a constant problem in my life, but he was a necessity we had to be able to deal with. To be totally honest, whenever I heard his name a shiver of disgust ran down my spine.

CHAPTER THIRTY-TWO

VENGEFULNESS

Whilst I was being driven from Harrogate to London, I had spoken to Sabah Al Salim for possibly thirty minutes or so, during which time I could hear his frustration rising with every passing minute.

He had exhausted his enquiries into who was behind the attempt on his life when coming out of my club in St James's. Members of his own Iranian intelligence organisation had been searching the files covering years of operations in the Middle East, Europe as well as in North America, uncovering literally hundreds of people who could have a motive for his death. Certainly none of those discovered would shed a tear had he died.

The list had been narrowed down somewhat when taking into account how many of those suspects were still imprisoned, but of course they could have relatives or close friends who could employ a killer. As could Alexi Vasilyev, I reminded myself.

Sabah's team of protection officers had been reinforced, with the places left vacant by the ones who had tragically died filled from some of his specially trained operatives flown in from Iran.

Once more, I'd asked my old friend Major-General, Sir Rupert Draycott to lend a hand. I needed his police mind to identify possible killers. It was true when he said it takes a person with an exceptional passion to engage another to kill a third party in cold blood. It would take an extraordinary person, he added, to complete that act, and it would take remarkable planning to get away with it.

It was obvious how there had been little planning involved in this attempt—which in some ways, Rupert argued, made the discovery of who was behind it more difficult. Rupert was more a police investigative officer than an intelligence-minded one, although the difference is minute, mainly in the state of mind, with his approach being moulded by years of detective work, some of which was spent in hunting down murderers.

The only intelligence I could provide Rupert with was the name of the shooter who died at the scene, Phillip Adams. As I've said, Adams had a sizeable criminal record, as did most of his immediate family. Two paternal uncles were serving prison sentences for murder, one had three more years of a recently reduced thirty year sentence to run, with the other, a younger uncle, at the start of a life sentence. An older brother was halfway through a fourteen year sentence for aggravated robbery, and not to be outdone by the masculine side of the family, one of Phillip's younger sisters was serving six years for causing grievous bodily harm.

There were parts to his investigation that crossed sensitive areas of national importance to us, as well as to Sabah's Iranian intelligence. There was one in particular I found very odd to speak about. There was another later in our cooperation, but this one concerned how the late Viscount, Winston Bottomly—he had been stripped of his title—was known by the person I can only refer to as Chevron.

Rupert had unearthed an audio tape from Chevron's final year in office, which had been logged into the MOD underground storage at Whitehall, not at Thames House, Millbank, where security would have precluded Rupert's search. The recording was of several top-floor intelligence officers, some named but not all, who had gathered to discuss a naval flotilla off the coast of South Africa with the visiting Russian and Chinese fleets, in what would be then, at the time of the discussion, four years' time.

The head of the SIS floated the idea of sending a detachment of SBS Royal Marines to carry out some 'research' on the Chinese vessels we were holding no intelligence about. Had Rupert been an agent of a foreign government, that information would have valuable. It's not always what you know that's of value, sometimes it's the fact you don't know, that's of value to someone else. As the session wore on, more facts of a general nature were spoken of until it came to discussing the actual South African Intelligence service.

Chevron was recorded as saying Bottomly was the worst of a bad bunch of South African intelligence officers. Bottomly was reckless, in the estimation of the traitor Chevron. It mattered little in the overall scheme of things.

Within two days of investigating, Rupert had a name. He was, in his words, eighty-nine percent positive he had the name of the initiator of the attempt. He could only provide the missing eleven percent after a few more 'in depth' enquiries, adding first quietly, then rigorously, being able to question the suspect.

There were a few details about this person which crossed the lines of hard-intelligence that I, as the only representative officer, was responsible for. One was to do with Page Boucher who was, as you know, part of the French Directorate for External Security. He was working out of their central offices in Paris, spending a great deal of his time in London, but for what purpose was left to guesswork for the two of us. Boucher had close ties to the area of the world known as the Levant. Rupert had indeed been busy. He had traced Boucher's travels back, all the way to his meeting with Valery Agapov in the Syrian capital of Damascus.

It seemed as if I couldn't get away from Agapov. His connection to Rupert's inquiries hinged on this geographical term of Levant, a part of the Ottoman Empire which identified with the life of Sabah Al Salim.

The British Sovereign RAF base areas of Akrotiri and Dhekelia on the island of Cyprus were part of this geographically-defined Levant, as well as being an area of significant Russian and American interest. I judged it safe to inform Rupert of this Pegasus bank, as he wanted to know why there was so much radio and text signalling about the island of Samothrace.

I told him how the two RAF bases were destined to be moved to Samothrace, with the Pegasus Bank staying on the island, potentially making the new commercial airport the hub of all things bad. I told him how the static cameras in the airport lounges would be filming every representative of the various terrorist groups having deposits in the bank, but, to the untrained eye, they would be impossible to spot, as they were constructed of a new material that actually blended into the wall-covering. If all went well, the future should be a lot safer when we knew who was doing what and where they were doing it.

That was precisely the way Jimmy Mercer saw it. He pictured the arrivals hall at the new Samothrace airport as his own personal picture gallery of these terrorist agents, just waiting for worldwide distribution. He was wringing his hands in anticipation, was the way I told Rupert. He may have been a retired member of Special Branch, but he had left a large portion of his heart there. He wanted to know if his old unit would have eyes on the cameras, as well as if they were to be installed at the port of Kamariotissa.

We were bouncing ideas off each other, with Rupert's main line of thinking focused on the Levant. He was of the mind that the attack on Sabah Al Salim and the murders at his apartment, inside the 199 Knightsbridge block, were related to that part of the world, but I asked how the murderer would know Boucher was at 199 Knightsbridge? He had no answer to that, unless Boucher was followed or he had told someone about his plans. If we were to chase those ideas, we would need an appreciable amount of either luck, or more help.

Another way of looking at it, was to look for someone coming for Sabah, finding Page Boucher there instead and, for some unknown reason, having to kill him along with the woman he was with. A random act of killing. A random act of any kind is the worst sequence of events for both the policeman and the intelligence agent. Or could it have been made to look as though it was a random killing? If that was the case, then Valery Agapov was my first suspect. He was that kind of operator, with a sharp, scheming mind.

I had asked him when we were walking in St James's Park why he used the name of Yuri Bogdan when dealing with the CIA at the bank. He said it was so long ago, he'd forgotten all the reasons behind his father's decision. Nevertheless, even allowing for time, I considered what he told me to be a load of rubbish. It was something to do with the letters in the word Baghdad, being taken from another word, which he couldn't recall, leaving the letters SAAD. A word in Arabic, as well as Urdu, which meant happiness.

Not a word I would immediately associate with Agapov. Apparently, he was born in Baghdad, but as his parents had taken him to Moscow before he was nine months old, he had always considered himself as Russian. I was pleased to get away from his version of logical truth.

Rupert had looked at the woman murdered at the same time as Boucher, a Deborah Simmons. One piece of solid information to come from the police was the time of death. At the post-mortem, it had been narrowed down to be between 2 and 4 am. But, as hard as we looked at the work the police had done, along with the work the Ministry of Defence intelligence side had done, we could find nothing on her. We had to assume Boucher was the target, and she was residual, at least, until we had any more intelligence.

Liam Gibson was a suspect, with his whereabouts being a topic occupying much of Rupert's time. He said he simply wanted him eliminated from his inquiries. Gibson was now in America, having been invited by Jimmy Mercer to stay on his personal staff as an advisor on Southern African affairs. When I heard of his appointment I inwardly applauded. I thought Gibson would be good for that position, he certainly had the knowledge. I sent a message of congratulations to Liam, wishing him well for the future.

As far as the double murder and the assassination attempt were concerned, they were both in Gibson's realm of capability, except I couldn't think of any reason for Gibson to use Phillip Adams as the assailant. He had plenty of other well-trained assassins who would have done an expert job, fulfilling another of Rupert's requirements of getting away with it, as well.

For some inexplicable reason, Serena came flooding back to the front of my memory. I wished times were better between us, but I was stuck, not knowing how to mend what was broken, then learning how to forget what had caused the rift. Most of what I could recall of our short time together was pleasant, if not wonderful at times, with Breno being a marvellous gift for which I will always be grateful. But I think the only reason I had to think of her was my loneliness, grasping onto whatever I knew rather than starting afresh, which I gauged as needing quite a bit of courage.

I found that often, disagreeable thoughts felt better for being rationalised, but this time I felt worse. I was thankful for having a busy day to take my mind away from her and Breno. No matter how busy I could make myself, some very disagreeable decisions needed to made, soon. Those matters didn't just rest with Serena. There was The Hall, with all that involved as well. There was a large part of me that wished I had someone close who could help in making the decisions.

A call from Sabah helped to bring me away from this latest malaise. I smiled as I thought I was developing a different habit when thinking of women. I said, "*C'est la vie*," in a normal voice into the phone as I was taking Sabah's call. Not unsurprisingly, he asked why. After I'd given some excuse, a long way from the truth, we arranged to meet at his apartment in Knightsbridge later that evening in order to discuss where we were, exactly, along his list of suspects. The list had been trimmed down to seven possibles.

I was to stay at my Chester Square address, thankful for its disguised size. There were three of us to accommodate, along with the three staff I'd hired.

There was one permanent housekeeper living at Chester Square who I'd hired a little while ago, perhaps in anticipation of moving to London permanently. I had asked the agency to send someone who would be looking for a permanent position rather than a short-term one, and it was on that basis I conducted the interview.

Chester Square is a Grade II listed terraced property, as are all in this part of the world, which is not to anyone's advantage, but being enormous inside, is. It was built by the Grosvenor family in the 1840s, who constructed the houses in Chester Square on five storeys, with a surfeit of rooms on each, which, with Sir Rupert staying there, along with Peter, my driver, then me, left little room for the agency staff I'd hired for a month. The shortest time for any contract. I had to supplement Mrs Whyte, the housekeeper, with a cook, a housemaid, a cleaner and a butler, all living-in positions. I'm sure the wage bill, for here, added to that of The Hall, could pay off the national debt of a medium-sized country.

Sabah was a lot calmer in the flesh than he was on the phone, the short while ago when we'd spoken. He was with his brother in the apartment, going over his past, looking more closely at those seven names he had mentioned. In Sabah's opinion, each of the seven had at one time been enraged enough to want to kill him. However, although not as consequential as having grounds to murder, Rupert, who had come with me, put forward the theory that the eligibility to become a suspect, or not, could hinge on knowing Philip Adams and how to contact him. From what Rupert had found, only two of them had that qualification.

Both were officers in the Islamic Revolutionary Guard Corps, principally stationed at the Sar-Allah Headquarters in Tehran, but, at one stage fairly recently, they were attached to the Guard Corps in London.

This was another example of where Rupert's research had impacted upon Sabah's and our own intelligence services. In this case, Sabah was highly impressed with Sir Rupert's thoroughness, praising him for it. It did cross my mind he might offer Rupert a fixed post! I wondered, if he did, how would Rupert react? I positioned myself near the front exit. I had no need.

A brother of one of the officers in this Guard Corps was the ambassador to the United Kingdom in the Iranian embassy at Prince's Gate, opposite Hyde Park in London. It was a place Sabah knew well, being just a short walk away from his apartment. He and the ambassador met often, playing squash in the court below the embassy.

On the ambassador's appointment, Sabah had

visited him strictly with business in mind, without any embellishment to it, but later, over time, Sabah had grown to like the man. On many occasions, the two would be in each other's company for formal events, of which there were more than many foreign postings, Sabah had noted.

The ambassador's brother in Iran held the rank of a two-star General. Sabah knew the man, having made a special detour to meet the General the last time he was in Iran, taking him a gift the ambassador had asked to be delivered.

The General, on the other hand, hid his dislike of the head of National Intelligence exceedingly well. He was versed in the art of deception, but his dislike came from an unusual place. It was born on the battlefront. At a particular place in the Iranian-Iraqi war, the General, whose rank was then that of a Major, lost a lot of men, due not only to the poor intelligence his battalion commander was given by Sabah's father, but his personal incompetence. The place was Kermanshah and the outcome was an Iranian victory, but the General thought his men would not have died had Sabah's father acted with less speed and more diligence.

He never spoke in anger, never spoke of the battle in public. He waited as his career moved to a different level, all the time trying hard to forget how he had committed his ground forces into a trap that should have been seen by the Intelligence Network

Sabah's father commanded. He might have forgotten his anger, if it hadn't been for one more example of sheer incompetence, or worse, treachery from the same family.

In the first week of Sabah Al Salim acceding to the position of the head of Iran's intelligence networks, he disclosed the hiding place of the top Iraqi General under Saddam Hussein to the American CIA. The two Generals were not friends, in fact, for eight years they had been sworn enemies during the war between their countries, but to betray another Muslim to the infidel Americans was a sin for which Sabah could never be forgiven.

Rupert had his information on the other officer at Sar-Allah from me. This officer qualified for attention by having his wife here in London. The officer concerned was not as high on the echelon of rank as the first, being just a lowly Colonel; however, his wife, Afra Khalaji, more than made up for that.

Afra was an active intelligence officer, one of the most valuable in Sabah's Ministry of Intelligence and National Security of Iran. At the time of the assassination attempt, she was living with a wealthy Scottish businessman, whose sexuality did not exclusively involve women. He spent a lot of his time in far-flung corners of the world wherever his life took him, and most of the time she would tag along with him. This man also served the British government in a recommendation capacity as the strategic advisor on all things Middle Eastern. In which capacity, of course, he kept his eye aimed firmly on commercial profit.

The Colonel knew every detail of his wife's arrangement, as he had spoken of it to Sabah when his wife was assigned. His words were to the effect that 'she viewed it as her solemn duty, as I viewed mine'.

"I doubt she sees her service in my command as her solemn duty nowadays," Sabah said without any explanation, then added, whilst I was looking at him in surprise. "Murder, yes! She would certainly be capable of putting things together for an attempt on my life. But why would she get a common British criminal to execute it? It would have been far easier, and more secure to fly over an Iranian specialist to use."

CHAPTER THIRTY-THREE

A BREAK

"How would this woman—what's her name? Oh yes, got it now," I had written her name down in a little notebook I had started to carry in order to remember these difficult to pronounce names, "Afra Khalaji, see her duty differently now, Sabah? What have you done to make her want to kill you?"

He poured two more glasses of my favourite whisky, which I knew he had purchased solely for my benefit. In return for such hospitality, I had promised to help in finding the person behind the assassination attempt. We sat facing each other, sharing the scenic view from the panoramic window across Hyde Park. I was a long way from anticipating what was to follow.

"Not her, no, although it could be. I was thinking it could be her sister. She was publicly flogged in the central square of Tehran for stealing cigarettes. There was some confusion about whether it was her or the man she was with who was guilty, but it was a judge who sentenced her to the punishment after hearing the evidence. I'm in no position to say why that was." With a shrug of his shoulders, he carried on.

"It could have been the evidence, or it could have been prejudice against a woman. Maybe it was a religious prejudice. There is that in my country. Perhaps she was Sunni and he Shia. In Iran, Shiites form the majority of Moslems, but as I say, I have no further knowledge, nor did I look any further. It is true my department is generally feared in Iran, with even the judiciary looking over their shoulders to keep us happy. So the judge may have delivered his verdict with fear of us foremost in his mind.

"I could have put pressure on the judge to decide it was the man who committed the theft of seven packets of cigarettes. Then I would have had to accept accusations of preferential treatment, even from people within my department, which, of course, it would have been.

"Had I taken that action, then my agent, this women's sister, stood a very good chance of being exposed as the espionage agent she still is today. What would have happened then? I'll take a guess, if you like. Western governments would have accused us of back-pedalling on our country's stated aim of achieving full and open democracy. If you're ready, I'll tell you what I can remember of the case, and I have a very good memory.

"The pair were stopped outside a busy grocery store with a full bag of shopping they'd paid for at the checkout. It's not important how or why, but they had acted suspiciously inside the shop. As a consequence of such actions, they were stopped in the street, taken back inside and then, when the bag was searched, these seven packets of American cigarettes were found.

"Apparently, they are very expensive for most Iranians. The packets were at the bottom of the bag with the other grocery shopping piled on top. The most condemning feature in all of this, was the printed receipt. It carried no mention of cigarettes. They both had the same excuse of buying them earlier in the day at another shop. When asked where the other shop was, they couldn't remember.

"What was I to do? I'm not normally in a position where my judgement is sought, but with this case, where corporal punishment was the sentence and the culprit a highly valued member of my inner departmental staff, I was expected to do something. I couldn't win." He shrugged his shoulders yet again, but this time more in defeat than doubt.

"It was said to me afterwards, by my brother, I think, that not only had I made enemies of the two sisters, I had made enemies of their whole families.

But had I decided to punish the man..." he held out both hands with the palms pointing up towards the ceiling, as if about to receive a large gift, "then it would have been impossible for me to count my enemies. I thought that was the truth."

Ruefully, he looked across the outside road, past the barracks of the Queen's Horse Guards, onto the green, pleasant park stretching away as far as the eye could see. As he was examining whatever it was he imagined to be out there, he was also trying to examine his thoughts by speaking them aloud.

"I did consider dismissing the charge altogether if only I could have found an outlet for the brand of cigarettes nearby, but despite my men looking, none could be found. I would have bribed a shopkeeper to say they had bought the cigarettes in his shop, if we had found one. I heard rumours there were some in my departments who expected a confession from the man to miraculously appear, but what if it had? Would it have been believed? No, it wouldn't be."

I asked why the woman was with the man, but apparently nobody had asked that question. Having obtained no answer to it, I decided it was best to leave things as they were. Even so, I was interested as to whether he knew where these two women were now, so I asked. I was no luckier with this question than the one before.

Mumbling something unintelligible, he shook his head in obsequious despondency, looking as if he'd been doing something similar, shaking his head that is, for a million years or more. Without any damage, presumably, he started to tell me a story.

After he had recruited Abu Saleh Al-Sabaid, a deputy leader of ISIS, he believed he had an opportunity whereby his intelligence agency could influence some of the decisions being made by the ISIS hierarchy. The first chance to see if he was right arrived when a part of the anti-government ISIS forces in Syria raided a supply facility at the al-Tanf garrison, driving away from the site with the entire compliment of the Turkish Bayraktar TB2 drones. These things were providing the Turkish-backed coalition with a huge advantage in hanging on to the north-western corner of Syria, bordering Turkey's Hatay province. Sabah wanted the drones used in a different way.

If ISIS could use these drones to defeat the Turkish-backed forces in this Idlib governorate, it would irrevocably disrupt Turkey's plans for the region and make the Ankara government more willing to trade a certain thing Sabah wanted for his own. Apart from the secret Sabah wanted from Ankara, he wanted an end to the civil war, to his country's advantage.

By way of showing his sincerity, he was willing to hand over the control he had established inside ISIS, along with his leverage inside the Turkish government, to the British SIS. He said he asked nothing in return other than the chance to live a peaceful existence in England, along with an entitlement to access his bank account in the Pegasus Bank on Samothrace at his convenience. That was gold-plated with his proviso. If, he said, the Bank of England would like a huge monetary deposit from Pegasus he would make that available.

He and I had spoken of his future arrangements a couple of times and I had met to discuss them with the government's Solicitor General, Sir Leonard Miles. Leonard was very much in favour of strengthening our ties with the Iranians, being careful not to trip over anyone's toes, as he succinctly put it. American interest would have to be a consideration.

Jimmy Mercer was encouraged by Sabah's continuing cooperation when it came to the financing for the construction of the airfield, together with the additional centres of operations, including all the obligatory, expensive storage installations, both civil and military, on the island of Samothrace. All aspects of this had become easier now the Greek government had signed off on its build. They had several reasons to be pleased the work would take place, involving Greek labour but no Greek money.

Another issue of the 'fluid' collaboration was with the 'solid' intelligence Jimmy was getting direct from Sabah on the ISIS operations in Somalia and on their operatives inside the Congo, where things were starting to 'rubble'.

Fluid' and 'solid' were two of the words in the

colloquial parlance I'd heard Jimmy Mercer loved to use, but this was the first time I'd heard him use the word 'rubble'. There was one more, which I must say I was fond of using, included here when he was talking about the Horn of Africa.

Apparently, the CIA had a considerable 'footprint' in the Horn of Africa, watching closely for incursions from recognised terrorist groups into the Djibouti area, where the Americans were building a base from where they planned to control the Gulf of Aden and then, ultimately, cargo movement through the Suez Canal.

"Didn't we once have a 'footprint' in Aden?" I asked of nobody in particular, merely smiling as the torch of proposed imperialism was picked up and carried forward.

That evening whilst I was having dinner, Katherine rang. Normally I would not have answered. I hate the thought of speaking on a telephone whilst my food is getting cold; however, this was a difficult time the two of us were living through. She wished to speak of a subject we had touched upon sometime earlier.

When I was discussing Sabah Al Salim's contributions in combatting Al-Qaeda and ISIS with Jimmy Mercer, I asked Jimmy that a permanent protection team be allocated to Katherine and Luca each time the two of them were in New York, which would happen whenever Luca's school was closed for holidays. I offered to pay for them, of course, but asked that they be allowed to carry firearms openly. Both Jimmy and Katherine wanted to know why I thought they were in danger. I tried, as best I could, to explain my thoughts on the disconcerting threats Alexi Vasilyev posed on us all.

I wanted a visible deterrent to Vasilyev with openly displayed firearms. Jimmy Mercer agreed to my request, but that wasn't the case in London. Even so, I did manage to provide some protection for Eaton Square.

I could supply any number of legally registered firearm holders to the inside of number 16 Eaton Square. I was told George and Sophie were entitled to leave their front door open with those firearm licence holders standing in the hallway with their guns on show. I had the same help from the Home Office when it came to asking the library section of the Royal Borough of Kensington and Chelsea to allow the provision of protection for Sophie on their premises.

When Katherine called, I was dining with a friend away from Chester Square. I had been friends with her and her husband for several years before he died in a tragic boating accident, near to the time I lost my brother and father. When her husband was alive, he was a prominent member of the Conservative Government. We had been close friends for several years before those devastating events occurred in our lives.

With the arrival of Serena into my life, followed by the birth of Breno, my time was spent considerably more at home or occasionally in Portugal, or even travelling with the Zabreno fashion show; wherever it was, it was most certainly not spent in London.

The demands of this matter of state had kept me in the capital for more time than I can remember, which could have been lucky for me. That's something I would not normally say. The extra time here had given me an opportunity to rekindle a friendship I had never forgotten, but had never thought of in any romantic way. Perhaps I should, as my friend had stayed single, professing a preference for that status rather than entering into anything more serious or binding.

I'm afraid my mind is wandering, for which I apologise. I drifted away from what I wanted to say, but in so doing, I've addressed some of the thoughts I've been having recently. Where I am now in life, is an issue I should tackle sometime soon.

The following evening, my lady friend and I were enjoying a glass of wine together in her London home, very close to the Royal Albert Hall, when Sir Rupert rang me. I made my apologies as I left the room to take his call.

Being the fine police officer he was, he had continued to dig around after he'd unearthed something that, at first glance, could be considered by someone less conscientious than he, as trivial at best. It was a possible relationship the man I'd shot dead at the assassination attempt, had to the murders in apartment number 75, at 199 Knightsbridge. I was all ears!

Though at first the clue Rupert had unearthed seemed, as I'd said, to be no more than a triviality, he contacted the department at Thames House who deal exclusively with tracing a person's lineage back through time, be it genuine or not. They are predominantly concerned with the construction of an authentic legend for people being relocated, people such as Judith Meadows. A legend that could stand up in front of any investigation. What they found, put together with what Sir Rupert had found, could be the answer to who murdered the two in the Knightsbridge apartment and maybe who was behind the attempt to murder Sabah Al Salim.

The woman who was murdered lying beside Page Boucher at Sabah's apartment, inside 199 Knightsbridge, Deborah Simmons, was a one-time model, as well as being the writer of a children's novella. Through a contact of Rupert's in the American FBI, it was discovered she was an American by birth. She was born in Chicago, Illinois, in June 1983, but christened Julia Simmons, not Deborah.

On leaving college, she worked for the Chicago Tribune on the features desk for almost two years.

Nearing the end of the first two years of her working life, her modelling life took over from her career at the newspaper as her photographs were appearing in more and more fashion magazines whilst her journalist career was, at best, stagnating, and at worse down the toilet, as the editor of the Tribune told Sir Rupert's contact.

According to Julia's best friend from college, it was just two photographs of her appearing in the French magazine, *Le Point*, that took Julia to France in order to meet her future husband. He had written a passionate letter to her, proposing marriage on the strength of the one facial and one silhouette photograph he said he'd seen in that magazine. He was older than Julia by over thirty years, being a twice-divorced French magistrate.

Their marriage did not last long. Which, apparently, her friend could have told anyone if they'd bothered to ask, but nobody had. It was ended shortly after Julia bumped into Page Boucher in a Parisian jewellery shop both had decided to browse. As they left the shop, arm in arm, they were followed by the *détective privé* hired by her husband to spy on his new wife's movements.

Those movements took her to an apartment near the Jardin Botanique that Boucher had, we assumed, 'borrowed' from a source in one of the capital's many foreign legations. They stayed in the apartment until late that night, the detective reported. Deborah's married name at that time had been Julia Toussaint and that was the surname that piqued the religious side of Rupert's interest. In French Toussaint means All Saints' Day and neither Deborah nor Page were displaying the behaviour of a saint!

Whilst the divorce was proceeding, the magistrate became very jealous and it was fair to say, he told Rupert, resentful of her having an affair. He even approached her one evening when she was dining with Boucher in a local restaurant, anxious for her to change her mind. She was adamant that she would not change.

Originally, it was he who had moved from the matrimonial home, but with each report from his private detective of her continued adultery, his jealousy grew more spiteful, until eventually he ordered her from the Paris apartment, changing the locks when she went shopping. The locks on each of his other properties were changed the same day.

Some of what now follows is speculation and some fact, but where it is supposition, it's based on years of investigative work Rupert has been engaged in and the lives of two experienced people, without any flowery embellishments.

In order to get through the French divorce proceedings as amicably as possible, she thought it best to not only change her name, but change where she lived. She adopted the name of Deborah Simmons, after arriving on British soil with Page Boucher. She hoped the subterfuge with her name, alongside the help from Boucher in relocating to Sabah Al Salim's apartment, would help her escape from her husband.

Page kept his relationship with the French Deborah ticking along as one does when dating married women: carefully. It was with the same extreme care that Rupert conducted his enquiries. At first, it was only a theory we had to go on as to why Phillip Adams became involved with Deborah, but later we found some information from Phillip's father, who had told the police virtually nothing.

To Rupert, Adams senior opened up, saying he didn't know much but what he did know he would share. He confessed how his son had told him he'd had an argument with a Frenchman at a club, the night before. The father didn't know which club, nor what it was over, but took a guess, saying it would be about a woman. He said when he'd next seen his son he had a badly bruised face. He said he was used to seeing Phillip after a fight, but this time it looked as though something harder than a fist had hit him.

Rupert took a small collection of photographs of each one, Phillip Adams, Deborah Simmons and Page Boucher, around all the top-drawer London nightclubs he knew. It didn't take him long before he found what he was looking for. At the Libertine Club, behind Oxford Street, one of the doorman recognised all three! When the girl and the Frenchman had left the club, they had been closely followed by Adams, who they knew, with two of his friends.

There had been a verbal altercation where Adams was being encouraged by his friends to do more. It was late, the doorman said, almost 2 am, when noise travels, so the two doormen stepped in to stop it escalating any further into a disturbance where the police would be called. This they did, without any trouble. Rupert did not leave it there. He asked if Adams had followed the woman and the Frenchman away from the club. At first, this doorman was very uncommunicative, but a fifty pound note altered his reticence.

The woman and man took a cab from the nearby rank in Winsley Street, with the doorman hearing the destination as Knightsbridge. With no cabs remaining, Adams and the other two ran the short distance into Oxford Street, flagging down a passing taxi. The doorman saw the taxi execute a U-turn, but couldn't say if the cab followed the other one or went off to drop the Adams party elsewhere.

It was Rupert who made a report to the police department dealing with the two murders at Knightsbridge—feeling, I'm sure, rightfully proud of himself because of his detective work. I apologised to my lady friend for leaving her on her own for the time it took to hear Rupert's news, but she would hear none of it.

I'm extraordinarily pleased to report she brushed my apologetic attempts away in a more than favourable manner, the details of which are not for sharing.

Neither Rupert nor I could be certain what happened next in this saga concerning Boucher and Adams. Had it been Philip Adams on his own, or with his friends, who gained entry to 199 and their way to number 75? But nobody came forward having changed their minds on hearing footsteps or gunshots in those early morning hours. Our problem did not end here. We had no motive for Phillip Adams to want to kill Sabah. What was his reason for going after him that day in St James's Street?

When the detectives in charge of what was first assumed to be a double murder case, called at the address in Battersea on the driving licence found in the handbag Deborah Simmons was carrying, nobody at that address knew her. The landlady of this five-storeyed block of five self-contained flats lived in the basement apartment, managing the property for a Frenchman whose name she knew only as Page. She did not know if that was his first or last name. It was the only name she had. She did not know all the tenants. They came and went, she said, with no word to her.

There was one apartment, she told the police,

where a single woman lived. The police inspected it, reporting it to be empty, but lived in. Her neighbours knew very little of her or the Frenchman who was there on occasions, with the very attractive woman.

As far as Sabah Al Salim was concerned, apart from not being in the country when Page and Deborah were murdered, as his diary attested to, he knew no woman named Deborah Simmons. He knew Boucher, of course. He knew of his philandering ways, being well aware of his reputation with women.

He told the police how Boucher had a key to his apartment at 199, of which some parts were securely locked. Then privately he told me how it suited his Iranian intelligence services to have Boucher use the apartment, precisely because of all the surveillance and audio equipment secreted there.

When he told me this, I asked why the Frenchman would want his affairs to be filmed? Surely Boucher would be aware of these steps? I guess I should not have been surprised by the answer, but I was. Boucher took copies of the films, which Sabah thought were either for his own gratification or, if the possibility existed, to extort money from the woman, or her husband!

* * *

It was the day after Rupert paid a visit on Phillip Adams senior that we got the break we were waiting for. The motorcyclist was found. He had stolen the bike the same day as the shooting from outside The Royal Free Hospital at Hampstead, changing the license plates in a garage he rented to store his car. He was also one of the two, who were with Phillip Adams at the Libertine Club the night of the disturbance with Page.

CHAPTER THIRTY-FOUR

MY TRUTH, YOUR LIES

The first odd arrangement about my summons was it came from Millbank, not from Vauxhall. Another element was how Sir Leonard Miles was representing MI5. Other than their peculiarity, I could find no importance to level on those two facts. However, that was not the same with the third factor: I was the only intelligence officer attending.

"Nobody from Five wanted to touch it," Sir Leonard had told me on the telephone. I hadn't bothered to ask him why that was, as I considered I would not have been told the truth, I would have been lied to.

As I approached the building in Peckham to fulfil my obligation to Sir Leonard, I wondered if the fairly new coats of blue and white paint to the exterior were an attempt to soften its austere presence. I doubted if paint alone could ever do that to a police station. In fact, I started to wonder if the eye could ever deceive the mind?

The sergeant behind the glass screen at the front desk was expecting me, he said, as he leant over to his side in order to press a button hidden beneath the counter, releasing the door to a brightly-lit corridor with six closed plain wooden doors off to my right, each with a plastic name tab attached announcing them all to be interview rooms.

At the end of the corridor stood a uniformed police officer, alongside a short but sturdily built man, with what I thought to be an appropriate name, Detective Inspector Small. "I'm the officer in charge of the case," he told me.

"I've followed all the procedure I could find," he declared, soberly. "I've reminded the police constable he signed the Official Secrets Act and not to repeat anything he heard the suspect say. That applies to either before or after being formally cautioned. I have torn out the page in his pocket book where he had made his notes. It's all been recorded in the station log, as well as being signed for, before being bagged up and put in the property room."

I looked at him first, then at the uniformed officer, wondering how often this sort of routine was carried out. If ever it had been, then they were certainly efficient. My mind was still wandering as he was continuing to speak.

"I was told to hand the suspect over to you, but to record your questioning as it may impact on the charge of either murder, or attempted murder. Apart from that, I think he's all yours, Mr Williamson. I'll be off. Tell the constable when you're finished with our man, please."

If an ending of anything could ever be called a beginning, then this was where a new beginning took place.

His name was Harout Ohanian. Harout, he told me, looking far from being poised or confident, was Armenian for Harry. Now there was a priceless coincidence, I thought, without mentioning it, but I'm sure I could feel the beginnings of a smile forming as I started the questioning, not daring to ask if Ohanian stood for Paterson, or even Williamson, in Armenian!

I can hear you asking why I was here in Peckham, which was not the most exclusive area of London, about to interrogate an Armenian over an assassination attempt of an Iranian in an exclusive area of London? At this stage I was the same as you are now, trying to understand what was happening. Let us begin together.

Harry, Harout Ohanian lived on his own in Peckham Park Road, within walking distance of the newly decorated, and smelling of paint, police station. He was with Phillip Adams on the motorbike he'd stolen in St James's Street when an attempt was made on Sabah Al Salim's life. Of that there is no doubt, but to understand why that came to be, we have to first go back in time to the Libertine nightclub.

Harry, Phillip and another friend, named Frankie, whose surname is not important to us, were at the Libertine Club when Phillip was chatting to a very attractive woman aged in her mid, to late-thirties.

Something completely unexpected happened that changed the whole end to the night. Harry was chatting to a woman when, without warning, Phillip grabbed hold of his arm and said, "Come on, I need the pair of you outside." With that, all three of them left the club.

"Outside, there was this biggish guy who I learned was French, with the same girl Phil had been talking to. Phillip was mouthing off about somefink or other, and it started to get a bit 'eated, as things do after a certain time, and after certain matters.

"All I saw was the bouncers stepping in front of Phil, as the Frenchie, with the girl, went off in a cab. Then he, Phil, that is, was running down the street, shouting for it to stop. Me and Frankie just followed. All three of us jumped in a cab in Oxford Street and followed the first one.

"We were all having a laugh before this 'appened, Mr Williamson. We'd all had a good night. Phil was saying he was having a good time before the Frenchman got a bit heavy with him. He said somefink, then pushed Phil away from the girl, before grabbing hold of 'er and walking off towards the exit."

I asked what this had to do with St James's Street and he said it had nothing to do with it—then, but, afterwards, everything. I looked at the police constable, who raised his eyes towards the ceiling. Once again, I was caught out. This time I was wondering what answer could be found on the ceiling as the police constable began to speak.

"It was about here, sir, when I was told to send it upstairs and the DI, the Detective Inspector, took over."

"I haven't heard anything to suggest why that should be, constable," I said, then asked, "What was said to cause so much fuss?" Inwardly, I was pleased it was passed on to the intelligence service.

The constable told how Harout Ohanian mentioned three Iranians outside the Knightsbridge address when both taxis arrived, one of whom he recognised as a spy. When Harout said that word, the constable followed standing orders, taking the case upstairs to the DI. It was he who said it had to be shifted on to Military Intelligence.

"Anyway, do you want me to go on with this, or what?" Ohanian asked, as he continued to look bored, but more so, whilst sitting with his hands cuffed to the table. I nodded, adding a quiet, "Yes, please."

"When we got to Knightsbridge, I paid the cab, as the other two were looking at three guys outside the front door, who were waiting for us. The Frenchman and woman were standing behind 'em. I knew one of those three to be Iranian and I thought the other two were as well. I also knew the name of the one I recognised and I knew him to be a spy with the Iranian Secret Service."

One of these three men waiting outside the address was indeed an Iranian, from a town named Tabriz, in north-western Iran. Harout Ohanian did tell me his name a little later, but once again, to pronounce it is difficult and not really worth your effort. He recognised a second man later from a newspaper report of the double murder that took place at 199, that night.

The important detail to all this is when Harout, along with Phillip and the other friend, left that place, Deborah Simmons and Page Boucher were still alive. Another pertinent detail was the time this took place. It was just after two in the morning when the three left the scene. Harout knew that to be true because he looked at his watch. It was 02:11.

I questioned him about knowing the Iranian from Tabriz, but Harry was absolutely sure, because his family came from a town a little north of there called Meghri, over the border into Armenia. He had visited the popular market in Tabriz on occasions during the many holidays he'd taken to the family home, having seen the man in the town several times. They had shared a drink together along with a chat, more than once.

Of the party of three waiting Iranians, two had guns which they threatened Harout's party with, telling them in no uncertain terms to leave the woman and Frenchman alone, as well as to leave the area.

Harry said Phillip was highly incensed by these threats. He was not the type to back down or to like being told what to do. Which I was later able to verify by the various records available on Adams. Apparently, until three and a half months ago, Adams was in the army, where he'd been accepted for the Parachute Regiment provided he passed the strict induction course. He didn't pass. He was thrown out for striking a drill sergeant. Whilst I was remembering some of the file on Adams, Harout Ohanian continued.

"Phil fronted-up the guy in the middle. He was standing almost touching nose-to-nose, spitting the words out of his mouth into his face. I don't know how the man did not hit Phil, who was saying—'tell the two monkeys to use the guns or put them away like good little f......g arseholes and f..k off.'

"He didn't get a chance to say any more, as the one I knew smashed him in the side of his face, with the gun still in his hand. I'd seen that Iranian guy have a row before. I was with my sister when one erupted one Saturday, in Tabriz. I won't go into details, but just take my word he's a nasty bit of work." He stopped for a second to take a breath.

"I've been in a few fights with Phil and I've never seen him hit the ground before, but he did that night. We left with Phil just about able to stand, but we found a cab driver to take us home after proving we weren't drunk. When he came round, Phil, that is, all he could think about was finding the guy who hit him. But first he wanted the guy in the middle as he'd seen his face in the newspapers, saying how he was a big noise."

An account of the double murder was carried the next day in the Sunday newspapers. The articles carried the woman's name and the name of the Frenchman, giving his job as a nightclub entertainer and hers the same. Sabah Al Salim's full name was printed in most of the newspapers either that Sunday morning, or in the daily newspapers of Monday.

Nobody in the Home Office considered issuing any 'D-Notice' or Defence and Security Media Advisory Notice, as its longwinded name is, to the editors of the newspapers, as they should have done. Maybe that was because it was a Sunday, or maybe the relevant duty officer was asleep, but Sabah was reported as being a 'millionaire philanderer' and owner of several properties in London and the Home Counties, including this Knightsbridge apartment.

As the article was expanded upon by the journalist's imagination, it was made to sound more and more self-indulgent. Sabah's reputation as an Arab Casanova was quoted as coming from a reliable source, who apparently added that he was regularly seen in the company of beautiful women.

Harout Ohanian was not sure, nor can anyone else be sure, whether it was a single word or phrase in the article Phillip read, or perhaps it was the fact of Sabah living at the Knightsbridge address, that pushed Phillip into taking the automatic weapon from someone in his family, possibly his father, then asking Harout for a ride so he could assassinate Sabah Al Salim. In order to cut his teeth in the family business, so to speak. First of course, he had to wait for Sabah's return to London.

When it came to the day outside my club, it was Philip Adams sat behind Harry Ohanian on the all-new Honda CMX500 Rebel sports motorcycle, following Sabah's Rolls Royce from the Knightsbridge address to Boodles then, fatally, choosing to wait until lunch ended that day, before he was the one who died.

* * *

Neither Phillip Adams, nor Harout Ohanian, nor the unnamed friend, murdered Deborah Simmons or Page Boucher. If you are like me, needing more proof than just Harout's word of them being alive when he,

Harout and friends left the scene at Knightsbridge, then I can provide you with more. But you won't like me for it.

I went to the apartment number 75, 199 Knightsbridge, to speak to the Iranian protection officer, the one whom Harout Ohanian had named.

The reason I have the name is because I promised Harry, Harout Ohanian, he would not face trial for the crime of murder if he told me. His cooperation in naming the man saved an immense amount of time, but unfortunately I learned how the man was not at the apartment. He was inside the Iranian Embassy, where he had diplomatic immunity. He was due to fly to Iran later that day with another two protection officers, presumably the two who were standing outside number 199 Knightsbridge the night of the murders.

* * *

Sabah Al Salim was lying on a divan being attended to by two very attractive young women, whisky glass in hand, ordering my favourite to be poured for my pleasure. As I stretched out on a similar sofa, I took the glass from the smiling girl, savouring each swallow as I outlined my proposal to him. Alas, it was quite complicated, meaning my glass needed refilling twice more before we had finalised his inauguration, as it were, into the British Secret Intelligence Service.

You see what happened was this—Sabah Al Salim killed Page Boucher when he decided he needed more friends. He killed Page because he had too much information about Sabah that had to be forgotten. Some of what Boucher knew, he used to secure the use of number 75, whenever he wanted the use of an apartment in Knightsbridge.

He knew, for example, where the evidence was that connected Sabah to the Mukhabarat, the Syrian Military Intelligence Division. It would be in America's interest to know where Syria was getting some of its logistical, technical and financial support in its civil war, but not if Page could show how Sabah's SAVAMA was responsible for the murder and torture of thousands of Sunni Kurds in order that some of that logistical, technical and most certainly the financial support, was getting through.

Sabah needed a clean sheet with no past indiscretions in order that Britain and America could welcome him into the fold. The only way he could be sure of that was to eliminate anyone who had a hold over him. Deborah Simmons was unfortunate in being with the wrong man. All of this, I knew. I also knew much more. I had to know, as it would be me who'd get sucked into the time-honoured shit if anything turned out to be wrong. Neither he nor I could risk that.

It was me who told Sabah about Rupert's findings, suggesting if Rupert, as conscientious as he was, managed to discover his past history with the Ba'ath Party, with him being a such a close relative of Saddam Hussein, or his present history with ISIS, then he could never be safe without taking severe precautions. I told him he needed to bury as much as the French and the Syrians knew of him as quickly, as well as silently, as was possible.

Page Boucher was also the person Alexi Vasilyev was referring to when he mentioned the risk to the British illegals operating in the countries of Afghanistan and Pakistan. It was Sabah who knew of them, but his knowledge was not as extensive as Boucher's. It was Boucher who had the microscopic details on behalf of the French intelligence service. Boucher not only had the names, but he knew the positions these British agents were occupying. He knew what they liked and what they didn't like. Page Boucher's knowledge of our operational agents was substantial, particularly about the two illegals we had inside the Pakistani Inter-Services Intelligence. Jerry Furley was happy when I told him that was no longer a problem.

Part of Sabah's attractions for Jimmy Mercer's departments was the information he had on the finances of ISIS. He knew where almost every penny of the money they collected had come from, but again there were the problems he'd generated that could sully the partnership paperwork. He had to coordinate with Jerry Furley, whilst our assets were removed from his path—a long way from it.

* * *

Jimmy Mercer had been closer in the spread betting than I, but not by much. Jimmy had wagered it would be between six and nine months, whereas I had speculated it would be between the time of inception and three months.

The actual time it took for Alexi Vasilyev to transgress from the oath of allegiance he'd taken when accepting the extended hand of American citizenship, along with his relocation to Glendive, in Dawson County, Montana, was five months, three weeks and three days. I was well out in the wager and I wasn't going to default on the bet just because Jimmy was short by a matter of days, but equally I did feel as though I could withhold payment for the alcohol consumed, other than for the first bottle of wine ordered. That seemed fair to me.

* * *

One fully encrypted email from th e unmonitored IP address accessible to Alexi Vasilyev was not intercepted before it went beyond its acknowledged perimeters and reached the intended destination.

That wasn't because it couldn't be stopped. No, that wasn't the reason. It could have been cancelled at anytime. It hadn't been because I had a very good idea where it was going and had no wish to spoil the party.

Vasilyev and Valery Agapov shared a secret that only one other person knew of, apart from me, but I wasn't supposed to know. The other person was Sergei Ivanov and the secret centred around his intimate knowledge of the governing family of Angola. The family was, it could be argued, the most corrupt of all the corrupted African rulers there had ever been, but an old proverb I was aware of—if you know a man is a thief, don't leave your valuables within reach—should have applied. It didn't! It obviously had not been translated into Russian.

Sergei knew about the corruption trail from the second largest oil production fields in Africa because he was the one who made sure it was navigable from Luanda to Havana. Then later, when the Angolan oil and diamond riches were more than poor Cubans could afford, he switched the exportable production to Beijing, in return for money and weapons from the rich Chinese business pioneers just waiting to plunder the meagre gross domestic produce of Angola.

The head of the ruling family was slowly dying. This was partially due to natural causes and partially due to the carcinogens he ingested each time he visited the love of his life; the zinc mine Sergei Ivanov gifted him last year. The mine was being sunk on the outside of a small town called Funda, twenty kilometres east of the home of the ruler of Angola, living in his grand, gated resident on the outskirts of the capital of Luanda, overlooking the South Atlantic.

Each day he visited his mine, he would take several cups of tea at the site with an oral zinc supplement as prescribed by his French doctors. However, due to the unforeseen events surrounding the initial encrypted signal received by the French, in the beginning of August, it was decided by the Agapov/Vasilyev/Ivanov axis that his death needed to be hastened. A trusted member of his staff was bribed by Sergei to add just enough zinc sulphate to the tea that it made his pancreatic cancer much worse.

And so Alexi's email to Sergei set out the programme to hasten the death, along with instructions on how to install the new leader, the one the tripartite coalition had selected.

* * *

From those far-off days of my youth when I first realised knowledge was power, I have been an avid learner. My learning urge has never ceased; in fact, the opposite is true, it has grown ever stronger as I've aged. The name Alexi sent to Sergei Ivanov was the one name I was waiting to know.

Ever since the specialist American signals officer, Lieutenant John Phipps, jumped from his field position in Turkey into Iraq, at Al-Qa'im, accepting idealism instead of the discipline of the American Defence Intelligence Agency, the highly secret post-quantum cryptography system to write emails has been available to those who know how to use the process. As of yet, time had not allowed me to become one, but Valery Agapov understood the programme and Agapov was one of ours, working in the field.

As a guarantee of Agapov's commitment to our side, not seeking to trade with anyone else, I had Sabah Al Salim devise a programme to insert into an IOMS unit that could decrypt Vasilyev's email before it reached Sergei Ivanov's secured sandbox. Once there, it would have been extremely secure had it not been for the malware the IOMS unit installed. Our unauthorised entry offered an opportunity for undetected penetration.

Before the signal had finished its journey, it passed through the coiled network of its first protocol at the operational, Soviet Red Banner Institute where the message on the screen read, *this email has no content*, then on to its second port of call, Valery Agapov's office of the Director of Foreign Intelligence where, by the time it was opened, it had inserted the same amount of malicious content, only this time with two added virus-features, thereby making both systems and consolidated networks ineffective for a considerable amount of time.

That single empty message was enough for Jimmy Mercer. It told him all he needed to know about the loyalty of a Vagabond. It also told me the whereabouts of a particular person I was waiting to find.

* * *

Unlike Sabah Al Salim, who had only a passing knowledge of his assailant in the ill-conceived attempt to murder him, Alexi Vasilyev knew his killer only too well. He had looked at this man's photograph time and time again when lying in his hospital bed after the first attempt to assassinate him.

He had, in fact, gazed at the same photograph, each time he was hospitalised for some measure to be taken as a result of the huge voltage he had been subjected to. He could not forget that face.In that respect, he and Sabah were similar; they had both survived attempts to do away with them.

Despite that analogy being true, there was a significant difference for Alexi. Russia had changed into America, but the face in the photograph was of the same person.

At three o'clock in the morning, the man in the photograph was standing at the side of the bed where Alexi Vasilyev lay, staring down at him this time, with a silenced gun in one hand, in the other a cushion to stifle the sound of the gun even more.

You see, I could not allow the threat this man portrayed to hang over so many people associated with me and loved by me for any longer. Yes, it's true, he never spoke any words carrying specific threats, but I knew what he was and he had never tried to hide it. As George Orwell once said—*once a whore, always a whore.* Alexi Vasilyev was the whore throughout this story, but what does that make me, eh? Perhaps I should ask Judith.

Vasilyev did not pass away to any Elysium Fields, nor did he enjoy the share dividend due from his holdings in the joint stock company known as The Iysium Complex. It had been Valery Agapov who had told me of the intricacies of this Iysium Complex, built up by Sergei Ivanov's shrewd handling of the affairs inside Angola, in exchange for passing all the blame for the Sarin canisters firmly on to Winston Bottomly.

When alive, Alexi Vasilyev owned one third of the share capital of this company, some four billion dollars, the remaining eight billion being owned equally by two people: Valery Agapov and Sergei Ivanov.

With everyone else in my family taken care of in a financial sense, I made it a stipulation that the cash value of one quarter of Alexi's share, some one billion dollars, went directly to Katherine and Luca, before I took care of Vasilyev. By killing Vasilyev, the remaining capital increased from eight billion to eleven billion dollars, an extra billion and half each for Sergei and Agapov. I did warn you I was not entirely, squeaky clean.

The End

ABOUT THE AUTHOR

Daniel Kemp is a prolific storyteller, and although it's true to say that he mainly concentrates on what he knows most about; murders laced by the intrigue involving spies, his diverse experience of life shows in the stories he writes both for adults and children.

* * *

To learn more about Daniel Kemp and discover more Next Chapter authors, visit our website at www.nextchapter.pub.

My Truth, Your Lies
ISBN: 978-4-82416-704-0
Large Print

Published by
Next Chapter
2-5-6 SANNO
SANNO BRIDGE
143-0023 Ota-Ku, Tokyo
+818035793528

27th January 2023

Lightning Source UK Ltd.
Milton Keynes UK
UKHW011920270223
417761UK00003B/81